### The *[Fashion Hound Murders]*

"I've read most of [M]...[mo]st of it excellent. This one...[wr]itten so far. My attention was caught from the ...[st]ayed caught the entire book. It is a wonderful cozy read. The characters are great, as are the relationships between the characters." —*Gumshoe*

"Elaine Viets does it again! . . . *The Fashion Hound Murders* is a hilarious story . . . [and] a fun-filled adventure. . . . Pick this book up if you are looking for a lighthearted read with great shopping tips!" —*The Romance Readers Connection*

### *Murder with All the Trimmings*

"Viets milks much holiday humor in her novel, pulling out all the wonderfully garish stops." —*Pittsburgh Tribune-Review*

"Elaine Viets writes exciting amateur sleuth mysteries filled with believable characters; the recurring cast starting with Josie adds a sense of friendship that in turn embellishes the feeling of realism." —*Midwest Book Review*

"[A] wonderful holiday read . . . a book to be savored by a cozy fire with a good cup of hot chocolate." —*Gumshoe*

### *Accessory to Murder*

"Elaine Viets knows how to orchestrate a flawless mystery with just the right blend of humor, intrigue, and hot romance. If you are looking to complete your wardrobe for the fall, you just found the most essential piece." —*Fresh Fiction*

"The writing and plot are superb . . . no wasted words, scenes, or characters. Everything advances the plot, builds the characters, or keeps things moving. It's what her many fans have learned to expect." —*Cozy Library*

"A funny, laugh-out-loud whodunit. Elaine Viets has created characters that you can identify with . . . This is one book you don't want to miss." —*The Romance Readers Connection*

*continued . . .*

**Also by Elaine Viets**

Josie Marcus, Mystery Shopper Series

Dead-End Job Mystery Series

# AN UPLIFTING MURDER

---

## JOSIE MARCUS, MYSTERY SHOPPER

---

## *Elaine Viets*

AN OBSIDIAN MYSTERY

OBSIDIAN

Published by New American Library, a division of
Penguin Group (USA) Inc., 375 Hudson Street,
New York, New York 10014, USA
Penguin Group (Canada), 90 Eglinton Avenue East, Suite 700, Toronto,
Ontario M4P 2Y3, Canada (a division of Pearson Penguin Canada Inc.)
Penguin Books Ltd., 80 Strand, London WC2R 0RL, England
Penguin Ireland, 25 St. Stephen's Green, Dublin 2,
Ireland (a division of Penguin Books Ltd.)
Penguin Group (Australia), 250 Camberwell Road, Camberwell, Victoria 3124,
Australia (a division of Pearson Australia Group Pty. Ltd.)
Penguin Books India Pvt. Ltd., 11 Community Centre, Panchsheel Park,
New Delhi - 110 017, India
Penguin Group (NZ), 67 Apollo Drive, Rosedale, North Shore 0632,
New Zealand (a division of Pearson New Zealand Ltd.)
Penguin Books (South Africa) (Pty.) Ltd., 24 Sturdee Avenue,
Rosebank, Johannesburg 2196, South Africa

Penguin Books Ltd., Registered Offices:
80 Strand, London WC2R 0RL, England

First published by Obsidian, an imprint of New American Library,
a division of Penguin Group (USA) Inc.

First Printing, November 2010
10  9  8  7  6  5  4  3  2  1

# Acknowledgments

Lots of people helped me with this book. I hope I've remembered all of you.

Special thanks to the helpful bra-fitters at the Intimacy store in Aventura, Florida, for their information and advice on lingerie. Susan Nethero's *Bra Talk* (BelleBooks) was also useful.

Rebecca Cohen and her mother, Golda Cohen, are St. Louis women. Like Rebecca in this novel, the real Rebecca loves art, theater, drawing and wants to be a writer. She is almost five years older than Amelia.

Doris Ann Norris is not a police officer, but she is a guardian of knowledge—a librarian. Thank you, Doris Ann, for letting me borrow your name.

Stuart Little is a real shih tzu. His owner, Bill Litchtenberger of Palm City, Florida, made a generous contribution to the Humane Society of the Treasure Coast fund-raiser auction to see Stuart's name in this book. I've seen Stuart's picture. He really is eleven pounds of personality.

Failoni's Restaurant, 6715 Manchester Avenue, is a St. Louis gem. Don't miss a trip there, especially if Alex Junior is singing.

Special thanks to Alan and Molly Portman, Jack Klobnak, Bob Levine, Janet Smith, Jennifer Snethen and Emma, my expert on nine-year-olds. In St. Louis, friendship is important. Sue Schlueter has been my friend since high school. Thank you, Valerie Cannata, Anne Watts and supersalesperson Carole Wantz, who could sell bus tickets at a NAS-CAR race.

Thanks to Jinny Gender for her soap opera expertise, and to Kay Gordy for her help with Alyce's son, two-year-old Justin.

Special thanks to Detective R. C. White, Fort Lauderdale Police Department (retired), and to the law enforcement men and women who answered my questions on police procedure. Some police and medical sources have to remain nameless, but I'm grateful for their help. Any mistakes are mine.

As always, thanks and love to my husband, Don Crinklaw, for his extraordinary help and patience. My agent, David Hendin, is still the best.

To my editor, Sandra Harding, and her assistant, Elizabeth Bistrow, thank you. Your critique made this a better novel. I appreciate the efforts of the NAL copy editor and production staff and its hardworking publicists.

Many booksellers help keep this series alive. I wish I had room to thank them all.

Thanks to the librarians at the Broward County Library and the St. Louis Public Library, who researched my questions. Please support your local booksellers and your libraries. The Internet may be packed with information, but it takes a librarian to sort out the gold.

# Chapter 1

"You want me to take off *what* for this assignment?" Josie Marcus asked. She stared right in the red, ratlike eyes of her boss, Harry the Horrible. They jumped like gigged frogs.

"Uh, your top," Harry said. The manager of Suttin Services was completely clothed, except for the little bulges of hairy fat that escaped through his gaping shirt.

"Is that all?" Josie knew Harry wasn't telling her everything. She had a ten-year-old daughter. Josie was an expert at ferreting out half-truths.

Harry flinched. "And your bosom thingie," he said. "Your bra."

"I'm supposed to strip naked for a mystery-shopping job?" Josie clenched her hands to keep from punching her flabby boss.

Harry took one look at her eyes and grabbed the St. Louis phone book. He held it in front of him like a shield. Josie was only five foot six, but she was mad enough to deck the guy.

"Just your top half," he said. "And there are no men around. It's all girls."

"Women," Josie said. "Grown women are not girls. Unless you want me to strip at a grade school."

"Okay, women," he said, quickly. "I need you for this job. All women wear bras. It's no big deal. Especially for you."

Josie's glare should have lasered every hair off his hide.

"I wasn't getting personal," Harry said. "I meant that

you—as a female person—are used to taking off your clothes in doctors' offices and when you get your annual chest squashing."

"What's that?" Josie asked.

"My mom gets them to make sure she doesn't have cancer," Harry said.

"Those are called mammograms," Josie said. "My mother gets them, too." She tried to hide a smile. From what her mom said, Harry had given an accurate description of the procedure.

"Please, Josie. I'm not talking dirty. I just don't know how to say it right." The big oaf was pleading now. He had the charm of an unkissed toad.

"You sure don't," Josie said. She looked through his office door into the main room of Suttin Services. Dust motes danced in the early-morning light, haloing the IT guy working on a computer. The sun gilded a muscular telephone repairman installing another inside line. None of the staff or other mystery shoppers had arrived yet.

"There are two men in the office now," Josie said. "Take off your shirt and show them your chest." Josie would have bet her next paycheck that his breasts were bigger than hers.

Harry clutched the phone book to his chest, horrified as a maiden aunt propositioned by a randy priest.

"I couldn't," he said. "That's different."

"Why?" Josie said. "They're strangers. And guys. You'll never see them again. You're a man. You can walk around at the pool without a shirt. I can't."

"I'm the boss," Harry said, trying to cover himself with a shred of dignity.

"And I'm a peon. So I should go naked?"

"No," Harry said. "Can I back up and start again? I didn't get off on the right foot. Desiree Lingerie, the fancy ladies' underwear chain, wants you to mystery-shop their store at Plaza Venetia. They've had a complaint about one of their saleswomen. I mean persons. Did I say it right?"

"Saleswoman is correct," Josie said.

"What I was trying to say is that every woman gets measured for a bra, so you'd be used to the process of undressing like that."

"Every woman with some bucks gets measured," Josie said. "The rest of us buy our bras off the rack at stores. Target doesn't have bra fitters."

"Desiree Lingerie is more upscale than that," Harry said. "But it's for women only. It's supposed to be a place where women feel comfortable with their bodies. They got a complaint that one of their saleswomen is making rude remarks about the size of the customers'—"

Harry stopped while he mentally searched for the proper word. "Chests!" he finally said.

"What do I get paid for these insults?" Josie asked.

"You'll make your usual fee," Harry said, "but there's an extra benefit. Desiree Lingerie is not returnable. You'd get to keep the bras and panties, up to two hundred dollars' worth."

Now, that was a bonus, Josie thought. She had a new boyfriend and lacy underwear was a frivolity she couldn't afford.

"Where's the store?" Josie asked.

"Plaza Venetia in West County, where the superrich shop. Nice atmosphere. Pleasant people. Good working conditions."

"That's the most expensive mall in the area," Josie said. "For two hundred bucks, I'll be lucky to get one bra."

"But it will be a great bra," Harry said. He knew he'd almost sold her on the job. He reached into his desk and pulled out a sheet of paper. "Here's the list of questions. You have to ask for Rosa. She's the saleswoman the company wants checked out. They have two complaints that she made rude comments about women's chests. She's a Latina, so they can't fire her. Political correctness, EEOC and all that."

"Plus she could be innocent," Josie said.

"Well, there's that," Harry said. "But Desiree is taking the complaints seriously enough to investigate. The company wants some ammunition, and they want it docu-

mented in writing. Maybe you'd like to take that friend of
yours. What's her name?"

"Alyce," Josie said. "Does she get paid?"

"No, but she can keep her bra, too. She's a big lady."
Harry pantomimed large rounds in the air. "And you're . . ."
He stopped, catching himself like a runner about to go
over a cliff. "And you're not." He made a small cup with his
hands. Very small.

"So between the two of you, you'd cover . . ." Harry
stopped and looked frightened.

Josie decided she'd take pity on the miserable worm.
"We'd cover two different body types," she said. "I'll ask
Alyce if she has time."

"Why wouldn't she?" Harry said. "She's just a housewife."

That remark made Josie seethe. But she remembered
that Harry was still her boss.

"Alyce is a full-time homemaker," Josie said.

"That's what you call a rich housewife," Harry said.
"She's got a house cleaner and a nanny, doesn't she?"

"And a two-year-old, a husband, and a dog," Josie said.
"She doesn't sit at home eating bonbons, waiting to go running around to stores with me."

"Isn't her husband some kind of rich lawyer?" Harry
asked. "It's not like she needs the money."

Josie wondered if Harry was reminding her that she
did need the money. She was a single mother with a ten-
year-old daughter to support. Josie and Alyce had met on
a civic committee. Both had volunteered to help beautify
Manchester Road, a major thoroughfare that tied their two
neighborhoods together. The committee had long since dissolved, but Josie and Alyce stayed friends.

On the surface, the two women seemed to have little
in common. Alyce loved the bucolic splendor of the Estates at Wood Winds, the gated community in an exclusive
western suburb. Josie thought the twisty country lanes and
bare-branched winter woods were lonely. She thrived in
the noise and variety of Maplewood, an old suburb on the
edge of downtown St. Louis.

The women were physical opposites, too. Josie was thin, short, and dark-haired. Alyce was pale and blond, a generous, full-figured woman who loved cooking. Josie could barely fry an egg.

Josie lived downstairs in her mother's two-family flat. Her home looked like the "before" side of a do-it-yourself project. She was fascinated by Alyce's white silk sofas with sensuous piles of pillows, soft rugs in muted grays and blues, and tall sunlit windows free of tiny finger smudges. Yet Alyce never fussed at her guests, or used plastic covers, coasters, or protective runners to spare her expensive decor.

Josie had never solved the mystery of how Alyce achieved this domestic perfection. Even if Josie had a nanny, a decorator, and a housekeeper, she didn't think her home would look as flawless or feel as comfortable.

Perhaps their differences were the key to their unlikely friendship: Josie liked to visit Alyce's well-ordered home, but didn't want to live there. Alyce was a bit bored by her own perfection and enjoyed Josie's zingy outings.

Josie guessed her friend would go along on this undercover underwear adventure, but she wouldn't let Harry take Alyce for granted. Not after he said she was "just a housewife."

"I'll call Alyce and see if she'll consider going," Josie said.

"Good." Harry looked relieved.

"But you're asking a busy woman to drop everything at the last minute," Josie said. "If you're not going to pay her, I want two bras with matching panties for both of us."

"You got it," Harry said. "There's just one hook."

"There always is," Josie said.

"You'll have to go this morning."

"That will depend on Alyce's babysitter," Josie said.

"Do I have to get her a bra, too?" Harry asked.

# Chapter 2

"You're not using a video camera on this assignment, are you?" Alyce asked.

"While we're trying on bras?" Josie asked. "Over my dead body. This is an old-fashioned written report, not a porn movie. No hidden cameras and no tape recorders. Thanks for joining me on such short notice."

"Don't thank me," Alyce said. "Thank Justin's nanny. She came to work even though we had six inches of snow last night. I'm glad the roads are open. Do I really get to keep the fancy bras and panties?"

"You bet," Josie said.

"That's so nice. I haven't pampered myself with pretty lingerie since before Justin was born."

Alyce rubbed the condensation off Josie's cold-fogged car window and said, "The driveway into Plaza Venetia has been plowed."

"Good," Josie said. "I won't ruin my suede boots. I'm trying to look upscale."

Josie wore her rich-lady outfit for today's mystery-shopping assignment: her good winter coat, dark suede boots, black pants, and a black cashmere sweater. Josie had wanted that luxurious sweater the first time she'd seen it at the store. She'd watched it for three months, carefully hiding it at the bottom of a pile of sweaters. After it had been marked down three times, she could finally afford it.

A fashionista might notice that brown-haired Josie

didn't have an expensive salon cut, but she'd have to look close. Josie had a gift for fitting into places. That made her a good mystery shopper.

Alyce was born rich. She didn't spend much on her clothes, but money couldn't buy her confidence. Josie's best friend was bundled in a blue wool coat that made her pale face look like porcelain. Except for her nose, which was slightly red from the January cold. Her white-blond hair stuck straight out. Alyce brushed it down with a gloved hand and the static electricity crackled.

"Remember when buying a bra was a big deal?" Alyce asked. "Mom and I spent a whole day at the department store picking out my first bra. She took me to tea afterward. I felt so grown-up."

"I had a different problem," Josie said. "I didn't wear a bra until I was fourteen. Even then I didn't need it."

"Then why wear one?" Alyce asked. "They're uncomfortable."

"Gym class. The mean girls made nasty remarks about me when I was getting dressed. Frankie, the only C-cup in our class, said I should change in the boys' locker room because I was so flat. Her snotty friends asked if those were mosquito bites on my chest."

"Ouch," Alyce said. "That had to hurt."

"I was in tears but didn't want Frankie's clique to see me cry," Josie said. "Thank goodness I had a nice gym teacher. Mrs. Hayes heard me crying in a shower stall. She called my mother and suggested that she buy me a training bra."

"How did your mother take that?" Alyce asked.

"Mom understood," Josie said, "even though she was never flat-chested. Jane calls herself buxom."

"Most women would sympathize with you," Alyce said. "Especially your mother."

"Mom was supportive, if you'll pardon the pun," Josie said. "Money was tight after Dad left, but she bought me a training bra. It looked like a bandage with straps, but I was thrilled. Now I wore a bra like all the other girls. Mrs. Hayes found things to do in the locker room for a few days while my class got dressed. The mean girls didn't dare make fun of me with her there. After a few days, they found someone else to pick on."

"Girls can be so unkind to one another," Alyce said.

"It's over," Josie said, and shrugged. "I survived."

Plaza Venetia, with its white pillared rotundas and pointless balconies, looked like a Southern plantation on steroids. Josie parked her gray Honda Accord between a hulking Cadillac Escalade and a mound of plowed snow, and turned up the heat.

"I can't take my questionnaire into the mall," she said. "I'd better review it here."

Most were standard mystery-shopping questions:

**Was the store neat and clean?**

**Were you greeted when you entered the store?**

**Were the counters, shelves, and display cases free of dust and fingerprints?**

**Were the sales associates dressed in a professional manner?**

**Who was your sales associate?**

Other questions were special for this assignment:

**Was the sales associate familiar with the merchandise?**

**Could she answer these questions about the product? Designer or country of origin? Price?**

**Did the sales associate tell you that alterations were free?**

**Did the sales associate mention the return policy?**

**Did the sales associate make you feel comfortable during your fitting?**

**Did the sales associate say anything that embarrassed you?**

**Was the sales associate's conversation appropriate?**

All reasonable questions. Josie hoped the sales associate behaved herself. She hated turning in bad reports and getting staff fired, but sometimes she had to do it. Josie checked her watch and noted the time: 10:07 a.m. The weather was minus two degrees and overcast.

"What do I need to know about this assignment?" Alyce asked.

"Desiree Lingerie is concerned about an employee named Rosa," Josie said. "One of us has to ask for her."

"You could ask for her, and we could share a dressing room," Alyce said. "I don't want to be alone when I face a dressing room mirror."

"Me, either," Josie said. "Are you warmed up enough to take off your clothes?"

"We really have to do that?" Alyce asked.

"It's the price we have to pay," Josie said.

"Let's go before I lose my nerve," Alyce said.

The two women ran for the pillared entrance, the wind stinging their faces. Inside, the mall was tropically warm and tastefully beige, except for the Venetian glass chandeliers—great iridescent saucers suspended by heavy silver chains. These gave Plaza Venetia its name.

Fountains trickled quietly. Marble planters sprouted colorful jungles. Wrought iron chairs and tables invited shoppers to rest and snack. Josie and Alyce powered past them.

Desiree Lingerie had a window full of lacy bras and panties displayed on slate blue female forms. Women shoppers studied the lingerie. Men scooted by, eyes averted.

Josie stared at the woman behind the store counter. She was slightly taller than Josie, about fifty-five years old, brown-haired, and chunky. Josie thought she recognized the woman. But that wasn't possible, was it?

"Josie Marcus, is that you?" the woman said.

"Mrs. Hayes?" Josie said. "Mrs. Laura Lavinia Hayes?"

"Not anymore," the woman said. "I've remarried. Now I'm Laura Lavinia Ferguson."

Josie tried to hide her surprise. Why was her favorite gym teacher working in retail? she wondered. Josie remembered Mrs. Hayes had left school in the middle of Josie's junior year, but never knew why. Mrs. Hayes—no, Mrs. Ferguson—had packed on some pounds since her days as a gym teacher.

"I recognized your eyes," Josie said, then wished she could take back her words.

"At least they haven't changed. I'm fifty pounds heavier than when I taught you," Mrs. Ferguson said.

"I meant you had kind eyes," Josie said, with an uncomfortable flashback to her awkward high school years. "Those haven't changed. Did you give up teaching?"

"I burned out, like so many other teachers," Mrs. Ferguson said. "Please, call me Laura. I've made a career change, but it wasn't that big a jump. I'm still in a people profession."

"I was just talking about you this morning," Josie said. "I told my friend Alyce how kind you were when the mean girls in my gym class tormented me because I was flat-chested."

"Those nasty little snips," Mrs. Ferguson said. "I'm sure their other victims still remember the wounds those girls inflicted. They're one reason I don't miss teaching. I guess I still am a teacher. I'm a C-cup counselor. But you didn't come here to talk about me. How may I help you?"

"We're lingerie shopping," Josie said. "This is my friend Alyce. We're two moms hoping to buy glamorous bras and panties."

"I'll be happy to wait on you," Laura said.

"Uh." Josie wondered how she could ask for Rosa, since she knew Laura.

Laura had heard her hesitation. "If that would make you feel awkward, I have two other sales associates. That's Trish." The thin blonde with the short hair and plump pink lips waved and smiled from behind a carousel of bras. "And the brunette is Rosa."

Rosa was about the same height as Laura, but curvier.

"You're right," Josie said. "We'd probably be more comfortable if we didn't know our salesperson. We'll take Rosa."

The shop bell rang as Josie and Alyce started for the dressing rooms. Josie thought the woman framed in the shop doorway looked vaguely familiar. She was more bosomy than she'd been in high school and thinner. Much thinner. She'd dieted to near starvation and upped her breast size to DDs at least. Were those real? Now she was built like a Popsicle stick with two cantaloupes. Her clothes dripped designer labels. She also wore a mantle of entitlement, as if the world should worship her stylish perfection. She carried a long red dress protected by clear plastic with the tags still on it.

"Francine?" Josie asked.

"Frankie," she said. "Do I know you?"

"I think we went to high school together," Josie said.

Frankie looked Josie up and down like a casting director rejecting an untalented actor. "Oh. Right. You're Josie somebody. I'm younger than you."

Frankie said that as if being younger were an achievement. She turned to Laura. The former gym teacher was frozen behind the counter. Her hands clutched the countertop.

"You!" Frankie said. There was an ocean of contempt in that one word. She started to walk out of the store.

"Wait!" Mrs. Ferguson said.

"I don't want you waiting on me," Frankie said.

"I can get another saleswoman for you," Laura said.

"One like you?" Frankie asked.

Josie was puzzled by Frankie's sneery tone and Laura's odd behavior. Why was Laura deferring to this creature?

"One who is well trained, yes," Laura said. Her voice was unsteady.

"Well, I've looked everywhere. I'm totally exhausted." Frankie drew out that word as only someone who'd never been exhausted could. "I can't find a bra for this dress. I guess I have no choice."

"You always have a choice," Laura said.

"You should know," Frankie said.

Josie looked at Alyce and raised an eyebrow.

Frankie turned back to Josie. "I guess you're here for a padded bra," she said.

"Oh, no," Josie said. "One blessing of motherhood is that it improved my cup size. Naturally." She stared at Frankie's oversized chest.

Frankie turned on Alyce. "Then I guess you must have a very *large* family."

"I—" Alyce was interrupted by the chime of the shop bell. A man in a black coat entered this den of femininity. He was no taller than Laura, but gave the impression of being bigger. He had a rugged sunburned face and dark brown hair. The man had a hunted air, as if he expected the police to leap out from behind the racks of panties and arrest him.

"My name is Cody John Wayne. I'm here to pick up my wife's order." He lowered his voice. "She's having a bra altered."

"I'm sorry," Laura said, "but her order won't be ready for another hour. Would you like to have lunch in the mall or do some shopping and then come back?"

Frankie blocked his way to the door. "You look awfully scared for a war hero, Cody," she said. "Maybe you could pick up some panty hose while you wait." She handed him a pair of extra-large control-top hose from a rack.

"My wife is petite," he stammered.

"Oh, these aren't for your wife," Frankie said. "Perhaps you'd like something for your hero son, Tyler. Imagine that. Two heroes in one family. Must be genetic. Or maybe Tyler gets his heroic genes from his mother."

Cody's face turned sunset red. "I need to go to the food court," he mumbled, and fled the store.

"Trish will be happy to wait on you, Frankie," Laura said.

Trish didn't look happy. She was making a big show of folding stock on the sale table.

"I'd rather have her." Frankie pointed to Rosa.

"We've got Rosa," Josie said, quickly.

The two saleswomen, unused to being the prizes in a tug-of-war, stayed silent.

"Whatever," Frankie said. "It's no big deal. Especially not in your case, Josie."

"Wearing oversized sacks of saline doesn't make you a better person," Josie said, as Alyce dragged her toward the dressing room door.

# Chapter 3

"If you ladies will take off your tops, you can put on one of those silk robes there," Rosa said. "I'll be right back."

"Are you getting your tape measure?" Alyce asked.

"Don't need one," the saleswoman said. "I can tell your size by looking at you. I could make an educated guess now, but it's better if I see the real you. I suspect that you, Josie, are a C-cup."

"No, I'm a B," Josie said.

"I don't think so," Rosa said. "But we'll know better when you try on some bras. Alyce, you're wearing a bust minimizer. You're squashing your poor breasts. That underwire has to dig into your chest. It's pushing your breasts out under your arms."

"My bust is too big," Alyce said. "If I don't minimize it, I look dumpy."

"In the right bra, you'll look curvy," Rosa said. "You'll have a waist and your hips will look smaller. I promise. I'm built like you."

Rosa gave a little hip-check. She had a lush figure, silky brown hair, and lively, humorous eyes the color of black coffee. She was overweight by fashion standards, but Rosa looked shapely in her pencil skirt and black sweater. A black leather belt emphasized her waist.

"All the women in my family are built like me, including my mama and my sister Maria. Mama still insists on squashing her chest with a minimizer, but Maria follows my advice, and let me tell you, the men follow her. It won't hurt to try on a bra, Alyce. I promise it will hurt a lot less than that minimizer."

"All right." Alyce was reluctant. "But I'm no Megan Fox. Armani isn't after me to model their underwear."

"No, you're not Megan Fox. You're a grown woman with a beautiful figure," Rosa said. "Do you want a stick figure like a child draws? Change into your robes, ladies, and I'll be back with some bras."

"Is that the saleswoman who got the complaints?" Alyce whispered.

Josie nodded yes. She didn't know how thin the walls were. Alyce got her silent message.

"This dressing room is the size of my entire bedroom," Josie said. "At least they keep the temperature warm."

"The slate blue suede-cloth walls make it seem cozy," Alyce said. "The mirrors aren't too awful. I don't look like a lump of lard."

"You're too rough on yourself," Josie said, though her own self-appraisal was equally brutal. She felt as old and saggy as her bra looked.

Rosa came bustling back with an armload of bras. She handed a lacy black one to Alyce.

"I can't wear lace," Alyce said. "I'm too big."

"Lace is a better support than those ugly industrial-strength bras," Rosa said. "Anyway, you're not that big. You're only a DD. We carry bras through size K.

"And you," she said, handing Josie a hot pink bra and a dark gray one, "are a definite C. A B-cup is too small for you."

Josie tried on the larger size, a sophisticated steel gray with an embroidered lace band and straps.

"You mentioned your sister. Does your family live in St. Louis, Rosa?" Josie asked.

"Yes. My sister and her husband have a Mexican restaurant near Cherokee Street, El Loco Burro. Good burritos, enchiladas, and taco salads. Good prices, too. They live nearby. There are many Latinos in that section of south St.

Louis. If you're in the area, stop by for a meal and tell them Rosa sent you."

"Do your parents live there, too?" Josie said.

"No," Rosa said. The warmth vanished from her voice and her face shut down. The bright, mischievous eyes avoided Josie. "I'll get you some panties." Rosa slid out of the dressing room door.

"Did I say something wrong?" Josie whispered.

"Didn't sound like it to me," Alyce said. "I'm definitely going with this black lace bra. She's right. It fits."

"So does this C-cup," Josie said. "If only I'd known in high school that this would be my future size. I wouldn't have wasted any tears on Frankie's insults."

Half an hour later, Josie and Alyce had made their selections. Josie was relieved that Rosa had survived the checklist questions. She peeked out of the dressing room.

"There's no sign of the insulting Frankie," Alyce said.

"Shh!" Josie said, and lowered her voice. She opened their dressing room a sliver and said, "The door is closed on the dressing room across the hall. She's probably in there. Here comes Rosa with our panties."

Rosa appeared with lacy lingerie in lush pink and peach and dashes of bold black and red.

A snarl issued from behind the closed door. "Who do I have to screw to get waited on around here?" Frankie shouted.

Rosa ran down the hall room. "I'll send in your saleswoman right away," she called.

Trish had been packing up the alteration order for Cody John Wayne, the shy hero. Laura the manager took the bra away from Trish and pushed her toward the dressing rooms. Cody eyed the store as if Frankie might ambush him behind a bra carousel.

He looked even more frightened when Frankie marched up to the counter, holding a sheer red crossed-strap contraption along with her plastic-bagged dress. She practically dangled the bra in Cody's face. He blushed.

"I decided not to wait for your salesperson," Frankie

said. She flopped her plastic-covered dress on the countertop, taking all the available space. Cody flinched as if it were poison instead of plastic.

Laura gently pushed the plastic-wrapped dress out of the way. "Thanks for waiting, Cody," she said. "You're a brave man to come in here and pick up your wife's order." She gave him a warm smile as she bagged his wife's bra.

"Good-bye, Cody," Frankie said. "We won't forget your heroism—or your son's." A shark would envy her smile.

Cody dropped his bag and backed away from Frankie. He stood in the center of the store, a blushing hero turned to stone, scrambling to pick up the lingerie bag.

"I can ring you now, Frankie," Laura said, trying to get Frankie's focus away from the bumbling hero. "Did you find what you needed?"

"This will do," Frankie said. She held up a fashionably fat Gucci purse. "Good thing I'm honest. I could have shoplifted this bra. Your saleswoman Trish certainly didn't stick around. Too eager to wait on a man, I see. I thought this store was supposed to be by women for women."

"I'm sorry you're not happy," Laura said. Josie noticed she didn't apologize for her saleswoman. "Trish is one of our finest sales associates. She was able to fit you when no other store could."

A white-faced Trish came around to the counter and began stacking lingerie hangers. Cody dropped the bag again.

"What is the address of your corporate headquarters?" Frankie asked. Her tone sounded like trouble.

Laura handed her a business card.

"And where's your bathroom? I need to pee."

Cody went a shade redder under his sun-weathered skin.

"There are restroom facilities two stores down on the left," Laura said. "Your total is seventy-six twenty."

While Frankie wrote a check, Rosa approached a young woman in the doorway. She was about as tall as Rosa, but dressed older than her years. She hid what looked like a buxom figure under a shapeless navy coat. Her shiny dark hair was pinned into a tight French roll.

"May I help you?" Rosa asked.

Miss French Roll looked around the lingerie store. Her eyes widened and she stammered, "Do I have to take off my top for a fitting?"

"Just for a moment," Rosa said. "We'll give you a robe to wear."

"Uh, no," she said, and left.

"We get some shy ones sometimes," Rosa said.

Everyone had stopped to watch the doorway drama with the shy woman in the French roll. "Excuse me," Frankie said. "You have customers here trying to buy things. Like me."

"I'll need your driver's license for that check," Laura said.

Cody dropped the bag for the third time. Trish ran out, picked it up and handed it to him. "You're all set," she said. "If your wife has any problems, please, have her call us. My card is in the bag." Cody sprinted for freedom as Trish went to the second register.

Out of respect for Cody's unease, Josie and Alyce had stayed in the doorway to the dressing rooms. Now that he was gone, they went to Trish's register with their lingerie. Neither woman stood close to Frankie, as if she might lash out and attack them.

Josie presented her credit card to Trish. The blond saleswoman had cushiony pink lips and hair so short it looked shaved, but stylishly so. Her skin was the color of skimmed milk. Standing next to Alyce, the two pale women were a whiteout.

Alyce was wearing her new black lace bra under her blue sweater. She admired her improved figure in the shop mirror. "Look," she said. "With my new bra, I have a waist for the first time since I was pregnant. I may even buy a belt."

"We can shop for one now," Josie said.

"Deep Designer Discounts at the west end of the mall has good buys on accessories," Laura said. "That's where I got this black-and-white scarf."

"Pretty. It looks like a Chanel," Josie said.

"It's my ten-dollar bargain," Laura said. "DDD has a pile of them. Where else can you get a Chanel for ten bucks?"

"It's a Chanel knockoff," Frankie said. "I have the real thing at home."

Laura hooked the bag for the newly purchased bra over the dress hanger and handed it to Frankie. She sailed toward the door, the plastic-covered dress billowing behind her.

"See you later," Frankie said.

"I hope not," Josie said.

# Chapter 4

Josie and Alyce strolled through Plaza Venetia's synthetic summer. The soft, warm air was an invitation to linger. The bright red and pink flowers were a promise that winter would end. The marble fountains could have been in a palace garden. Plaza Venetia made shoppers believe they could buy their way into heaven.

"That was an unusual bra fitting," Alyce said. "But I like the results." Alyce was carrying her heavy winter coat to show off her improved figure. Her shoulders were thrust back and her bosom jutted proudly.

"Rosa was right," Josie said. "That new bra does bring out the curves in your figure."

"Nobody will mistake me for Jennifer Aniston," Alyce said. "But I do have a waist now. I want to show it off with a new belt."

"Deep Designer Discounts is straight ahead through the forest of ficus trees," Josie said. "Shall we go in and get one? This is my kind of store. Deeply discounted designer clothes and accessories, as well as good knockoffs."

DDD's accessories, displayed at its mall entrance, were an attractive lure for shoppers. Alyce pulled a beige leather belt off a sale table and fastened it around her waist. "What do you think?"

"I like how it sets off your blue sweater," Josie said.

"I mean, how does it look on me, Madame Chunk?" Alyce asked.

Josie winced. "Don't beat yourself up like that," she said. "The belt looks good on you. If it didn't, I'd say so. Friends don't let friends buy ugly."

"I can't believe you ran into your old high school gym teacher and Frankie the mean girl, both in the same day. How weird is that?"

"Not very," Josie said. "Not in St. Louis. This is a big small town. Everyone stays in their own neighborhoods. I only go to Plaza Venetia when I'm mystery-shopping. I can't afford to buy here on a regular basis."

"Plaza Venetia advertises itself as 'where the best people shop the best stores,'" Alyce said.

"They mean the richest," Josie said. "It would make sense that an expensive lingerie store would be located here. Mrs. Hayes—I mean Laura Ferguson—was the best of the best when I was in school. She was good at dealing with difficult situations. She'd be a natural fit for an upscale-store manager. As for Frankie . . ."

"I'd hardly call her one of the best people," Alyce said.

"Definitely not," Josie said. "But she's decorated with designer logos like a Christmas tree covered with ornaments."

"And she looks just as flashy," Alyce said.

"Meow!" Josie said.

"I hope Rosa the bra fitter will get a good mention in your report," Alyce said.

"Absolutely," Josie said. "The whole store will get top marks. The sales staff stayed courteous, despite Frankie's vicious attacks."

"What's with her?" Alyce asked. "I felt like I walked into a play without having the script."

"I was trapped in a time warp in high school," Josie said. "What the hell was wrong with me? I don't care what Frankie thinks."

"You shouldn't stand there and meekly take her insults," Alyce said. "Frankie attacked you for no reason. She insulted me and Cody, too."

"I guess she was insulting Cody," Josie said. "Her voice sounded like she was taunting him, but the words weren't that mean. Why would she call Cody a hero? Was that some kind of subtle insult?"

"No, Cody is a real hero with the medals to prove it," Alyce said. "Didn't you recognize Cody John Wayne? He's the carjacker hero."

"Never heard of him," Josie said. "Cody sure didn't enter Desiree Lingerie like a hero."

"That's a guy thing," Alyce said. "Lingerie scares married men. If I rinse out my stockings and hang them in the shower, my husband, Jake, acts like I've let loose live snakes. I have to go in and remove the offending underwear."

"Ted actually likes live snakes," Josie said. "I haven't tested his reaction to stockings in the shower."

"Does he bring his pets when he visits you?" Alyce asked.

"Only the dog," Josie said. "Ted's love of snakes is his one flaw, but he never brings his slithery friends around me."

"Glad the romance with your hunky vet boyfriend is still on," Alyce said. "Think you'll be Mrs. Dr. Ted Scottsmeyer?"

"It's been three months," Josie said. "My daughter likes him. My mother likes him. Even our cat likes him."

"You've found the perfect man," Alyce said. "He's even the perfect age. Thirty-five is just right—young enough for fun, but not too cranky and set in his ways."

"I'm waiting for something to go wrong," Josie said. "You never answered why Cody is a hero."

"You must remember the story," Alyce said. "He saved a newlywed couple. They lived in the subdivision near mine. Ten years ago, you couldn't turn on a television without hearing about the carjacker hero."

"Amelia was a baby then," Josie said. "I was trying to cope with colic, three a.m. feedings, and no sleep. My daughter cried so loud, I was sure she'd be an opera singer."

"Cody was a decorated veteran of the Gulf War," Alyce said. "He came home and tried to find a job in construction, but didn't have any luck. He worked in a convenience store for a while, then landed a guard job at a warehouse near Manchester Road."

"Those ones along the railroad tracks? They need guards," Josie said. "That area is deserted at night. You can hear the wind howling around the buildings when you wait at a stoplight. I wouldn't want to walk around there late at night, even if I was armed."

"Well, Cody had a gun and it was a good thing," Alyce said. "This young couple went to a party in Rock Road Village and made a wrong turn trying to get back to the highway. The couple got lost and wound up driving past Cody's warehouse at one in the morning.

"Two men tried to carjack them. They dragged the husband out of the car and pistol-whipped him and were trying to rape the wife. Cody heard her screams, called 911, then ran out and confronted the carjackers. They ran away after firing six shots at Cody. He took a bullet in one lung and his right leg. It's a good thing Cody had called the police. By the time they arrived on the scene, he'd passed out.

"Television loved the story about the veteran who'd come through the Gulf War unscathed and was wounded at home. They had nightly updates on Cody's condition and interviews with the cute couple he'd rescued. Cody needed surgery. He had to go through months of rehab. A fund was started to cover his medical bills and support his wife and little boy while he healed. The carjackers were caught and Cody limped into court to testify against them. A year later, the young woman he saved was pregnant and the couple named their baby after Cody, the man who saved the mother's life."

"Cody didn't limp when we saw him," Josie said.

"He recovered, though he'll never be strong enough to work in construction," Alyce said. "But his story has a happy ending. He got a medal for bravery and a check for one thousand dollars. Cody's wife and seven-year-old son were at the ceremony. A big store hired him as their director of security for more money than he made as a guard. TV even covered his first day on the new job. The building had a banner on it that said, 'Welcome, hero.' Cody dropped off the radar after that."

"Why did Frankie call Cody's son a hero?" Josie asked.

"Haven't a clue," Alyce said. "A lot of what Frankie said didn't make sense. Hey, there are the Chanel scarves Laura talked about." She dragged Josie to a sale table.

"I'll get one for Mom and one for me," Josie said, pulling two black-and-white scarves out of the pile of jumbled stock.

"Even though they're knockoffs?" Alyce said.

"They're good knockoffs," Josie said. "The only way you can tell they're fakes is if you study the design details—and only Ted is getting that close."

After they paid for their accessories, Josie said, "Let's get some coffee."

"Not till I find a restroom," Alyce said. "There it is, on the left."

They walked to the restroom near the lingerie shop. There was barely room to squeeze through the door into the utilitarian gray room. A woman in a wheelchair blocked the entrance. Her long blond hair hung over the back of her black chair. She wore a long black coat and plain black wool gloves. A Bluestone's shopping bag was hooked on the back of her wheelchair. The blonde had the face of a fashion model, with clear skin and large blue eyes, but a bulky body.

"Hi," the wheelchair woman said. "Sorry I've blocked your way, but there's not much room for me to maneuver. My name is Kelsey. I'd been trying to get into that handicapped stall. The door is either locked or blocked from the inside."

Kelsey backed up her wheelchair in slow, awkward movements so Josie and Alyce could enter. The handicapped stall took up most of the restroom. Josie knelt down on the gray tile floor and tried to look under the door. "I can't see anything. I'll crawl under the door and open it."

"Ew, don't do that," Kelsey said. "It's a bathroom floor. There's another restroom in the mall. I'll use that one."

"It's okay. I'll open the door," Josie said.

"No, no, it must be out of order. I'll just go." Kelsey tried to roll past them.

Alyce stood in front of her. "The other restroom is at the other end of the mall. You might not get there in time."

"I'm wasting time here," Kelsey said. "Please, let me leave."

"Nonsense," Josie said. "I'll get under that door in a second. The floor doesn't look too dirty."

"Wait!" Alyce tore off long strips of brown paper from a towel dispenser by the row of sinks. "Put this under your chest and your hands, so you don't touch that floor."

"I'll be fine," Josie said.

"It will save you a dry cleaning bill," Alyce said.

"Please," Kelsey said. "Don't go to all that trouble. I don't mind using the other restroom."

Alyce ignored her. She spread the paper strips on the floor. Josie lay down on them and put two more pieces under her hands, then slid under the wide metal door.

She was halfway under when Josie started screaming.

# Chapter 5

"She's dead," Josie said. "Frankie's dead."

She was shaking so badly, Josie could hardly drag herself out from under the stall door.

Alyce reached down and helped her friend off the dark gray bathroom tile. The paper towels Josie had used as a quick shield were scattered across the floor.

"You're pale as unbaked pastry," Alyce said. "And there's something icky on your coat."

"If I'm lucky, it's water." Josie sat on the edge of a sink and tried not to look at the stall door. It seemed to grow bigger, darker, and wider as she stared at it, like the entrance to a metal mausoleum.

"I don't understand," Alyce said. "How can Frankie be dead? She was fine when we saw her an hour ago. Did she do an Elvis and die on the john?"

"No, worse. She . . . she's . . ." Josie couldn't say the words.

"Is there a lot of blood?" Kelsey asked. Her eyes glittered with unnatural interest. "Was she shot? Knifed?"

Josie could see Frankie clearly in her mind. Her mouth was open and her eyes were wide. She seemed to be pleading for help. Blackness started to close in around Josie, as if her mind was trying to blot out the horrific vision.

"Don't faint." Alyce grabbed Josie's arm to steady her, then reached over and turned on the water in the next sink.

"I'm not some wuss." Josie's voice was a ragged whisper.

"I didn't call you one. But you've had a shock. Run cold water over your wrists." Alyce looked shocked, too. Her face was bleached bone white.

Josie pushed up her sleeves and dutifully held her wrists under the water. She shivered, but not from the chilly water. She took deep breaths until she was calm enough to talk.

"It's horrible," Josie said. "Remember when Frankie came in the store with that dress in a plastic bag? Now the bag is wrapped around her face."

"She suffocated?" Alyce asked.

"It looks that way," Josie said.

"Why couldn't this woman tear a flimsy plastic bag away from her face?" Kelsey asked. She'd parked her wheelchair back in the narrow passage by the door. "Was she old or sick? Was she disabled?"

"She seemed healthy," Josie said. "She couldn't rip off the plastic bag because her hands were tied with that strappy bra she'd just bought. I didn't get a good look at her, but I think she tried to fight. She's definitely dead. Alyce, please, call 911."

Josie didn't like the quaver in her voice.

"I'm trying," Alyce said. "My cell phone doesn't work in this bathroom."

"Look, ladies, I really do need to find a working john," Kelsey said. "Please, let me out. I can't wait much longer."

"This place is going to be a crime scene, Kelsey," Josie said. "The police will want to talk to you."

Kelsey pulled out a tiny notebook from the purse in her lap and scribbled on a sheet of white paper. "Here's my contact information for the police. Now I have to get rolling."

Kelsey handed Alyce the paper. Alyce, still trying to call 911, absently stuck the paper in her pocket.

Kelsey hit the wall plate that opened the door for wheelchairs and rolled briskly toward Bluestone's department store at the other end of the mall. Josie noticed Kelsey's powerful arms. She might be unable to walk, but Kelsey didn't seem helpless.

"I give up on this cell phone," Alyce said, slamming it shut.

"I'll call the police from the Desiree store phone," Josie said.

"I'll stay here," Alyce said, "and keep more women from stumbling inside."

"There's no one else in this bathroom, is there?" Josie asked. "I don't want to leave you alone with a killer." She checked the other stall. "It's clear. I'll be back as fast as I can. Are you too creeped out to be alone with a dead woman?"

"Go!" Alyce said. "I didn't like Frankie when she was alive. She can't hurt me now that she's dead."

Josie ran all the way to Desiree Lingerie. She felt oddly disconnected, as if she were watching a movie. She was relieved to see her former gym teacher standing behind the counter.

"Quick!" Josie said. "Call 911. It's an emergency."

"Are you hurt?" Laura said. "What about your friend?"

"Alyce is fine. It's Frankie. Someone killed her."

Laura's face turned white as a bridal trousseau. "No! This is awful." The big woman swayed. Josie hoped she wouldn't collapse. She wasn't sure she was strong enough to catch Laura.

"It is pretty bad," Josie said. "But I didn't like Frankie much."

"Neither did I," Laura said. "I meant this is bad news for me, personally. I'll be arrested for her murder."

"You? Why?"

"I'm the most likely suspect," Laura said.

"Frankie isn't a regular customer, is she?" Josie asked.

"No, this is the first time I've seen Frankie since high school."

"That's good," Josie said.

"No, that makes it worse," Laura said. "When the police know our history, they'll blame me for her death. That girl was wicked. Frankie ruined me once. She destroyed my career and my marriage. It took me years to rebuild my life.

Now when it's finally back on track, Frankie will destroy me again."

A woman has been murdered, Josie thought, and Laura is worried about herself. She didn't remember her former teacher having this selfish side. But what did any student know about someone she saw a few hours a week?

Laura must have read Josie's face. "I must sound heartless," she said, "but I have a hard time feeling sorry for Frankie."

"It's easy to see why you wouldn't like her after today's performance," Josie said. "How did she ruin you?"

"It would take too long to explain now. I'll need to sit down and talk to you. All I can say is I was innocent. I should have fought her and I didn't. She would have ruined more lives than mine. I couldn't have let that happen then."

"You have an alibi for today, don't you?" Josie asked. "Alyce and I have been shopping for the last hour. Weren't you in the store?"

"No," Laura said. "I was on my lunch break. After you left, I put on my coat and went for a walk outside—two laps around the mall."

"When it's two degrees?" Josie said.

"I take lunch walks, no matter what the weather. You burn more calories walking in the cold. After my walk, I came back here."

"The other saleswomen must have seen you when you came back," Josie said.

"No, Rosa and Trish were both in the fitting rooms with customers. I didn't want to disturb them. Bra sizing is a delicate process and interruptions can kill sales. I hung up my coat in the office and had lunch in the food court."

"Then you're safe," Josie said. "Your receipt will show the time you paid for your lunch."

"I don't have a receipt," Laura said. "I brought my lunch from home: grilled chicken, fruit salad, and a bottle of water. I'm on a diet, not that it does any good."

"Someone must have seen you eating at a table."

"Who notices a fat middle-aged woman?" Laura asked.

"I didn't know any of the shoppers in the food court. No one said hello. How will the police track down witnesses?"

"I don't know," Josie said. "But we'd better call them now. Alyce is alone in the restroom with the dead Frankie."

"I'll do it," Laura said. "Though it's like a knife through my heart." She stabbed 9-1-1 on the phone keypad.

"This is Laura Ferguson, manager of Desiree Lingerie at Plaza Venetia," she said into the phone. "A customer says there is a dead woman in the mall restroom. She was murdered. It's the public women's restroom two doors down from my store. Desiree Lingerie is store number one fifteen on the first floor, near the escalator."

There was a pause while Laura listened.

"Yes, the woman who found the body is here with me and she's safe. Another woman is standing guard inside the restroom. I'm sure she is, but let me ask."

Laura turned to Josie. "The operator wants to know if Alyce is safe." She handed the receiver to Josie.

Josie took the phone with shaking hands. She said, "We checked the other stall, and it was empty, operator. I left the handicapped stall door locked from the inside and didn't touch the woman's body. I don't think she needs paramedics. She looked really dead. Yes, I realize the killer could come back."

"Please, tell the woman still inside to leave the restroom immediately, ma'am," said the 911 operator in a professionally calm voice. "She can stand in front of the door and wait for the police. They'll be right there."

"I'll stand with her," Josie said, and handed the phone back to Laura.

"No, I won't hang up," Laura said into the phone. "I'll stay on the line until the police arrive."

Josie ran for the restroom, wondering how Frankie could ruin Laura's life twice.

She looked up and down the mall and saw no sign of Kelsey in her wheelchair.

# Chapter 6

"Is this your bra, Ms. Marcus?"

Josie's lacy steel gray bra dangled from Detective Michael Yawney's index finger. He arched his eyebrow. The empty C-cups bulged, as if accusing her of intentional embellishment.

In the drab little back office at Plaza Venetia, Josie's bra looked more sleazy than sophisticated. She tried not to think about Yawney unhooking that bra.

Now that her love life was hot again, Josie found herself giving men appraising looks, sizing them up for encounters she knew she'd never have. She wondered what Detective Yawney's thick brown hair felt like, and if his jutting jaw would be slightly scratchy with beard stubble. His ironic smile said he wouldn't take himself too seriously. His wedding ring said he was off-limits. She shut down her wandering thoughts and wished he'd get his hands off her bra. She could feel a blush burning her cheeks.

"It's a simple question," Detective Yawney said. "Is this your bra?"

"Yes, I bought it this morning," Josie said.

Yawney started to reach for the Desiree Lingerie bag again. If he takes out my thong panties, I'll strangle him, she thought. Josie added quickly, "All that's mine. The other bra and the underwear."

Was he smirking? Those scraps of lace hardly deserved such a sensible noun as "underwear."

"I bought them for a mystery-shopping assignment," Josie said. "I work for Suttin Services on Manchester Road."

"You bought lingerie as a secret shopper?" he asked.

"My paperwork is in my car. I'll be happy to get it." Josie stood up and pushed back her scuffed chair.

Detective Yawney's desk chair creaked and he sat up straighter. "That's okay, Ms. Marcus. Sit down. I can check later."

"Those are my black-and-white scarves in the other bag," she said.

The detective didn't seem interested in the scarves. She wished he'd put down that quizzical eyebrow. He did, and his ironic smile disappeared. "I'd like to go over your discovery of the victim again. Why were you in that restroom?"

Josie swallowed hard and repeated the story for the third time for the homicide detective.

Plaza Venetia was in the exclusive enclave of Venetia Park. The town did not want anything threatening its main source of income. The police would move fast when there was a murder at the mall.

Josie's voice was scratchy. She wanted a drink of water, but then what if she needed a restroom? Josie didn't even want to think about using a public bathroom.

"Alyce and I were shopping and she needed a bathroom. We opened the door and the entrance was blocked by a woman in a wheelchair. She said her name was Kelsey. She wanted to leave because she couldn't get into the handicapped stall. The other restroom was at the other end of the mall. I offered to crawl under the stall door and open it."

"Did you know this Kelsey woman?"

"I never saw her before this morning," Josie said.

"Did you look under the stall door first to see what was blocking it?" the detective asked.

"Yes. I rattled the door, too. It wouldn't open."

"Did you see the victim on the floor when you first checked underneath the door?"

"Of course not," Josie said. "I couldn't see anything but

the gray floor. It was a big stall and Frankie was wedged in the far corner alongside the toilet."

"How well did you know the victim?"

"I went to high school with Frankie," Josie said. "She was a year younger. I didn't see her after I graduated until she walked into Desiree Lingerie today."

"When was the last time you saw the victim alive?"

"When she left the store this morning, about eleven or so. Frankie had carried in a red dress covered with a plastic bag. She bought a bra and left. Alyce and I had made our selections. I put our purchases on my credit card. We walked around, then left to do more shopping at Deep Designer Discounts. That's where I bought the scarves." She pointed to the DDD bag. He ignored it.

"I'm having trouble understanding something," Detective Yawney said. "You say the handicapped-stall door was locked and you volunteered to crawl under it."

"Yes."

"Did you know this Kelsey?"

"No," Josie said.

"But you volunteered to crawl on a filthy bathroom floor for a stranger?"

"She needed help," Josie said. "Any woman would have done it. The floor didn't look too bad."

"What happened when you slid under the door?" Detective Yawney asked.

"I was halfway through when I saw Frankie. Her eyes were bulging and her mouth was open like she was screaming. Her face was swollen and horrible. Thin plastic covered her face. I thought it was the bag from her new dress."

"Where was the dress, if its protective plastic was suffocating her?"

"I don't know," Josie said. "I didn't take time to look for it."

"Describe this dress."

"It was a long, red dress with a high front and a low back. It was made out of silky material. The dress still had the tags on it. That's why Frankie came to Desiree Lingerie, to find a bra to wear with it. I didn't spend more than a second or two in that stall. I panicked, pushed myself backward, and got out of there."

"You didn't check to see if the victim was alive?" Detective Yawney asked.

"Frankie was definitely dead. Her eyes and mouth were open. Her color was funny. Grayish. It was frightening."

"You weren't too frightened to crawl across a dirty bathroom floor to help a woman you didn't know, but you wouldn't stop to check on a high school friend?"

"She wasn't a friend," Josie said.

"An enemy, perhaps?" Yawney's eyebrow was up again.

Josie realized she'd made a mistake and tried to correct it. "No. She wasn't either one. I never thought about her from the time I left school until she walked into the store today."

"When you saw that the victim was dead, why didn't you unlock the stall door and walk out instead of crawling under it?"

"I panicked," Josie said. "I didn't expect to find a dead person in the stall. I didn't want to get too close to the body. I could mess up a crime scene."

"Very thoughtful, Ms. Marcus. But suffocation isn't catching. Funny, the crime-scene techs didn't find your palm prints aimed inward on the floor, just your prints going out. In other words, they didn't find any evidence that you crawled into that stall."

"Alyce gave me some paper towels to protect my hands and the front of my coat. I slid under the door, saw Frankie, and pushed myself back out. I guess that's when I lost the paper towels."

"You should be used to dead people by now," Detective Yawney said. "The victim isn't the first dead person you've encountered at Plaza Venetia."

"That other woman died a couple of years ago," Josie said. "She attacked me. Her death was an accident."

"I know. I was a detective on the case. You know, Ms.

Marcus, my daughter has a knack for finding four-leaf clovers. You seem to stumble over dead people."

"Only two," Josie said. "Here. At this mall, I mean." Josie was afraid her stupid stumbling would land her in jail.

"Let's talk about your relationship with your long-lost classmate," Detective Yawney said.

"There isn't one," Josie said. "She should have stayed lost."

"Were you happy to see her again?"

"No," Josie said.

"What did you talk about when you saw Frankie after all these years—your children, your jobs, marriages?"

Josie hesitated, then decided to tell the truth. Yawney would find out anyway. "She insulted me," Josie said, cautiously.

"In what way?"

"She made a remark about me being flat-chested," Josie said.

He looked at the tag on the gray bra. Josie thought it was the color of slate and ashes. "Flat?" Yawney asked. "Isn't this a C-cup?"

Hot rage burned away the last scraps of Josie's caution. "It is, and you know it. What does my bra size have to do with her murder? This is harassment."

"Then let's get back to a more professional topic. Tell me about the woman in the wheelchair. How old was she?"

"Midtwenties, maybe," Josie said.

"Describe her."

"Clear skin, pale complexion, blue eyes, long blond hair. Her legs were hidden by her long black coat, and she had on dark pants."

"What kind of wheelchair was she using?"

"It was black. It wasn't an electric one."

"Was it a lighter sports model like athletes use?"

"No."

"Was she wearing gloves?"

"Yes, plain black wool ones."

"Did they have leather palms, like driving gloves?"

"No, I don't think so. They were regular gloves."

"Interesting. Anything printed on the wheelchair? Any writing, stickers, flags, flowers, ribbons?"

"Nothing personal on it at all. It had a black plastic seat and rubber tire wheels."

"And she said her name was Kelsey?" the detective asked.

"Right," Josie said.

"Did she decide to leave the restroom after you discovered the body?" Yawney asked.

Josie thought she heard a change in his tone. It was suddenly harder. "No. She wanted to leave as soon as she saw us. But the other bathroom was way at the other end of the mall. I said I'd open the stall door for her. She said I didn't need to."

"But you ignored the woman's wishes and crawled under the door anyway," Detective Yawney said.

"That's when I discovered the body," Josie said. "I told Kelsey this stall would probably be a crime scene and she might want to find another bathroom."

"Did you, now? You suggested she leave the scene of a crime?"

"Well, yes." Josie was floundering for an answer. "But she gave us her contact information. She printed her name, address, and cell phone on a piece of paper and handed it to my friend Alyce."

"We checked it. One Hundred South Central Avenue is the address of the St. Louis County Jail," he said. "The phone number is for a Game Piece Pizza."

"But she rolled off toward Bluestone's," Josie said. "She has to be here in the mall."

"We haven't found any sign of this Kelsey. There was no red dress, either."

# Chapter 7

Alyce stumbled out of the temporary interrogation room at Plaza Venetia like a bomb-blast survivor. Her coat was buttoned crookedly, her lipstick was chewed off, and her blue eyes were wide with shock.

Josie was waiting for her friend in the narrow hallway leading to the mall. "Are you okay, Alyce?"

"Just peachy," Alyce said, then burst into tears. "I'm sorry." She wiped her eyes with her gloved hands.

Josie dug in her purse for a tissue. "Why? You've had an exhausting morning." She tried to steer her friend toward the warm, flower-bordered food court. "Let's get some coffee."

"Let's get out of here," Alyce said, still sniffling.

"We can have coffee at my house," Josie said. "Mom had another cooking class for Amelia last night. She taught her how to bake a chocolate marble cake. I've had two pieces already. My kid aced that exam. She's only ten, and she's already an accomplished cook."

Josie couldn't keep the pride from her voice. She was worthless in the kitchen, but her daughter had real culinary talent.

"Do we have time for coffee before you have to pick up Amelia at school?" Alyce asked.

"We have a whole hour before I have to politely muscle my way into line at the Barrington School," Josie said. "And dark chocolate is good for your heart."

"Then let's not waste time," Alyce said. "I need some medicine."

They crunched carefully across the salted steps of Plaza Venetia as a harsh wind reddened their faces. The door to Josie's car creaked from the cold as she opened it.

Inside, waiting for the heater to warm up, Alyce said, "There's no such thing as a free bra. I paid for this one in sweat."

"Now it's my turn to be sorry," Josie said. "I thought this would be a treat. Who interrogated you, that smart-aleck Detective Yawney?"

"Worse. Detective George Waxley. He wore this lumpy suit that kept shifting around on his fat frame like gerbils were inside."

"Waxley was the detective who worked with Detective Yawney when I had that other problem at Plaza Venetia. Does he still have that bald dome?" Josie asked.

"Yes, but it's not as shiny as it used to be. I was tempted to Lemon Pledge it," Alyce said. "The wispy hair around Waxley's ears drove me nuts. I want to do a complete make-over on that man."

"His clothes are awful. But if I remember right, Detective Waxley is a lot smarter than he looks."

"He's smart all right," Alyce said. "Waxley remembered how I tried to help you when he and his partner wanted to take you into custody for murder. And by the way, that wasn't a problem you had at Plaza Venetia. It was murder. The killer tried to murder you, too, and you nearly got killed getting away. You solved the crime, too. He didn't."

"You didn't tell Waxley that, did you?" Josie said.

"No," Alyce said. "I practiced great restraint. Even when he accused me of impersonating a lawyer."

"You didn't!" Josie said. "You just said you were my representative."

"That's what I told Waxley," Alyce said. "It's not my fault he thought I was an attorney."

"What did he ask you this time?"

"The same things over and over," Alyce said. "How long

did I know the victim? What was I doing at Plaza Venetia with you? Did you look under the door to check for a body? What could I tell him about the woman in the wheelchair?"

"She gave us bad information," Josie said.

"So I heard. Now they can't find her or that red dress," Alyce said.

"We'll never find her now," Josie said.

"I have a surprise," Alyce said. "While I was waiting for Waxley to interview me, I copied down the address she gave me."

"Brilliant," Josie said. "You think of everything."

"No, I remembered what happened last time. If this investigation gets sticky, we'll be shut out. I'll put the copy in your purse."

Alyce dropped in the paper while Josie studied the traffic on busy Lindbergh Boulevard. "You're never going to get out of here with all those cars," Alyce said. "The drivers are going too fast on these half-cleared roads."

"St. Louis is still a Southern city when it comes to winter driving," Josie said. "We don't understand ice and snow require a different driving style."

A speeding SUV hit a patch of ice and went into a three-hundred-sixty-degree spin.

"Did you see that?" Josie asked.

"He's going too fast for these conditions," Alyce said. "If there had been a car in the lane next to him, he'd be dead."

They watched the speeder come out of the spin. "You don't suppose Kelsey, or whatever her name is, killed Frankie?" Alyce asked.

"Kelsey was in a wheelchair, but she didn't look helpless," Josie said. "She seemed young and strong."

"We couldn't see her legs," Alyce said. "They were covered with her long coat. Maybe they were shriveled and useless."

"Maybe she wasn't able to walk long distances," Josie said. "My grandmother spent her last months in a wheelchair. She couldn't walk for long stretches in supermarkets and malls, but she could shuffle around her home."

"We know for sure that Frankie was mean enough to insult a disabled woman," Alyce said. "Here's how I think she was murdered: Frankie said something ugly. Kelsey rolled into the stall behind her, trapped her in the corner, wrapped the bra around her wrists, ripped the bag off the dress, and suffocated her."

"Single-handedly?" Josie asked.

"People in wheelchairs can have extraordinary upper-body strength," Alyce said.

"Then how did Kelsey get herself and her chair out of the stall?" Josie asked.

"Maybe Kelsey could walk a little, like your grand-mother. She's disabled, but looks superstrong. After Kelsey killed Frankie, she pushed her own wheelchair out of the stall, locked the door from the inside, and then crawled out. She was prepared to leave when we came in, so she pre-tended to be locked out of the stall and asked for help." Alyce's voice trailed off.

"What happened to Frankie's red dress?" Josie asked.

"That sounds far-fetched, doesn't it?" Alyce asked.

They were on Manchester Road in downtown Maple-wood. Josie loved driving this section of her little city. Ma-plewood was an early suburb of St. Louis. It was like time travel into midcentury America. Most of the buildings were one- and two-story brick with big plate-glass windows. They passed fine restaurants, including Monarch and Acero, and inviting little shops such as Eddie's Guitars, Cheryl's Herbs, and Paramount Jewelers. Shops were rich with music, good smells, and sparkling gifts.

"I like your downtown," Alyce said. "No boring mall stores. Each one is unique."

"Now that Amelia is interested in cooking, she's hang-ing around Penzeys Spices," Josie said. "I guess I should be happy she's snorting coriander."

She turned off the main street into the side street. The car slid and Josie pumped the brakes.

"These big old houses belong on Christmas cards," Al-yce said. "Look at the porch on that one."

"You should see it in the summer when it's overflowing with white wicker and plants," Josie said.

"Your home looks pretty," Alyce said.

Fluffy white snow decorated the eaves of Josie's two-family flat and trimmed the bare-branched trees. A light glowed in an upstairs window at 131 Phelan Street, warding off the gray winter day.

"I see a light on in Mom's flat. I'm glad she's inside. She shouldn't be out in this snow. She could fall and break a hip. I wonder who she got to shovel our walk?"

They crunched up the salted walk. Her daughter's cat, Harry, greeted Josie at the door. The big-eared tabby with the swirly dark stripes grumbled and mumbled as he rubbed against Josie's boots.

"He's marking me as his territory," Josie explained.

"He's so friendly," Alyce said, hanging her coat by the door. "Like a puppy."

"He's especially friendly if his food bowl is empty," Josie said. "Amelia fed him this morning. She can give him more food when she gets home. He's not going to starve in the next hour."

Soon they were settled in Josie's warm kitchen with two cups of hot coffee and two plates of marble cake.

Alyce took a bite from an enormous wedge of cake. "Rich and moist," she said.

"I think Amelia learned to cook in self-defense," Josie said. "She spends a lot of time upstairs in her grandmother's kitchen. She hangs out with good kids, too."

"How's she doing since her father's death?" Alyce asked.

"Pretty good," Josie said. "Considering."

"Considering what?"

"Nate didn't die, as you so nicely put it. He was murdered, and that made it worse for Amelia."

Josie felt herself tear up and swallowed a forkful of cake. Alyce reached over and squeezed her friend's hand.

"I keep asking myself how I could have been so stupid about Nate," Josie said. "I was so in love, I never bothered to see the real Nate. I didn't ask where his money came from. I was thrilled when I found out I was pregnant with Amelia. I was all set to tell him the news, so we could get married."

"Except that never happened," Alyce said. She sipped her coffee and listened to a story she already knew. Alyce was a good listener.

"No," Josie said. "Nate was arrested for drug dealing when he went home to Canada. He went to prison and I became a single mom. I didn't see him for nine years. I told Amelia that her father's helicopter had been shot down in the war. I lied."

"You lied for your mother's sake," Alyce said. "You had to. This is an old-fashioned neighborhood. The church ladies would have made your mother miserable when they found out you were never married."

"Fat lot of good it did," Josie said. "Nate showed up on our doorstep last year, alive, drunk, and looking for trouble. I was so afraid, Alyce. The whole time he was in St. Louis, I thought he would run off to Canada with Amelia. It's a terrible thing to say, but I'm glad he's dead."

"At least you didn't marry him," Alyce said.

"Amelia never saw his bad side," Josie said. "He was the ideal father the few times he was around her and I'm glad for her sake. When he was dying, Nate told Amelia that he loved her. She lost her father, but gained a wonderful Canadian grandfather. He helped Amelia through the dark time after Nate's death."

"Amelia is strong, like her mother," Alyce said. "She seems her old self again."

"She isn't, not quite," Josie said. "She's more serious. But she's made a good recovery. I knew Amelia was getting better when she wanted a cat. She fought for that animal. Amelia chose Harry because he looked like the cat Nate had when he was a boy."

"And thanks to Harry the cat, you met your hunk of a vet," Alyce said. "That man is a good match for you."

"I hope so," Josie said. "I've made some bad ones. But it's too soon for matchmaking."

The conversation died in awkward silence. Alyce took another bite of marble cake. "This almost makes up for the terrible morning with Frankie and the detectives. Your daughter is turning into a real cook."

"She's also turning into a real woman," Josie said. "I'm going to take Amelia to Desiree Lingerie for her first bra."

"Already?" Alyce asked. "She's only ten."

"And well developed," Josie said.

"I hate that word," Alyce said. "It makes women sound like photographs."

"I'm glad my girl takes after her grandmother. Amelia won't be flat-chested like I was at her age."

"Being busty is not a reason to rejoice," Alyce said. "I was a C-cup at age twelve. The boys would stare at my chest, or yell 'Great knockers!' when I walked down the hall. I hated that line from *Young Frankenstein*. If any teachers were around, the boys would make a big show of pretending they were talking about the school doors."

"Little pigs," Josie said.

"I started walking with my shoulders hunched. I held my books against my chest to hide my breasts."

"Boys couldn't get by with that behavior now, could they?" Josie asked. Her encounter with Frankie had revived old, unpleasant memories. "I want to protect my daughter from snotty remarks by the kids at school."

"Can any mother protect her child from that pain?" Alyce said. "We had to put up with mean girls—and mean boys."

"No point giving the meanies extra ammunition," Josie said. "I want Amelia fitted for a bra before kids start making ugly comments. She'll get a real bra, not the ugly white training bra I had. My daughter will wear something pretty."

"Victoria's Secret has pretty bras," Alyce said.

"Uh, not that pretty," Josie said. Victoria's Secret meant sexy to Josie. She wasn't ready for a tween vamp. "Did you wear a training bra?"

"I went straight to the big leagues," Alyce said. "I heard a lot of sniggery remarks about 'over-the-shoulder boulder holders,' 'happy nipples,' and 'headlights.' I spent my allowance on shields to stick in my bras and hide my nipples."

"I found creative uses for Kleenex and gym socks," Josie said. "Mom would catch me trying to leave the house wearing my overstuffed bra and make me take them out. You'd think she would have let me keep the homemade padding. I used to wrestle my high school dates who tried to unbutton my blouse and get my bra off. They called me a door hugger and a prude. They didn't know I was terrified they'd find out I wasn't as well built as I seemed."

"Ah, the good old days," Alyce said. "Those don't seem like real problems now."

"Nothing on a par with who killed Frankie, the former mean girl—and used a bra to bind her wrists," Josie said. "That's going to develop into a real problem."

# Chapter 8

The Barrington School for Boys and Girls looked quiet—and quietly moneyed. The snow-covered lawns were barely disturbed by footprints. The evergreens were tastefully flocked with snow. The solid redbrick buildings promised security.

The curved drive was free of ice and snow, protecting the offspring of the city's premier movers and shakers—and litigators. Josie took her place in the pickup line. Her gray Honda was not anonymous in this crowd of BMWs, Escalades, and Lexuses. It stood out like a beggar at a society ball.

Josie opened her cell phone to call Dr. Ted Scottsmeyer at work. He answered. She could hear blood-freezing howls in the background.

"Torturing one of your patients?" Josie asked.

"Fred thinks so. Our new vet is giving the basset hound a manicure. Fred carries on like his nails are being pulled out with pliers."

More howls.

"I'd like to crawl into the next cage and howl with him," Josie said.

"Your day was that bad?" Ted asked.

Josie heard the warm concern in his voice. She wished he could hold her now. She would put her head on his muscular shoulder. Ted smelled like coffee and cinnamon with a faint tang of woodsmoke—at least when he wasn't tending to his hairy patients.

"I mystery-shopped a lingerie store this morning," Josie said. "A customer was killed after she left the shop. She was suffocated in a mall restroom."

"Good Lord! Are you all right?"

"I'm fine. Just shaken. I found the body."

"Let me cook dinner for you and Amelia tonight," Ted said. "You need comfort food."

"I do. But I also need to have a mother-daughter talk with Amelia tonight. We're still on for dinner at Failoni's Friday night, aren't we?"

"Wouldn't miss it. We have reservations. Josie—" He was interrupted by louder howls and spirited curses.

"What's wrong?" Josie asked.

"Fred escaped. He's waddling down the hall now. I'd better catch him."

The bell rang, but children did not explode out the school doors. Barrington students were handled like the heirs they would someday be. Each child's recognized ride had to be in the school driveway before the principal called a name. Josie watched the impeccably dressed mothers waiting for their offspring. She didn't care that she didn't fit in with this crowd. She wanted to give her daughter the best education. Josie endured their sly snubs for Amelia's sake.

Amelia's intelligence, plus a small legacy from her aunt Tillie, earned the girl a scholarship to the city's classiest private school. Amelia was part of the Barrington "diversity" program. Diversity meant Amelia lived in Maplewood, an old brick suburb on the edge of St. Louis. That made her "urban." Many Barrington children had never been in the city except for chaperoned school-sponsored field trips. Many of their mothers bragged that they never set foot in St. Louis. There might as well be a brick wall around the city limits.

Josie was startled when Fiona Henderson-Dobbs tapped lightly on her car window. A suburban snow queen in her full-length white fur coat, Fiona didn't give an ermine tail about animal cruelty. Her white-blond hair was pulled so tight into a chignon her eyes were slanted—unless Fiona had had an eye job.

She bared her teeth in a skeleton smile as Josie rolled down her window.

"Fiona," the snow queen announced. "I met you at the school book fair. Do you know the name of a good exterminator?"

"No, I just buy a can of Raid," Josie said. "It kills the occasional roach who wanders in."

"I don't think Raid would work on night squirrels." Disdain dripped from Fiona's lips.

"What are night squirrels?" Josie asked.

"They're small gray brown animals that look like squirrels, except for their long, skinny tails," Fiona said. "I've never seen one, but our gardener has. Pedro says the night squirrels have been eating the dog food we store in our garage."

"These night squirrels have long, skinny tails?" Josie asked. "Hairless tails?"

"Yes, kind of pink and naked." Fiona gave a small dramatic shudder.

"I don't think those are night squirrels," Josie said. "They sound like rats."

"We don't have rats," Fiona said. She gave Josie a frosty stare. "We live in Ladue."

"That's the ideal place for rats," Josie said, unwisely. "Rats go where the money is and you have money. I mean, your neighborhood has. Ladue has those big estates, lots of woods and creeks. Rats love waterways. Everybody has dogs, too. Those bring rats."

"Hewitt is a pedigreed Labrador," Fiona said. "He has nothing to do with rats."

"Maybe not," Josie said. "But I bet the rats love the dog food you probably keep in the garage. They'll gnaw right through plastic storage bins. Trust me, you have rats."

"You would know," Fiona said. "You live in the *city*." She made it sound like an insult.

Before the rat fight could continue, Josie heard the principal, Mrs. Apple, announce, "Pamela Henderson-Dobbs!" A thin blond girl with whirling windmill arms burst out of the door. Even her heavy navy backpack didn't slow her. She jumped into the snow queen's BMW.

"I have to go," Fiona said. Her smile looked painful.

"Amelia Marcus!" Mrs. Apple called.

Josie admired the easy way her daughter ran down the sidewalk. Last year Amelia nearly dwarfed by her enormous green backpack. Josie had bought her a rolling backpack, but Amelia refused to use it. Now she carried her monogrammed backpack effortlessly. Josie could see the elegant nose and the high cheekbones emerging on her daughter's round childish face. Amelia would be a heartbreaker soon.

Josie was glad she'd stood in line to get those black boots by Alice + Olivia for Payless. They'd been fifty bucks, but they were warm and stylish. She'd found the leopard-print coat on eBay—the virtual garage sale—and the warm wool scarf and gloves at Target. She made sure Amelia was dressed as well as her classmates. Maybe better.

"Hi, Mom." Amelia tossed her backpack into the backseat. She brought in a rush of cold air and warm energy. "Were you talking to Pam's mom?"

"She asked me a question about city life," Josie said. She kissed her daughter on her freckled nose. Amelia permitted this liberty. For now.

"You're all dressed up," Amelia said. "Did you go mystery-shopping?"

"At Desiree Lingerie at Plaza Venetia," Josie said, "with your aunt Alyce." Alyce was an honorary aunt. "We bought bras."

"Cool."

"Not really. A woman from my high school came into the shop, insulted me like she used to when I went to school with her, and wound up dead in the restroom."

"That will teach her," Amelia said.

"This isn't funny," Josie said. "I found her body."

"Sorry." Amelia looked contrite.

"Alyce and I spent most of the day with the police. I'm free. Alyce was upset, so I took her home for coffee and your marble cake. She said you're an amazing cook."

"It was good cake," Amelia said. She waved to her friend Emma as Josie inched down the school driveway. Her nightmare was that a careless student would dash in front of her car.

"How's Harry?" Amelia asked.

"Hungry," Josie said. "But he's always hungry."

"I'll feed him as soon as we get home," Amelia said.

"And clean his litter box," Josie said.

"Aw, Mom. Do I have to?"

"Only if you want to keep your cat," Josie said. "You know the deal."

Amelia had promised she'd do anything to have a cat. She'd kept that promise for about four weeks. Now she was shirking litter box duty.

"It's disgusting," Amelia said.

"Lots of cute creatures are disgusting. I should know. I changed your diapers."

"But I've outgrown that," Amelia said.

"You're almost a grown-up. That's what I wanted to talk to you about. It's time you were fitted for a bra."

"I figured we'd have this conversation soon," Amelia said. "I've been wearing two undershirts, a blouse, and a sweater to hide the speed bumps."

Josie let those last words go.

"I know the kind of bra I want. I tore the picture out of a magazine." Amelia turned around and unzipped a pocket in her backpack. "Here."

"Honey, let's wait till we're at a stoplight. I'm trying to drive. And put your seat belt back on."

Two miles later, Josie examined the ad for Alexander Wang underwear. To Josie, the gray cotton "athletic in-spired" bras and boy shorts looked almost as ugly as her old training bra.

She searched for something positive to say.

Amelia misread her hesitation. "I know seventy-two dollars is a lot to pay for a bra. But you're good at finding bargains and knockoffs. We could get something that looks like these."

"Don't you want something lacy and pretty?" Josie asked.

"Satin and frills are kind of old—"

"Fashioned?" Josie said.

"Lady," Amelia said.

"Oh," Josie said. Her sophisticated steel gray bra had been mauled by Detective Yawney. Now it was dissed by her daughter. "You don't like lace?"

"Maybe when I'm older." Amelia forced a smile.

She's trying to make me feel better, Josie thought. That makes me feel worse. I need to remember this isn't about me. It's about giving my daughter the bra she wants and needs. First I shied away from getting Amelia something sexy. Now, when she doesn't want lace, I'm disappointed.

"I'm sure the shop will have something you like," Josie said. "Let's go tomorrow after school. Is there anything you want to know about why your body is changing?"

"Is this where I get the sex talk?" Amelia asked. "I already know the basics and the words: 'penis,' 'vagina.' The guy puts it in, and the girl likes it."

"When the time is right, when you're in love, and when you're married," Josie added. "Babies need two parents."

Amelia had been conceived in love, but not in wedlock. Josie regretted the circumstances, but not her daughter.

"And you need protection to prevent the babies," Amelia said. "I know about birth control and the free pass."

"What free pass?"

"You can't get pregnant the first time you have sex," Amelia said.

"Who told you about the free pass?" Josie asked.

"Zoe," Amelia said.

"Figures," Josie said. Zoe was the class's fount of misinformation, the first girl to try everything from alcohol to junior-hooker outfits.

"You know what you call a girl who believes in the free pass?" Josie asked.

"A slut?" Amelia asked in a small voice.

"Pregnant," Josie said.

# Chapter 9

The phone was ringing.

The shrill sound destroyed Josie's deep sleep. She crawled into consciousness like a drowning woman dragging herself onto shore. Josie reached for her bedside phone, found the receiver, and croaked, "Hello."

"Josie? Josie Marcus?" The voice was a woman's, frantic and frightened. "It's Laura."

"Laura who?" the befuddled Josie asked.

"Laura Ferguson. Mrs. Hayes. Your old gym teacher."

"Oh. Right. Sorry."

"Did I wake you up?" Laura asked.

"No, I shouldn't have been asleep." Josie sat up in bed and checked the clock: eleven a.m. She'd lost the entire morning.

Last night had been difficult. She'd made hot chocolate and talked with Amelia about pregnancy and sexual myths, stepping around the subjects as carefully as if she'd landed in a nest of alligators. Josie thought she'd navigated the treacherous sex swamp fairly well. A chastened Amelia now knew there was no "free pass" and that Zoe's information was dangerously inaccurate.

After the talk, Josie had fixed her daughter her favorite meal of burgers with no pickles. Then they'd finished the last of the marble cake, while Josie added generous helpings of praise for Amelia's cooking abilities. Hamburgers and cake weren't the most nutritious meal, but Josie thought

Amelia needed comfort food on a cold night. So had she, for that matter.

Amelia had helped clear the table without complaint, a good gauge of her mood. Then they played with Harry, dragging a catnip toy around the kitchen while the cat pounced and rolled on it.

About eight that night, Amelia had retired to her room to IM her friend Emma. Harry followed like a puppy and curled next to her by the computer. Josie filled out her report on Desiree Lingerie and faxed it to Suttin Services.

Josie had made sure Amelia was tucked into bed, then spent a nearly sleepless night, tormented by maternal fears and flashbacks of the murdered woman's face. Frankie's silent scream echoed in Josie's mind, a plea for help that would never come.

She had fallen asleep as a drab dawn rudely poked through the window. Josie slept through the alarm, then awoke at 7:12. She'd hustled Amelia into her clothes, fed her child and her cat, and hurried to the car. There hadn't been time for coffee.

Josie had delivered Amelia to the Barrington School with two minutes to spare, then carefully made her way home on the slippery streets. Once inside, Josie thought she'd lie down for a minute. She'd been asleep until Laura Ferguson called.

"Josie, you have to help me." Laura's voice was hoarse with desperation. "I think the police are going to arrest me."

"You? Why?"

"I'm the most likely suspect for Frankie's murder. They have a video."

"They caught you killing Frankie on camera?" Josie voice rose to a shriek. Harry peeked in the bedroom door, ears up and alert.

"Not quite, but it looks bad. I didn't do it, Josie. I wished her dead a thousand times, but I would never kill her. I'm over that now."

"Tell me what happened," Josie said. Harry, satisfied

there was no crisis, settled next to Josie on the bed for an
ear scratch.

"I can't go into it on the phone. I'm at the shop. I need a
big favor. Can you meet me at Plaza Venetia to talk?"

"Sure," Josie said. "I wanted to bring Amelia in for a fitting this afternoon. It's time for her first bra."

There was a long hesitation. "Bring her in, of course. I'll
be happy to help. If I'm still here. But I need to talk to you
privately. This topic isn't fit for a young woman's ears."

"I can come over now. We could have lunch or coffee,"
Josie said.

"My break is at twelve fifteen. Lunch is my treat. I'll
meet you at the Venetian Coffee Bar in the food court."

Josie fortified herself with coffee before she went for coffee, a move that was redundant but necessary. She couldn't
face the cold morning again without hot caffeine. While she
drank her first cup of the day, Harry curled next to her on
the couch, shedding companionably on her brown sweater.

"At least I'm learning to wear cat-colored clothes," she
told the cat. Harry gently bumped her elbow, asking for another scratch.

Plaza Venetia was a self-contained world, tropically
warm and inviting. When Josie arrived at the coffee bar at
12:10, Laura was waiting. The shop manager was still large,
but Laura now seemed collapsed at her core. Her eyelids
were red from crying and her nose was raw.

"Do you have a cold?" Josie asked.

"No, I'm crazed with worry," Laura said. "I expect the
police to show up any minute. Let's order. I can at least eat
a decent lunch. I hear jail food is terrible."

They ordered grilled-chicken salads and coffee. Laura's
hands shook slightly as she lifted her coffee cup. She waited
until the waitress left, checked the nearby tables for potential eavesdroppers, then said, "I think the police are going
to arrest me."

"Are you sure?" Josie asked.

"Of course I'm not sure," Laura said. "But the way
they're asking questions, they definitely see me as a person

of interest. That's what they call someone they're going to arrest, right?"

Josie leaned forward. "Tell me why they're interested. I can't help if you keep being mysterious."

"I haven't told this story to anyone but my husband," Laura said. "Husbands, actually. My first husband left me in the lurch, so he doesn't count. But he knows, too."

She sipped her coffee as if it could give her courage. "Frankie ruined my teaching career. She got me fired."

"Was that during my junior year in high school?" Josie asked. "You just up and left."

"And you never knew why?" Laura asked.

"We were told it was for your husband," Josie said.

"I guess my story didn't get into the rumor mill." She took a bite of her grilled chicken. Josie noticed her ex-teacher's sharp white teeth. "Frankie wanted to be a nurse. She was on track for a scholarship. With her grades, it seemed like a shoo-in. Frankie took this honor as her due. She seemed to think she could do anything she wanted and the scholarship was guaranteed. She'd had two warnings about smoking and drinking on campus. The school was strict back then. It had a zero-tolerance policy.

"One Wednesday, I went for my lunchtime walk. I caught Frankie sitting on the hood of a blue Camaro, laughing and drinking beer with three boys in the student parking lot. The boys didn't go to our school. They took off like scalded roaches.

"I reported the incident to the principal. This was Frankie's third offense. Frankie was looking at expulsion. That would have ruined her chances for a nursing school scholarship.

"I figured the issue was over. She'd been warned twice and this was her third offense. Most of the teachers would have been glad to see her go. She was nasty to the other students and disruptive. No one liked her but the principal, who was proud of his future scholarship winner. She made him look good and he got bonuses if the school produced scholarship winners.

"I thought I'd caught her red-handed, but Frankie fought back. She told the principal that I'd touched her 'inappropriately' in gym class. She said I'd watched her undress in the locker room and invited my gay sister to see her get dressed after the mandatory showers."

"But that's not true," Josie said. "Not when I was there. Frankie was mean to me when we were in class. You stayed in the locker room to make sure she didn't make any more ugly remarks."

"I tried to say that, but she sat there like little Miss Perfect. Members of her clique backed her up. They said my 'creepy' sister stared at their breasts, and so did I.

"The principal didn't want to believe his scholar was a liar. Frankie wasn't lying about my sister. Not entirely. Pat did stop by my office at the gym to give me two tickets to a theater performance. She'd signed in at the administration office. That was on the record. Pat waved at me and left the tickets on my desk. She didn't stay long enough to ogle anyone.

"Frankie knew about my sister, or guessed it. Pat looked rather butch. Pat is a lesbian, though she hadn't come out of the closet back then. She kept her sex life quiet, because of the prejudice against gays. Pat worked at a kindergarten run by a church nursery school. They would have fired Pat if they'd known her sexual orientation. I was afraid Frankie's false accusations would hurt my sister's career.

"Frankie told the principal, 'It runs in the family. Mrs. Hayes may be married, but it's a cover for her perversion.'

"I was allowed to quietly resign without references. I was too heartsick to fight back. A year later, I was no longer Mrs. Hayes. My husband left me, saying, 'No smoke without fire.' He abandoned Kate, our ten-year-old daughter.

"I took jobs in retail. I met my husband, Langley Ferguson, while I worked for a dry cleaner. He's a broker in Clayton. Lang came in to pick up his shirts and started dating me. It was a whirlwind courtship. My life has been good ever since I met him. Until Frankie turned up in my shop yesterday."

"But why do the police think you killed her?" Josie asked. "Why would you ruin your new life?"

Laura sipped more coffee. "That's what I told the detectives. But they said a video camera outside the bathroom door captured me going inside. They showed me the video, thinking I would confess. This person has dark hair. She's wearing that black-and-white scarf, the one you admired, except it's covering her head, babushka-style."

"Can you see the woman's face?" Josie asked.

"No." Laura fortified herself with more coffee. "The video is grainy. All you see is a dumpy woman in a dark coat and print head scarf opening the door to the bathroom, then coming out fifteen minutes later."

"She could be anyone," Josie said. "Those scarves are on sale at this mall. I bought two."

"I said that. But the police claim the murder is premeditated. They say I sent Frankie to that bathroom so I could ambush her."

"It's a public bathroom in a mall," Josie said. "Any woman can use it."

"We have a restroom here in the store and our customers are allowed to use it. The police know that. I didn't tell Frankie about it. She was insulting the other customers and upsetting my staff. I wanted her out of here. I may pay for that petty act for the rest of my life."

"Why would you use a yucky public bathroom when you had one in the store?" Josie asked.

"The police say I wore the scarf to hide my face and killed Frankie in the restroom. The person who's supposed to be me is seen entering about two minutes after Frankie went inside at eleven twelve. She never came out. The police figure she died between eleven twelve and eleven thirty, when the person who looks like me left."

"You went for a walk around the building on your lunch hour, didn't you?" Josie said. "Won't the mall cameras show you outside?"

"The closed-circuit system malfunctioned in the cold,"

Laura said. "It wasn't fixed until two that afternoon. There is no video of my walk."

"Oh," Josie said.

"It gets worse," Laura said. "My fingerprints are all over the plastic bag that killed Frankie. I told them I touched the bag. She'd flopped it across the counter, and I moved it to make room for another customer."

"I saw you do that," Josie said. "I can testify."

"Testify," Laura said. "I'm praying this won't go to court. What do you think?"

"Do you know the name of a good criminal lawyer?" Josie said.

# Chapter 10

"Mom, can I ask a favor?" Amelia said.

Josie and Amelia were in the car after school, Amelia's favorite time and place to ask difficult questions. The old Honda was a warm cocoon, a small, private world for Josie and her daughter.

Also, Amelia, the little slick, knew her mother couldn't overreact if she was watching the road and trying not to run down Amelia's classmates.

"What favor?" Josie asked. She eased out of the Barrington School driveway, the major distraction zone, and headed for a four-lane road. She tried not to sound wary, but she'd been ambushed by her daughter before.

"Can I get measured for my bra without you this afternoon?"

"You don't want me in the store?" Josie asked.

"No, no, you can stay in the store."

"That's big of you." Out of the corner of her eye, Josie saw her daughter flinch and regretted her sarcasm. This is a sensitive issue, especially for a young woman, she reminded herself.

"I mean, can it just be me and the saleswoman in the fitting room?" Amelia asked. "Without you? It would be less embarrassing."

Less embarrassing.

Josie had breast-fed her daughter, bathed her, and wiped strained prunes off her face, but now it was embarrassing if she was present when Amelia was fitted for her first bra. Josie was hurt but tried not to show it.

Of course Amelia doesn't want you in the fitting room, she told herself. Did you ask your mother to go with you when you bought that steel gray lace number? Amelia is a normal preteen, despite her single mother and murdered father.

The self-administered psychobabble was no comfort. Amelia's request still stung.

"Let's make a deal," Josie said. "I won't go in the fitting room if you promise to buy a bra with real cups, not a sports bra."

"But—" Amelia began.

"It doesn't have to be a lace bra or an underwire. It can be any color or design you want. But a sports bra doesn't have enough support if you wear it all day and you need support. Also, you have to stay within the budget. I'm giving you fifty dollars. You may have enough left over to get panties."

"Awesome," Amelia said. "I brought some of my money in case."

Amelia was willing to spend her own money? The kid guarded her gold like a miser. She probably had more in her savings than Josie did, thanks to gifts from Jane and her generous Canadian grandfather.

"Then we have a deal?" Josie asked.

"Deal," Amelia said. "We're here." She raced out of the car in case Josie changed her mind. They met at the entrance to Desiree Lingerie. Amelia eyed the lace-frosted lingerie display doubtfully.

"They have lots of different styles." Josie gently steered her daughter inside the store, where they were greeted by Laura Ferguson.

"This is an important day for you, Miss Marcus," Laura said. "Trish, our best bra fitter, will wait on you."

Amelia looked pleased at this adult treatment. She eyed Trish's chic, nearly shaved blond hair, and smiled.

"Let me show you some styles," Trish said.

"No lace," Amelia said.

"No problem," Trish said. "Are you coming with us, Josie?"

"I'll wait here and talk to Laura, if she's not too busy," Josie said. "Remember our agreement, Amelia."

Josie watched her daughter go back toward the fitting rooms, as if she was seeing Amelia depart on a long journey. She was, in a way.

Laura looked at Josie and said, "Let me guess: Your daughter didn't want you to come into the fitting room and you're hurt?"

Josie nodded.

"Congratulations," Laura said. "You've produced a healthy young woman."

"She doesn't want lace," Josie said. "She called my sexy bra 'old lady.'"

"That's how young girls think, Josie. Did you have a crush on Mr. Sullivan, the American-history teacher?"

His picture popped into Josie's mind: dark hair, crooked smile, flat stomach, a muscular chest that strained his freshly ironed shirts, and brown eyes the color of unwrapped Hershey's Kisses. Mr. Sullivan was the object of schoolgirl fantasies. Josie's classmates dreamed of ripping that shirt off Mr. Sullivan through the Puritans' struggles, the endless Constitutional Convention, and countless wars.

"Of course. He was incredibly handsome for an older man."

"Do you know how old he was when you were in high school?"

"Fifty?" Josie guessed.

"Thirty-five," Laura said.

"Four years older than I am now," Josie said. "But he seemed ancient back then."

"Just like I must look ancient to Amelia now," Laura said.

Laura did look older than her years, Josie thought, and not because of her weight. Laura's shoulders were bowed under the burden of official suspicion. Her skin sagged from worry. Her weary eyes nested in dark circles.

"What's happening with you and the police?" Josie asked.

"Nothing good. They stop by here every couple of hours. They've already told me not to leave town. My husband agrees with you. He says I need a lawyer. But we don't know any good criminal lawyers."

"I can help," Josie said. "Alyce, my blond friend, is married to a lawyer. She'll know a good one. I'll call her."

Josie stepped to a back corner and speed-dialed her friend on her cell phone. She watched Trish come out of the fitting room with a pile of rejected lace-free lingerie, then return with more selections. Trish was still smiling, so Josie hoped the bra fitting was going well.

She was relieved when Alyce answered her phone. "Jake always says if he needed a criminal lawyer, he'd go to Renzo Fischer. Renzo has offices in Clayton near the county courthouse. He's good but expensive. Don't be put off by Renzo's flamboyant dress. A good trial lawyer is part actor."

"Flamboyant how?" Josie asked. "Does he wear pink tights and feathers? Purple caftans? Sequins and stage makeup?"

"He has a white ten-gallon hat, a bolo tie, and cowboy boots," Alyce said.

"That's not flamboyant," Josie said.

"Not in Texas," Alyce said. "But it's a bit much for downtown Clayton."

Josie hung up and relayed the information to Laura.

"A Clayton lawyer. He'll be expensive," the store manager said, and sighed. "My husband has some money. We didn't lose as much in the Great Recession as some people. Lang is a good broker. But I'd rather use my money for this. I inherited some property in St. Charles County from my grandmother. I'll have to sell it, but at least I have something to sell. I'll call Lang now."

Josie backed away to give Laura privacy. She saw Trish come out again, another load of rejects dangling from her arms. Josie thought the saleswoman's smile might be slipping. Trish hung the rejected bras back on the carousel and selected four more, then disappeared into the fitting room. Josie was starting to feel grateful she wasn't involved.

Laura finished her call and said, "Lang says thanks. He's heard of Renzo Fischer. He'll call him now."

Josie went back to the front counter to continue their chat. "If worse comes to worst and the police arrest you—" she began.

Laura winced.

"I hope it doesn't happen," Josie said quickly. "I know you're innocent, but we need to know our enemy. What else can you tell me about Frankie?"

"Nothing," Laura said. "I had no contact with her after she got me fired."

"Did she go to nursing school?" Josie said.

"So far as I know, yes. But I never saw her again until she walked back into the store, and I've lost contact with the other teachers. Wait! One of my college friends is a nurse. She used to work at Holy Redeemer Hospital. Edith Terna has stayed my friend through all my troubles. She was my maid of honor when I married Lang. Edith and I have lunch or dinner about twice a month. Edith might know where Frankie was a nurse. Edith is no gossip, but she notices people. She'll give you good information about Frankie."

Laura pulled out her cell, checked the digital display, and started writing on a business card. "Here's her number. Tell her I sent you. That's my home phone number underneath. Thanks for helping, Josie. We haven't seen each other in years. You don't have to save me."

"Hey, you were there when I needed help," Josie said.

The fitting room curtain parted and Amelia came out, holding a bra over her head with both hands like a pro wrestler's championship belt. "Tah-dah! We have a winner."

Trish was smiling but slightly frazzled.

"The bra is green with hearts and skulls," Josie said, trying to sound enthusiastic.

"And no lace," Amelia said, her smile growing wider.

"It's an Ed Hardy. I'm getting the matching panties with my own money."

"That's nice, honey," Josie said. No advice in her child-rearing books had prepared her for this mother-daughter moment. Her baby was wearing hearts and skulls like a biker chick.

"Are you happy with your choices?" Josie asked.

"Definitely," Amelia said.

"Let's ring them up," Laura said. She sensed this conversation could go south quickly.

Josie took out her wallet and Amelia pulled out a crumpled twenty-dollar bill to cover the rest of the purchase.

"I'll wrap your lingerie," Trish said.

Could you call something decorated with skulls lingerie? Josie wondered. "Thanks for your help, Trish," she said out loud.

"My pleasure," Trish said. "I had a nice talk with Amelia."

"Do you know Trish wants to go to the police academy?" Amelia said. "She's going to be a cop just like—"

Venetia Park detectives Waxley and Yawney appeared at the shop door with two uniformed officers. Amelia saw the handsome Yawney, blushed, and shoved her bra back in the bag.

Both detectives looked grim as death.

"Laura Lavinia Ferguson," Detective Yawney said.

Laura looked as hollow-eyed as one of Ed Hardy's skulls. She nodded.

"We're arresting you for the murder of Francine Angela Martin," Yawney said.

# Chapter 11

Somewhere in hell, Francine Angela Martin was laughing. Josie knew it. She could practically see her former classmate wearing her missing red dress and howling amid the flames.

Frankie had succeeded in disgracing Laura Ferguson. Her ex-teacher's arrest was the lead local story in print and on radio and television. The TV stations showed the Desiree Lingerie manager being bundled into the back of a police car like a common criminal.

In a story headlined NEW TWIST IN FORMER-STUDENT MURDER, a reporter said, "Unnamed sources revealed Laura Ferguson left her teaching job under a cloud after she sexually harassed Frankie Angel."

That was Frankie's new nickname. She was nearly thirty, never was and never would be an angel—except in the media. Some even used her high school photo in the stories and called her a "former student." All the news stories painted Laura Ferguson as a predatory closet lesbian seducing a sweet student.

The day after Laura's arrest, Desiree Lingerie announced that Laura Ferguson was no longer in their employ. A company spokesperson formally apologized to their customers for hiring Laura. "This would have never happened if Mrs. Langley Ferguson had not concealed part of her previous employment history."

TV stations endlessly replayed the grainy gray video of

a lumpy figure in a print scarf and dark coat opening the Plaza Venetia restroom door. An "expert"—in what field was never clear—declared the "killer's head scarf" was the same type as the one worn by Laura the day Frankie was murdered.

Josie thought the person in the video could have been Laura Ferguson. Or Josie's next-door neighbor, Mrs. Mueller. Or any large, dowdy woman. She taped the video and decided she'd study it later.

With a sinking heart, Josie watched the morning-show news video of Laura arriving at her arraignment. Her ex-teacher looked defeated and guilty in her drab dress. Her lawyer, Renzo Fischer, strutted at Laura's side, loudly proclaiming his client's innocence. Even in high-heeled cowboy boots and a white Stetson, Renzo was shorter than Laura. He probably weighed less, too. Could this little clown save Laura?

Josie had her doubts. She said so to Alyce, when her friend called after the news report.

"Trust me, Josie, Renzo is the best," Alyce said. "Short lawyers are tough. They have a lot to prove."

"What if he fails?" Josie asked. "Missouri is a death penalty state. I have to save Laura."

"Why?" Alyce said. "Because she used to be your gym teacher ages ago?"

"Yes," Josie said. "She helped me when I needed it. The other teachers let Frankie and her friends do what they wanted. Those girls were bullies. Even teachers were afraid of Frankie."

"For good reason," Alyce said.

"Laura was the only adult who stepped in and helped me, and Frankie used that to ruin Laura's career. So I do feel obligated. The police won't investigate the case anymore now that Laura's been arrested and charged. It's up to me."

"It's up to Renzo," Alyce said.

"Renzo can handle the legal side," Josie said. "But we were there the day Frankie was killed. So were the two saleswomen, Trish and Rosa, Cody John Wayne, and that shy woman who stood in the doorway."

"Don't forget Kelsey in the wheelchair," Alyce said.

"I'll never forget her," Josie said. "She's the reason I found Frankie's dead body." She shivered at the memory.

"I realized last night that Jake has a connection with Frankie," Alyce said.

"He does?"

"A business connection. A distant one. Her late brother, Charlie, was a client at Jake's law firm. I met him at a firm party. He was as obnoxious as his sister. Charlie owned the big Mexican restaurant on Page Avenue, Fiesta San Luis."

"Wasn't there a fatal holdup there at Christmas?" Josie asked.

"That's the one. Charlie was shot and killed. I'm not giving you privileged information. Charlie got drunk and told everyone at the party. He'd gotten in trouble several years ago for hiring illegals at his restaurant. After that, he used Jake's firm to vet his new hires. The firm turned the information over to their in-house private eyes. They did the actual investigative work. Charlie bragged that it was still cheaper than the government fines.

"Charlie said that an older man—maybe in his seventies—tried to get hired at his restaurant. The man's name was Hector Maria. Charlie thought it was hilarious that a man would have Maria as a middle name."

"What a jerk," Josie said.

"An ignorant jerk," Alyce said. "Men in Italy, France, Spain, and other Catholic countries have Maria as part of their name. You know what Charlie's middle name was? Darwin. Anyway, just a thought. And here's another one: Remember the last time you meddled in a murder. Please, be careful."

"You got yourself a really cute dog named Bruiser," Josie said. "How is he?"

"Don't change the subject, Josie Marcus," Alyce said. "You were nearly killed. You have a daughter to consider."

"I'm not doing anything dangerous," Josie said. "I'm

just going to talk to a good friend of Laura's named Edith
Terna. Laura said to call her if I needed more information
about Frankie. Edith is a nurse. If anyone hurts me, I'll have
medical attention right next to me."

"What if this Edith is the murderer?" Alyce asked.

"I doubt it. Anyway, I'm meeting her soon at Chris' Pancake House on Southwest Avenue," Josie said. "That restaurant is always packed. There will be a crowd to protect
me. Gotta go."

At ten thirty that morning, Chris' breakfast crowd had
dwindled to two gray-haired couples shoveling in pancakes
and a table of six businessmen all talking at once. A sturdy
waitress was refilling their coffee cups.

Sitting alone in a booth was a slender woman in her fifties. She smiled tentatively when Josie entered the restaurant, waved, and said, "Miss Marcus?"

Edith Terna inspired confidence, Josie thought. Her hair
and nails were short and sensible. Her manner was brisk.
Josie would want this woman at her bedside if she was in
the hospital.

Josie ordered pancakes and drenched them in syrup.
Edith had the fruit plate and coffee. "No grapefruit," she
told the waitress. "I take Zocor."

Josie wolfed down her pancakes. Edith ate her fruit
plate carefully, slicing each piece with surgically precise
cuts. She finished her food, positioned her fork and knife
at three o'clock on her plate, and said, "Now, what can we
do to help Laura?"

"Did you know Frankie Martin?" Josie asked.

"Oh, yes." Edith sipped her coffee and made a face, but
Josie thought it was the mention of Frankie, not the coffee,
that triggered the grimace.

"I worked with Frankie in the ER at Holy Redeemer.
That's where she met her husband, a plastic surgeon. Dr.
Tino was called in to stitch up some poor woman's face
after a terrible car crash. Frankie married the surgeon. She
finally left the hospital last year. Frankie said she was retir-
ing from nursing. I was at her good-bye party. The whole

staff was. We all celebrated when she left. We were terrified she'd change her mind and stay on."

"Was she a bad nurse?" Josie asked.

"No, Frankie was competent and careful. She did everything by the book. But she was mean. If she had to take off a bandage, she'd say 'This is going to hurt,' and the patient would scream in agony while she slowly pulled the adhesive away from the skin.

"Other nurses could remove bandages from the same patients without the suffering. If patients complained, Frankie told them they were ... what were her words? Oh, yes. She called them 'pansy asses.' She made them ashamed to report her to someone in authority."

"There had to be more than ripping off Band-Aids," Josie said.

"There was. Frankie was no healer. She liked power. She liked pain. She also liked getting sensitive information about people and tormenting them with it. Naturally, she gravitated to the ER. People in trauma let slip lots of personal information. Frankie seemed to feed off it."

"I'm not sure what you mean," Josie said.

Edith looked around the restaurant. The other diners were engrossed in their own conversations. The waitress was across the room, delivering plates of eggs to the businessmen. Edith still lowered her voice.

"We had a young man undergoing gender transformation come into the ER. He'd had an allergic reaction to one of the drugs he took in preparation for his final surgery. Frankie told him, 'I don't know whether to call you miss or mister. Maybe I should call you both.' You can hear everything through those flimsy ER dividers. He was mortified.

"Frankie told a young woman who nearly OD'd that she should do a better job next time. 'You've wasted my evening. I could have been helping a sick person.'"

"Good Lord," Josie said. "Didn't the families complain?"

"The drug user's parents were eager to hush up the incident in case it hurt their daughter's chances for college. The gender-transformation candidate wanted to keep his sex change as quiet as possible. He planned to move to another state after the final surgery.

"Frankie even told her husband-to-be, Dr. Hugo Agustino Martin, that his first name was for a hurricane. She started calling him 'Tino.' Said it made him sound like a Latin lover. We thought he'd object, but Tino let her change his name. He seemed flattered. Tino made new business cards and a new sign for his practice. He's been Tino ever since."

"Frankie was mean when I was in school," Josie said. "She was wild, at least by high school standards. How was her behavior as a nurse?"

"Some of those young nurses lived pretty fast, but Frankie was a handful. She managed to avoid getting caught by anyone in authority. I never saw her study much, but she passed her exams. Holy Redeemer hired her right after graduation. They're a small hospital, no competition for top-notch institutions like Barnes-Jewish or St. Louis University Hospital.

"The other staff nurses wanted to get rid of her. We watched Frankie, hoping we could catch her blackmailing a patient with the information she collected. But we never caught her asking for money or stepping over the line in an obvious way. She was careful to say her ugly things when she thought no one was listening. We tried to nail her. Believe me, we wanted her fired. Frankie had a charmed life."

"If Frankie liked pain and power so much, why did she quit nursing?" Josie asked.

"Her biological clock was ticking," Edith said. "Frankie was turning thirty. Rumor said Dr. Tino was attracted to his new receptionist, who was sweet, shy, stacked—and younger than Frankie. The new receptionist doted on babies and fussed over every child brought into his office. She might as well be wearing a sign that said, 'Want a baby? I'm ripe and ready.' Frankie wasn't stupid. She knew she'd lose her meal ticket if she didn't have a child."

"Do you think this new receptionist killed Frankie?"

"I don't know. There are easier ways to kill doctors'

wives. Less risky ones, too. I think Frankie said something nasty and the woman fought back."

"Any idea who it could be?"

"No," Edith said. "I saw the tape on television. Could have been anyone. But if you catch the woman, let me know. I want to shake her hand."

# Chapter 12

"I'd like an appointment with Dr. Tino Martin," Josie said into the phone.

"Why do you want to see the doctor?" said a sultry voice.

To find out if he killed his wife, Josie thought. Husbands are always the prime suspects, and any sane man would want rid of Frankie Angel. So why didn't the police arrest her husband?

"Ma'am?" the receptionist said, interrupting Josie's internal monologue. Her voice was a shade less velvety. Was this the receptionist who was supposed to be having a fling with Dr. Tino? "Why do you need an appointment, please?"

What body part should I say needs sculpting? Josie wondered. I'm not taking off my top again, so a boob job is out. My nose looks okay.

"I'd like to talk about a face-lift," she said.

When Dr. Tino Martin saw Josie was only thirty-one, he'd probably throw her out of his office, but at least she'd get a look at Frankie Angel's husband—and Frankie's possible rival behind the reception desk.

"Dr. Martin has a cancellation for three o'clock today at our Clayton office," the receptionist said.

"I'll take the appointment." Josie wrote down the address.

Josie would have to ask her mother to pick up Amelia at school. Jane had her moments, but she never complained about helping out with Amelia. Josie felt too lazy to run upstairs to ask her mother in person, so she made a second call.

Jane sounded uncommonly cheerful when she answered. "I'll be glad to pick up my granddaughter. But why can't you? Are you working again today?"

"I need to see a doctor." Josie tried to stave off a barrage of motherly concern with "Nothing serious, I promise."

"Are you sure?" Jane asked. "You don't usually go to doctors unless you're really sick. Were you upset finding that dead woman? That would make me sick."

"Just a routine checkup," Josie lied.

"Good," Jane said. "You're finally getting some sensible habits. I've been after you to start getting an annual checkup since Amelia was born. If you're feeling under the weather, I still have some homemade chicken soup left over in the freezer. It's better than penicillin."

"Your chicken soup is better than anything," Josie said.

"Amelia and I are making stuffed green peppers in our cooking class after school today. Would you like to come upstairs for dinner?"

"Thanks, Mom. Ted and I are going to Failoni's tonight. Alex Junior is singing, and Ted has reservations for seven o'clock."

"That Alex sounds just like Sinatra," Jane said. "An evening of music and Sicilian cooking will cure what ails you. If you want, Amelia and Harry can stay overnight with me, so don't worry about coming home early. Amelia and I can make waffles for breakfast together, since she doesn't have school on Saturday."

A double gift. Jane didn't like cats until she met Harry. She actively disliked Ted at first, calling him the "animal doctor," as if he had four legs and fleas. Now Jane loved these two new additions to Josie's life.

"Thanks, Mom," Josie said. "I'm lucky to have you."

"Don't forget that," Jane said. "Time for my soap opera." She hung up.

Josie was glad her mother was watching soap operas.

Not too long ago, Jane had been a serial-shopping addict, buying everything from cubic zirconias to collectible dollars on the shopping channel.

Josie called Ted at his office. In the background she could hear barks and an outraged meow.

"Sorry," he said. "I'll shut the door so I can hear you better. My partner is wrestling a twenty-pound feline. That cat doesn't like visiting the vet."

"I do," Josie said. "I have a babysitter for tonight. Mom is letting Amelia stay overnight."

"So I can come over to your place?" Ted asked.

"Uh, my mother lives upstairs and she has sharp ears," Josie said. "Also, my daughter will see your car." Josie was careful to shield Amelia from her sex life.

"Then maybe you can stop by and see Festus and Marmalade," Dr. Ted said. "I'll try to get as much dog and cat hair off the couch as I can."

"I'm used to pet hair," Josie said.

Her day was improving already. Josie put on a flattering pink sweater and a little lipstick and decided she looked good. She was ready to meet Dr. Hugo Agustino Martin.

The plastic surgeon's Clayton office was hushed and plush. The walls were a summer sky blue. In the soft waiting room light, Josie studied framed ads featuring attractive, ageless women. "Radiesse," said one. "For the treatment of facial folds."

Was that what plastic surgeons called wrinkles? Josie wondered.

Dr. Martin's receptionist seemed familiar, but Josie wasn't sure why. Lustrous brown hair fell past her shoulders in dark waves. She seemed sweet, shy, and "stacked," as Edith said, a word Josie thought was used only in old movies. Were the receptionist's curves real or the work of Dr. Tino Martin? Her name tag said she was Shannon.

An impressively built nurse in a trim blue uniform showed Josie into an office. Again, Josie wondered if her amazing chest had been enhanced by her employer. The plastic surgeon's desk was big as a parking lot and empty except for a telephone. There were no family photos. The fat volumes on the bookshelves looked like they'd cause serious reading wrinkles.

Dr. Hugo Agustino Martin bustled in. He was probably in his fifties, but was eerily youthful. Even the gray at his temples looked like an artful addition to make him seem serious. His white coat crackled from the starch when he sat in his leather chair.

"So, Miss"—he checked his notes—"Marcus. How can we help?"

"I'm thinking about a face-lift," Josie said, "but I don't know if it's too early."

"Oh, it's not too early." Dr. Tino's smile revealed blinding white teeth. Josie wished she had sunglasses to protect her eyes.

He stood up and came over for a closer look at her face. Josie could smell his citrusy aftershave. "Time, stress, and sun exposure take their toll, even in the midtwenties," he said. "I estimate you are in your early thirties."

"Thirty-one," Josie said.

"Hm." He studied her face. "You need a little tightening around the jawline and your eyelids could use some work. The wrinkles are starting to come out on your forehead and around the mouth. The lines at your lips should respond to collagen. A rhinoplasty could reshape your nose."

Josie's face fell as he talked. She could feel the wrinkles grow deep as ruts in a country road while Dr. Tino listed all the work that needed to be done on her face.

He brushed her hair back lightly. "Your ears are fine."

Terrific, Josie thought. I cover up the one part that doesn't bag or sag.

"I might be able to get your insurance to pay for the blepharoplasty—that's an eyelid lift," Dr. Tino said. "But you'd have to pay for the face-lift, collagen, and rhinoplasty. However, we do have financing and an easy payment plan."

"Thank you," Josie said. "You've given me a lot to think about."

"Don't delay," he said. "These problems don't cure themselves. They only get worse."

Josie staggered down the hall to the reception desk. She could practically feel her jowls swinging as she walked.

Shannon, the sweet, shy, stacked receptionist, said, "That will be two hundred dollars, please."

Josie numbly wrote a check, still staring at the receptionist. She'd seen Shannon before. She knew it. Where?

Josie shivered on her way to the parking lot. She'd wasted her time and spent a lot of money for nothing. No, wait. The visit wasn't a total loss. The new widower was seeing patients when his Frankie Angel had been murdered days ago. He didn't have any photos of his wife in his office. He hadn't bothered closing his practice.

Dr. Tino Martin was not overcome with grief.

# Chapter 13

"I did it my way," Alex Failoni Jr. crooned. If I close my eyes, Josie thought, it sounds like Ol' Blue Eyes himself is in this neighborhood restaurant.

Josie liked the way Alex sang "My Way" in Failoni's. Sinatra's signature song had been mangled too often in karaoke bars. Alex Failoni didn't draw out the last phrase with inflated emotion or fill it with ersatz drama.

Many restaurant patrons thought Alex could have a career as a full-time entertainer, but Alex seemed as proud of his pizza as he was of his music. Maybe prouder.

The star of Failoni's Restaurant was as skinny as a young Sinatra. His fans were almost as fanatical in their subdued way. St. Louisans did not go for public displays of emotion, except when the Cardinals were in the play-offs.

Josie thought the audience was part of the show at Failoni's. She liked watching them. Some of the older women could have been bobby-soxers swooning for the teen-heartthrob Sinatra. Some of the couples could have applauded the mature Sinatra on one of his many farewell tours. Some young men in the restaurant dressed like Rat Packers in narrow ties and skinny-brimmed hats.

Many customers enjoyed Alex's singing—and Failoni's food. The restaurant was one of St. Louis's hidden gems.

Josie applauded as the song ended. Ted took his arm from around her shoulder to join in the clapping. Josie admired her date's rugged good looks. Tonight Ted had

traded his green veterinarian scrubs for khakis and a blue
cotton shirt. He still had that outrageously noble chin and
deep brown eyes. They were eyes a woman could get lost in.
Josie had been lost for months.

"Would you like coffee or dessert?" Ted asked.

Just you, Josie thought. We only have tonight and then I
turn into a responsible mom again.

"No, thanks," she said. "The rosemary chicken was delicious."

Ted signaled for the check. Josie watched the other
women in the restaurant eyeing him and thought, He's
mine.

"You seem distracted," Ted said. "Is something wrong?"

"Do you think I need a face-lift?" Josie asked.

"A what!"

Josie was gratified by his surprise. She could hear it
wasn't faked.

"What moron said you had wrinkles?" Ted said.

"Dr. Hugo Agustino Martin," Josie said. "He's a plastic
surgeon."

"He's an idiot," Ted said. "Why were you seeing a plastic
surgeon? You don't need one."

"Dr. Tino is the husband of Frankie, my former classmate."

"Oh, right. The murdered woman," Ted said. "You discovered her body in the mall bathroom. Do you still believe your ex-teacher is innocent?"

"I know Laura Ferguson is innocent," Josie said. "The
police arrested the wrong woman. I've heard the husband
is supposed to be the main suspect when a wife is murdered. They didn't arrest Dr. Tino. I wanted to know why."

"Was Frankie killed during his office hours?" Dr. Ted
asked.

"Between eleven twelve and eleven thirty in the morning," Josie said. "How did you know?"

"I see patients, too," Ted said. "Mine have fur or feathers, but their appointments are all in the clinic computer.
Dr. Tino's appointments give him an airtight alibi. The po-

lice may have checked the times, interviewed his staff and patients, and concluded he wasn't guilty."

"Oh," Josie said. She could have saved two hundred dollars if she'd thought. At least she'd verified that Dr. Tino and Shannon couldn't have killed Frankie.

"The killer has to be someone besides Laura Ferguson," she said. "I just need to find her."

"Before you suspected Frankie's husband murdered his wife. Now you're calling the killer a 'her.' Are you sure about the gender?" Ted said.

"Frankie was found dead in a women's restroom in the mall," Josie said. "There's a mall video showing a large woman in a dark coat and head scarf entering just after Frankie did. The head-scarf woman came out. Frankie never did, except dead."

"I saw that video on television," Ted said. "The killer looks like a large woman."

"That describes Laura," Josie said. "But it could fit many women. The police arrested the wrong person." She reached into her purse and said, "Here's my share for dinner."

"Put that away," Ted said. "This is my treat."

Josie was secretly relieved. She was going to be short of cash for a while after her visit to Dr. Tino and her splurge for Amelia's first bra. She enjoyed dating a man who wasn't a nickel squeezer.

"Shall we go?" Ted whispered in her ear. "My place?"

"Definitely," Josie said. "Amelia is staying with Mom tonight. That's one less worry."

They left the warm restaurant, stepping into the cold night. Josie carefully picked her way along the shoveled walk. The air was crisp and the black sky looked velvety. They could see their breath. Failoni's had been a Dogtown neighborhood institution for more than seventy-five years. An ancient sign on the brick building proclaiming Failoni's "air-conditioned" was from the days when that was a luxury. New awnings said the owners kept the restaurant updated.

"Is she a worry?" Ted said. "She seems so smart and together."

"She is," Josie said. "She's always been good. You're awfully patient with her."

"I like kids," Ted said. "Your daughter is smart, curious, and funny. She makes me see things in a whole new
way—like her mother. I'm not good with babies. They leak
at both ends."

Josie laughed. "You deal with leaky pups and kittens all
day," she said.

"I know," Ted said. "But babies make me feel helpless.
Once kids can talk, I'm fine. And your Amelia has a lot to
say."

A man who likes children, but not babies, Josie thought
dreamily. He's too perfect. I don't want another baby, but I
enjoy watching my daughter grow up. He seems to appreciate her, too.

"What's your plan to help Laura?" Ted asked.

He's taking me seriously, Josie thought, and held on to
his arm tighter. "If we rule out her husband as a suspect,"
she said, "I want to talk to the people who were in the store
right before Frankie was murdered. There are two other
store employees, plus a man named Cody John Wayne."

"What was a guy doing in a bra shop?" Ted asked.

"Picking up his wife's alterations," Josie said.

"He's a brave man to go in there alone," Ted said.

"Actually, he is brave. Alyce said he was a decorated
hero. He was shot saving a couple who'd been carjacked."

Josie felt uneasy as they walked toward Ted's 1968 Mustang, parked on the street. This stretch of Manchester Road
was mostly empty. On Failoni's side were small businesses
closed for the night. Across the street was a struggling
shopping center with a moonscape of deserted asphalt.
Josie slid on a small patch of snow and Ted drew her closer.
Josie didn't mind at all.

"Who else was in the shop besides the hero?" Ted asked.

"There was a woman who appeared in the doorway of
the shop for a moment," Josie said. "She was too shy to get
fitted. There's no way to track her down. In the mall restroom, Alyce and I talked to a blonde. I crawled under the

handicapped stall to unlock the door for her. That's how I discovered Frankie's body. The blonde said her name was Kelsey. She gave us a bad address and phone number, then disappeared before the cops showed up."

"Every mystery needs a disappearing blonde," Ted said.

"This one was in a wheelchair," Josie said.

"That makes her more mysterious," Ted said.

"Unless I can look up handicapped plates in a DMV database, I don't know how I'll find her," Josie said.

"She might not have driven herself to the shopping center," Ted said. "You'll probably have to write her off as lost. This is where the police have the advantage. You don't have the resources to look for her."

"I'm down to Cody the hero and the saleswomen, Rosa and Trish," Josie said. "I want to start with Rosa. I'm guessing she'll be at Desiree Lingerie most days now that Laura is in jail. But I'd like to do some research first. Her family has a restaurant off Cherokee Street, El Loco Burro. Would you like to go to lunch there tomorrow? My treat?"

"I never turn down a free lunch," Ted said, "but why do you want to see her family's restaurant?"

"I want to get a feel for her family. I might even see her working there. People act differently around their families."

"You're on," Ted said. "I have tomorrow off at the clinic. My partner, Chris, has emergency duty this weekend."

A trio of lean dogs trotted across Manchester toward them. Even from a distance, the animals looked starved. The smallest one was missing a back leg.

Ted froze. "Don't move," he said to Josie in a low voice. "They may be a pack of feral dogs."

He reached in his pocket.

"What are you going to do?" Josie asked. "Shoot them?"

"Yes," he said. "If I have to."

The dogs glanced Ted and Josie's way, then trotted off in the other direction, toward the nearly empty shopping center.

Ted relaxed. "Fortunately, most feral dogs are afraid of humans." He pulled out the cylinder and handed it to her. "Dog repellent. Mail carriers use it. Here, take this one."

"What is it made of?" Josie asked. "Is it poison?"

"It's mostly pepper spray," he said. "I hope you never get close enough to a dangerous dog that you have to use it. If you think you're going to be attacked by a dog, the best thing is to freeze. If the dog charges you, spray it with this. The drawback is you have to aim for the dog's face. Go for the nose. Dog noses are extremely sensitive."

"Do I really need dog repellent?" Josie said. "We don't have wild dogs in Maplewood."

"Feral dogs are everywhere, in every city. I'm sorry to say the feral-dog situation is getting worse. More people can't afford to care for their dogs. The kind ones take the dogs to animal shelters. The bad owners turn the dogs loose. The poor animals soon die of disease and starvation. House pets don't survive long in the wild."

"That's so sad," Josie said.

"It is," Ted said. "I have an abandoned dog at the clinic now. His owner brought him in for a broken leg, then refused to take him home. I offered to forgive the debt, but the guy said he couldn't afford to feed his pet. Stuart Little is healed now. He needs a good home."

"He named a dog for the mouse in a children's tale?" Josie asked.

"I don't know where the name came from. But Stuart Little is a shih tzu. He's a sweet animal. I can't take on another dog. I spend too much time in the mobile clinic."

"Harry would never tolerate a canine rival."

"Cats and dogs do get along, you know," Ted said.

"I had a tough enough time getting Mom to accept Harry," Josie said. "A dog might send her over the edge. She's not a dog person."

"If she saw Stuart Little, she couldn't resist," Ted said. "He needs a home. There are so many good dogs and so few places for them."

"I'll try," Josie said. "But I can't make any promises."

Ted looked so sad, she threw her arms around him and kissed him. "Ted, you can't save everyone."

"I know. I just want to make a difference in my little world. I'm failing." His shoulders sagged.

"No, you're not," Josie said. "You're doing everything you can. You have to remember that."

Free advice costs nothing, Josie thought as she kissed Ted. Maybe I should take some. The price is right.

# Chapter 14

"Josie Marcus, I need to talk to you!"

Mrs. Mueller was waiting at the end of Josie's shoveled walk, clipboard in hand. Josie's neighbor looked like the killer in the grainy mall video: large, lumpy, and gray. She was ready for a winter war. Her hair was sprayed into an iron gray helmet. Her coat could belong to a Russian general. Her boots were suitable for Siberia. Mrs. Mueller planted them in Josie's path, blocking her way.

Josie buried her face deeper in her wool scarf. Only her brown eyes were visible between the scarf and her hat. They shifted left, then right, looking for a way around Mrs. M.

It wasn't going to be easy. Shoveled snow was heaped on both sides of the sidewalk, and Josie was slowed by her load of groceries. She'd stopped at the store on her way home from Ted's this morning.

Josie hoped the groceries would distract Amelia from discussing her mother's overnight absence. Josie knew she couldn't fool Mrs. Mueller. The neighborhood gossip had already noted Josie's car had not been parked outside her flat last night and mentally condemned her. Mrs. Mueller had disapproved of Josie almost from the day the Marcus family had moved next door.

"Excuse me," Josie said. "I have to get these groceries inside."

"Those eggs won't spoil," Mrs. Mueller said. "Not in this cold. Snow won't hurt that can of coffee."

"These groceries are heavy," Josie said.

Mrs. Mueller snorted like a Clydesdale. "For a strong girl like you? If you must go inside, we can discuss this issue there. But I won't leave this property until I've talked with you, Josie Marcus. And it isn't your yard. It belongs to your mother."

Jane admired Mrs. Mueller, local committeewoman and neighborhood fixer, for reasons Josie could never fathom. *No way I'll let that woman inside my flat*, she thought.

"What do you want?" Her mother would have disapproved of Josie's tone, but Jane wasn't facing Mrs. Mueller with the windchill at two below.

"I want your signature on this petition." Mrs. Mueller's sturdy gloved finger pointed to the clipboard. Nearly every line on the form was filled with signatures.

"What for?" Josie asked. She was getting icicles on her eyebrows.

"It bans the use of our church basement for Narcotics Anonymous meetings."

"What's wrong with that?" Josie asked.

"We'll have drug addicts at St. Philomena's," Mrs. Mueller said.

"Recovering drug addicts," Josie said. "Big difference. Narcotics Anonymous members want to quit using. They'll drink coffee, discuss their problems, and stay clean. That's what churches are for. To help those who are tempted."

"Exactly," Mrs. Mueller said. "Some people can't resist temptation. Our church has many items that can be easily fenced. What if those drug addicts steal the gold candlesticks off the altar and hock them for drugs?"

"The church has insurance," Josie said.

"Few drug users reform," Mrs. Mueller said. Her chins were wobbling with indignation. "Most of those people are incorrigible. I've seen the figures on recovery. Only one in eight drug users beat their addiction. What do we do about the other seven?"

"God will forgive them," Josie said. "You should, too. I won't sign that petition. It's the church's duty to provide a place for Narcotics Anonymous meetings. Now, if you'll excuse me, I need to go inside before I freeze."

Mrs. Mueller didn't move. Josie stepped around the stubborn woman into a snowdrift higher than her boot tops. The cold snow filling her boots was a chilling shock and spurred Josie on. She sprinted for her front door, her outraged neighbor behind her squawking like an angry hen.

Amelia held the door open. Inside, Josie relished the warmth as she hung her coat by the door and slipped off her boots. She kissed Amelia, then bolted the front door shut.

"Good teamwork," she told her daughter.

"What's Mrs. M complaining about this time?" Amelia asked.

"Narcotics Anonymous meetings. She thinks they'll bring addicts into the neighborhood."

"Isn't her daughter a gambling addict?" Amelia said.

"That's different. At least to Mrs. Mueller."

Amelia carried the groceries into the kitchen and set them on the table. Harry jumped up on the table and gave her arm a polite forehead bump.

"Hey! Off the table, big guy," Josie said. Harry gave her an extravagant purr as she dumped him on the floor.

"So, how was your sleepover, Mom?" Amelia asked.

"Dinner at Failoni's was lovely," Josie said. "It was nice to see Ted."

"How much of him did you see?" Amelia's shoulders were back and her fledgling breasts were thrust out as she put the eggs away in the fridge.

"I'm entitled to my privacy," Josie said, sharply. "You are a young woman and should act that way."

Amelia looked contrite. "Sorry, Mom. I appreciate your efforts to hide Ted."

"I'm not hiding Ted," Josie said.

"I said that wrong," Amelia said. "I mean it's nice that you don't flaunt him. Callie's mom has turned their house into cougar town."

"Who's Callie?"

"Callandra Simmons," Amelia said. "She's new at school. Callie's mom even wears a cougar ring."

"What's that?" Josie said.

"It's lame," Amelia said. "Her mom's got this silver ring with a cougar head to show she's prowling for younger men."

"Where's Callie's dad?"

"Out. Her mom found out he was having an affair at work and made him leave the house. She gets her revenge by hooking up with younger men. Callie never knows who she'll find frying eggs in the kitchen on Sunday morning. Her cougar mom did it with the postman, the dishwasher repairman, and the pool boy."

"She has a pool boy in the winter?" Josie couldn't hide her interest.

"He shovels snow in the winter. You'd be surprised how fast he can clear her driveway."

Amelia saw her mother's frown and said, "I'm glad you're not like Callie's mother. I'd be embarrassed if Ted wandered into the kitchen in his boxers."

"Me, too," Josie said. "How's the new bra?"

"It bothers me when I wear it all day."

"Maybe we should get you one that fits better," Josie said.

"No!" Amelia said. "I like this one. Emma thinks it's awesome. I'm not used to it, that's all. Grandma says I have better posture when I wear a bra."

"Did she see it?"

"Not yet," Amelia said. "I don't think she's an Ed Hardy person. She'd get the hearts, but not the skulls. Is it okay if I go over to Emma's house this afternoon and watch a movie? It's G-rated. Emma's mom won't even allow her to watch PG-13 movies unless she's seen them first."

"I should think not," Josie said. The two women had similar views on child rearing. Emma's home was a safe place for her daughter to hang out. "I'll call Emma's mother and check. If Liz says it's all right for you to visit, I'll drop you off. I'm taking Ted to lunch."

"Didn't you two just have dinner?"

"That was last night," Josie said. "Want to make something out of it?"

Amelia giggled and put on her coat and boots while Josie checked with Emma's mother. Liz offered to bring Amelia home by five o'clock. Emma's house was two highway exits away from Ted's place.

Ted rented a two-bedroom home on the edge of Maplewood, a redbrick bungalow with a round-topped wooden door that belonged on a fairy-tale cottage. Josie studied the churned snow where Ted had been playing with Festus, his black Lab.

Ted loped out of his house, wearing a fleece jacket over a red lumberjack shirt and sturdy Timberland boots. He filled her overheated car with a rush of cold air and sexual static.

"I missed you," he whispered in her ear.

The conversation died after that promising opening. Twenty minutes later, they were almost at El Loco Burro when Josie said, "You're quiet. Are you tired?"

"Worried," he said. "Stuart Little, the abandoned shih tzu, won't eat. I have to find him a home. Do you think your mother would adopt him?"

"I haven't had time to ask her yet, Ted. She's not an animal lover."

"No one could resist that dog's big eyes and lovable personality." He fluttered his own eyelashes at her.

"Mom could," Josie said.

"How about if I throw in a year's worth of dog food and free medical care? It won't cost Jane to look at him."

"You can try," Josie said. "It's on your head if she goes ballistic."

"A risk I'll take. Your mother loves me. She'll love Stuart Little, too."

"She won't have to walk you twice a day," Josie said. She spotted a shoveled parking space in front of the restaurant and slid into it—literally.

El Loco Burro's stolid brick storefront gave no hint of

the warmth and color inside. The restaurant looked like every tourist trap between St. Louis and Tijuana—bright Mexican blankets, bouquets of red paper flowers, and a yellow piñata. Latino music blared. The air was fragrant with grilled meat and spicy sauce.

Josie and Ted sat at the only empty table. A statuesque woman in a long skirt carried out menus, salsa, and a basket of chips. "My name is Rosa," she began, "and I'll be your ..."

She stopped. "Josie, is that you? Laura's friend?"

"It is," Josie said. "I'm seriously in need of a margarita and a chicken fajita."

"I'll have a Tecate beer and the Big Burro beef burrito," Ted said.

Rosa delivered a brimming margarita. Ted's burrito was big as a rolled bath towel and smothered in cheese. Josie and Ted once more lapsed into silence, this time in appreciation of their food.

Rosa ran back and forth, fetching chips, bringing plates, and pouring coffee. She stopped for a moment at their table and Josie asked, "How's the store now that Laura's—" She wasn't sure what to say next: Gone? Arrested? In jail?

"I'm the new manager," Rosa said. "I don't want Laura's job. I used to have weekends off to help out at my family's restaurant. Now I can't until Laura is free. I have to leave here at three o'clock to work at the lingerie store."

"You must be run ragged," Ted said. "This place is packed."

"And mortgaged to the hilt," Rosa said.

"It seems so successful," Josie said.

"It is," Rosa said. "My sister and brother-in-law are good managers. But they're paying Papa's medical bills after his heart attack. He's not well enough to wait tables, but he still comes to work. That's Papa at the register—Hector Maria Albagato."

Rosa's father was short, stocky, and weary-looking. His hair was frosted white. His skin was a sickly yellow.

Propped against the counter behind Hector was a metal orthopedic cane.

"He's getting better," Rosa said. "We almost lost Papa in two thousand eight. He was coming home from dinner at my aunt Carmen's. He blamed her arroz con pollo for his heartburn. Thank heaven my mother recognized that warning sign. They were near Holy Redeemer and she insisted Papa go straight to the ER. The hospital saved his life, but we're buried in bills."

"Medicare doesn't cover much," Ted said.

"For those who have it," Rosa said.

"Miss! More coffee!" The man at the next table raised his cup. Rosa bustled off to fill it.

"I wonder if Rosa knows about the resident-alien program?" Josie said. "Her father could buy Medicare coverage."

"How would you know about that?" Ted asked. "You're too young to worry about Medicare."

"I heard Mom and Mrs. Mueller discussing it."

"She's your nosy neighbor?" Ted asked.

"That's her. Mrs. M found out that a Russian immigrant working at a local store got Medicare and she wasn't a citizen. Natasha is nearly seventy and works six days a week. Mrs. Mueller complained to our representative about a 'foreigner getting a free ride.' The representative said resident aliens didn't have to be U.S. citizens, but they did have to be in this country legally."

"Dessert? Coffee?" Rosa asked.

"No, thanks," Ted said, patting his flat stomach. "That was good."

"Rosa, do you know resident aliens can buy Medicare insurance?" Josie asked.

Rosa's smiling face turned stone hard. Josie started fumbling with her words. "I mean, it's not my business, but it might help if your father needs more medical care."

Rosa slapped down the check. "You're right," she said. "It's not your business." She walked away, her back rigid with indignation.

"I didn't mean to upset her," Josie said. "I didn't think low-cost health insurance was a touchy subject."

Ted lowered his voice. "What if Rosa's parents are illegal? What if they came here on a visit and never went home? No wonder the family is struggling to pay the hospital bills. One phone call and ICE would bust through that door."

"ICE?" Josie asked.

"The new name for immigration," Ted said.

"Right. The margaritas must be getting to me. I was thinking ice as in snow and winter."

"Hector would be deported," Ted said. "Somebody at the hospital would know Rosa's father didn't have health insurance. It would be easy to figure out why his family is struggling to pay those bills, instead of walking away from them like so many people do. I bet Frankie saw Hector's paperwork and found out."

"Maybe," Josie said. "But Frankie had an easier way. Her late brother, Charlie, owned a Mexican restaurant, Fiesta San Luis. The feds rapped Charlie's knuckles for hiring illegals. After that, Charlie used a law firm to vet all his staff—Alyce's husband is a partner. Charlie told Alyce at a party that an old man called Hector tried to get a job at his restaurant with a forged green card. Hector's middle name was Maria. Charlie thought it was a big joke that a man had a woman's name."

"Charlie may have owned a Mexican restaurant," Ted said, "but he sure didn't understand the culture. Maria is a traditional name for men in a number of Catholic countries."

"Hector Maria might have laughed at Charlie's middle name—Darwin," Josie said. "He and his sister weren't so highly evolved."

"Frankie and her brother sound like a nasty pair, laughing at a desperate old man," Ted said.

"I wonder if that information died with Frankie," Josie said.

# Chapter 15

"Josie, you have to help me," Jane said. "My car won't start. I'm stranded."

Josie could hear the fear in her mother's voice. She sat up on the couch, sending Harry skittering to the floor. Her sixty-eight-year-old mother shouldn't be out in a night like this: It was black as the inside of a coal mine, the temperature was dropping below zero, and the streets were slick with fresh snow.

"Where are you, Mom?"

"I've just come out of the Altar Society meeting. I stayed behind to talk to Father Murphy. The other committee members have left. I tried to start my car, but it makes a clicking sound when I turn the key. I've called Triple A. The nice girl on the phone asked if I was in a safe place. I told her I was in a dark parking lot surrounded by drug dealers."

Drug dealers? The church wasn't in an iffy neighborhood.

"Did you park your car at St. Philomena's Church?" Josie asked.

"Of course," Jane said.

"Then how can you be surrounded by drug dealers?"

"There's a Narcotics Anonymous meeting at the church."

"Mom, those people are *recovering* drug users. They're not going to bother you, no matter what Mrs. Mueller said."

"They don't look like our parishioners," Jane said. "I saw a skinny woman in black who could use a bath and a large scary man going into that meeting room. One has a tattoo on his face—a black widow spider. Who would do that to his face? Get here soon, Josie. Please, don't leave me here alone with those people."

Josie could see her small sturdy mother in her sensible wool coat, shivering in fear from imaginary drug lords and their ladies.

"Mom, I'm leaving now. Go inside the church vestibule and wait for me. Keep your cell phone on. I'll talk to you while I drive there."

Josie had her coat on and was running out the door.

"No, I can't keep talking to you," Jane said, her panic rising. "I have to keep the line open so Triple A can call me."

Josie unlocked her car and slid inside. "Mom, I'm in the car. That's my engine starting. I'll be there before you know it," Josie said. "The NA meeting is in the church basement. They'll use the side door. You stay inside in the front of the church. I'm on my way. Triple A should be there any moment."

Josie snapped her phone shut and drove to St. Philomena's as quickly as she could safely manage. She was at the old redbrick and stone church in twelve minutes, even going twenty-five miles an hour. The church's pointed Gothic towers loomed over a snow-filled playground where dark shadows chased one another. The parking lot was a desert of salted asphalt, quickly being covered with more snow.

Under the orange brown mercury-vapor lights, a burly tow truck driver was hooking the front end of Jane's car onto his flatbed truck. The man looked like he could have carried the car under one muscular arm.

The tow truck driver labored patiently, attaching hooks and checking chains. He puffed out great bursts of air like a steam engine. Jane stood behind him, supervising and making smaller puffs of air. My mother, the Little Engine That Could, Josie thought.

She gave her car horn a friendly tap and waved. To make sure the tow truck driver had room to maneuver, Josie drove around by the church's side entrance. A handful of cars were huddled near it, including a dented green Neon.

The tiny car's back window was crammed with stuffed animals. Josie wondered if it belonged to a recovering Ecstasy user. She'd read that X users liked the feel of soft things such as velvet, plush, and fur.

A neat black Honda pulled into the slot next to the Neon and a blonde climbed out. The woman looked vaguely familiar. The lot's brownish lights distorted her skin color, but Josie could tell she was milk pale with plump lips. The woman wasn't wearing a hat, and Josie saw her hair—what there was of it. Her hair was stylishly shaved and gelled into waiflike wisps. It was Trish, the saleswoman who'd waited on Amelia at Desiree Lingerie.

Josie opened her door and started to say hello, then wondered if Trish wanted to be recognized when she was going to a Narcotics Anonymous meeting. They had an awkward, nearly wordless encounter.

"Hi," Josie said. The sound died on her lips.

"Uh, hello," Trish said, vaguely.

Josie was sure Trish didn't recognize her. Trish is too distinctive to miss, she thought, and I'm too anonymous to remember. I should be grateful. Good mystery shoppers need to blend in with the crowd. Better let Trish believe she really is anonymous.

Josie wondered what drug Trish used to take and whether she'd been addicted to prescription or street drugs. Had she stolen to support her habit? A tiny thought burrowed into her mind like a worm: What if Mrs. Mueller was right?

Mrs. Mueller was never right, she told herself firmly. People deserve another chance. It's none of my business what brought Trish to a Narcotics Anonymous meeting. Maybe she got addicted to painkillers after a bad car accident. Josie headed into the cold wind toward the front church entrance and her stranded mother, warmed by her virtuous thoughts.

"Thank goodness you got here," Jane said. "This nice man is ready to leave." She hugged her daughter and hung on as tightly as if they'd been separated for months. Josie hugged her mother back.

Jane threw the tow truck driver a smile warm enough to melt the nearby pile of plowed snow.

"I think your car has a bad starter, ma'am, but your mechanic will know for sure," he said to Jane. "You want it towed to Pete's, right?"

Jane checked the repair shop's address and signed the forms. Her nose was red from the cold. "I'm frozen," she said. "Let's go home. I'll make hot chocolate and peanut butter cookies. Amelia can help."

"I'll help eat them," Josie said.

Back at their home, Amelia followed her grandmother upstairs for another cooking lesson. Harry trailed behind his friend, his striped tail raised in a question mark, the signal of cat curiosity. Harry suspected Jane might feed him from the stash of treats she kept upstairs.

Josie started to go with them when her phone rang. She heard whimpers when she answered. "Ted? Is your dog hurt?"

"Festus is fine," Ted said. "You're listening to Stuart Little, the abandoned shih tzu. I've got him on my lap. He's lonely. Can I bring him over tonight to meet your mother?"

"Not a good idea," Josie said. "Mom just had her car towed this evening. It wouldn't start and she was stranded in the snow."

"Tomorrow?" he asked.

"You can try," Josie said. "Come over for dinner then."

"I'll cook," he said.

Had he volunteered to fix dinner to avoid her cooking? Josie wondered. No reason to feel hurt. Ted was as good a cook as he was a lover. She was better in bed than in the kitchen—she hoped.

"How about a winter meal of white chili?" he said. "It has a little cayenne pepper for a mild kick, white beans, chicken breasts, and Monterey Jack cheese. I'll make corn bread, too."

"Sounds hearty," Josie said.

"Do you think your mother will like it? Can she come to dinner, too?"

Josie thought of her mother glaring at the poor dog while everyone tried to eat. Not a good idea, she decided. "Let's have her come downstairs after dinner," she said. "That will give Stuart Little time to calm down and get used to a new place. What kind of wine goes with white chili?"

"Beer," Ted said. "I'll start the chili tonight. The flavor will rock by tomorrow night. Amelia will be there, won't she?"

She wouldn't miss the chance to flirt with you, Josie thought. "Amelia is at Mom's making peanut butter cookies right now," she said. "There should be enough left over for dessert tomorrow night."

"It just gets better and better," Ted said.

It certainly does, Josie thought. I'm in love with a hottie who begs to cook for me. He likes my daughter. My mother is crazy about him. I hope she still likes Ted after he springs that dog adoption on her.

Life seemed nearly perfect until she remembered Laura Ferguson, locked in the county jail.

Why was Laura's sales associate going to a Narcotics Anonymous meeting? Was Trish a recovering drug user? Did she go to the meeting masquerading as a user to get a better perspective for her future police work?

Going undercover in that amateur way was risky if she wanted to be a police officer. The wrong person could see Trish going to that meeting. Mrs. Mueller wasn't the only snoop in the neighborhood.

Did Frankie, the former mean girl, stumble on Trish's drug use at the hospital? Did Trish go to the emergency room because she had OD'd? That would make a tasty tidbit for the power-hungry nurse. What if Frankie taunted her and Trish killed her to save her future career?

How about if I find out some facts first? Josie thought. One more person was in the store the day Frankie was murdered. One I can identify, anyway.

I need to talk to Cody John Wayne, the bra-fetching hero.

# Chapter 16

"You want me to eat broccoli?" Josie screamed into her phone. She didn't bother hiding her outrage. She couldn't believe Harry the Horrible was giving her this assignment. Good thing she wasn't in the Suttin office. She'd snap his neck like a green bean.

"Not just broccoli," Harry the Horrible said, his voice oozing suppressed glee. "Vegetables. Some broccoli is included in the sampling, but you won't be eating all broccoli."

"Any broccoli is too much," Josie said. "You did this on purpose."

She could almost see him in his dusty lair of an office, little tufts of hair poking triumphantly through his gaping shirt buttons, smug smile on his fat face.

"I don't eat broccoli," Josie said.

"You said you wouldn't take off your bra, but you did," Harry said. She heard a glooping sound in the background.

"I only did it for the money," Josie said, then realized that wasn't a good argument.

"And you'll do this for the money, too," he said. "You'll get paid a nice fee. Ten dollars more than usual."

"Not enough," she said.

"Most kids would be happy to get paid to eat broccoli."

"I hate broccoli," Josie said. "So does my daughter." She sounded like Amelia, only not as mature.

"Work isn't supposed to be fun," Harry said. "That's why we pay you for it. I need a mystery shopper." His voice turned hard as a head of cabbage. "Jobs are in short supply these days. I could give this one to someone else."

Josie thought of her daughter and her hungry cat. She'd do anything for them—even eat broccoli.

"You have to mystery-shop the Veggie Madness restaurant in downtown Clayton. Just one. That's all." Harry was back to pleading. The salad bar chain must have requested Josie for this job. He hated to admit that. "Nice business-type neighborhood, professional clientele. It's not that big a deal. Their Bonkers for Broccoli salad is only one selection."

Josie heard a sucking noise, like an elephant pulling its foot out of a mud hole.

"The Veggie Madness salad bar chain says they must serve the freshest food," Harry said. "Your mission is to check for freshness."

"How would I know what a fresh vegetable tastes like?" Josie said.

"By the sound, I guess," Harry said. "Don't they go snap, crackle, and pop?"

"That's Kellogg's Rice Krispies," Josie said. "When's the last time you even ate a vegetable?"

"I'm eating a cherry tomato right now." Harry's voice was larded with righteousness.

Josie heard a small popping sound, like a grape being run over. "Don't tell me you're having a salad for lunch."

"No, I'm having a hot beef sundae," Harry said.

"Roast beef and ice cream? That's disgusting."

"There's no ice cream. The hot beef sundae is today's special at the Carnival Diner. A hot beef sundae is a soup bowl of creamy mashed potatoes covered in chocolate sauce, which is really beef gravy. The mashed potatoes and gravy are piled with tender roast-beef chunks and cheese 'sprinkles.' A cherry tomato tops off the hot beef sundae."

Josie's mouth watered at the thought of roast beef and gravy, though she'd probably skip the cherry tomato.

"Why can't I mystery-shop the Carnival Diner?" she asked. She'd stooped to whining.

"Because there's only one," Harry said. "The chef used to work at the state fair and he cooks fairground favorites. You should try his funnel cakes.

"But I'm not calling you to discuss my lunch. Here's what Veggie Madness wants you to eat at their restaurant: the Bonkers for Broccoli salad, the Zucchini Zip-a-Dee-Doo-Dah."

"What's that?" Josie asked.

"A cheesy medley of zucchini, onions, and roasted red peppers," Harry recited.

"Cheesy is right," Josie said.

"Hey, you might like their Obsessive-Compulsive Onion Soup. You have to eat that, too. The desserts are supposed to be fantastic and you can have any one you want."

"Nothing will take away the taste of broccoli," Josie said.

"A little broccoli won't kill you," Harry said. "It's not like your last assignment, when that Frankie Angel got offed. I saw her photo on TV. What a babe. A waste of a primo pair."

"You're so sensitive," Josie said.

Her sarcasm sailed over his head. "Do you think the manager, Laura What's Her Name, killed Frankie Angel?" Harry asked. "She looked big and fat. Maybe she killed a babe like Frankie Angel out of jealousy."

"No," Josie said, shortly. "And Frankie's no angel, dead or alive."

"I'll fax you the checklist for Veggie Madness," Harry said. "Oh, one more thing. They want you to bring a guest, a woman between fifty and sixty years old."

Alyce is too young, Josie thought, and Mom is too old. But nurse Edith Terna is the right age. She ate a fruit plate at a pancake house. A salad restaurant would be Edith's kind of place. We could talk about Frankie's murder again. Did Frankie threaten to report Rosa's father to ICE? Did she know that Trish had a drug problem and wanted to be a police officer? Did Frankie go after a certain type of patient? Did Frankie have a natural talent for finding victims—until she became a victim herself?

Josie could take Edith to lunch and get paid for helping Laura. She found her boss, Harry, irritating, but mystery-shopping was the perfect job for her. The hours were flexible enough that Josie could take Amelia to school and pick her up. Jane took over that chore when there was a problem. Plus, Josie felt she defended consumers who were quietly abused or neglected by businesses, the people who couldn't or wouldn't complain. Josie was there for them. She could right the wrongs of shoppers snubbed by rude salespeople, directed to the wrong aisle, ignored at the cash register.

Today, with the help of Edith, she would brave a plate of broccoli.

Two hours later, Josie walked into the Veggie Madness restaurant with the wariness of a lone woman entering a biker bar. Edith was waiting under a WELCOME TO THE GARDEN PARTY! sign.

The sensible nurse got straight to the point. "Can I get a beer?" Edith asked.

"Looks like a soft drink kind of place," Josie said. "Sorry."

"You're telling me," Edith said. "At least I like veggies."

Josie picked a green cafeteria tray from a stack. A limp lettuce leaf was stuck on the back. She dropped the tray and grabbed a blue one. The two women joined a line of soberly dressed suits from the nearby offices and pushed their lunch trays past bowls of salads buried in ice.

Edith filled her plate with precise movements, as if she were preparing for surgery.

Josie took a tiny, tentative spoonful of Bonkers for Broccoli. The cranberries in the salad looked like blood spots.

"What's with the names?" Edith asked, reading the sign beside the Krazy for Kale entrée. "Is mental illness supposed to be a joke? What's next: Apeshit over Asparagus?"

A woman in a navy coat turned and glared at Edith. Edith glared back. Josie watched enviously as Edith constructed a well-shaped mountain of Nutty Wonton

Chicken, then made room for a Batty Baked Potato neatly topped with chopped scallions and bacon. None of these items were on Josie's list.

Josie dutifully added a thimbleful of Obsessive-Compulsive Onion Soup to her tray. *Maybe if I pick the cheese out of the Zucchini Zip-a-Dee-Doo-Dah and spread it on the Wacky Wheat Bread, I won't starve,* Josie thought.

"I knew it!" Edith said when they reached the dessert section. "They have Chocolate Suicide cake."

"Thank God." Josie cut herself a thick wedge, admiring the rich chocolate icing dotted with chocolate chips. Edith took a low-fat Bananarama muffin.

Josie followed Edith to a booth in the crowded restaurant. "You didn't get much food," Edith said, as she crunched her wonton chicken salad.

"I'm supposed to be mystery-shopping this place," Josie said. "I haven't a clue about vegetables."

"I can help you," Edith said. "The first tray you picked up had old lettuce on it. Salad dressing was dribbled down the pots. That looked messy. The staff was talking to one another instead of cleaning the salad bar."

She pointed at her chicken salad with her fork. "The romaine lettuce and the wonton pieces are crisp. The dressing is well blended. The cheese is fresh and there's lots of it. Your broccoli salad—may I?"

"Please," Josie said.

Edith took a clean fork from her tray and speared a floret. "Al dente. That's not a used-car dealer, Josie. It means the broccoli is slightly crunchy, properly cooked. This Veggie Madness gets high marks on freshness, low marks on cleanliness."

"Piece of cake," Josie said, taking a big bite of her dark chocolate dessert.

"Have you been able to help my friend Laura?" Edith asked.

"I've made some progress," Josie said. "At least I've

come up with possible motives. One of Laura's saleswomen may have a drug problem. She wants to be a police officer. I'm pretty sure Rosa, the other saleswoman, has parents who are illegal aliens from Mexico."

Edith gave her a shrewd appraising look. "Pretty sure? No proof?"

"Not so far," Josie said. "But having your parents deported and losing your chance at your dream career are powerful motives."

"But you don't have enough to go to the police and help Laura, do you?"

Josie watched as Edith enthusiastically cut up her baked potato. "No," Josie said. "There are still two possible suspects. One is a woman who stood in the doorway at the shop. She was too shy to take off her blouse and try on a bra. Nobody seemed to know who she was."

"Not worth looking for," Edith said. "Laura gets two or three of those every week."

"A blonde was in the bathroom when I discovered the body. She was in a wheelchair and the handicapped-stall door was locked. She was gone before the police got there. She gave us bad contact information."

"That sounds suspicious," Edith said. "But I'd let the cops look for her."

"They didn't," Josie said. "They arrested Laura instead. She was an easier target."

"Could be." Edith took a bite of baked potato. "Could be they eliminated her and didn't tell you. They don't have to, you know."

"There's also Cody the hero," Josie said.

"I thought police were looking for a woman?" Edith said.

"They are. But I want to know what he's like. Cody John Wayne was the last person in the shop to see Frankie alive. What do you know about him?"

"He is a real hero," Edith said. "They pinned the medal on the right man. Those carjackers had served time for murder. Cody saved that young couple and took a bullet in his leg and in his lung."

"Were you his nurse at the hospital?"

"No," Edith said. "Cody wasn't my patient. Frankie was his nurse, but she didn't blab anything bad. All I know is that Cody is a customer of Laura's."

"You mean his wife is," Josie corrected.

"No, he is, too. I stopped by Desiree Lingerie near closing time one night—before the carjacking. I was meeting Laura for dinner after she got off work. Cody was at the register. I heard him stammer, 'I need to pick up that thing for work. It's cold at night around those warehouses.'"

"Was he buying long underwear?" Josie asked.

"Didn't look like it," Edith said. "Bag wasn't fat enough. Besides, Cody turned redder than a stoplight when he saw me in the doorway. I'm good with faces, and well, he's a memorable man. I don't usually forget good-looking men. A few days later, I saw him on TV and he was a hero—and at our hospital."

"Why would Cody go to Desiree Lingerie when he could walk into Sears and buy long underwear there?"

"I asked Laura about it," Edith said. "She said the man had been in the war and deserved his privacy. She keeps her clients' secrets, better than some doctors. She never would tell me. I asked her again when I saw her in jail two days ago. She turned all noble on me and said he was a brave man who didn't need more grief."

"Another mystery." Josie finished the last of her cake. "This just gets more complicated. Do you think Cody is a cross-dresser? If Frankie wanted to reveal that secret, it would be a good motive for murder."

Edith shrugged. "We get some in the ER. Mostly guys who'd been in accidents. I could never tell till we cut off their clothes and saw they didn't have female parts. But the nurses who worked on Cody said he's all man."

"Do you know where Cody lives?" Josie asked.

"No, but he's director of security for the Sale Away Store on Manchester Road."

"That big ugly store near the failing shopping center?" Josie asked. "I don't like to shop there."

"Not many do, with muggers and wild dogs roaming the parking lot. Sale Away would need an army of heroes to guard that place. I don't think they can afford enough security to keep it a safe place for shopping. We get Sale Away's dog-bite and mugging victims at the hospital."

"Maybe I'd better see Cody right after lunch," Josie said.

"Better hurry," Edith said. "I wouldn't be surprised if that Sale Away closes soon. Don't forget your pepper spray. You have to be crazy to go there, even in daylight."

# Chapter 17

A steel wool sky scraped the flat roof of the Sale Away building. The store looked like a monster beige packing box abandoned in acres of dirty gray asphalt. Josie steered her Honda around a car-swallowing pothole and pulled in beside a salt-crusted SUV.

A long, sad howl split the cold afternoon air.

A coyote on the edge of St. Louis? Josie couldn't tell what kind of doglike creature was wailing under a light pole, but it had a long snout, skinny legs, and yellow teeth. Two more scrawny dogs straggled across the Sale Away lot and sat by her car door, teeth bared. How was she going to get out without being attacked?

She remembered Ted's advice: Most feral dogs are frightened of humans and will run away. Most. What if these were the exception to that rule?

Josie reached into her purse for the dog repellent Ted had given her. She hoped she wouldn't have to spray the starving creatures.

The chilling howl was cut off by a soft *putt-putt* sound. A golf cart trundled around the side of Sale Away and the dogs scattered.

Cody was riding to Josie's rescue. The man couldn't help being a hero. Josie thought he should be riding on a white horse instead of in a white golf cart. He parked his vehicle beside her car and dismounted. Josie had to restrain herself from batting her eyes and gushing, "My hero."

Once again, Cody gave the impression of being bigger than he was. Today his blue-gray uniform jacket added the bulk. His flapped cap protected his cold-reddened face. There was nothing timid about Cody now. He spoke with a cowboy's "aw-shucks" ease. "Sorry about that. Animal control can't keep up with all the stray dogs. May I escort you to the door so you can shop?"

"Are you Cody?" Josie asked.

"Cody John Wayne," he said. "At your service. My father was from Iowa. He was a big fan of two Iowans, Buffalo Bill Cody and John Wayne."

"It makes for a manly name," Josie said.

"I'm just lucky he didn't admire Herbert Hoover, another Iowan," Cody said.

"I'm not here to shop," Josie said. "I want to talk to you. Does your store have a food court? I'd like to buy you a cup of coffee."

"It does, but I wouldn't drink that swill they call coffee," he said. "I have a better brew in the thermos in my office. We can split a cup there. I'm due for a short break."

"Deal," Josie said. She felt guilty about taking the man's hot coffee on a cold day, until she remembered Laura in the county jail. She had to help her former teacher. Besides, what if Cody was guilty? Josie wished he wasn't so likable.

The inside of Sale Away was even dingier than the parking lot. Josie gave it a professional inspection. The aisles were dimly lit and needed mopping. The "on sale always!" lamps, sinks, and ceiling fans were jumbled on metal shelves. They looked like cheap knockoffs of better merchandise.

The cashiers outnumbered the customers. Josie trailed behind Cody to his office in the back of the store. Cody took off his coat as he walked. Josie checked his back for the telltale signs of a bra under his uniform shirt. Nothing. If he was a cross-dresser, it didn't show.

The only decorations in Cody's office were pictures of his wife and son on the walls. He hung his jacket on a hook

already loaded with dark coats and sweaters. Cody sat behind his desk. Josie perched on the edge of a wobbly chair.

"How can I help you?" Cody asked.

"I'm a friend of Laura Ferguson, the manager of Desiree Lingerie in Plaza Venetia," Josie said. "I was at the
store the day you were there."

"I don't go to lingerie stores," he said. "I'm a dude, in
case you haven't noticed." A smile flickered across his face.
The man was either forgetful or a skilled liar, Josie thought.
He'd been in Desiree Lingerie more than once. Nurse
Edith had seen him there, too.

She didn't smile back. "You were in that store."

"Never been in a ladies' lingerie store in my life." Another smile, this one clearly faked.

"You were there. I saw you," Josie said. "You picked up
a bra that had been altered for your wife. A woman complained that the blond salesperson, Trish, was helping you
and she couldn't get waited on."

"Oh, that." Cody made such a show of remembering, he
nearly slapped himself on the forehead. "Right. I forgot.
Must have wiped the painful experience out of my mind. I
remember now. I was embarrassed being the only guy in a
store that sold ladies' frillies."

"The woman who complained about you was Frankie
Angela Martin. She was murdered sometime after you left
the store."

"She was?"

Josie thought he was faking more surprise. "You must
have seen the TV coverage," Josie said. "The local stations
played and replayed a video of the person the police think
killed her."

"Sorry. I can't keep those stories straight. They're all
alike: First, they show the victim's photo, then a gray video
from some store, followed by interviews with weepy family
and friends. Finally, the police promise to catch the killer.
Then the murder is forgotten.

"I mean no disrespect to the dead, but I can't tell the

victims apart. They're all sad and they're all the same. Wish I could help you, but I don't know any Frankie."

"But you know the manager, Laura Ferguson," Josie said. "She needs your help."

"That the big lady? She was nice to me when I picked up my wife's bra, but I wouldn't say I know her. I'm sorry she's in trouble, but I don't see how I can help."

The more earnest Cody sounded, the more *LIAR* seemed to flash over his head in red neon.

"Did you go straight back to work that day after you left the lingerie shop?" Josie asked.

"That's none of your business," Cody said. "But the answer is no. It was my day off and my wife, Renee, declared it a 'honey-do' day. You know, 'Honey, do this' and 'Honey, do that.' I spent the day running errands. Picking up her bra was one of them. Why do you want to know where I was? Do you think I offed the lady because she was rude?"

"I am trying to help Laura," Josie said. "I owe her. She helped me when I needed it. Now a customer at her store has been murdered and Laura has been arrested for killing her. I think she's innocent."

"I'm sorry your friend is in jail," Cody said. "But I don't know anything about a murder. Now if you'll excuse me, I'm working here single-handed today. I have to get back to protecting customers."

He stood up and pulled his uniform jacket off the hook, herding Josie toward the door. She caught a brief flash of black and white as the coats and other clothing swung on the overloaded hook.

Josie had no choice but to leave. She never did get that coffee.

# Chapter 18

"What do you think of my hair?" Amelia asked.

Josie hadn't noticed her daughter's new style. Jane had picked up Amelia at school, and the girl had holed up in her room, IMing her friends. Josie had said hello and gone into a frenzy of dusting, polishing, and vacuuming to prepare for Ted's visit.

Amelia had tracked her mother down in the kitchen, where Josie was arranging peanut butter cookies on a pretty plate.

"Mom? Do you like it?"

Josie's ten-year-old daughter had slicked her rich brown hair into a sophisticated French roll. Amelia assumed a pout suitable for a thirtysomething siren and twirled on the living room carpet. "Do I look older?"

Josie stopped and studied her daughter. "Much older. With that hairstyle, I'd say you were pushing eleven."

"Mom!" Amelia drew out the word to show her displeasure. "Be serious. Do you like my hair up?"

"Maybe in a few years," Josie said. "I like the way you wear it now—chin-length."

Josie wouldn't admit it, but she was startled by how adult Amelia looked with an updo. She caught a glimpse of the woman Amelia would soon be. Her daughter looked older—and ridiculously young at the same time. Josie wanted her little girl back, at least for a while.

She kissed Amelia and said, "It's fun to experiment with your hair, sweetheart, but I like you just the way you are."

"What about Ted?" Amelia asked. "Do you think he'll like this style?"

"Ask him," Josie said. "He'll be here shortly. He's bringing white chili with chicken and homemade corn bread. Your peanut butter cookies will be dessert."

"Yay!" Amelia danced around the kitchen.

"There," Josie said, half to herself. "The cookies are ready. I have six bottles of Schlafly Pilsner cooling in the fridge. I hope beer brewed in Maplewood will go well with Ted's white chili. Now, if you'll set the table, please."

She didn't have to ask twice. Amelia loved Ted's visits.

Josie needed a few moments alone. She'd been racing around since she got home, hoping to distract herself with cleaning. It didn't work. She felt shell-shocked and confused after her encounter with Cody. She still suspected the hero was lying, but she couldn't quite believe he'd killed Frankie. Cody had said he wouldn't kill someone for being rude, and he was right. At a store like Sale Away, he must encounter rude people every day. Maybe Ted could help her figure Cody out. She needed a man's perspective.

Josie changed into a crisp white blouse and jeans and put on fresh lipstick. She'd just combed her glossy brown hair when she heard a car crunching on the snow at the curb, then a door slam, a short bark, and heavy booted feet on her porch.

Harry growled and crawled under the couch.

Josie opened the door to a flurry of cold kisses, warm hugs, and friendly yaps. Ted was juggling a heavy cardboard box and a curly-coated dog.

"Take Stuart Little before I drop the chili." Ted handed off the dog to Josie. "I carried him so he wouldn't get muddy paws on your floor."

The shih tzu was the color of whipped cream and caramel with chocolate brown eyes.

"Stuart Little, we meet at last," Josie said. "He feels so light. Hardly bigger than Harry."

Josie heard another growl come from under her couch.

"Eleven pounds of personality." Ted set the box with the chili pot on the kitchen counter.

Stuart Little wagged his feathery tail at Josie and she scratched his ears.

"Let me hold him! Let me, Mom!" Amelia said.

Josie handed her the warm canine bundle and followed Ted into the kitchen. She opened two beers, one for him and one for herself. He was heating the chili on the stove and the foil-wrapped corn bread in the oven.

"What can I get Stuart?" Josie asked.

"He's had dinner," Ted said. "Put down a bowl of water, if you want. Think your mom will like him?"

"I sure hope so," Josie said, though she wasn't sure at all.

Amelia carried the dog into the warm kitchen. "Stuart Little is so handsome. Look at those bright eyes."

Josie heard another growl from under the couch, loud enough to reach the kitchen.

"Can we keep him? Can we?" Amelia asked.

"No," Josie said. "Harry's top cat in this house, and one pet is all we can handle. You have school and I have a job. We have to persuade your grandmother to adopt him. That will take work. She doesn't like animals."

"She likes Harry," Amelia said.

"Harry doesn't live with her," Josie said. "It took weeks for her to warm up to him. We don't have that time with Stuart Little."

"What can we do to change her mind?" Amelia asked.

"We'll have to help Grandma. That means we'll walk Stuart Little and clean up after him."

"Yuck-o," Amelia said.

"Then Stuart has to go to the pound, where he may not get adopted," Josie said.

"He can't. He'll die!" Amelia hugged the small dog closer. "I won't let anyone hurt you, Stuart. I'll clean up your mess. I'll walk you in the cold. I want you that much. Right, Mom?"

"You don't have to persuade me," Josie said. "You have to convince your grandmother."

They were interrupted by more angry growls.

"Harry is not happy with your new love," Josie said.

"Hey, where is the big guy?" Ted asked. "Harry always comes out to see me."

"He's sulking under the couch," Josie said.

"We'll see about that." Ted got down on the living room floor and peeked under the couch. "Harry, what's wrong, old man?"

A louder growl, as if an angry tiger were wedged under the couch.

"Come out and say hello," Ted said.

Silence.

Ted reached into his pocket and set a fish-shaped treat inches from the couch. Twitching whiskers and a red rubber nose appeared, followed by a striped face with enormous ears and angry green eyes. Harry slid out far enough to sniff the treat. Josie, Ted, and Amelia waited. No one dared to talk. Even Stuart Little was silent.

Harry gulped the treat and scooted back under the couch as if he were on rollers. Ted put out another treat, this one a full foot from the couch.

"We have to be patient," Ted whispered. "Cats don't like change."

"They don't like dogs, either," Amelia said.

"They can learn to get along. We have to introduce Harry to his future friend in the right way." Ted set a second treat beside the first. Then a third.

The triple temptation was too much. Harry rushed out to gobble the treats. Ted grabbed him. The cat squirmed, furious at being caught. Harry calmed as Ted fed him the three treats, one at a time, while scratching the cat's short, striped fur. A fourth treat earned a loud purr.

"Let's put Harry in his safe place now," Ted said. "That's your bathroom, right, Amelia?"

"He likes to hide under the claw-foot tub," Amelia said. "I keep his litter box in my bathroom, too."

"Is there a soft rug in there?"

"The bath mat," Amelia said.

"Good. Put down food and water, in case this introduction takes a while. I'll hold Harry."

Ted stroked the cat, talking to him and feeding him treats, while Amelia scurried to prepare Harry's room. Josie sat in a living room chair petting Stuart Little, enjoying the feel of his soft ears. The shih tzu whimpered and licked her arm.

Harry's enormous ears rotated, catching the sound of his canine rival, but he didn't growl.

"Room's ready," Amelia said.

Ted continued to pet the cat while carrying him to Amelia's purple bathroom. He gently placed Harry on the rug, left two more treats, and closed the door.

"Now what?" Amelia said.

"Now they'll get acquainted while we have dinner," Ted said.

"But the door's shut," Amelia said.

"Wait and see. Meanwhile, let's eat chili."

The white chili was slightly spicy and rich with chicken. It was meaty enough to erase Josie's memory of her all-veggie lunch. The three emptied the entire chili pot.

"That was amazing," Amelia said. "Can I have your recipe?"

"Anytime," Ted said. "Maybe we can cook something together."

"I'd like that," Amelia said. "What do you think of my hair?" She patted her new style and fluttered her eyelashes.

"It's perfect for special occasions," Ted said, "like introducing a new dog to your grandmother. But for every day, I like your hair down. Simple and uncomplicated—like me."

"You're neither one," Josie said, and kissed his cheek. She liked the slightly scratchy feel of his freshly shaved beard.

They heard a thud and a yelp. Josie, Ted, and Amelia tiptoed to the hall. Harry was poking his paw out from under the bathroom door. Stuart Little twirled in excited circles, then licked the cat's striped paw. Harry pulled his paw back, then stuck it out again, while Stuart tried to catch it.

"They're playing a game," Ted whispered. "Let's leave them alone."

"We'll have coffee and cookies in the living room," Josie said.

"I'll clear the table," Amelia said.

"We'll help you," Ted said.

"No, you and Mom figure out how to get Grandma to adopt Stuart Little. I can clean up on my own."

"Amelia really wants my mother to keep this dog," Josie said as she settled next to Ted with her coffee. They heard another thud, this one louder, followed by a sharp bark.

"The animals are getting noisy," Josie said. "Mom's going to hear Stuart Little before she meets him."

"Then it's time to introduce Harry to Stuart."

In the hall, they saw Stuart Little dancing in excited circles, yapping at Harry's outstretched paw. Ted opened the bathroom door. Harry emerged cautiously. The shih tzu sat down in front of the cat. Harry slowly sniffed the dog from ears to paws, then licked his forehead. Stuart Little stayed still as a stuffed animal.

"Harry's grooming him," Ted whispered. "That's good."

Harry swatted the dog playfully. Stuart Little streaked down the hall toward the kitchen, Harry running after him. When the dog and cat raced out of the kitchen again, Stuart was chasing Harry. Amelia was laughing so hard, she had to sit down.

"They're like an old Warner Bros. cartoon," Josie said.

"We'll let them play," Ted said. "Once they calm down, we'll call your mother so she can meet her new dog."

Josie and Ted settled on the couch in comfortable silence, waiting for the animals to run off their energy. Josie closed her eyes, and leaned back against his outstretched arm. She had to ask him about Cody. It was important.

"Mom! Look!" Amelia said in a stage whisper. Josie snapped her head up and saw her daughter pointing under the coffee table. Harry and Stuart Little were curled up asleep. Harry had his head on Stuart's shoulder.

"They're adorable," Josie whispered back. "Let's call

Grandma. We'll tell her we have someone for her to meet. Battle stations, Amelia. She may not react well to this surprise."

"She'll love Stuart. She has to," Amelia said. It was a prayer, not a statement.

Jane promised she'd be right down. Amelia paced while she waited. "What's taking Grandma so long?"

Josie guessed her mother was adding another layer of Aqua Net to her hair, fresh lipstick, and Estée Lauder perfume.

Finally the front door opened. Stuart Little and Harry scrambled to sit up, looking as guilty as caught lovers.

Jane had done everything Josie suspected and more. She wore her new pink pantsuit and a smile for Ted. He was the current front-runner in the son-in-law sweepstakes.

"Well, who do you want me to meet?" Jane asked.

"Uh," Josie said.

"Don't keep hiding him. What's his name?" Jane's smile was starting to fade. She saw Josie's guilty look. Jane's face was a slide show. The smile died in her eyes. Then it turned into a stare, and finally a glare when she saw Stuart Little and Harry under the coffee table.

"What's that?" Jane said.

The dog whimpered.

Josie's courage failed. "Dust?"

Jane pointed at Stuart Little. "I've never seen a four-legged dust bunny. What is that thing?"

Stuart Little wagged his tail and looked at Jane with melting brown eyes. She was rock hard with anger.

"I said, whose dog is that?" Jane demanded.

"Yours?" Josie asked, and gulped.

# Chapter 19

"Oh, no. No dogs," Jane said. "You know I don't allow animals in this house."

"What about Harry?" Amelia asked.

"I let him in against my better judgment," she said. "That cat can leave anytime."

Her glare could have lasered the fur off Harry. He crawled under the couch again. Stuart stayed under the coffee table. Josie wished she could join them.

Ted stepped in and tried to help. "Mrs. Marcus, this is Stuart Little. He's a patient at my clinic. His family abandoned him and he needs a home." Ted used the same soothing tone he reserved for furious dogs and spitting-mad felines.

"And Josie's going to adopt him?" Jane was outraged. "This is my house, not the pound, young woman. You can't take in strays just because your boyfriend is a veterinarian."

"We were hoping you would take him," Ted said.

"Why don't you add him to your own menagerie, Ted?" Jane said.

"My Lab, Festus, plays too hard. He'll hurt this little guy. Stuart Little is only eleven pounds. He's a lapdog. A people animal. He needs you to love him."

Stuart continued thumping his plumed tail like a cheerleader shaking pom-poms at a losing game.

"And I need him like a hole in the head," Jane said. "What's wrong with that dog? Why was he abandoned?"

"His owner couldn't afford to feed him," Ted said.

"Hah! Do I look made out of money?" Jane asked.

"No, but you are a generous person," Ted said. "If you'll take him, I'll give you free food and veterinary care for a year. Stuart will give you unconditional love."

Stuart Little tilted his head and kept wagging his tail.

"Look, Grandma, he's smiling at you," Amelia said. "Isn't he cute?"

"Real cute," Jane said with a snarl. "Especially when I have to walk him on a cold night."

"I'll walk him," Amelia said.

"And who's going to clean up the messes in my yard so Mrs. Mueller doesn't get upset?"

Jane didn't seem to realize that she'd declared Mrs. Mueller the overseer of her property.

"I will. I'm real good at cleaning Harry's litter box," Amelia said. "Just ask Mom."

Josie said nothing. She wouldn't admit she nagged Amelia into litter box duty. She'd walk Stuart herself, if she had to.

Jane was wavering. "Well, he is a cute little thing." Stuart wagged his tail with extra enthusiasm. "But he looks like he needs a lot of grooming. That's expensive."

"I'll throw in a year's worth of grooming at our clinic," Ted said.

"Please, Grandma," Amelia begged. "Can't we keep him?"

Stuart sat up and begged, too. That did it. "Okay, we'll keep him. On trial. But that animal is *not* sleeping in my flat on my furniture. I'll fix him a basket in the basement laundry room."

"It's cold down there," Amelia said.

"He can have a pillow in the basket," Jane added. "And a blanket."

Amelia looked as big-eyed as the dog. Jane caved. "I'll put his bed by the furnace so he'll be nice and warm."

"Yay!" Amelia said. "Let's go down now, Grandma. I'll help you fix it."

Amelia hurried down the basement steps. Her grandmother followed at a slower pace. Stuart trotted behind them.

When the trio was out of sight, Josie collapsed on the couch. "That was exhausting," she said.

"I knew your mother would say yes," Ted said. "She's a generous woman."

"You gave her free food, vet care, and grooming for a year. Wouldn't it have been easier to pay Stuart's owner to keep him?" Josie asked.

"His owner wanted to abandon that sweet dog. He didn't appreciate him. Stuart is better off with your mother."

"I need your help," Josie said, seriously. "I want to ask you about the man who was at Desiree Lingerie the day of the murder. Something was going on there, but I'm not sure what it was."

"Tell me what you remember," Ted said. "It helps to relax."

Josie snuggled against his flannel shirt, breathing in his manly scent of woodsmoke and hot coffee. She closed her eyes and tried to recall the morning at Desiree Lingerie. "Cody John Wayne came into the shop to pick up his wife's bra. He looked scared."

"Lingerie shops frighten most men," Ted said.

"I know men can be shy, but it was more than that," Josie said. "There was some sort of tension. The late, not-so-great Frankie was there. I think she was taunting him, but I can't figure out how. She handed Cody a pair of extra-large panty hose from a rack. He said his wife wore a small size. She said the panty hose were for him. Frankie mentioned Cody's son, Tyler, and said heroes must run in the family."

"Cody and his son are heroes?" Ted asked.

"I don't know about Tyler, but Cody has the medals to prove it," Josie said. "He's the security guard who saved a young couple from a carjacking ten years ago. Cody had served in the Gulf War and came home unscathed, then got shot in the leg while working in his hometown."

"I remember that story," Ted said.

"Cody's wife sent him to pick up a bra that had been

altered. It wasn't ready. Laura asked him to come back an hour later. Cody ran out of that shop like terrorists were after him. Frankie was up to something, but I don't know what."

"Could be he was a cross-dresser and bought his underwear there," Ted said.

"I know he bought something from Laura in secret, but she won't say what. Edith, one of her friends, saw Cody in the store once and he was very uneasy—and Edith didn't say anything to him."

"Maybe she imagined that?"

"Edith is a nurse and good observer," Josie said. "I don't know if Cody gets his kicks from wearing women's underwear. I tracked him to his job today and tried to check. I didn't see the outline of a bra under his uniform."

"You checked a man for bra straps?" Ted said. "You're adorable." He kissed her ear.

"I wasn't being cute," Josie said. "I wanted to know. I didn't think to look for panty lines in his slacks."

"Maybe his shirt material was too thick to show bra straps," Ted said. "Maybe he doesn't wear the underwear to work."

"Maybe he's not a cross-dresser after all," Josie said. "Is there another reason why Frankie would hand a man panty hose? She made a big show of it. She wanted an audience."

"Cody was in the Gulf War, huh?" Ted asked. "I knew two guys who wore panty hose over there. Both asked their wives to send them in their 'care packages' from home. They wore L'eggs control tops, if I remember right."

"You're kidding," Josie said. "Panty hose in the desert? Even I don't wear them, especially not in the summer. They're too hot in the St. Louis humidity."

"Humidity wasn't a problem in the desert," Ted said. "But nasty, disease-carrying sand flies were. Some soldiers wore the panty hose to protect them from sand fly bites. Others wore panty hose as protection from the cold. Desert temperatures can drop to near freezing at night. My friends said they liked panty hose because they were lighter and easier to carry than long johns. These men didn't give a damn what anyone thought. They were battle-scarred veterans. Could be Cody kept wearing panty hose once he got home and worked as a security guard. It gets cold walking rounds at night. In the St. Louis summer, the mosquitoes would eat him alive."

"Why wouldn't he wear men's long underwear?" Josie asked.

"Panty hose keep your feet warm," Ted said. "They don't stop at the ankle, like most long johns I've seen. Don't bulk up your clothes, either, so you can wear them under your uniform. Put a couple pairs of socks on over the panty hose and a man can work outside in comfort."

"I can't picture our troops in panty hose," Josie said.

"Not everyone wore panty hose," Ted said. "Just some. The others denied it and were angry at the mention of soldiers wearing them. The subject launched more than one bar fight. This Frankie was a nurse, right?"

Josie nodded. She felt so comfortable in the crook of Ted's arm she didn't want to move.

"Maybe she cut the panty hose off him when he got shot on duty," Ted said.

"Would Cody kill Frankie if she spilled that information?" Josie asked.

"Depends on how secure a man he is," Ted said. "His wife had to know he wore them. She was probably the only female whose opinion he cared about."

"I don't think Cody worries about his manhood. He doesn't brag or swagger. He worked some lousy jobs to feed his family. He faced two armed carjackers and saved a young couple."

"Sounds like my definition of a real man," Ted said. "I'm no psychologist, but I'd guess that information wasn't worth killing Frankie."

Josie sighed. "I'm getting nowhere. Laura will never get out of jail."

# Chapter 20

"Mom?" Amelia appeared in Josie's bedroom door, a pale ghost on a winter night.

Josie struggled out of a sound sleep. "What's wrong, honey? Are you sick?"

"Stuart Little is crying in the basement," Amelia said. "Listen. He's lonely."

Josie heard a thin howl rise up from the depths of the basement. "Didn't Grandma put him in his basket with a blanket and pillow?"

"We tucked him in and left Stuart food and water. Grandma put his basket near the furnace so he'd be warm, but not so close it could catch on fire."

"Then he's fine." Josie put her head back on her warm pillow.

"But what if he's not, Mom? What if he's sick?"

"He's just lonely," Josie said. "He'll be okay. Go back to sleep. You have school tomorrow."

Amelia padded back to her room. Josie settled into her pillow and pulled the covers around her, hoping to fall back asleep. Now she could hear the dog whimpering. What if he was sick? What if he woke up her mother and Jane sent him back to Ted? She'd better get up.

The floor was cold as an ice-skating rink. Josie buried her feet in warm slippers, pulled on a fleece robe, and dragged herself downstairs. The furnace pilot light revealed Stuart burrowed into his warm basket, whining. He stopped and wagged a greeting.

"What's your problem?" she asked as she picked up the dog.

Stuart snuggled in her arms and looked at her with melting brown eyes. "You are not going upstairs tonight," she said, stifling a yawn. "You'll be fine. I'll stay with you a few moments until you fall asleep."

She carried Stuart to the old overstuffed chair her mother kept next to the dryer, and gently rocked the dog. As soon as he fell asleep, she'd go back to bed. It should only take a moment. He was quiet already.

"Josie Marcus! Why are you sleeping in the basement?" Jane's voice was like a slap on the head.

"Huh? What time is it?" Josie sat up in the chair. Stuart had sneaked back into his basket sometime last night. Now he was sitting under his blanket, looking innocently curious.

"It's six thirty," Jane said. "How long have you been down here? Aren't you cold?"

Josie was chilly and stiff from sleeping in the butt-sprung chair. Jane was somewhere under all those winter clothes. She could make out her mother's eyes between the hairy muffler wrapped around her face and her squashed knit hat.

"Hi, Mom. I heard a noise and went downstairs to investigate," Josie said. "I sat down a minute and must have fallen asleep." She was afraid to rat out Stuart Little. He was still on probation. "Should I walk Stuart before I get Amelia up for school?"

"No, I'll do it," Jane said. "I need an invigorating walk." She held up a red leash, another gift from Ted.

"Walkies, Stuart?"

The dog yapped. Jane attached the leash to Stuart's collar and the two of them raced up the stairs. Josie followed, cold and creaky. She needed coffee.

Josie watched her mother step briskly toward the sidewalk, the shih tzu charging ahead on his leash. Jane took the route away from Mrs. Mueller's home. Josie wondered how the old biddy would take the news that a dog was living next to her precious lawn.

Josie returned to the kitchen and found Amelia making toast and pouring herself a glass of milk. Harry sat at her feet, looking hopefully at the milk. He rarely left Amelia's side.

"Did Stuart sleep well after you checked on him, Mom?"

"Like a baby," Josie said.

"I got up early so I can walk the dog before school." Amelia carefully spread grape jelly on her toast so all four corners were covered, then took a huge bite.

"Grandma already beat you," Josie said. "She's out walking Stuart now."

"Does that mean Grandma will keep him for good?" Amelia asked.

"I hope so. But we'd better take this one day at a time. Speaking of time, now that you're up early, you have time to clean Harry's litter box."

"But, Mom—" Amelia began.

"Unless you want me to tell your grandmother how often I remind you to rake Harry's box."

Ah, blackmail, Josie thought. What family could survive without it?

"Come on, Harry," Amelia said. She dropped her glass and plate in the sink, and sulked off to her chore. The striped cat trotted behind his friend.

The drive to school that morning was silent. Josie was tired from sitting up with the dog. Amelia was unhappy she had to clean the cat box. Too bad, Josie thought. You promised you'd do anything to have Harry. At least the silence avoided a fight.

Josie returned to an equally silent house when her phone rang. She kicked off her boots and caught the phone on the fourth ring. It was Harry the Horrible, her boss.

"Wanna go to a movie?" he asked.

"Is this a date?" Josie said.

"Of course not," Harry said.

He didn't have to sound so offended, Josie thought.

"I want you to mystery-shop a movie theater, Chick Flickers, in West County. You've seen the ads: 'All women, all the time.'"

"Sounds like a strip club," Josie said.

"Can't I tell you anything without getting slammed?" Harry asked. "You whined about the salad place and complained when you had to shop a lingerie store."

"Where a customer was murdered," Josie said.

"So? It wasn't you," Harry said. "Now I want to pay you to watch a movie and I get sarcasm."

He's right, she thought. Jobs are scarce these days. "What's the movie?" Josie asked in a softer voice.

"*Ursula Unbound,*" Harry said.

"Never heard of it," Josie said.

"It has all the stuff chicks love: shopping, hair, guys groveling to get back in bed with them after a big fight."

I could spend the rest of the day straightening out this lamebrain, Josie thought. Or I could take the assignment and shut up.

"What do I have to do?"

"Go to the afternoon show. Buy a ticket to *Ursula Unbound*. If anybody wants to sell you 3-D glasses, buy them and remember what happens. Order a large popcorn."

"That's it?" Josie said.

"Take your friend what's-her-name, too. As long as she asks for 3-D glasses."

"Alyce has a little boy," Josie said. "I don't know if her nanny is working today."

"Chick Flickers has free babysitting."

"I forgive you for the broccoli," Josie said.

"Yeah, yeah, just remember to take notes and fax the results as soon as you get home."

By noon, Alyce was parking in the movie-theater lot. Josie sat next to her in the front seat. Alyce's toddler, Justin, was strapped in the child-safety seat in back, crowing his new word: "Boozer. Boozer! Boozer!"

"Who's Boozer?" Josie whispered.

"Bruiser," Alyce said. "He can't quite get the *r* in our Chihuahua's name. At least he doesn't pull the poor dog's ears so much anymore."

Alyce looked back at her son. "Brrruiser," she said, rolling her *r* like a Spaniard. "Your doggy's name is Brrruiser."

"Boozer!" Justin said.

Alyce rolled her eyes.

"Brrruiser is your friend, Justin," Josie said.

"And we're going to meet some more new friends." Alyce unbuckled Justin from his safety seat and adjusted his hat. He held his mother's hand and chugged through the plowed parking lot toward the Pepto-Bismol pink building.

A fuchsia sign proclaimed, "Free babysitting! Movies when Mom wants them! Get your quality time, ladies, and we'll get you out in time to pick up the kids!" A pair of pink high heels danced next to the words.

"You would know they'd paint the theater pink and stick a giant pair of heels on it," Alyce said. "As if any mother in high heels could run after kids."

At the box office, Josie paid for two tickets.

"Can I interest you in our special 3-D glasses for one dollar each?" the cashier asked. She wore a pink uniform and a name tag that said DENISE.

"It's a 3-D movie, right?" Josie asked.

"Definitely," Denise said.

"We'll take two," Josie said.

Justin could hardly wait to get inside the playroom. "Ball! Ball!" he yelled, excited that he knew the word for the blue toys in a yellow bin.

"That's right," Alyce said. "And you can play with one." She gave her contact information to Gina, the playroom employee watching four preschoolers.

Gina gave Alyce a beeper. "Just in case, but I know this little sweetie won't be a problem." Justin was so enraptured with his ball, he didn't notice when his mother and Josie left.

"Our next assignment is to get a large popcorn," Josie said.

"I like this job," Alyce said.

There was no one behind the concession counter in the hot pink lobby. Josie and Alyce waited. "Even the ceiling is pink," Alyce said. "I feel like I've been swallowed by a giant mouth."

"Hello," Josie called after a long wait. "Anybody here?"

A fiftyish woman emerged from a back room wearing earbuds and a pink uniform that clashed with her red Jell-O hair. Her name tag said SUE.

"Help you?" Sue asked.

"A large popcorn," Josie said, "and two waters." She took the water bottles out of a self-serve cooler. Sue scooped popcorn into a big pink box and handed it over with insolent indifference.

"Ya need any 3-D glasses?" Sue asked, with slightly more animation.

"Got 'em," Josie said, and held up hers.

Josie and Alyce walked into a pink cave, put on their glasses, and watched the movie. Josie didn't recognize the star, a cute brunette with her hair twisted in a French roll. She thought the shopping spree and ritual guy groveling were dull. She had trouble focusing in the 3-D glasses. Josie took hers off, waited for her eyes to adjust, then said, "Alyce, the movie looks the same without the stupid glasses. In fact, it looks better."

"Then why charge a buck for these things?" Alyce asked.

"I bet it's a scam," Josie said.

"Sh!" said the woman sitting in front of them. She turned around and glared. She was not wearing 3-D glasses.

Josie and Alyce sat in silence for the rest of the movie. They stopped by the playroom to pick up Justin. The little boy ran to his mother and buried his head in her coat. Justin's hair was silky with a slight curl. Josie remembered Amelia at that age and felt a pang of longing. Amelia had been such a happy baby.

"Someone's tired," Alyce said, gently buckling her son into his car seat. Justin was asleep almost before the car left the lot.

"So what did you think?" Josie asked.

"The popcorn tasted like salted foam and the concession service was terrible," Alyce said. "The chick movie didn't do much for this chick. The heroine was an airhead. I also didn't realize that shopping was a contact sport."

"You've never been to a 'final markdown' sale," Josie said. "This should have been an action movie."

"It was pretty amazing when Ursula leaped a counter to corner the last sale purse," Alyce said.

"And she did it for her mother," Josie said. "She was a hero."

"I didn't like her hair," Alyce said. "When Ursula wore it down, she looked like Medusa. Maybe it was the 3-D."

"I thought she looked better with long hair," Josie said. "She certainly got more men that way. Was that the meaning of *Ursula Unbound*—she was a freer woman when she let her hair down?"

"Moviemakers can't possibly think we're that shallow, can they?" Alyce asked. "What was with that French roll style? In 3-D, it looked like a sausage."

"Did I tell you that Amelia put her hair up in a French roll?" Josie asked.

"How'd she look?"

"Older. More mature. Completely different, actually. Oh, my God, that's it! I know who the strange woman was in the doorway!" Josie said.

"What doorway?" Alyce said.

"Remember that woman who came into Desiree Lingerie the day of Frankie's murder? The one who wanted to know if she had to take off her top? When the salesperson said yes, she disappeared. I thought someone I saw later looked like her, but I wasn't sure. It was the hair. I know who she is and where to find her. Let me see how long she'll be there."

Josie opened her cell phone and called a number from the menu. "How late will your office be open today?" She listened, then said, "Six thirty. Thank you.

"Hurry!" Josie said. "I need to get home, then pick up

Amelia at school before I go. You have to take Justin home
for his nap."

"You'll have to go alone," Alyce said. "That's not safe."

"Clayton is perfectly safe at that hour," Josie said. "I
don't think the man she's with will use his knives tonight."

# Chapter 21

Josie found a free parking spot during rush hour in downtown Clayton, a modern miracle. It was a few minutes past six o'clock. Josie had been running nonstop since she leaped to her conclusion about Frankie's killer.

After Alyce had dropped her at home, Josie had picked up Amelia at school, faxed her mystery-shopping report to Harry, then sent her daughter upstairs to Jane. The two planned to make pecan-encrusted catfish and chocolate volcano cupcakes. Amelia would spend the evening with her grandmother, cooking, eating, and lobbying for Stuart Little.

That gave Josie enough time to confront the mystery woman and visit the St. Louis County Jail.

Fine mother I am, Josie thought, fobbing off Amelia on her grandmother so I can go to jail. At least the kid is doing something creative instead of staring at a computer screen.

Josie fought against the herd of homebound suits pushing toward their cars on the shoveled Clayton sidewalks. Her legs were sideswiped by sharp-cornered briefcases, but Josie barely noticed. She arrived at the office of Dr. Tino Martin at 6:06.

Even the silence in the plastic surgeon's medical suite seemed expensive. One woman waited on a blue chair. She frowned as she read a fat document, no doubt creating more lucrative work for Dr. Tino.

Shannon, the same full-figured receptionist, was guarding the gates to Dr. Tino's sculpting service. Today, her rich brown hair was plaited into a crown. Josie was sure this was the same mystery woman who'd appeared for a moment at Desiree Lingerie.

The frowner put down her reading and whined, "How much longer do I have to wait, Shannon? My appointment was for six o'clock."

"I'm sorry, Mrs. Craig," Shannon said. "The doctor is running a few minutes behind." She turned to Josie. "May I help you?"

"I hope so," Josie said. "You were at Desiree Lingerie. It was a day I won't forget. Dr. Tino Martin's wife, Frankie, was murdered soon after you left the shop."

The receptionist's head snapped back as if she'd been slapped. "What shop? Where? I never went shopping."

Josie heard the fear in those lying words. She raised her voice loud enough to attract the frowning Mrs. Craig.

"I have three witnesses who can place you there," Josie said. "Answer a couple of questions and I won't tell the police."

Now Mrs. Craig was obviously listening and the receptionist was definitely panicked. "Step out into the hall," Shannon said, her voice barely audible. "As soon as I show in this patient, I'll talk to you. I'll be there in two minutes."

Josie left, followed by Mrs. Craig's stare. In the hall, she stood between two doors. One was the patients' entrance. The other was marked STAFF ONLY. Unless Shannon climbed down the outside of the building, Josie would get her.

True to her promise, the receptionist came out two minutes later. Her braided crown had slipped and she seemed ready to burst into tears. "Please," she said. "What do you want?"

"Answers," Josie said. "You're having an affair with Dr. Tino."

"Uh ..." Shannon was hyperventilating. She towered over Josie, but was so frightened she couldn't speak.

"I know you're having an affair," Josie said. "Lie to me, and I'll go to the police."

Shannon seemed to shrink into herself. "Yes, we're in love. We're getting married now that Tino is free."

"Did you help speed up your marriage by murdering his wife, Frankie?" Josie asked.

Shannon's vivid coloring went white as new-fallen snow. Her lipstick looked like a blood clot.

Josie waited.

Shannon gulped and said, "No. Never. I was following Frankie around that day. I was trying to get some useful information for Tino. She knew about us. He'd told Frankie he wanted a divorce. The marriage had been over for some time, even before he met me. Tino expected her to be trouble, but Frankie went crazy when he told her. She said she'd ruin Tino."

"How could she do that?" Josie asked.

"A patient filed a malpractice suit against Tino. His lawyer says it's a nuisance suit. Plastic surgeons get these all the time. The woman claimed he botched her nose job. Her nose looks fine—even a jury would agree. Well, most juries. The lawyer says juries can be tricky. Tino's lawyer thinks the plaintiff wanted money to go away. He says some people try that. They think the threat of bad publicity will make doctors pay off, even if they are innocent.

"Frankie knew about the lawsuit. She told Tino she'd testify for the plaintiff. She was going to lie and say that Tino took tranquilizers the morning he did that nose job. As a nurse, Frankie could do Tino's case a lot of damage. She wanted to destroy him. I swear she'd enjoy it. She was like that."

"So I've heard," Josie said.

"Frankie kept hinting she knew something that would ensure the woman would win her lawsuit. I wanted to help Tino. I took off for an hour and followed her, trying to see where Frankie went and who she met. I trailed her into Plaza Venetia, then lost her. I stumbled into that bra store and there she was, standing at the cash register. I was shocked. I had to get out before she recognized me. I said something and left."

"We thought you were too shy to try on a bra," Josie said.

Shannon shook her head. "I was sure Frankie didn't recognize me," she said. "I thought I'd gotten away with following her. I didn't learn anything. After the scare at the store, I went straight back to work. It was a close call. I felt lucky to escape.

"That afternoon, the police came to this office to tell Tino that Frankie had been killed at Plaza Venetia. I was horrified. I thought the detectives knew I'd followed Frankie there. I was afraid for Tino—and for me. I'd tried to help and only made it worse.

"The police never found out about me. I've been so scared. I keep waiting for them to arrest me. Tino is already worried sick, even though he's no longer a suspect."

"How do I know you didn't kill her?" Josie asked. "You have a good reason to want Frankie dead."

"Our office records give me an alibi," Shannon said. "I have to clock in and out. I have to sign in with a password on my computer. I left right after I encountered Frankie, and I'm glad I did. I was back at the office before the killer followed Frankie into the women's restroom. The staff and patients told the police I was here."

"Show me," Josie said. "Let me see your appointment records for that day and the times you clocked in and out."

"I can't show you patient records," Shannon said. "That's confidential."

"Can you get a printout?" Josie asked.

Shannon nodded.

"Then get one and cross out the names. I'll go back inside with you. There's no one in the waiting room, is there?"

"No, our last patient is with Tino."

Josie followed Shannon behind the reception desk and watched her make a printout of the schedule. The date at the top of the sheet was correct. Shannon used a pen to cross out the patient names. Josie saw that all the slots were filled.

Shannon tapped more keys on her computer, then

handed Josie a time-clock printout. Shannon had clocked back in at 11:01 a.m. Frankie had been alive then.

"What about Tino?" Josie asked. "What's his alibi? Did the records show he was here?"

"He wasn't here. He was at the hospital," Shannon said. She swung her computer monitor around so Josie could see it, and slid her thumb over a patient's name. "There's his schedule. He did a rhinoplasty that morning. And he didn't botch it."

I've certainly botched this, Josie thought, as she rode the elevator down to the lobby. I've wasted more time and I haven't helped Laura one bit. The county jail is two blocks away. I made the calls and arranged a visit tonight. I'd hoped to bring Laura good news after I met with Shannon.

Now I have to tell her I've failed. Again.

# Chapter 22

Laura was staying at a four-star jail.

Josie had seen the ratings on Citysearch.com. The Web site's readers rated Clayton's haute hotels, pricey bars and restaurants, and upscale shopping—and the St. Louis County Jail, located on a prize piece of real estate.

She was startled at the idea of rating a jail with stars, like a hotel. Josie read the jail's reviews and couldn't tell if they were send-ups or not. While she waited in the visitors' line along with the inmates' friends and families, she reread the printouts she'd stuffed into her purse.

She thought "toadtws," whoever he—or she—was, had done genuine jail time. The tip-off was the second sentence.

"Excellent location right in the heart of beautiful downtown Clayton," Josie read. "Easily accessible by public transportation (by the way, ST.L.Co. P.D. police cars have excellent legroom in the backseat)."

The rest of the miscreant's review was a parody of a hotel rating:

"Excellent staff who remember your name each time you come back. They always do their best to make you feel welcome. The presentation upon arrival meets and exceeds that of all other similar facilities I have ever experienced. The accommodations were more clean and spacious than other places I've stayed in the past. No detail is too small to be overlooked. Cannot say enough good things about my recent stay from the location, the views, the other guests, the dining fare ... Everything met and even exceeded my expectations. Even though I am a frequent guest, I always look forward to my stays. Will return again and again."

That should thrill the uptight, upright taxpayers of Clayton, Josie thought, who had to live with the county jail in their midst. Citysearch provided helpful maps and information about parks, restaurants, and other spots suitable for muggings and purse snatchings.

"Toadtws" also listed the jail's pros and cons:

"Pros: Best Baloney Sandwich in the State. Cons: Lack of a Frequent-Guest Program."

A possible repeat offender called "mwshakespeare" was almost nostalgic about the time at the county lockup: "I feel that over the yeras [sic] it had become a little rundown; it adds to its charm. I will always remember the tender service offered by the guards, the intimate guest rooms, and chic modern decor.

"It's where me and Blaine had our first kiss.

"Highly recommend.

"Pros: Location, everything you need right there.

"Cons: Hard to get out of quickly."

Score another point for St. Louis County, Josie thought, as she shuffled forward in line with the rest of the visitors. Slumped shoulders and bent heads showed how tired they were. Many wore hospital scrubs or uniforms. Some had one or two children, eager to see "Daddy," "Auntie," or "Momma." The energetic kids were quieted with shushes and promises of McDonald's Happy Meals.

What kind of lives do these poor families have? Josie wondered, and said a prayer that Laura would soon be released. It was close to the seven o'clock visiting hour. Josie read the last starred jail review to pass the time.

This third reviewer, "schendel," seemed to be teasing St. Louis County with his rating: "One of the finest jails in Missouri. Excellent educational programs, GED opportunities, low-cost laundry service. Located in desirable downtown Clayton, just blocks from gourmet eateries (although takeout can be difficult). Visitors welcome.

"Pros: Extended weekends, Laundry service, Private rooms.

"Cons: Surrounded by them, Limited rec time, YOU'RE IN JAIL."

Those last three words cut off Josie's chuckle at the starred review. Laura was in jail. A real jail. Josie was surrounded by weary, suffering families. There was nothing funny about that.

Josie wouldn't rate the booth where she talked with Laura as four-star, but it wasn't as grim as she'd expected. It was white and slightly scuffed, with a telephone and a plastic glass window. The floor was a pleasant blue-and-white check.

Laura's appearance was shocking. The confident, robust store manager Josie had seen a short time ago was gone. Laura's face was sickly yellow and haggard. Loose skin hung on her arms and at her jawline. Her gray roots were nearly an inch long.

"Laura!" Josie said into her phone. She hoped Laura couldn't read her face. "How much weight have you lost?"

"Six pounds, I think," Laura said. "I needed to lose it, but not this way. I'm so worried that I can't eat."

"Of course, you're worried," Josie said. "You're going on trial for murder. What does your lawyer say?"

"Renzo says juries are unpredictable. I think he's preparing me for the worst, Josie. I've seen the TV news stories. Even the inmates think I'm guilty. LaCinda asked me how I could have offed that nice Frankie lady. The whole city sees me as the teacher with the tarnished reputation who killed sweet Frankie Angel."

"But she isn't an angel," Josie said. "She never was."

"I know that. So do you. But too many people don't. All it takes is twelve citizens to agree with LaCinda."

"I'll tell the jury what she was like," Josie said. "They need to know the truth."

"You can't testify," Laura said. "Renzo told me we can't attack a dead woman. It will backfire against me. This case can't go to trial, Josie. I have to get out now. My daughter, Kate, is eight months pregnant with her first child. She started spotting a few days ago and her doctor ordered her to bed until the baby is born.

"Kate's husband, William, can't take any more time off from his law firm. He's an associate and he has crushing student loans. William hired a nurse to be with Kate. I'm sure the nurse is competent, but my daughter needs me. Her father abandoned Kate after our divorce and she's facing this difficult pregnancy alone. I should be with her. You have a daughter, Josie. You understand."

All too well, Josie thought. "I'm trying to help. But I keep running into dead ends."

"Oh, Josie." Laura attempted a lopsided smile. "You're a good girl—woman—but what can you do?"

"Ask questions the police won't," Josie said. "I know they've arrested the wrong person. I have an advantage. I look like an ordinary mom. Well, I guess I am. But that's a disguise, too. People tell me things because I don't look important or official.

"The police have to read people their rights or follow department procedure. They can't knock on doors and ask questions like I can. Nobody's afraid of me. They tell me things. I may learn something that will help you."

"Have you?" A flash of hope lit Laura's sad face.

"No, not yet," Josie said.

"Oh."

"But I'm getting there," Josie said. "I found the mystery woman who was in the doorway at Desiree Lingerie the day Frankie was killed—and the police never did. Her name is Shannon. She's engaged to Frankie's husband and wants to marry him."

"That's a good reason to kill Frankie," Laura said.

"It is, but Shannon and Dr. Tino both have alibis. I've talked to everyone who was in the store that morning. I found out that Trish, your saleswoman, goes to Narcotics Anonymous meetings."

"That's her business," Laura said, her voice cold enough to frost her phone.

"It could be yours, too," Josie said. "Trish told my daughter she wants to be a police officer. If the academy found out she had a drug problem, she'd never get in."

"That depends, Josie," Laura said. "My husband told me that police departments can be more flexible than you'd think on that subject. What if Trish's addiction was a teenage mistake? Or she got addicted to painkillers after an injury or accident? If the force has a quota for women officers or she has a powerful sponsor inside the department, they might overlook that."

"I think Rosa's parents are illegal aliens," Josie said.

"But you don't know for sure."

"No. Well, maybe yes. Rosa mentioned that her father had had a heart attack and went to the ER at Holy Redeemer—Frankie's hospital. She said the family was still paying off his hospital bills. Rosa clammed up when I mentioned her father was eligible for Medicare if he was in the country legally."

"Money is a touchy subject," Laura said, "especially for immigrants. Rosa is proud. She doesn't want anyone to think she would take charity. Her family would rather pay than ask for help and they may not want to use the government. You don't know Rosa like I do. She's strong, generous, and endlessly patient with fussy customers. She wouldn't have killed Frankie."

"But Frankie's brother owned a big Mexican restaurant. He told everyone that an old man named Hector Maria tried to get a job with bad papers at his restaurant."

"And you think Rosa's father is the only Hector Maria around?"

"In St. Louis, yes."

"We have a lot of Latino immigrants here," Laura said.

Josie could see she didn't want to listen. "Why does Cody the hero come to your shop? Don't say to pick up his wife's alterations. He's been your customer for some time. Edith saw him there."

"He's entitled to his privacy," Laura said, her five words short and clipped.

"Your daughter is entitled to her mother's comfort," Josie said.

"I know that, Josie, but I can't tell you."

"Then let me tell you," Josie said. "You can nod your head if I'm correct: Cody is a cross-dresser."

Laura burst out laughing, then shook her head. "Nothing like that."

"Then why did Frankie hand him a pair of . . . ?" Josie stopped, remembering what Ted had told her. "Cody wears panty hose, doesn't he? Some Gulf War soldiers wore them—at least that's what my boyfriend, Ted, said."

"Ted is right," Laura said. "Frankie cut a pair of control-top panty hose off Cody in the ER after he was shot. He told me that. But it didn't bother him. He even joked about not having to shave his legs when he wears his panty hose. Cody is a decorated hero. He's been my customer for years. He's sent two male security guards to me. Cody loves his wife and son. He is too secure to kill Frankie because she needled him about something so silly."

"Then I'll have to keep searching for the killer," Josie said. "I've located everyone but the blonde in the wheelchair."

"What blonde?" Laura asked.

"The woman Alyce and I talked to when we went into the mall restroom. She was trying to get into the handicapped stall when I found Frankie's body. She said her name was Kelsey. She gave us false contact information and left before the police arrived. Actually, Alyce and I helped her get away."

"Do you really think someone in a wheelchair could have killed a healthy young woman?" Laura asked. "Frankie could have easily escaped from her."

"The wheelchair woman had remarkably strong arms," Josie said. "People in wheelchairs aren't necessarily weak. Some are amazing athletes."

"But you forgot the mall video, Josie. It showed a large woman wearing a black-and-white scarf like I wore that day going into that restroom. She was walking, not rolling, in there."

"I guess it was a dumb idea," Josie said. She turned away to avoid Laura's lost, hopeless face.

Josie didn't need to see another reminder of her failure.

# Chapter 23

"Hey, congratulations, you caught two crooks," Harry the Horrible said.

"I did?" Josie said. "Harry, you aren't calling to congratulate me, are you?"

"Why sound so surprised?" Harry asked. *Crunch.*

Because you never tell me I do a good job, Josie thought. "I don't remember catching any crooks, that's all," she said.

"You nabbed them with your shopping report for Chick Flickers." *Munch.*

Through noisy crunches, crackles, and chomps, Harry told Josie the story: "Chick Flickers' head office suspected a scam involving their 3-D glasses, but they couldn't catch the employees who were ripping off the customers. So they sent you. They didn't tell you what was going on, just asked you to take notes."

"So Denise at the box office was running a scam," Josie said. "I thought so. I took off those glasses in the theater and the movie looked better."

"She's the one. She ratted out the broad at the concession stand."

"Sue!" Josie said.

"Naw, the company won't sue them." *Chomp.*

"I meant her name was Sue," Josie said.

"Whatever. Both women had to resign and return the money," Harry said. "They got fired, too, with no references."

"Bad time to be out of work," Josie said. "Why did they risk their jobs?"

"Sue and Denise had been turned down for raises. They were pissed and cooked up this scam to get their own raise. *Avatar* made 3-D movies a big deal again. Sue found an old box of glasses buried in the Chick Flickers' storeroom. They were left over from some horror movie. She and Denise sold them to unsuspecting customers for a buck each, cash only."

"Clever pricing," Josie said. "Few people would object to paying a dollar."

"Chick Flickers thinks the pair raked in nearly five hundred bucks before you caught them."

"What happens to the five hundred dollars when the company recovers it from those two?" Josie asked.

"It's going to charity," Harry said.

Josie heard a tremendous crunch, like a kid landing in a pile of fall leaves. "What are you eating, Harry?"

"A hamdog," he said. "It's today's special at the Carnival Diner. Delicious."

"It's made out of ham?" Josie asked.

"Hamburger," Harry said. "A hamdog is a hot dog wrapped in a hamburger patty. Then the chef deep-fries the hamdog, pours on chili, adds grilled onions, and tops it with a fried egg. This one has all that, plus extra-crispy bacon."

"I could hear it," Josie said. "Aren't you worried about cholesterol?"

"As my granny used to say, nobody gets outta here alive. She fried everything but her beer and lived to be ninety-six. Gotta go. I'll have another assignment for you soon."

*I'm some detective,* Josie thought. *I caught two thieves and didn't know it, but I can't find Frankie's killer. Maybe I'll have better luck finding Kelsey. The woman in the wheelchair is still worth investigating, no matter what Laura thinks. I just have to find out where Kelsey hangs out.*

Josie was prowling the Internet for disabled women's support groups when Amelia burst into her office. That was

Josie's grand name for a computer and fax machine on a garage sale table in her bedroom.

Amelia interrupted her search. "Mom, can you sign my permission slip for the school field trip?"

"Sure," Josie said. "Where are you going?"

"The Fabulous Fox Theatre."

"That old theater is fabulous," Josie said. "All red and gold and fantastic statues. Wait till you see the twisty columns, the terra-cotta rajas, and the staircase with the lions' heads. It's a true movie palace."

"The other cool part is we get to ride on a school bus," Amelia said.

"That's a treat?" Josie asked, then realized that Barrington students were driven to school in their parents' cars. They rarely rode buses.

"I've already decided who I'm going to sit with on the bus—Zoe, Emma, and Rebecca."

Josie knew Zoe all too well. She liked Emma. She'd never heard of Rebecca.

"Who's Rebecca?"

"Rebecca Cohen. Very smart, likes art and acting. She's excited about visiting a real theater. After the field trip, Rebecca wants to go to Bluestone's department store at Plaza Venetia to look at prom dresses. Is that okay? Rebecca's mom will drive us."

"Is Rebecca going to a prom?" Josie asked.

"No, she's our age. We just want to see the dresses."

First a bra, now prom dresses. Her girl was growing up. Josie wasn't entirely pleased with Amelia's shopping foursome. "Is Zoe going shopping, too?"

"Yes, but Emma and I will keep her in line," Amelia said. The little slick knew what Josie thought of Zoe. "Rebecca is quiet and gets good grades."

"I'll have to check with Rebecca's mother first."

Amelia handed Josie the phone. "I've predialed her number," she said. "Her mom's name is Golda."

"Go rake the cat box while I make the call," Josie said.

Amelia didn't argue. Josie chatted with Golda, warning

her that Zoe could be a trouble magnet. Golda promised to be on guard.

When Amelia had finished her least favorite chore, Josie said, "It's all set. Mrs. Cohen will take you to Plaza Venetia after tomorrow's field trip. She'll be shopping, too. Don't think you girls can pull anything. At the first sign of trouble, Mrs. Cohen will take you right back home."

"Yay!" Amelia said, ignoring the warning. She thrust the permission slip at Josie. "Please?"

"Where's a pen?"

The pens seemed to have disappeared. Josie searched her desk, the kitchen counter, and finally the bottom of her purse. She pulled out crumpled Kleenex, a fuzzy cough drop, and a piece of paper.

Amelia picked up the paper and asked, "What's a Clayton address doing with Big Al's phone number?"

"Kelsey the wheelchair woman gave me that," Josie said. She read the address out loud and recognized it now. "One Hundred South Central. That's the county jail. I was just there."

"What were you doing in jail, Mom?"

"I wasn't in jail. I was visiting Laura, my friend who was arrested for Frankie's murder. Your aunt Alyce and I ran into this Kelsey when I found the body in the restroom. Kelsey gave me this address and phone number and said it was hers. That information is obviously fake. I'm guessing Kelsey isn't her name, either."

"But how did she get Big Al's real phone number?" Amelia asked.

"Who's Big Al?" Josie asked.

"Our pizza deliveryman. All the Game Piece Pizza stores in the St. Louis area have phone numbers ending with 4040. This number is for the Maplewood store. Big Al almost always delivers our pizza."

My daughter knows the pizza delivery number by heart, Josie thought. No wonder she's learning to cook.

"I didn't know that was our pizza number," Josie said. "Kelsey has disappeared. Even the cops can't find her."

"They would if she'd given them a doughnut-shop number," Amelia said.

"Hey, that's no way to talk," Josie said.

"You already said the police arrested the wrong person. So they can't be good."

Josie thought the Venetia Park police weren't smart, but she didn't want her daughter to openly disrespect the law. She tried a small distraction: "If Kelsey knows the number for a Maplewood pizza place, she must live near here."

"Let's call for a pizza," Amelia said. "If Big Al shows up, we can ask if he knows her."

"You want pizza for dinner again?" Josie said.

"We haven't had it for weeks," Amelia said. "I've been cooking with Grandma, remember? Last night we had catfish and that's healthy."

"We want a large pepperoni, right?" Josie said, dialing the number on the paper.

"No anchovies," Amelia said.

Big Al arrived twenty-eight minutes later. It was obvious where he got his nickname: Big Al was tall and so broad-shouldered he filled their doorway. If he hadn't been smiling and carrying a pizza, Josie would have hesitated to open her door.

"Al! Do you have a blonde in her twenties on your route?" Josie asked. "Long straight platinum hair, blue eyes, white skin, black wheelchair."

"Oh, you mean Blond Babe," Big Al said. "Gorgeous hair, great legs. Lives in the house with the purple shutters."

"And uses a wheelchair," Josie finished.

"No, she doesn't," Big Al said. "People with wheelchairs have ramps, not steps."

"There must be some mistake," Josie said.

"I don't think so," Al said. "She orders two large sausage-and-green-pepper pizzas every weekend, and tips me five. She lives next to One Buck Chuck. He's a thin older man who lives in a two-story charcoal gray house on Palmer Avenue. On the other side is Busy Mom. She's thin, too, from running after four kids. Her white house has a wide front porch. She tips five to eight dollars."

"Are you sure about Blond Babe?" Josie asked.

"Positive, ma'am. That long hair is hard to forget."

"But you must have a lot of blondes on your route."

"Not with white-blond hair," Big Al said. "One Buck Chuck is bald. Busy Mom is a brunette. I have some gray-haired and white-haired customers, a redhead who gives me a lot of green, and two blondes with hair that's a weird yellow. But Blond Babe is my only regular with long, straight hair. She's hard to forget."

"What's her real name and address?"

"Sorry." Big Al looked down at his shoes. "I can't say. Against company policy. I have to go. More pizzas to deliver."

Josie paid for the pizza and tipped him a five.

"One more thing," Big Al said. "Pizza delivery drivers know the neighborhood streets better than anyone, except maybe the cops. If you're ever lost, stop at our pizza stores. We'll help you find where you want to go with our big map. Sorry I couldn't be more help."

But you were, Josie thought. Only one house on Palmer Avenue has purple shutters and sits between a gray house and a white one with a big porch.

I've found the mystery woman.

# Chapter 24

The mystery woman lived two blocks from Josie's flat. She could picture the house with the purple shutters in her mind. She wanted to see it with her eyes. After Josie dropped Amelia off at school for her field trip, she drove down Palmer Avenue.

There it was.

"Yes!" Josie yelled, alone in her car. The tall, skinny house with the deep purple shutters looked like it was bruised. It was hunched between a charcoal gray home with a red door and a sprawling white house with an elegant jigsaw Gothic porch.

Josie didn't see any cars in the driveway of the purple shutters house. She parked her Honda at the curb, then walked up fourteen steps to the front porch. Steep steps led to the side entrance. There were no ramps. If this really was Kelsey's home, she definitely didn't use a wheelchair.

Josie knocked on the purple front door. No answer.

She knocked harder until the door glass rattled. Silence.

A bald, older man ambled out of the gray house next door. He wore a barn jacket. One Buck Chuck, Josie thought. Chuck wore slippers in the snow. He must have been eager for gossip.

"Good morning," he said. "You looking for Victoria?"

So that's her name, Josie thought.

"You must be Charles," she said.

"My friends call me Chuck."

So does Big Al, Josie thought. If you only tip him a dollar to run up those stairs with a pizza, I doubt that he considers you a friend.

Chuck moved closer to the porch for a chat.

"Is Victoria home?" Josie asked. "I'm trying to find her."

"She just left," Chuck said. "She'll be back about two o'clock. She's home by that time most days."

"Is that when she gets off work?" Josie knew that was a risky question, but decided to chance it. Chuck seemed like a talker who might volunteer useful information.

"I think so," Chuck said. "Don't know what she does exactly, but Victoria brings home plenty of shopping bags from the fancy malls. She must be some kind of model. She's certainly pretty enough. Are you one of her shopping-party friends?"

Josie hesitated and Chuck obligingly filled in the blanks. "Victoria is a real bargain hunter. She holds shopping parties. Victoria mixes a bunch of margaritas and a lot of young women come over and buy her clothes. She keeps them in her living room."

"You've seen the clothes?" Josie asked.

"I can't see in the windows," Chuck said. "But we have a new letter carrier and he gets the mail mixed up. I took her light bill over the other afternoon. She must be getting ready for another sale. She had sweaters and scarves sitting on a couch and a rack of new-looking dresses.

"Her sales are by invitation only. They attract gorgeous women. I can hear them giggling from my upstairs window. I never complain. An old geezer like me couldn't ask for a more interesting neighbor."

Victoria is definitely interesting, Josie thought. I have an idea how she hunts those bargains.

Chuck was still chattering. "She has her sale parties once or twice a month."

"That's what I wanted to ask her about," Josie said.

"I see lots of happy ladies leaving her house afterward,

and not because of the margaritas," Chuck said. He looked at ease, prepared to gab the morning away.

If I don't get back into my heated car, I'll be as purple as Victoria's shutters, Josie thought. "Nice talking to you. I'll come back after two," she said.

"No problem," Chuck said. "If you see a yellow Miata in the drive, you'll know Victoria is home."

On the short drive back to her flat, Josie fretted about the enforced wait until after two o'clock. That meant another day in jail for Laura, who needed to be with her pregnant daughter.

Josie was almost grateful when Harry the Horrible called with a last-minute mystery-shopping assignment.

"I need you to shop another Veggie Madness," he said. "This time, it's the restaurant in Chesterfield."

Josie bit back a snarky remark about more vegetables. Too many stores and restaurants were going out of business. Too many companies were cutting back on mystery shoppers. Josie couldn't afford to turn down a job. She'd eat lettuce to make lettuce.

"Same food as last time?"

"New choices," Harry said. "Today Veggie Madness wants you to try the Looney for Lettuce salad and the Go Bananas nut bread. You can bring a guest, a female between thirty and thirty-five. Veggie Madness wants you to look for food freshness and restaurant cleanliness."

At one fifteen, Josie and Alyce were in the Veggie Madness in Chesterfield, a well-heeled western suburb of St. Louis. The restaurant was packed with expensively dressed women grazing on greens.

Alyce savored a bowl of Crazy for Cauliflower soup. Josie picked at her Looney for Lettuce salad, using her fork to pull a thin purple strip out of the ranch dressing.

"The shutters on Victoria's house are the same color as this lettuce," she said.

"That's cabbage," Alyce said. "You can't get Victoria out of your mind, can you?"

"She's the killer," Josie said. "I know it. She lied to us. Why else would she give false information? She's not disabled if she lives in that house. She's big and strong enough to surprise Frankie and kill her.

"I know how she did it, too. Victoria wheeled herself into the restroom, got out of her chair, surprised Frankie, pushed her into the handicapped stall, and smothered her with the plastic bag. Then Victoria left her body in the locked stall and crawled out. When we blundered in, Victoria jumped into her wheelchair, played the poor little cripple, and escaped."

"What about the large woman in the black-and-white scarf?" Alyce said. "The one on the mall security tape?"

"She's just someone who had to use the bathroom," Josie said. "She wasn't wearing an unusual scarf. You saw the pile on the sale table at DDD. Anyone could buy one. There's nothing on the tape that shows the scarf lady killed Frankie."

"Why would Victoria want her dead?"

"Everyone wanted to kill Frankie," Josie said.

"So when do we meet this murderer?" Alyce asked.

"Her neighbor Chuck says she's usually home after two," Josie said. "Amelia's on a field trip today, and then she's going to Plaza Venetia with her friends, so I don't have to pick her up at school."

Alyce checked her watch. "We'd better get moving if we're going to meet Victoria. I'm going with you."

"We?" Josie said.

"Don't even think of confronting that killer alone, Josie Marcus. I know you want to help Laura because of her daughter, but you need to think of your own child."

"All right," Josie said. "We'll go together. I've nearly finished my banana-nut bread."

"We'll use my car," Alyce said. "You live too close to her house. You don't want her finding out you live two blocks away."

By two thirty, Alyce was cruising down Palmer Avenue. Josie saw a yellow Miata parked in Victoria's driveway.

"Nice car for a killer," Alyce said. "She has style."

"Let's go catch her," Josie said. "Laura needs to get out of jail."

They marched up the stairs together. Josie knocked on the door. They heard footsteps inside on the hardwood floor. The door swung open and there stood Victoria, straight and sturdy. She was tall—about the same height as Laura Ferguson—but slimmer than Josie remembered. When she'd been in the wheelchair wearing her dark coat, she'd had a matronly figure. Josie, who'd spent many hours in malls, had an idea what had bulked up Victoria.

No wonder One Buck Chuck liked watching her, Josie thought. With that platinum hair and vampire-pale skin, Victoria was stunning. She could have been a model.

Victoria's wide blue eyes studied Josie and Alyce. She did not seem to recognize them.

"May I help you ladies?"

Josie took a step forward, crowding Victoria on her doorstep. "Yes, I want to know about your miraculous recovery."

"My what?" Victoria still looked clueless.

"The last time Alyce and I saw you, you were in a wheelchair. Now look at you, so tall and healthy. It's amazing."

Victoria's mouth gaped.

"You must remember us," Alyce said, inching closer. "You were in the Plaza Venetia bathroom. Josie crawled under the stall to unlock it for you and found a dead woman. You gave us your contact information."

"Fake information," Josie said. She pushed her way into the wide foyer. Alyce followed. Victoria didn't try to block their way. She seemed rooted to the rug.

Inside, Josie caught a glimpse of a living room sofa piled with fluffy sweaters like gathering clouds. A rainbow of dresses and blouses hung on a plain metal rack. A flurry of white tags dangled from the clothes. Now Josie was sure what Victoria did every day.

"The Venetia Park police are looking for you," Josie said. "You're a person of interest in a murder. We have to tell them where to find you, so an innocent woman can get out of jail."

"It's our duty," Alyce said.

"I'm sure the cops will be interested in your living room," Josie said. "Those cashmere sweaters piled on your sofa cost a fortune. If you buy them."

"I didn't kill her," Victoria said in a raven's croak.

"Then what were you doing in that restroom?" Josie said, her voice harder. "Where is the new red gown Frankie was carrying?"

Victoria turned even paler, if possible. "I—" She stopped.

Josie pulled out her cell phone. "The police are a phone call away."

"I stole the dress. It was brand-new," Victoria said. "I could see that." Now the words came out in a rush. "I took her diamond tennis bracelet, too."

"What tennis bracelet?" Josie said.

"I never saw it mentioned in the news stories, but she wore a nice one," Victoria said.

"The police like to keep back some information to find the real killer," Alyce said.

"You take trophies," Josie said. "Like a serial killer. How many other women have you murdered?"

"No! I didn't kill her," Victoria said. "I'm a thief, not a killer. I took the tennis bracelet and the dress. I admit that. I'm not proud of it, but she was already dead. She didn't need them."

"Where are they?" Josie asked.

"I sold the tennis bracelet at a pawnshop. I sold the dress to a friend who needed it for a date. She couldn't wait until my next shopping party. I can invite you to one. I sell a lot of designer clothes that I . . ."

"Shoplift," Josie finished. "The parties are over, Victoria. These clothes go back to the stores or I call the police. I should call them now. They're looking for you."

"Please, don't!" Victoria said. "I lost my job and can't find another. This is my mother's house. She had a small heart attack. She's in rehab at a nursing home and it costs a fortune. Her Social Security only pays for part of her treatment. I'm trying to make the mortgage and the utilities so she'll have a place to come home to."

"Which home is she in?" Josie asked.

"Carlson Place in Chesterfield."

Alyce raised her eyebrows. "That is pricey. What's the number?"

Victoria rattled off a number and Alyce keyed it into her cell.

"Give me your last name and your mother's," Alyce said.

"Garbull," Victoria said, and spelled it. "My mother is Justine Garbull."

Alyce pressed the call button, then said, "Is Mrs. Justine Garbull a patient at Carlson Place?" There was a pause. "When is she expected to return home? You can't give out private information? I understand. Thank you."

"There is a Mrs. Garbull," Alyce said. She kept her cell phone out. It looked like a threat.

"Keep talking," Alyce said. "If you tell us the truth, we won't call the police."

"Do you live in this neighborhood?" Victoria asked.

"No," Josie said. "But I know Chuck, your next-door neighbor. He's been watching you. One word to him, and he'll spill everything if the cops ask."

"That old busybody," Victoria said. Chuck would have been hurt by her venomous look.

"Men can be worse gossips than women," Josie said. "You thought he was admiring your blond hair—but he's been watching your parties. He'll make a good witness."

"Where did you get the wheelchair when we ran into you in the restroom?" Alyce asked.

"It belongs to Plaza Venetia," Victoria said. "The center keeps a couple stashed in an alcove behind the escalator. I use them sometimes to . . . get merchandise. No one ever suspects me. I wheel myself into the dressing room with a lot of clothes and keep talking so the saleswoman forgets to count the items. I always refuse her help because I'm so independent."

"Clever," Josie said.

"Hey, it works," Victoria said. "I put on the clothes in the dressing room, then put on my oversized coat. I've rolled out wearing as many as six sweaters and two skirts. Sometimes I buy a sale item if it's cheap enough, to avoid suspicion. It doesn't matter if it fits. I resell it at my parties."

"What were you doing in the mall bathroom?" Josie asked.

"I needed to take off the clothes I'd . . ." She stopped.

"Shoplifted," Josie said.

"And put them in shopping bags, so I could leave," Victoria said. "When it's time to leave the mall, I fold up the chair, put it away, and walk out. I never had any problems until that day. Then I opened the stall and found that dead body. I couldn't change clothes. I did see her dress and bracelet and I took them. I stumbled out and slammed the door so hard, the bolt slid shut. I sat down in the chair and tried to get out. That's when you came in."

Alyce glared at her. "Why didn't the police find your fingerprints on the stall door?"

"I wore wool gloves," she said. "Please, put away your cell phone. I'll stop the parties. I'm a shoplifter, not a murderer. I'm not a bad person, really."

"You just rob the dead," Josie said.

# Chapter 25

Jane was lounging on her pale green living room couch, a pillow under her head and the shih tzu on her lap. Bright-eyed Stuart Little wagged his tail when he saw Josie.

"Excuse me," Josie said. "There must be something wrong with my eyes. I see a dog on your couch."

"Stuart is not a dog," Josie's mother said. "He's a member of the family. He likes the soaps."

"He likes getting his ears scratched," Josie said.

"We're watching *The Young and the Restless*. They're dealing with the mix-up of Sharon and Nick's baby with Ashley's baby."

"Didn't Ashley miscarry?" Josie said. She didn't watch her mother's soaps, but she remembered some of the plots. Jane discussed the characters' accidents, arrests, and amnesia as if they were real people.

"She did," Jane said. "But Ashley thinks Sharon and Nick's baby is hers. We hope DNA will prove they are the true parents, don't we, Stuart?"

"Woof!" the dog said.

"Are Nick and Sharon married?" Josie asked.

"No," Jane said. "Nick is married to Phyllis. He used to be married to Sharon. She was his first wife and they share a child. He has a child with Phyllis, too. Ashley thought she was pregnant by Victor—he's Nick's father—but she was really being manipulated by Adam, who is Nick's half brother."

Josie struggled to follow her mother through the swamp of the soap's plot and lost her way. "So Adam is the bad guy." Josie sounded like a C student guessing at an answer.

"Adam is a terrible person," Jane said. "Stuart recognized that right away."

"Who's Stuart?" Josie asked.

"He's right here," Jane said. She patted the dog's head. "Every time evil Adam appears, Stuart Little growls. He wags his tail for poor Ashley, who needs some encouragement. Stuart knows the plot."

"Better than I do," Josie said.

"Are you hungry, sweetie? Would you like some roast chicken?" Jane asked.

"That would be nice," Josie said.

"I was speaking to Stuart," Jane said. "But help yourself, Josie. There's a whole bird in the fridge."

Great. The dog gets waited on and I get the bird, Josie thought. She heard a car door slam and looked out her mother's living room window. "Thanks, Mom, but Amelia's home. I want to see how her field trip and shopping expedition went. Can I walk Stuart Little for you?"

"No, thanks," Jane said. "We want to finish our soap. Then we'll go for a walk. Maybe I'll let Amelia walk the dog. She's been begging to take him out."

Josie tried to feel happy that Stuart Little had won her mother's heart and forget that she'd been displaced by a dog. She made her way carefully down the back stairs to her winter-dark kitchen.

Josie didn't see Amelia but she could smell her daughter across the room.

"Yuck. Amelia, where have you been?"

Josie flipped on the light. Amelia was wearing her coat, but she'd taken off her boots.

"Shopping at Bluestone's." Amelia widened her eyes to look innocent. It didn't work.

Josie sneezed. "You smell like you fell into a vat of perfume."

"It's not my fault." Now Amelia was talking too fast. "Zoe—"

"I should have known," Josie said.

"It's not Zoe's fault, either, Mom. Bluestone's had the new prom perfumes on display. We were looking at the bottles. I liked Michael Kors's Very Hollywood. Zoe said she loved Vera Wang's Glam Princess because the bottle was shaped like a heart. Rebecca thought Versace's Versus rocked and said she'd buy it just for the purple bottle.

"Zoe said they were selling perfume, not bottles. She sprayed some Glam Princess on her wrist. Then she sprayed my wrist, but she sprayed too hard and it stunk.

"I sprayed her back with Very Hollywood. Rebecca was laughing and saying, 'More! More!' so we both sprayed her. Then she sprayed us with Versus and it kinda got out of hand."

Josie sneezed again. "Amelia, I knew this would happen if you went shopping with Zoe."

"Mom, the salesclerks were right there. Nobody said anything to us. Nobody got mad. Ask Mrs. Cohen."

"I will," Josie said. She sneezed a third time. "You stink. Put your coat and scarf on a hanger and leave them on the back porch to air out. Then take a shower while I call Rebecca's mother."

"Can I still see Grandma after my shower?" Amelia asked. "We're cooking broiled flank steak tonight."

"She can have you for the evening," Josie said, and sneezed again. "Now, go shower. I'm allergic to my own daughter."

Harry the cat trailed his gal pal into her bathroom. Josie dialed Golda Cohen.

"I know why you're calling," Golda said. "I bet you smelled your daughter."

"She reeks," Josie said.

"You should get a whiff of my car," Golda said. "I made the girls ride home with the windows rolled down. I almost choked on the perfume fumes."

"I'm sorry Amelia misbehaved."

"She didn't," Golda said. "None of the girls did. They were at Bluestone's looking at the perfume testers. The girls got carried away. The sales staff was busy talking to one another and didn't notice. The girls stopped as soon as they saw me. Amelia's going to have trouble getting rid of that odor. Rebecca has had two showers so far and her hair is still pungent."

"Amelia is in the shower now," Josie said.

"She'll need at least one more before school tomorrow. Don't worry, Josie. The girls were good, even Zoe."

Josie could hear the water running in Amelia's bathroom when she hung up. The phone rang again. This time it was her boss, Harry the Horrible.

"Got another job for you," he said.

"Good," Josie said. "My January heating bill is going to be a bear."

"You'll love this one," Harry said. "I want you to get your hair cut at Cheap Chick."

"That's the name of a salon?" Cheap Chick sounded like an insult to Josie.

"It's a chain. You've seen their ads on TV—'High Fashion at Low Prices.' They're like Supercuts, only better."

"Oh, you mean Cheap Chic Cuts," Josie said.

"That's what I said."

Not quite, but Josie wasn't going to split hairs. "Harry, I'm not sure about this. Angela cuts my hair every four weeks at her beauty shop on Manchester Road. She's good. I don't want to go to an unknown stylist and wind up with my hair ruined."

"Cheap Chic stylists are trained in New York," Harry said. "They're better than the local slobs."

Josie heard versions of this way too often: If you were any good, you'd leave the city. She felt it was a self-fulfilling prophecy. As for "local slobs," that inelegant description definitely fit Harry.

Josie's mind flashed on a mental picture of her troll of a boss, his fingers greasy from some artery-busting snack.

Hair—at least on his head—wasn't something Harry had to worry about. Too bad he couldn't transplant those furry growths from his chest, nose, and knuckles to his scalp.

Josie remembered her monster heating bill. Sorry, Angela, she mentally told her stylist. I have a utility giant to feed.

"Cheap Chic promises customers will never wait more than fifteen minutes for high style," Harry said. "The main office wants you to drop by either today or tomorrow and test the wait time."

"With my head?" Josie said.

"What's the problem? They guarantee a high-style cut or your money back."

"I'm mystery-shopping this salon. Isn't headquarters paying for my haircut anyway?" Josie said. "If I get a bad cut, how do I get my money back?"

"Jeez louise, do you want the job or not? First I got you and your friend new underwear. Now you get a free New York haircut. If you don't like the cut, write a report and get the stylist fired. It's just hair. It will grow back."

It won't grow back on your bald head, Josie wanted to say. But Harry had slammed down the phone. Just as well, she thought.

Amelia emerged damp from the shower and still stinking of prom perfume.

"What do you think, Mom?" she asked.

"A couple more showers might drown out the perfume," Josie said. "Tell Grandma hi for me. I have to run to the store. We'll talk about dinner when I get back. Go straight upstairs."

Outside, the air felt fresh and crisp after Amelia's penetrating perfume. Josie breathed it in gratefully, taking deep lungfuls of carbon monoxide–laden air. Then she held her breath.

What was that on her car? Something red was spattered on the windshield.

It looked like someone had upended a strawberry shake.

No, it was darker. Maybe cranberry. Or a raspberry drink. Except it didn't smell like raspberry.

Josie examined the gunk frozen on her windshield, then picked off a piece and sniffed it.

This wasn't a fresh-fruit smell.

It was raw and harsh. An iron scent, like . . . blood.

Cold blood.

Someone had thrown blood on her windshield.

# Chapter 26

Officer Doris Ann Norris studied the blood on Josie's windshield like a collector examining a rare find. The afternoon light was fading and she used her flashlight.

"Less than a cup of blood," the officer said. "Doesn't look like an arterial spurt." Norris was a fit thirty. She was tall, but everything else—from her brown hair to her fingernails—was short and practical.

"Is that good?" Josie asked.

"For the victim," Officer Norris said. "Cut an artery and you're dead unless you get medical attention fast."

"Then no one was murdered?" Josie didn't bother hiding her relief.

"I wouldn't say that," Officer Norris said. "An injury with low blood loss can still be fatal. Any blood drips down the side of your car?"

She shone her flashlight on the driver's door. The patrol officer's leather gun belt creaked when she bent for a closer look at the car. "Ah, it is a murder," she said. "The body is under your car."

Josie grabbed the fender for support and braced herself for a new horror. Officer Norris reached under the car and pulled out a bloody mass of gray feathers.

"It looks like a pigeon," she said, aiming the flashlight at the bird. "Look at this left wing here. I think the pigeon was injured, possibly hit by a car. Someone took the dying bird and splashed its blood on your windshield."

Josie's stomach turned. "That's so cruel."

"It is," Officer Norris said. "I'm no fan of pigeons. You won't believe how they mess up my patrol car. Nothing but flying rats. I'd like to see them all dead." She seemed to be aware of the gathering crowd. She added, "In a humane way, of course."

"Absolutely," Josie agreed.

"Well, now we know that there's no human victim, this is a lot easier," Officer Norris said. "Looks like a nasty prank. Someone got it in for you?"

"No," Josie said.

"What about your boyfriend?"

"Ted and I are just fine," Josie said. "My former boyfriend Stan lives in that house right there. His fiancée's blue VW Bug is in the driveway. They're getting married. I'm out of that picture."

"How about the boyfriends before him?" Officer Norris asked.

"Mike and I parted on good terms." And his ex is in jail, Josie thought. She didn't mention the man before Mike, who'd supplemented his income with drug dealing. She was still trying to forget Josh. Josie knew she'd made some bad choices when it came to men, but she dumped them as soon as she found out they were seriously flawed. Just as well not to mention Josh to the police. She hadn't seen him in months, anyway. Maybe he'd found a new way to make extra money.

"Know anybody mixed up in Santeria?" Officer Norris asked.

"What?" Josie asked.

"Santeria. It's a Caribbean religion. They make animal sacrifices."

"In Maplewood?" Josie didn't bother hiding her disbelief.

"You'd be surprised," Officer Norris said.

Josie could see trouble coming straight at her. Mrs. Mueller marched across the lawn in her Russian-winter outfit, moving through the yard like a snowplow.

"Absolutely nothing would surprise me, Officer," Mrs. Mueller said, loudly. "I've lived next to this young woman since she was nine years old. The things I could tell you. I saw this whole incident."

"What incident, ma'am?" Officer Norris asked. She looked deceptively wide-eyed, like Amelia.

"The bird. I saw the woman who did it." Mrs. Mueller puffed herself out like a giant pigeon. "I can describe her, too. She was wearing dark gloves, a dark coat, and a black-and-white scarf. Josie has a scarf just like it."

"Are you saying Ms. Marcus vandalized her own car?"

"No, this woman was bigger than Josie."

"How much bigger?"

"She was taller and bigger around."

"As big as you?"

"I wouldn't say I am big," Mrs. Mueller said. "Stately would be more accurate. This was a generously built woman."

"Could you tell her race?"

"She was a white woman," Mrs. M said.

"Young? Old?" Officer Norris said.

"I couldn't tell. I didn't get a good look at her face."

"Blonde, brunette, or redhead?" Officer Norris asked.

"She had brown bangs. Ordinary brown. Josie's color, I think. The rest of her hair was hidden by the scarf. But she was carrying a box, a pink shoe box. She took the lid off and I saw something flapping inside the box."

"You saw this from your living room?" Officer Norris sounded skeptical.

"I was upstairs in my bedroom. I'd been napping, but I was awakened by a sound of some sort."

Right, Josie thought. Mrs. Mueller spent every afternoon watching who went up and down the street and whether the person walked, drove, or rode a cycle. Her description was so detailed, Josie wondered if Mrs. M used binoculars to spy on the neighborhood.

"I woke up suddenly and went to my window," Mrs. Mueller said. "The sun was out. I watched the woman take the lid off the box. I could look down and see inside. There was a creature bleeding and flapping, like a wounded bird. The woman sort of squeezed it over the windshield, wringing out the blood."

Josie hissed in horror. Even a pigeon didn't deserve that.

"Then she threw the bird under the car and left," Mrs. Mueller said. "She must have heard the black car."

"What black car, ma'am?" Officer Norris asked.

"It was a black Lexus. The driver was a woman and she had several young girls inside. One of them was Josie's daughter, Amelia. They were driving with the windows rolled down and it's cold out."

"Yes, I know that, ma'am," the police officer said. "The woman in the black coat who painted this windshield with bird blood—did you get a look at her car?"

"She didn't drive. She walked here. I saw her come from the west. She went back that way and around the corner." Mrs. Mueller pointed in that direction.

The officer followed her wool-gloved hand. "The sidewalk is shoveled and salted," Norris said. "There's no way we can get footprints. You saw this person squeezing blood from a wounded bird on a windshield and you didn't call the police?"

"It didn't look like a police matter," Mrs. Mueller said.

"It was an act of animal cruelty, ma'am. You should have reported it."

"Well, it was just a pigeon." Mrs. Mueller was deflating like a week-old balloon.

"You do understand that killers enjoy acts of animal cruelty?"

"No," Mrs. Mueller said. "I don't associate with killers."

"You didn't warn your neighbor that someone had vandalized her ride?"

"No," Mrs. Mueller said. A touch of malice tinged her voice. "I can't keep track of everything Josie does. She has so many men in and out of her house. Men who are not of the highest character and reputation. Neither is Josie. She's not married and she has a child out of wedlock. The father of her child was a drug dealer."

"He was pardoned," Josie said.

"He still spent time in a foreign jail," Mrs. Mueller said, firmly. "The father of her child died on that very front porch."

"He was murdered," Josie said. "He was poisoned. The killer is in jail."

"I seem to remember that incident," Officer Norris said.

"Well, then, you understand my problem, Officer," Mrs. Mueller said. "That's why I don't associate with Josie Marcus. With the caliber of people she knows, it's hard to tell what's out of the ordinary at her place. Do you want me to come down to the station and sign a statement?"

"Thank you, ma'am, but no," Officer Norris said. "You witnessed an act of animal cruelty and vandalism. You saw nothing useful. You failed to warn your neighbor or call the authorities. You let a potentially dangerous person go free. I won't take up any more of your time. If I need a statement, I'll contact you."

Mrs. Mueller slunk off to her home. Josie heard the older woman's front door slam, then saw her mother and Amelia running toward her.

"Josie!" Jane cried. "Are you all right?"

"She's fine, ma'am," Officer Norris said, holding up her hand like a traffic cop's to stop Jane. "I need to ask her one more thing. Then you can take her inside to warm up.

"Anything else you want to tell me?" Officer Norris said to Josie. Her eyes were watchful.

"No," Josie said. She didn't want to tell the police about her private investigation. The cops were clueless. They had the wrong person in jail. Those two Venetia Park detectives had never even found the mysterious blonde in the wheelchair.

I did that, Josie thought. Alyce cleverly established that the shoplifter was telling the truth with a phone call. I must be getting somewhere. I'm close to solving this. I can do it on my own.

"I find that hard to believe," Officer Norris said, as if she'd heard Josie's thoughts.

Josie's eyes shifted. The cop knew she was lying.

"Here's my card," the police officer said. "When you're ready to talk, call me. If anyone threatens you, call 911. Watch out for your daughter. Whoever is after you may decide your daughter is the way to hurt you. If you get a message from this person, let me know, hear?"

"Yes," Josie said.

She already had the message. She was a dead pigeon.

# Chapter 27

"More tea, Josie?" Jane asked.

Josie's mother had run out to the car and folded her daughter into her arms. Small, fierce Jane led her daughter inside, away from the police officer and the prying eyes of sidewalk spectators. In Josie's warm kitchen, Jane made rafts of buttered toast and strong Lipton tea.

Josie was a dedicated coffee drinker, but her mother's toast and tea were a soothing throwback to childhood comfort food. Josie had wolfed down six slices so far, each golden brown and dripping butter. The dark bitter tea was heavily sugared.

The caffeine, fat, and sugar had revived Josie. She'd finally stopped shivering.

"Who would do such a thing?" her mother asked for the fourth time.

"To me or to the pigeon?" Josie said.

"Be serious," her mother said. "This isn't funny. Only a horrible person would torture a bird like that, even a pigeon. I don't want that monster coming after my daughter. Or my granddaughter."

"I don't know who did it," Josie said again.

She didn't. She'd riled up too many people. Any one of them could have smeared blood on her windshield: the two Desiree Lingerie associates, Trish and Rosa. Or Shannon, the receptionist who had followed Frankie to help her lover, Dr. Tino, get free of his marriage and avoid a lawsuit. There was also Victoria, the neighbor who held monthly sales of her shoplifted bargains.

Josie had four people angry at her. Five if you counted Cody the hero. Except it couldn't have been Cody. The killer was a woman wearing a black-and-white scarf. The killer knew where Josie lived. And Josie's daughter, Amelia. Josie shivered again. The cold feeling was back, and all the tea in Maplewood wouldn't take it away.

"It has to be someone, Josie," Jane said. "Why would that person pick your car?" She slammed down a third mug so hard tea slopped over the side.

Josie was saved from answering by a knock on the door.

"Why, it's Ted!" Amelia cried in poorly faked surprise. "What are you doing here?"

Josie guessed that her daughter had called Ted and told him what had happened. She was glad Amelia was so bad at lying.

"Hold this for me, will you, Amelia?" Ted handed her a cardboard box, then dropped a gym bag on the floor. "Where's Josie?"

"Right here," Josie said, running out to greet him in the living room.

Ted wrapped his arms around her. His shoulders were hard and muscular. He smelled of woodsmoke, cinnamon, hot coffee, and hot man. Josie wished she could have stayed in his arms for the rest of the day. They were far more comforting than tea and toast.

"How are you?" Ted asked.

"Fine," she said.

"No, you're not. Let me look at you."

He held Josie away from him and appraised her carefully. "Your face is too pale. You have dark circles under your eyes and there's a blood streak on your cheek."

"That's bird blood," Josie said. "I picked some off my windshield. The blood was frozen. It must have melted when I touched it and I smeared some on my face."

"You're talking too fast," Ted said. "That's a sign of

shock in humans." He quirked an eyebrow. "Unless you're lying to me."

"I'm hyped on adrenaline and caffeine," Josie said. "I'm a little scared, but I don't think this is anything to worry about."

"I do," Ted said. "Anyone cruel enough to hurt a dying bird has no conscience. I'm concerned about you and Amelia both. I'm spending the night on your couch. That gym bag has a change of clothes in it."

"Good!" Jane said.

Josie was surprised. Her mother usually worried what the neighbors thought. This time, Jane's concern for her family's safety won out over her fear of Josie's lost reputation. Besides, Josie thought, mine is already ruined, thanks to Mrs. Mueller.

"I'm driving Amelia to school tomorrow," Ted said.

"Yay!" Amelia said. Arriving with the hunky vet would impress her friends. She had a schoolgirl crush on Ted.

"There's a problem, Amelia," Ted said. "I'm on call in the Mobo-Pet van from six till two o'clock. Will you be embarrassed riding in a big blue van with a cat, a dog, and a bird painted on the side?"

"I'm cool with it," Amelia said. "Your van is better than Zoe's red Hummer. That energy hog is butt ugly."

"Language, young lady," Josie said.

"I'm just warning you that your social life could be ruined," Ted said.

"It won't be," Amelia said. "Anybody who makes fun of my ride isn't my friend."

Josie remembered how embarrassed she'd been when Jane had worn an ugly brown knit cap and picked her up at school. The mean girls had chanted, "Hi, Patty, Patty, Cow Patty!" and waved at Jane, slyly pointing at her head. Josie's mother thought they were being friendly and waved back. Josie had never said anything, but the shame still burned in her.

*My daughter is more mature at ten than I was sixteen,* she thought.

"Can we take Harry with us when we go to school?" Amelia asked. She was testing them, going for the double goal of handsome escort and cute cat.

"Harry is an indoor cat," Ted said. "Most cats don't like riding in cars. Their eyes don't adjust properly to the road as it rushes by and they get upset. He'll be more comfortable at home."

"You will have to take Mom, though," Josie said. "The school will not let strangers drop you off or pick you up, Amelia. You know that. I'll have to be there to reassure Mrs. Apple that you are with someone safe."

The wealthy Barrington students were prime targets for kidnappers and custody fights. The school had strict safeguards. A phone call would not be enough to clear the way for Ted. Josie would have to ride along with them.

"I'll drive the Mustang when I pick you up after school," Ted said.

"Yay!" Amelia said. His vintage tangerine Mustang was almost as handsome as he was. Amelia thought the old car outclassed the shiniest new BMW and Mercedes anyone else drove.

"Can it be just us in the afternoon? Mom can do the paperwork in the administration office when you drop me off in the morning. Then you can pick me up without Mom."

Josie was crazy about Ted. She thought he would make a good father, but it was too soon to be forcing him into that role. Too much responsibility too soon could make a man run.

"Sorry," Josie said. "Your mother is riding shotgun after school, too."

"But the backseat of a Mustang is small," Amelia said.

Does my daughter really think I'll crawl in the backseat so she can sit up front with Ted? Josie wondered. "You'll fit in it just fine." Josie's tone squashed that hope.

Ted changed the subject quickly. "What are you going to do tomorrow, Josie, if I have to answer a house call?"

"I have to go for a haircut tomorrow morning," Josie said. "It's a mystery-shopping job. I'll fax my report to the office afterward. Then I can ride with you. When it's time to take the van back to the clinic, we can get your car and pick up Amelia together. I'll be safe at a hair salon. It has scissors and razors. I'll come straight home and file my report."

"Deal," Ted said. "How about if I make dinner tonight? Do you like pasta with Italian sausage, peppers, and onions? I thought I'd cook up a batch."

"Love it," Josie said.

"Can I watch?" Amelia asked.

"You can help."

Josie, Jane, and Amelia followed Ted into the kitchen. He pulled a pot out of the box and handed it to Amelia. "Fill this with water and put it on to boil, please. Then we'll start cutting up peppers and onions."

"Onions make me cry," Amelia said.

"I have a way around that," Ted said. "No tears, I promise."

"Do you put the onion under water and then chop it?" Jane asked.

"No, that's a good method, but the wet knife could slip and Amelia could cut herself."

"Do you chill the onion?" Josie guessed.

"That one works, too," Ted said. "But this onion is now room temperature and I don't want to wait for it to get cold again. I didn't bring a lime, either. The acid in the lime juice, Amelia, reacts with the gas in the onion and cuts down the tears. Instead I got this."

He reached in for a box of sugar cubes.

"Sweet!" Amelia said.

"Indeed," Ted said. "Start chopping while you chew sugar cubes."

Amelia and Ted chopped and chewed sugar cubes. The girl's eyes didn't redden or water.

"It worked," Amelia said. "Why?"

"Because when you're chewing the sugar, you breathe through your mouth and that stops the onion's 'tear' gas from getting in your nose."

"Let me try," Josie said.

She chewed a sugar cube while she worked with an onion and a knife. Sugar to stop the crying. Such a simple, pleasant solution. Josie hoped she and her daughter could get out of this trap she'd created—without tears.

# Chapter 28

Josie sat up in bed, awakened by a brittle crash. Her sleep-logged brain registered a sound like glass breaking. In the front of the house. Only two rooms were there: Josie's living room and her daughter's bedroom.

"Amelia!" Josie cried.

She rushed to her daughter's room. In the glow of the night-light, she could see Amelia sleeping. Harry the cat sat up by her, eyes wide and ears alert.

"You heard it, too, didn't you, boy?" Josie whispered.

Amelia slept undisturbed. Josie decided it was safer if she stayed that way.

Upstairs, Stuart Little sounded the alarm with frantic barks. Josie ran back to her room and pulled the dog repellent from her purse. If the spray could stop rabid dogs, it should work on robbers. She threw on her robe, slid into her slippers, and crept down the hall to the living room.

"Ted?" she called softly.

He wasn't on the couch. His blanket was thrown back and his pillow was on the floor. The front door was wide open. Ted had run outside in a hurry. A light popped on upstairs at Mrs. Mueller's house.

Stuart Little's barks grew louder and deeper until he sounded twice his size. The lapdog had turned into a fierce protector.

Josie grabbed the living room phone out of its cradle in case she had to call 911. Armed with the phone and the dog repellent, Josie ran outside and was hit by a blast of chill wind. She froze when she saw a man standing under Amelia's window. Josie moved into the shadows along the porch and raised the spray, hoping to hit him in the eyes. Then she saw it was Ted, dressed in the same blue flannel shirt and jeans he'd worn last night.

"What is it?" she asked, joining him on the snowy lawn. "What's wrong?"

"Looks like a big chunk of snow slid off your roof," he said.

"I heard a sound like glass breaking," Josie said.

"The snow slide took the icicles on the gutter along with it. I don't want to worry you, but you should see this."

He pointed to footprints leading from the sidewalk to the pile of snow under Amelia's window. More footprints led back to the sidewalk, forming a deep V in the yard. Ted's footprints made a third track beside them.

"Oh, my God, someone was trying to steal my girl," Josie whispered.

Ted put his arm around her. "He won't get past the two of us," he said.

He? Or was it "she"? Josie wondered. Officer Doris Ann Norris's warning replayed in her mind: *Watch your daughter. Whoever is after you may decide your girl is the way to get to you.*

"I'd better call Officer Norris," Josie said. "Do you think a man or a woman left those prints?"

"The shoe soles are flat," Ted said. "Could be a man or a large woman."

A large woman in a black-and-white scarf, Josie thought. The footsteps ran to the sidewalk to the west— the same direction as the woman who'd bloodied Josie's windshield.

Jane appeared on the front porch in her chenille robe, her head crowned with pink rollers. Stuart Little was at her side.

"Josie, what's going on?"

"Someone walked across the lawn to the window here,"

Ted said. "Whoever it was is gone now. Let's go inside and talk. Josie has to call the police."

"The police!" Jane said.

"It's all right," Ted said. "No one was hurt. We chased them away. I'll stay with you until help arrives."

He was careful to step only in the footprints he'd made. When he reached the broad porch, Ted ran up the stairs and put his arm around Jane. Josie's mother seemed small and shrunken next to the broad-shouldered veterinarian. Stuart Little trotted at Jane's side, eyes bright with curiosity.

Josie followed them, shivering. Her slippers were stuffed with snow. "What time is it?" she asked, and yawned.

"Five o'clock," Ted said. "I'll have to leave soon to get the van. I'll stay with you until Officer Norris arrives."

Josie found the police officer's card and dialed her number. She sounded sleepy at first, but rapidly grew alert as Josie described the situation.

"Do you have someone with you now?" Officer Norris asked.

"Yes, my friend Ted stayed overnight. He has to get his vet-clinic van, but he won't leave until someone gets here."

"I'm on my way," Officer Norris said.

Josie made coffee. Ted made stilted conversation with a worried Jane. "Where is Stuart Little sleeping these days?" he asked. "In the basement?"

"Absolutely not!" Jane conveniently forgot that she'd banished the dog there his first night. "He has a basket in my bedroom."

"They watch soap operas together," Josie said.

"Shih tzus are natural soap lovers," Ted said. "They're intelligent and loyal."

"He can follow the plot," Jane said.

Josie had just poured three cups of coffee when Officer Doris Ann Norris knocked on the door. She was in uniform. Josie didn't see a patrol car parked out front and wondered if Officer Norris had rushed over in her own car.

"Come outside," the officer said. The three abandoned their coffee and dutifully followed Officer Norris outside.

"Are those the footprints, the ones running from the sidewalk to the front window and back?"

"Yes," Josie said. "They make a V at my daughter's bedroom window. The straight line of footprints along the edge there belong to Ted."

"Looks like the person walked slowly and deliberately to the window," Officer Norris said. "You can see the whole footprint on this side of the V. There are no prints or marks in the snow on your windowsill. Then something startled or surprised the perp. Maybe it was the snow slide."

"Or my dog barking," Jane said.

"Could be that, too. A noisy dog can be good protection. Either way, they took off in a hurry."

Officer Norris pointed at the other half of the V. "Those footprints were made by someone running fast. They end at the sidewalk, where the snow has been shoveled and the concrete is heavily traveled. Looks like the person wears a size eleven or twelve shoe. Can't say if it's a man's foot or a woman's, but the person wasn't wearing high heels."

"Are you going to make a cast of the footprints?" Josie asked.

"Casting prints made in the snow is tricky, but possible," Officer Norris said. "Given the fact that there wasn't really a crime committed other than perhaps trespass, I can't call in CSI. You're sure you didn't receive any threats?"

"Positive," Josie said.

"Then all I can do is advise extreme caution. Call if there are any further disturbances or you see anything suspicious. Is your friend Ted staying over again tonight?"

"No," Josie said.

"Yes," Ted said at the same time.

"If it was me," Officer Norris said, "I'd want him here."

"Ted can't move in with us," Josie said. "He has to work. He has a home. He needs his sleep, too."

"It may not be for long, ma'am," Officer Norris said. "Just a few days. Sometimes trouble lands on a house for a while. We'll get two or three calls about noises and minor vandalism and then the problem goes away, or looks for an easier target. We never find out what caused it."

"The couch is comfortable," Ted said. "I'd sleep better here knowing Josie and Amelia are safe. I can nap this afternoon when I get off work."

"What if Amelia slept upstairs in my guest room for the duration?" Jane asked.

"That's a good idea. If someone is after your granddaughter, she'll be harder to reach there."

"He'll have to get past me first," Ted said.

Josie knew she'd miss her daughter if Amelia slept upstairs. But this wasn't about her comfort. This was for Amelia's protection. Jane's suggestion was a good one.

"I have to go," Officer Norris said. "You have my number. Program it into your cell. Never hesitate to call me or 911 if anything looks or feels wrong."

"Would you like a cup of coffee?" Josie asked.

"Thanks, but I need to report to work."

Officer Norris was out the door. Josie saw the blinds move in Mrs. Mueller's upstairs bedroom window, and knew the busybody was watching. She waved from her porch. The blind slat slid back into place.

"I have to pick up the clinic's Mobo-Pet van," Ted said. "Will you be all right while I'm gone?"

"We'll be fine," Jane said. "We'll keep our phones in our hands and we have Stuart Little here."

"Woof!" Stuart said. He looked as fierce as a teddy bear.

"I'll be back in half an hour at the most."

He kissed Josie and ran for his car.

"I must say, I am impressed with that young man," Jane said. "You could do worse."

"Mom, it's too early to be measuring him for a wedding suit," Josie said.

"What's too early?" Amelia said. The sleepy girl stood in the hallway in her flannel nightgown with Harry at her side. Her dark hair was tousled. Josie's heart turned over at the sight.

Stuart barked at the cat and Harry slid under the couch.

"Was that the policewoman from yesterday? Why was she here?" Amelia asked.

"We found footprints on the lawn last night," Josie said. "Ted scared off whoever it was and we called the police."

"I didn't hear anything," Amelia said, rubbing her eyes.

"They're gone. We think it would be better if you slept upstairs with Grandma tonight. Ted will stay here with us."

"On the couch?" Amelia asked.

"He can sleep in your room," Josie said. "It will be more comfortable than the couch."

She didn't mention that the footprints led up to Amelia's window. She hoped her girl wouldn't notice.

"Do you think someone wants to hurt me?" Amelia said.

"Of course not," Josie said. "It's just a precaution. Now go get dressed and feed Harry. Ted will be back shortly and we'll all go to school together."

Fear gripped Josie's heart like a cold hand. Who had been under Amelia's window last night? What did that person want? Was it Frankie's killer?

# Chapter 29

"Breakfast, Harry!" Amelia called. "Come and get it."

Harry poked his head out from under the couch and looked both ways for the shih tzu, as if he expected the dog to rush out and body slam him.

"Stuart Little went upstairs with Grandma," Amelia said. "He wasn't going to hurt you. He just wanted to play."

Harry slid out from under the couch, carefully sniffed the carpet, then followed Amelia into the kitchen. He moved cautiously, a tiny tiger on the prowl, still waiting for the canine ambush.

He overcame his caution when he saw the bowl of cat food beside the fridge. Harry gobbled his food as if it would be outlawed in half an hour. The smelly stuff had a bouquet only a cat could appreciate. Josie was glad Amelia handled this chore. She couldn't stomach it this early.

Harry polished off his breakfast and moved to his water bowl.

"I thought Stuart Little and Harry were friends?" Josie said.

"They are," Amelia said. "Harry just doesn't feel like playing right now. He wants to finish breakfast."

Harry didn't even look up from his water when Ted returned.

"That was quick," Josie said.

"I'll take you up on that coffee now," he said. "Then I'd like a shower."

Josie poured him a cup and said, "Drink this while I get you fresh towels."

She raced to her bathroom, checked the tub and toilet, swiped the sink with a sponge, and stripped her clean lingerie off the towel rack. Then she hung up two fluffy bath towels and a washcloth. Josie dumped the wastebasket into the one in her bedroom and was back in the kitchen in five minutes.

Ted was still sipping his coffee. "Was Harry a feral cat?"

"Don't know," Josie said. "We adopted him from the Humane Society. His original family gave him to the shelter when they had to move. We never found out where they got him. Why do you ask?"

"Look how he drinks his water," Ted said. "He dips one foot in his bowl, turns his paw over, and licks the water off the pads."

"I know. Makes a mess on the floor," Josie said.

"That's how some wild animals drink water," Ted said. "A domesticated pet will lap the water out of its bowl."

"That's how Stuart Little drinks!" Amelia said. "He laps his water."

"Shih tzus have been lapdogs for centuries," Ted said. "No pun intended."

"I'm doing a report on cats for school," Amelia said. "I can use the information about how Harry drinks."

"Can I fix you some eggs for breakfast, Ted?" Josie asked.

"I can make biscuits," Amelia said.

"Coffee is fine," Ted said. "I'd better shower if we're going to get Amelia to school on time." He carried his coffee cup to the sink, then hauled the gym bag he'd brought last night into Josie's bathroom.

Amelia loaded the dishwater without being asked. Josie could practically see the halo over her daughter's head. She enjoys having a man around the house, Josie thought. And so do I, for that matter. But I don't want to rush into this romance. That got me in trouble last time. I nearly had Mike's ring on my finger when I realized our two families would never blend. I'd better put the brakes on now. I want to keep this man, not scare him away.

Josie waited until she heard the water running in her shower, then called her friend Alyce. It was only 7:10, but Alyce had a toddler and a husband who had to be in his law office by eight o'clock. Alyce answered her phone on the first ring, a sure sign she was up.

"Of course you didn't wake me," Alyce said. "I've been awake since six. Justin is busy applying oatmeal to his face. Hold on a second, while I make sure some of his breakfast gets into his mouth."

Alyce put down the phone. Josie heard cooing and coaxing noises that made her long for the time when Amelia had been a fat, laughing baby and Josie had loaded up her spoon with cereal and said, "Here comes the airplane."

"I'm back," Alyce said. "What's wrong? You rarely call this early."

"We've had a minor disturbance," Josie said. "There's been a prowler around our house. We found footprints across the lawn to Amelia's room."

"Is she okay?"

"She's fine," Josie said. "Whoever it was never got to her window. Ted was staying here with us."

"Whoa! Back up. Ted has moved in with you?"

"No," Josie said. "His stay is temporary until things calm down. Ted is taking Amelia to school this morning and I'm riding with them. He wants to stay with me all day until we pick up Amelia after school. I like Ted. No, I think I love him, but it's too soon for twenty-four-hour togetherness. Can I see you for an hour or so without my bodyguard? I'll give you the full story then."

"You can come over now, if you want."

"I need to get my hair cut first and file a mystery-shopping report. It will be about eleven before I can make it."

"Good," Alyce said. "That's time for me to fix brunch. Josie, is your romance going sour?"

"No," Josie said. "Ted's perfect. That's the problem."

"Most women would love to have your problem, but you don't have to explain. We'll have some food and talk. Then, if you want, I'll call Ted in officially for his veterinary service. I can ask him to see Bruiser."

"Is your dog sick?" Josie asked.

"No, but I'll make up something if I have to," Alyce said. "Josie, do you think the vandal was Victoria? She was furious when you shut down her shopping parties."

"I don't know," Josie said. "Mrs. Mueller saw a woman wearing a black-and-white scarf."

"Like the kill—uh, the woman—in the mall video?"

"Exactly," Josie said. "And we both know that woman was up to no good. You can say killer. I've already thought it."

"Josie, don't throw Ted out too soon," Alyce said. "The scarf woman is dangerous. The police say she killed Frankie."

Josie heard the water shut off. Ted's shower was over.

"Gotta go," Josie said. "We'll talk later."

Josie hung up. Her mind flashed on the grainy video of the woman with the black-and-white scarf. Something nagged at her. So far as she knew, Victoria didn't have any idea where Josie lived. Alyce had driven the day they'd confronted the shoplifter at her house on Palmer Avenue. But it was possible Victoria may have remembered she'd seen Josie before. They lived only two blocks away.

The scarf woman could also have been Rosa, whose parents were in this country illegally. Or Trish, afraid that her future career would be crushed if word got out about her drug-abusing past. Shannon, Dr. Tino's fiancée, was another good candidate for the scarf stalker. She and her doctor lover benefited from Frankie's untimely death. If Shannon had been cleared by the police, she wouldn't want Josie stirring up trouble by asking questions. That made four suspects.

Five if you counted Cody the hero. Except Mrs. Mueller had seen a woman, not a man, and Cody was all man, even if he did wear panty hose. He was married, too. Maybe his wife had killed Frankie. A woman would do a lot to protect her family. If ever a person deserved killing, it had been Frankie.

Josie could hear a hair dryer roaring in the bathroom. She flipped on her computer and Googled Cody's name, hoping to find a photo of the hero's wife. She saw twelve stories.

She printed out every news story she could access. Josie caught glimpses of photos with the articles and hoped one included a picture of Cody's wife.

The hair dryer stopped. Ted strolled out of the bathroom, whistling. Josie joined him in the hall. He gave her a damp kiss. "Where do I drop you after we take Amelia to school?"

"Back here, so I can pick up my car and drive to the salon," Josie said.

"I thought I'd take you there. It's safer that way."

"Nothing is going to happen to me at a beauty shop," Josie said, "except that I might get a bad cut."

"What about after that?"

Josie didn't like being accountable for her time. "I have to see my friend Alyce. You've met her. She adopted Bruiser. Alyce lives in a gated community. I'll be safe there. The guards are good."

"I really don't think . . . " Ted began.

"I'm a grown woman," Josie said, kissing Ted on his damp ear. "I've been alone for a long time. Amelia will be safe at school and that's what I really care about. I'm not worried about me."

"Well, I am," he said, kissing her on the mouth.

Um, Josie thought. I could get used to this.

"Then stop by Alyce's, if you're not on duty. You can check out her Chihuahua, Bruiser."

"Deal," Ted said. "Do you think she'll mind?"

"She already said she'd like to see you." She kissed Ted again. His lips were soft and warm and he smelled of mint toothpaste and Dial soap.

The kiss was interrupted by loud throat clearing. Amelia was suited up in her coat and boots. "Mom, we need to get going. I'm going to be late for school."

"Right," Josie said, pulling herself away from Ted. "Let me get my purse."

Josie ran into her bedroom, ripped the pages out of her printer, and stuffed them in her purse. She made certain the dog repellent was in there, too. She felt ready to confront any threat on two legs or four.

She was not going to live like a scared rabbit. Frankie died because she'd been surprised. Josie was prepared to fight.

# Chapter 30

"Josie Marcus, is that you? I haven't seen you since high school!"

Josie stared at the blond stylist in the black jeans and Cheap Chic T-shirt. Did she know this woman? She seemed vaguely familiar. If it was who Josie thought it was, she'd definitely changed, and for the better.

"Donna?" Josie asked in a tentative voice.

"That's me."

"Wow!" Josie said.

Back in high school, Donna's blond hair had looked like a haystack. She'd worn plum lipstick and raccoon eye makeup. Now her chin-length style was sleek. Her hair color had changed from bottle blond to warm honey. Her makeup was stylish and subdued. Two things stayed the same: Donna was still slender and her green eyes sparkled with mischief.

Donna had been Josie's friend in high school. They'd lost touch after graduation when Josie went to college.

"You always said you wanted to be a hairstylist," Josie said. "Here you are at Cheap Chic Cuts and trained in New York, too."

Donna rolled her eyes. "I'll tell you about that later," she said. "Let's talk about your hair. What do you want me to do?"

"I'm not sure," Josie said. "I don't want my hair short but—" She took a deep breath and surprised herself by saying, "I'm tired of this look. I haven't changed my hairstyle since Amelia was born, and my girl is ten now. I'd like something that's not so soccer mom."

"You're too hard on yourself," Donna said. "You have a simple cut that's right for the shape of your face. I can make the style edgier without a drastic change."

"That's what I want," Josie said, and laughed. "The same, only different."

"Hey, that's Cheap Chic," Donna said. "How do you feel about highlights?"

"No, thanks." Josie knew they'd be expensive to maintain on what a mystery shopper made.

"Follow me," Donna said. "My station is in the back."

Josie picked her way through a maze of mirrored stations, rolling equipment carts, and electrical cords. Skinny black-clad stylists wielded blow-dryers and scissors. Clouds of hair spray filled the air.

Donna's station was near a row of black porcelain washing bowls. Josie sat down in a black chair and Donna unfurled a styling cape.

"I can't believe I haven't seen you since high school," Josie said. "Are you married?"

"I was," Donna said. "Remember Tim, our basketball center?"

"The blond with the muscles? You were dating him senior year," Josie said. "He was such a star."

"Not off the basketball court," Donna said. "Tim was one of those guys who peaked in high school. I got pregnant the night of the prom and we got married that summer. We were both too young. We divorced three years later, after I graduated from beauty college. We have one son, Paul.

"My son inherited his father's athletic prowess. I think Paul will make the school team when he's older. I hope he doesn't inherit his father's drinking habit. My son is thirteen. I'm holding my breath that I can get him safely through the wild years."

"My daughter is ten," Josie said. "I have two years

before Amelia is abducted by brain-altering aliens and changes completely. At least, I hope I do."

"The good part about this job," Donna said, "is that I can arrange my hours to be there when Paul gets home from school. I don't let my son hang with his friends unless I'm home and I know who the kids are."

Josie heard that "my son" and assumed Paul's father had little or no say in the boy's upbringing.

"What do you do?" Donna asked.

Josie couldn't say she was mystery-shopping her old friend. "I'm in retail," she said, and yawned, signaling a subject too dull to discuss. "How did you wind up one of Cheap Chic's New York–trained stylists?"

"That's a trick to impress the folks in the flyover."

"The what?" Josie said.

"The flyover is what some New Yorkers call the Midwest. Cheap Chic thinks we're all hicks in the sticks. They did send me to their New York headquarters for training—for one whole day.

"I took a six a.m. flight. The company picked me up at JFK and I spent an intense day at their Manhattan salon learning the Cheap Chic style. I flew home by eight that same day. So it's technically true: All Cheap Chic stylists are trained in New York. And the receptionist can tell everyone that I am just back from Manhattan."

"If I want to conclude you worked at a high-priced New York salon," Josie said, "I jump to that conclusion all by myself."

"You got it." Donna pulled a black ring binder from a drawer. "Do you want to look at some style photos or trust me to start cutting?"

"Go for it," Josie said. "From the way your hair looks, you know what you're doing."

"I hope none of the yearbook pictures of my Farrah Fawcett mane are still floating around," Donna said.

"Hey, you were in style then, too," Josie said.

She wondered if Donna could make her "edgier," as she promised. Josie had always looked ordinary. It was an asset in her job to blend in with the crowd. Maybe she shouldn't change her hair.

What are you? Josie asked herself. Woman or wallpaper? Make the change and enjoy looking stylish.

Donna was studying Josie's face carefully. She pulled back Josie's brown hair. She felt the texture with her hands. She combed her bangs to the right, then to the left.

"You have a nice natural wave we should use," Donna said. "Do you straighten your hair with a curling iron?"

"I try to," Josie said. "But it doesn't work well."

"It makes your hair dry," Donna said. "I'll wash it and give you a silk cap to make your hair shinier."

"Sounds glamorous," Josie said.

"It's not," Donna said. She settled Josie at a washing bowl. "Scooch your head down a bit. There's no charge for the silk cap. It's my gift to a high school friend."

"In St. Louis, where we go to high school marks us forever," Josie said. "Amelia's father was from Canada. The first time a St. Louisan asked Nate, 'Where did you go to school?' he told the guy the name of his college. The man really wanted to know what high school Nate went to. Nate never understood that St. Louis is such a settled town, we can tell a person's religion, race, and family income by their high school."

"You said 'was,'" Donna said. "Are you divorced, too?"

"He died," Josie said. She didn't want to go into Nate's sad history. Donna seemed to sense that. She washed Josie's hair until it squeaked, then massaged her temples.

"Mm. You can do that all day," Josie said.

"All good things have to end," Donna said. "Do you want a hot or a cold rinse?"

"Hot," Josie said. "It's cold enough outside."

After a warm-water rinse Donna said, "I'm going to paint something cold on your hair. It has to stay there for ten minutes, but I promise that your hair will look good. I'll cover your head with a plastic shower cap while it sets. That's your silk cap treatment. Do you want a magazine while you wait?"

"Thanks. I brought something to read."

Donna set a timer and disappeared. Josie pulled her sheaf of news stories about Cody John Wayne from her purse. The first showed a photo of Cody and his wife, Renee. The small brunette smiled proudly at her husband while the police pinned a medal on his chest. Renee barely came to Cody's shoulder. She weighed maybe a hundred pounds.

So much for my theory that Cody's wife was the large, lumpy scarf stalker, Josie thought.

Unless he'd divorced her since then.

Josie skimmed two more stories. Neither had photos. A fourth article was two years old. It reprinted the same photo of Cody and Renee at the medal ceremony, plus high school yearbook pictures of two boys. Both had acne spots and goofy grins. Their pictures looked out of place under the headline, HEROES RUN IN THIS FAMILY: HERO'S SON RESCUES FRIEND FROM BURNING CAR.

The story was the kind that gave parents nightmares: Randy, a high school sophomore, had been driving around with his friend Tyler Dylan Wayne. Randy lost control of the car. It hit a curb and collided with a parked car. Both cars caught on fire.

Tyler suffered second-degree burns while pulling his friend from the wreckage, Josie read. Randy died in the emergency room without regaining consciousness. Tyler was in a coma, but expected to recover.

A timer dinged and Donna came back to wash out the hair solution. "What are you doing with a picture of Tyler Wayne?" she asked.

"You know him?" Josie asked.

"I know *of* him. Tyler lives in our neighborhood. Paul looks up to him, especially after that story. Paul knew the dead boy, Randy, too. I was glad Paul was too young to hang around with those boys. The newspaper said Tyler was a hero like his dad. Believe me, that kid was no hero unless you counted his heroic drinking. I wasn't surprised that Tyler's best friend was killed driving around with him."

"Why didn't someone tell the newspaper Tyler wasn't a hero?" Josie asked.

"How?" Donna said. "The dead kid's photo was all over the papers and television. The parents were weeping on TV. Do you think I'd call the *City Gazette* and say, 'Ms. Reporter, you know that kid you praised as a hero? He's a teenage drunk and so is his friend. Yeah, I know he's dead, but the truth is the truth. The public has a right to know.'"

"Oh," Josie said.

"I couldn't do that," Donna said. "No one with half a heart could. So Randy was buried as the poor boy who died in a fiery car crash, and Tyler left the hospital a hero who'd burned his hands while trying to save his friend. And nobody said a word to the press.

"But if I catch my son even talking to that 'hero,'" Donna said, "Paul is grounded for life."

# Chapter 31

"Josie!" Alyce met her friend with a big smile. Little Justin clung to her jeans leg, and Bruiser the Chihuahua stood behind the toddler, just out of ear-grabbing range.

"Hi!" shrieked Justin.

"Hi, back," Josie said, hugging the boy. His hair stuck out in duck-down fluffs. He had inherited his mother's milk white skin and floaty blond hair. "You're such a big boy."

"Big!" caroled Justin. "I big. Big. Big." He repeated the word as if tasting it.

"Yes, you are," Alyce said. "Also, noisy. Sit down and play while Mommy fixes lunch. You can pat Bruiser, but nicely."

Justin gave Bruiser's short brown fur soft strokes with a single finger.

"Good boy," Alyce said. "Look at him wag his tail. He likes that. Keep doing it."

Alyce turned to her friend. "It's so good to speak to an adult. I sound like I'm talking to my dog when I talk to my son, and vice versa. The nanny will be downstairs shortly and take him to a playdate. Is that a new hairstyle? I like it. You look like that actress, the *Catwoman* star. I can't think of her name."

"Halle Berry," Josie said. "All we have in common is a hairstyle."

"Hey, it's closer than I get to her," Alyce said. "I'm marooned in suburbia."

"On a very comfy island," Josie said.

Alyce's huge oak-paneled kitchen was her creative haven. She enjoyed cooking complicated recipes for her family and friends in a kitchen a top chef would envy. Her cabinets and drawers were stuffed with arcane kitchen gadgets.

"Pour yourself a cup of coffee and go sit in the breakfast room," Alyce said, "while I finish our brunch."

Josie sat down at a sunny table set with red-checked place mats and a bright geranium.

"Now, tell me why Dr. Ted is sleeping at your place these days," Alyce said. She held her wooden spoon like a scepter.

Josie told her the frightening story of the blood on her windshield and the footprints leading to Amelia's window.

"And the police can't do anything?" Alyce asked.

"There's no crime," Josie said. "Well, nothing big enough to concern the police. I'm praying it doesn't. Ted volunteered to stay with us until it blows over. We took Amelia to school this morning and we'll pick her up this afternoon. Tonight Amelia sleeps upstairs in Mom's guest bedroom. If anyone tries anything, she'll have to get past Ted and me both."

"This is horrible," Alyce said, and shivered. She was stirring a thick white sauce. "I don't want to add to your troubles, but the way Mrs. Mueller describes her, she sounds like the woman in the mall video. The one the police think killed Frankie."

"Exactly," Josie said. She was suddenly afraid. Reciting the facts out loud made them seem worse. She wanted desperately to change the subject. "That smells delicious."

"It's a breakfast skillet," Alyce said. "Roasted Yukon Gold potatoes with applewood-smoked bacon, spinach—"

"Spinach," Josie said. "It sounded good till you got to that."

"You'll love it. Trust me. It's fried, then topped with Gouda cheese. Now I'm adding poached eggs and hollandaise sauce with a little Tabasco for zip. And don't even mention the word diet. You need comfort food. You can't worry on an empty stomach."

"You're a true friend to give me brunch and rationalizations."

"And you're evading the subject," Alyce said. "What are your reservations about Ted?"

"I'm grateful for his help, but I'm worried our romance is heating up too fast."

"At the risk of sounding like my mother, love doesn't happen on schedule," Alyce said.

"And it's hard to find a good available man," Josie recited in a singsong voice. "And I'm thirty-one years old. With a daughter. And he has a good job. And he's kind to animals. And my mother and daughter adore him. And . . ."

"And what?" Alyce said. "I still haven't heard anything bad about the man." She carried two small skillets into the breakfast room.

"Comfort food" was the right term for this dish. Josie reveled in the mix of poached eggs, smoked bacon, and roasted potatoes, with the sophisticated twist of hollandaise and a hint of Tabasco. She didn't notice the spinach.

"You didn't answer my question," Alyce said. "What's wrong with Ted?"

"I was savoring your food," Josie said. "It's not Ted. It's the other men I've dated before him. I've made some bad choices."

"I agree Josh was no prize," Alyce said. "Once you found out about his hobby job, you never saw him again. Nate, Amelia's dad, had legal problems."

"Legal problems?" Josie said. "Nate did time in a Canadian prison for selling drugs."

"But he was pardoned," Alyce said.

"The pardon couldn't change what Nate had become. He was a drunk. He was murdered on my doorstep. I can really pick 'em."

"He developed the drinking problem in jail, Josie. Nate's father has been the ideal grandfather for Amelia. You had nothing to do with Nate's murder. Besides, how old were you when you met Nate?"

"Twenty," Josie said.

"We all make dumb decisions at that age," Alyce said.

"I was a grown woman when I started dating Mike the plumber," Josie said. "In fact, I met him right here in your kitchen. He put in that pot filler over your stove." She nodded at the tap over the burners.

"That saved me from lugging huge pots of water across the floor," Alyce said. "Mike is a good plumber, a hard worker, and a good man. He wasn't a bad choice."

"I couldn't tie myself to a man with a psycho daughter," Josie said.

"So you didn't," Alyce said.

"It took me a while to figure out that Mike and I couldn't marry," Josie said. "Amelia would have had the worst stepsister this side of Cinderella. It hurt terribly when I said good-bye to Mike."

"But now you have Ted," Alyce said.

"Ted seems like a good choice," Josie said. "Too good to be true. But I don't know enough about him. I've never met his mother or his father. I don't know if he has brothers or sisters. I don't know if he has a temper."

"You and Ted have been together under trying circumstances. If he hasn't erupted in anger yet, Ted is even-tempered."

"I've been on my own all my life," Josie said. "Maybe I'm not marriage material."

"You don't look like someone who's given up on men," Alyce said. "And they definitely haven't given up on you. If you don't feel comfortable with Ted at your house, you and Amelia can stay here. We have two guest rooms. There's a guard at the subdivision gate. Jake, Bruiser, and I will watch you."

"You also have a little boy," Josie said. "It's too risky. We're better off in our home, with Ted watching us and Amelia sleeping with Mom upstairs. I hate to sound like a cliché when I talk about Ted, but I need some space."

"It used to be only men said that," Alyce said. "Now I hear it from women."

"I like my life," Josie began.

"And you don't need a man," Alyce finished.

"I may need this one," Josie said. "But I need time to find out. Maybe Ted staying at my house is a good test. I'm not ready to make him a permanent resident—yet."

"Let's call and invite him to join us for brunch," Alyce said. "You can tell a lot about a man by the way he behaves with your friends."

Josie dialed Ted's cell phone. It rang four times before Ted answered.

"Josie," he said. "What's wrong?" He sounded harried. Josie could hear barks and whimpers in the background.

"I'm fine," Josie said. "Do you want to join me at Alyce's for brunch?"

"Sorry, I can't. My partner is doing spays and neuters all morning. Chris called me into the clinic to perform emergency surgery on a beagle hit by a delivery truck."

"Is that him whimpering? Will he be okay?"

"He'll make it, but Buddy will be hurting for a while."

"Sounds like you're busy," Josie said. "Alyce and I are safe here. How about if I meet you at your clinic at two thirty this afternoon? Then we can drive to school together to pick up Amelia."

"Deal," Ted said. He was interrupted by a hair-raising howl. "That's my patient. See you soon."

Josie clicked off her phone. "Let me guess," Alyce said between bites. "Not only is Ted perfect—he's giving you that so-called space this afternoon."

"He has emergency surgery," she said. "A dog got hit by a car. It was an accident—for the dog and me."

Josie sipped her coffee, took another bite from her skillet, and said, "This twenty-four-hour bodyguard duty has to end. Let's figure out how to find the woman in the black-and-white scarf. She's the killer and the car vandal. There are three main candidates."

"I think I know who they are," Alyce said. "Rosa, the Desiree Lingerie sales associate whose parents may be illegal aliens. Trish, who may have drug addiction in her past. And Dr. Tino's fiancée, Shannon."

"Shannon is definitely out," Josie said. "She has a rock-solid alibi for the murder. There's also Victoria, my shoplifting neighbor. We put a stop to her income."

"I drove you to her house," Alyce said. "We made sure she didn't see your car. She didn't follow my SUV after we left her place. I checked. How would she know where you live?"

"So she's out," Josie said. "I had to rule out Cody, too. The police and Mrs. Mueller said the scarf stalker was a woman. I had a brainstorm that she could be Cody's wife until I saw her photo in the newspaper. Renee doesn't weigh much more than a hummingbird."

"Then Rosa and Trish are our prime suspects," Alyce said. "How are you going to prove which one is Frankie's killer?"

"St. Philomena's has Narcotics Anonymous meetings every Thursday at seven o'clock in the basement," Josie said. "I called Desiree Lingerie and found out Trish gets off work on Thursday at four. I thought I'd follow her from work to the NA meeting and see where she goes."

"I don't like that idea, Josie," Alyce said. "The woman deserves her privacy. What if she spots you? Trish wants to be a police officer. If she's any good, she'll see you tailing her."

"You forgot my wig collection," Josie said. "I can look like white trash in that curly blond wig."

"Didn't you have a rhinestone-studded T-shirt to go with that one? It will be cold in January."

"I'll wear my winter coat. Nobody will see anything but that fake blond hair down to my waist. I can also wear my Fashion Victim outfit. That red Escada jacket with the gold braid is scary. I look like Michael Jackson meets Joan Rivers."

"It's hard to chase someone in stiletto heels," Alyce said.

"I have my short curly black wig, too. My own mother doesn't recognize me in that."

"Who would? You look like you have a dead poodle on your head. It's still a dumb idea. Even if you're disguised, the killer will see your car."

"That gray Honda is so anonymous, even I can't find it sometimes," Josie said. "I have disguises for it, too. I can put a tennis ball on the antenna one day, a bunch of fake flowers the next, and a magnetic bumper sticker when I wear my white trash disguise."

"What's it say?"

"'Kiss my grits,'" Josie said. "Alyce, I need your help."

"I am not going along with your harebrained scheme to tail Trish." Alyce's pale skin was flushed with anger.

"I'm not asking you," Josie said.

Alyce softened her voice. "How about if you check in with me every half hour while you tail her? You shouldn't do that alone. Calling me will provide some backup. But that doesn't mean I approve."

"That would help," Josie said. "I really need you to go with me when I see Rosa at Desiree Lingerie. She's the temporary manager now. When I called the store, Rosa said she was working ten to six o'clock every day but Monday. Will you go with me? It's the only way I can find out more about Rosa. You told me that Jake's law partner blabbed about Rosa's father being illegal. We went to lunch at her family's restaurant and got more information to support the illegal-alien theory."

"How did you do that?"

"Rosa's a talker," Josie said. "She doesn't realize how much she tells people when she's chattering. If she sees you with me, she may let down her guard and say something useful. I wondered if you'd like to go with me to Desiree Lingerie."

"Today's Tuesday," Alyce said. "I could maybe get away tomorrow."

"Then I'll tail Trish on Thursday. With any luck, we'll have Laura out of jail by the weekend."

"Unless we wind up in jail," Alyce said. "Good thing I'm married to a lawyer."

# Chapter 32

"Is that a man coming out of Mrs. Mueller's house?" Ted asked as he carefully parked his nineteen sixty-eight tangerine Mustang in front of Josie's home.

"Can't be," Josie said. "There are rumors of a Mr. Mueller in the distant past, but I've never even seen a photo of the man."

"Maybe she buried him in the basement," Amelia said from the backseat. She'd been snappish and sulky when Josie had insisted her daughter crawl in the cramped space. Amelia could barely hide her bad temper from Ted.

"My car's back bumper isn't hanging over her property line, is it?" Ted asked. "I don't want her screaming at me again."

"I'd better check," Josie said. "She'll scream at me, too. The law says we can park anywhere on this street, but Mrs. Mueller lives by her own rules."

Josie got out of the car, which made her slightly closer to the tall, lumpy figure in the long dark coat, boots, and Soviet-style hat. Now the person was stomping across Mrs. Mueller's snowy yard. Their difficult neighbor would have a fit over this trespasser.

Then Josie realized who it was. She knocked on Ted's window. He rolled it down and Josie whispered, "You're parked fine. That's Mrs. Mueller in her Russian-winter outfit."

"You're kidding," Ted said. "I could have sworn she was a man."

Josie giggled. "Sh!" she said. "If she hears you, there will be hell to pay."

Ted climbed out of the car, then helped Amelia out of the narrow backseat. "Can we have hot chocolate?" she asked.

"With little marshmallows?" Ted said.

"And some oatmeal-raisin cookies?" Amelia asked.

"Please," they chorused together, howling like hungry cats.

"Okay," Josie said, laughing. "As long as you save room for dinner. It's beef stew, courtesy of the Jane and Amelia cooking school."

"Good afternoon," Mrs. Mueller said briskly as she strode past them on the sidewalk. "Lovely winter day. Perfect afternoon for exercise. I have the constitution of a horse."

Josie thought Mrs. Mueller had other equine attributes, too. She swallowed a smart-aleck reply and said, "I'm planning a run myself."

Well, she was about to run into her house for hot chocolate and cookies.

Inside her cozy kitchen, Ted warmed the hot chocolate, slowly stirring the milk on the stove. "I'm making it the old-fashioned way," he said. "Hot chocolate is better heated slowly than nuked."

Josie put out cookies and napkins. Amelia sat at the table with a pile of computer printouts, ready to discuss her cat research paper with Ted. He poured three cups and set them on the table. Josie added the miniature marshmallows.

"Guess what kind of cat Harry is?" Amelia asked.

"Alley?" Josie said.

"He's a classic tabby," Amelia said. She couldn't keep the pride out of her voice.

"Of course he is," Josie said. "Ted's Mustang is a classic, too."

"No, it's a special type of tabby pattern." Amelia brandished a printout from Wikipedia in her mother's face. "It says here there are four patterns: mackerel, classic, spotted, and ticked. The classic tabby—that's Harry—has 'a whirled and swirled pattern with wider stripes that make a "butterfly" pattern on their shoulders and a bull's-eye on the flank.' "

Harry, exhibit A in Amelia's cat lecture, entered the kitchen, looking for food. Amelia handed her mother the printout and picked up her cat. "See, Mom, there's the butterfly mark on his shoulder." She pointed to a winged brown-and-black design.

"And here's the swirly bull's-eye on his side." She lifted Harry higher to show off that marking. Harry's brown paws kicked in the air.

"Are you sure?" Josie asked. "Harry looks like the photo of the mackerel tabby."

"No, Mom, you're not *looking*," Amelia said with passionate intensity. "That cat in the picture has an *M* on his forehead, like a McDonald's *M*, and straight stripes down his sides. He's a mackerel tabby. Harry has swirly stripes and no *M* on his forehead, just some dark lines."

"Looks about the same to me," Josie said. She handed the printout to Ted. "Doctor, may we have a second opinion?"

"Harry is definitely a classic tabby," he said.

"See, Mom, *you* weren't listening," Amelia said. "It's the little stuff that makes a big difference. You don't see the details."

Josie didn't like her daughter's tone—a sort of superior whine—but decided to write it off to the upsets in their household. She hoped it wasn't a foretaste of the teen years.

Josie's marshmallows had melted into a creamy froth. She took a sip. "This is perfect."

All three clinked hot chocolate cups and drank.

"Can't say I'm any better at details," Ted said. "I mistook Mrs. Mueller for a man."

Amelia snorted. "Anybody can make that mistake."

Harry, tired of being an exhibit, squirmed to get back to his food bowl. Amelia placed him gently on the floor. Josie heard the cat happily crunching his dry food. The three humans munched cookies and drank their hot chocolate.

Suddenly, Harry looked up, alert to a different set of sounds. Josie heard them, too: the patter of dog feet on the back stairs, followed by a slower, heavier tread. There was a knock on her back door.

"It's Grandma with Stuart Little," Amelia said, and ran to open the door. Harry left his food bowl for the safety of the couch.

Jane's eyes peered from a mound of winter wool. "Stuart and I are going for a walk before we start dinner," she said. "Who'd like to go with us?"

"I would!" Amelia said. Her grandmother had cleverly made dog walking a privilege.

"I'll go with you," Ted said. Josie was relieved he'd be their bodyguard. She didn't want her daughter walking in the gathering dark with only her sixty-eight-year-old grandmother.

"I'll go, too," Josie said. "As backup." She had the pepper spray in her purse.

Amelia already had on her coat. "Can I hold Stuart's leash while you get ready?"

Jane handed her the red leash. "Stay on the porch until we join you," she said.

The empty chocolate cups were abandoned on the table. Ted started to carry them to the sink. "Thanks, Ted, but we can clean up later," Josie said. "We'd better get going."

Harry had been sitting on the back of the couch like a mountain lion waiting on a rock. As Amelia passed him with Stuart on the leash, Harry jumped on the dog's back, riding him like a circus pony. Stuart yelped in surprise. Amelia was opening the front door when Stuart tossed Harry off his back, yanked his leash out of Amelia's hand, and dashed outside. Ears flat and short legs racing, he ran straight for Mrs. Mueller's yard.

"Stop! Stuart, don't go there!" Amelia cried.

Josie and Ted heard the yowls and barks, then the front

door slamming. "Uh-oh," Josie said. She and Ted both grabbed their coats. Jane was already out the door.

Josie heard Amelia's shrieks followed by short, sharp barks. Then a voice like thunder rolled across the lawn.

"WHAT IS THAT BEAST DOING IN MY ROSES?" Mrs. Mueller was back from her constitutional and bristling with outrage.

Frightened yips, yaps, and inarticulate phrases followed: ". . . He didn't mean it. . . . Didn't do it on purpose . . . He's just a little dog. . . . I'm sorry. He's sorry. We're sorry." Amelia sounded small and scared.

"That animal has no business doing its business in my yard!" Mrs. Mueller roared.

Amelia was frozen on the edge of Mrs. Mueller's lawn like an ice statue.

"Amelia Marcus, you are as worthless as your mother," Mrs. Mueller shouted. "No wonder you've turned out the way you did, with men running in and out of your house at all hours."

Josie ran to her daughter's side. Jane was already facing down their battle-ax neighbor. "What do you mean speaking to my granddaughter in that tone?" Jane drew herself up to her full height, which still made her six inches shorter than Mrs. Mueller.

"That thing—" Mrs. M pointed to the cowering Stuart Little. "That thing urinated on my roses."

"Of course he did," Jane said. "You scared the pee out of the poor animal. Now you listen to me. That dog didn't hurt your precious yard."

"He did, too. Look at the yellow spots on my snow!"

"Your snow?" Jane said, her voice dangerously low. "It's God's snow, and every dog in the neighborhood has been walked on this street. You can't blame my Stuart Little. Besides, it's just a small puddle. He probably improved your roses. Last year they were infested with aphids."

"They were not," Mrs. Mueller said. "My roses win prizes."

"Only because you run the garden club," Jane said.

"May I remind you, Jane Marcus, that I am the chair of three major church committees *and* the garden committee and responsible for the selection of next year's members?"

"That doesn't give you the right to criticize my daughter," Jane said. "Or my granddaughter. My girls are polite and well behaved. Certainly better behaved than that gambler daughter of yours."

"She's in treatment," Mrs. Mueller said.

"She should be, and you should be, too. The idea! Attacking my grandchild, my child, and a little dog."

Josie was lost in admiration for her small, irate mother. Jane had kowtowed to the old bat for too many years. She'd lusted for those committee positions and lived in fear of Mrs. Mueller's good opinion. Today, she was undoing years of caution.

"You know what you can do with your committees?" Jane asked. "And your criticism of my family? You can shove them right up your—"

Jane stopped.

Josie held her breath. Jane never used off-color words.

"Up your—"

Josie waited. Would her mother say "ass"?

"Your floribunda!" Jane said. "Come along, Stuart, Amelia, and Josie. Let's go somewhere civilized."

# Chapter 33

"I could just kill that woman!" Jane was sharpening a fearsome butcher knife in her kitchen.

Josie giggled. "Better take your rage out on the stew meat, Mom."

Josie, Amelia, and Ted were upstairs in Jane's flat, celebrating her encounter with Mrs. Mueller as a crushing verbal victory.

"You were awesome, Grandma," Amelia said. She fed Stuart Little scraps of leftover roast chicken and scratched his silky ears, which seemed unscathed by the fiery battle.

"The nerve of that old bat!" Jane safely stowed the knife next to the cutting board. Now she paced her kitchen in ever slower circles, like a windup toy that was running down.

Josie gave her mother another hug. "Thanks, Mom. You fought the good fight. Mrs. Mueller is one tough woman."

"She's tough? Hah! I'm tougher," Jane said.

She felt small and fragile in Josie's arms. She noticed that her mother's gray hair was thinning at the crown. Josie felt sad and hugged Jane again, inhaling the old-fashioned fragrance of her Estée Lauder.

"I don't know what I saw in that interfering old shrew," Jane said.

Josie wisely didn't respond, though those words felt like balm on a painful wound. She'd waited more than twenty years for her mother to come to her senses. Josie had been nine years old when her lawyer father abandoned Jane and his daughter to start another family. He went to Chicago. Josie and Jane moved from pricey Ladue to Maplewood, a neighborhood considered low-rent back then. Now Maplewood was fashionably funky.

Jane, friendless, penniless, and reeling from her unwanted divorce, had fallen under Mrs. Mueller's witchy spell, following her with sheeplike devotion.

Today, at long last, Jane had defended her daughter from their overbearing neighbor—loudly and publicly.

"Stuart's walk was interrupted by the fight," Josie said. "Would you like me to take him outside again?"

"He doesn't need it," Amelia said, and snickered. "He gave Mrs. Mueller's bushes a good watering."

Ted's shirt pocket started barking. "Oops. That's my phone," he said.

"Your phone barks?" Jane asked.

"My clinic partner's son programmed the ringtone." Ted looked endearingly embarrassed. He checked the display and said, "It's the clinic. I have to answer."

Ted politely took his call in Jane's living room. He seemed upset when he returned. "Buddy the beagle is having complications after his emergency surgery this morning. I need to see him. Will you be okay if I leave for a short time?"

"I can handle anyone," Jane said. "Amelia and I are making beef stew. We'll be armed with knives." She brandished the butcher knife.

"They'll have to get by me first," Josie said. "Go see your patient." She kissed Ted and pushed him toward the stairs. "I've put 911 and Officer Doris Ann Norris's number on speed dial in my cell phone. I'll call them both if there's an emergency."

"Then you'll call me," Ted said, rushing for his Mustang.

"Promise," Josie said.

"Come back for stew," Jane called after him.

"Wouldn't miss it," Ted said.

"Are you staying up here with us, Josie?" her mother asked as she closed the upstairs door. "You might learn something watching us cook. Your stew tastes like a boiled boot."

"I'm hurt you think that," Josie said, laughing. "But I'll stay." She didn't want to leave her mother and daughter alone. It was five o'clock and darkness was falling fast. Josie hoped it was too early for troublesome home invaders, but she was taking no chances.

Josie sat at the kitchen table watching her mother and daughter do an elaborate dinner dance. Both washed their hands at the kitchen sink. Then Jane set out the ingredients on the counter and Amelia got the cooking equipment. Her mother had used the same pots, knives, and measuring cups for decades. Josie enjoyed their worn, homey familiarity.

"Josie," Jane said, as she dug potatoes out of the bin, "if you let that man get away, you're making a big mistake."

"Won't be the first one," Josie said.

"I see that stubborn look on your face." Jane tossed a bag of carrots on the counter. "But Ted is a good man."

"Yeah, Mom," Amelia said. "Harry likes him. And Stuart Little. And me."

Josie felt cornered. She said nothing.

Jane, not normally sensitive to Josie's moods, seemed to know she'd pushed her daughter far enough. She switched the subject back to cooking. "This is how my mother made stew, Amelia. I'm leaving the turnips out of her recipe, knowing how you and Josie feel about vegetables."

"Ew," Amelia and Josie said together.

"In my opinion, turnips produce a richer stew, but I will honor your prejudices. The carrots and celery stay."

Jane and Amelia chopped stew meat, carrots, celery, and potatoes on adjoining wooden cutting boards. Then Amelia volunteered to chop the onion. She wanted to try Ted's "no tears" method again. Jane gave her a sugar cube to chew.

"You get one, too, Josie, though you aren't doing a thing but sitting there," Jane said.

"I'll set the table," Josie said, and reached for the dishes.

"Be careful with those soup plates," Jane said. "You're sleepwalking around this kitchen."

Her mother was right about that: Josie was in a daze.

This afternoon's events nagged at her. Something was forming in her mind, like a face through wisps of fog. She could almost see it. She had to know who killed Frankie and spattered blood on her car. The answer was at the edge of her mind. But when she reached for it, the fog rolled in and obscured everything.

Josie desperately wanted Amelia to be safe. She wanted her life back to normal, or as normal as it could ever be. She wanted Ted to return to his own home. She didn't want him to go away permanently. She wanted that voice whispering "too soon" to shut up. Most of all, she wanted Jane to quit pushing her into marriage.

Josie laid out napkins and silverware for four while she sang off-key the old Rolling Stones song about how you can't always get what you want.

"I hope that horrible yowling isn't about my dinner," Jane said, attempting to lighten Josie's mood.

"Never," Josie said. "GBH."

That was the family rule. Those letters stood for Great Big Hug. If you said "GBH," you had to hug the person, no matter how mad you were at her—or she was at you.

Josie hugged her mother, and the foggy picture she'd been trying to see vanished.

It was close to seven o'clock when Ted returned from the clinic. The vet looked pale and his shirt was rumpled. Fluffs of short brown hair decorated his jeans.

"Sit down, Ted. You look tired," Jane said. She tested the potatoes and carrots with a fork. "The vegetables are tender. All we have to do is thicken the stew. It will be ready in five minutes." Jane gave him a dazzling future-son-in-law smile, which terrified Josie.

Maybe I'm resisting Ted because Mom wants me to marry him, she thought.

Josie knew that was ridiculous. She'd be married to Mike now if Amelia and his daughter had gotten along. Jane had disapproved of Mike from the beginning.

"Good timing on my part," Ted said. "What can I do to help?"

"Relax. It's under control," Jane said. "How is your patient?"

"Buddy is young and strong. He'll be fine. The beagle's temperature spiked a bit and our new assistant vet panicked."

"Do you like your stews thick or thin?" Jane asked.

"Thin," Ted said.

"Good." Jane didn't bother hiding her approval. Josie suppressed a childish desire to say, Just because you and Ted agree about stew doesn't mean I should marry him.

"I use a tablespoon of flour for every two cups of liquid," Jane said. "Otherwise, it's too much like gravy. We'll use the jar method to thicken the stew, Amelia. That was another of your great-grandmother's tips."

"Can I watch?" Ted asked.

"Of course," Jane said. "You put a little cold water in the bottom of a glass jar." She held the jar under the tap. "Then add the flour and the liquid from the pot. I use a Mason jar and make sure it's tightly closed before I start shaking it."

Jane wore her rubber-grip kitchen mitts and gave the jar a vigorous shaking. "See? No lumps. Now keep stirring, Amelia, while I add the liquid to the pot. Then dinner is served."

The stew was meaty and fragrant. Josie barely tasted it. She kept trying to see through that fog in her mind. Mrs. Mueller was part of the picture. And Harry. And Amelia. And the woman in the black-and-white scarf. The killer.

Did Rosa or Trish murder Frankie? Did Trish kill that terrible woman to protect her future career in law enforcement? Did Rosa want Frankie dead because the nurse knew her Mexican parents were in this country illegally? What about Victoria? Why was she in that handicapped stall? Did she find Frankie? Or kill her?

"Josie?" Ted said. "Are you feeling okay? You've hardly touched your dinner."

She looked down at her plate. She'd taken two bites and then rearranged the ingredients.

"Sorry," she said. "I'm tired and preoccupied. I'd like to go to bed. Alone."

Ted looked stricken. Amelia seemed ready to burst into tears. Jane had a wounded look.

Terrific, Josie thought. Now I've hurt everyone.

"I wasn't implying," Ted began.

"Of course you weren't," Josie said. "We're all glad you're here to protect Amelia. We need you. I'm just a little tired, that's all. It's hard to eat with my foot in my mouth."

She fixed on a smile, then kissed her mother and her daughter. "Remember, Amelia, if you need anything tonight, just yell. Ted and I will run right upstairs. Do you have everything for school tomorrow?"

"Packed and ready to go, Mom. I've fed Harry dinner, too. Will you take care of his breakfast?"

"I promise. Ted, I'll see you downstairs." She gave him a quick, sexless, in-front-of-her-family kiss. "Sleep well. And thanks for putting up with me, all of you. I'm going to turn in."

Undressed and in bed, Josie couldn't sleep. Rosa, Trish, or Victoria? Trish, Victoria, or Rosa? The names chased one another inside her head like cartoon cats and mice. She heard Ted come down the stairs to her flat. The water came on in Amelia's bathroom while he showered. A final soft click, then Ted went into Amelia's room.

Harry padded down the hall, meowing sadly for his friend. He came in to see Josie.

"Hi, guy," she said to the cat. "You miss her, too, don't you? Tonight you'll have to settle for second-best. Let's put our heads together and find the killer."

She scratched Harry's big, warm ears until the cat fell asleep. Josie was still awake, her mind still turning over the same three names. Which was the woman in the black-and-white scarf?

Then, suddenly, the picture came together.

Josie knew who the killer was. Everything made sense. All she needed now was a motive and she knew where to get it.

She got out of bed and switched on her computer.

# Chapter 34

Josie typed "Victoria Garbull"—the name of her neighborhood shoplifter—along with the woman's street address in her computer's search bar. That produced a "0 matches" message.

Rats. Josie hadn't expected that. She was sure this information would be an easy find. Victoria told Josie and Alyce that her last name was Garbull, and her mother, Justine, was recuperating in a nursing home. Alyce had called the home on her cell phone and confirmed that Mrs. Justine Garbull was a resident there. Maybe Josie had spelled Victoria's last name wrong.

Josie couldn't risk going back to Victoria's house and checking her mailbox—or her mail. Not with chatty One Buck Chuck watching every person who went up on Victoria's porch.

A cross-directory service popped up on Josie's computer screen, offering to find Victoria's last name for a fee. Josie decided to use that option as a last resort.

Instead, she typed in "Victoria" and "Maplewood." That produced strings of news stories about women who lived in Maplewood, New Jersey, and Maplewood, Minnesota, as well as her own town of Maplewood, Missouri. Josie read sad stories about Victorias who'd died in car crashes and "after a long illness." Two were murder victims and one unfortunate woman hanged herself.

Josie knew her Victoria was definitely alive. She believed in the not-too-distant past, her Maplewood Victoria had had something life-threatening happen to her.

She refined her search terms for the third time: "Victoria," "Maplewood, Mo.," "Holy Redeemer Hospital."

There it was! The fourth news story said MAPLEWOOD WOMAN INJURED IN HIT-AND-RUN ACCIDENT. No mistaking the photo of Victoria with that eye-catching blond hair. She stared from the news story with sultry, hooded eyes. This was definitely Josie's shoplifter neighbor.

Josie felt triumphant as she read: "Victoria Eva Malliet, age twenty-six, was hit by a black SUV while crossing Manchester Road three p.m. Wednesday," the story said.

Malliet? That wasn't the name Victoria gave Josie and Alyce yesterday. She said she was Victoria Garbull. Did the newspaper get her name wrong?

Josie kept reading. "Ms. Malliet was taken by ambulance to nearby Holy Redeemer Hospital, where sources say she remains in serious condition with head injuries, a broken arm, and a dislocated shoulder."

Ouch, Josie thought.

"A witness reported that the SUV driver ran a stoplight, hit Ms. Malliet, and continued driving east on Manchester. Police found the vehicle abandoned in a no-parking zone on North Market Street near Jefferson Avenue. Both the SUV and its plates had been stolen."

A tip hotline asked for information leading to the arrest and conviction of the driver.

Josie tried a fourth search. The hit-and-run driver was never brought to justice, as best she could find. There was no correction on Victoria's last name. Further searches using Victoria's complete name and address produced no information about Victoria's shoplifting. She'd managed to stay off the police radar. So far.

Josie checked the accident date again. The story was three years old. Frankie had been working at the hospital during that time. Had she been on duty the afternoon Victoria was brought to the ER? Josie couldn't prove it. But she knew Frankie had a penchant for poking around in high-profile hospital cases, such as Cody's shooting injury.

Did Frankie know about Victoria's secret source of income? That information wouldn't stay hidden in the fishbowl world of a hospital. Victoria had been brought to the hospital seriously injured. If she'd slipped an expensive watch or bracelet into her pocket or had clothes with the tags still on them stuffed in her purse, Frankie could easily leap to the same conclusion Josie had. The nurse would let Victoria know she knew, slyly tormenting her patient during a long hospital stay.

Victoria would want to get rid of the problematic Frankie, just like she was trying to get rid of Josie. Josie knew Victoria had lied about her real name. She wasn't just a shoplifter. She was also a liar.

Victoria had succeeded in murdering her tormentor, Josie was sure. The woman wearing the black-and-white scarf in the mall video was simply an ordinary shopper who needed a restroom. Victoria, pretending to be disabled, had rolled into the bathroom in her wheelchair and waited until the scarf woman left. Then she'd strangled Frankie, robbed her dead body, and disappeared with Alyce and Josie's help. The police still hadn't found her.

But Josie had. She shivered. She heard a noise. A soft rhythmic sound. Was someone scratching at Amelia's window?

She rushed to Amelia's room. Ted was lying in her daughter's bed, but he wasn't asleep. He sat up as soon as he saw her figure in the doorway. "Josie, what's wrong?"

"I heard a noise. A soft, steady noise like scratching or something."

Josie and Ted ran to Amelia's window and looked out. A cold moon revealed the snowy lawn with its V of footprints—V for Victoria. The footprints looked like purple pools. No lights were on in nearby houses. No cars drove down the silent street. Even Mrs. Mueller wasn't watching.

"No one there," Ted said.

Josie was suddenly aware that he was wearing only a white T-shirt and blue boxers. His hair was adorably tousled. She had on only a nightgown and a robe.

This is no time to be distracted, Josie told herself. "I still hear the sound. Listen!"

They both listened. Under the furnace clanks and house creaks was a softer *shush*ing sound with a slight wheeze. The thing was alive.

"It's coming from your room," Ted whispered. "I think I know what it is. Keep quiet."

Softly, swiftly, they crept back to Josie's bedroom. Harry was sprawled on his back in her bed, paws out, snoring.

"I didn't realize the cat snored," she said. "He usually sleeps with Amelia."

Harry jumped up, staring at them with big, round eyes.

"It's okay, old man, go back to sleep," Ted said. He scratched the cat's back until Harry put his head down and closed his eyes.

Then Ted put his arms around Josie, who realized just how thin her nightclothes were. Ted felt good. Too good. And hard. Reluctantly, she slid away from him.

"I can't, Ted. Not here. Not tonight. My mother and daughter are right upstairs and sound travels in this house."

"I'm sorry, Josie," he said. "You're just so beautiful. Did I say how much I like your new haircut? You feel so soft and smell so nice."

"You do, too," Josie said. "I mean, you smell nice. You don't feel soft. You feel—" She stopped and felt a fiery blush race from her neck to her face. "We can't be distracted. We have to protect Amelia."

"I woke up as soon as you walked into the room," Ted said. "You've been working."

The pile of printouts sat next to her computer like an accusation.

"I couldn't sleep," Josie said. "I know who made those footprints on my lawn. She killed Frankie, too."

"Let me put on a robe, and we'll talk about this," he said. He checked her bedside alarm. "It's only four in the morning. I'm wide-awake and hungry."

"Maybe an early breakfast will help us catch a couple more hours of sleep," Josie said.

She brewed coffee and made toast. Ted scrambled eggs. She liked sharing these familiar domestic tasks with a man. Her doubts about her relationship with Ted were lifting. He was easy to be with. She remembered reading somewhere that men reached their peak at age thirty-five. Ted certainly had.

Your daughter is your first priority, she told herself, and dragged her thoughts away from a connubial future. Over coffee, eggs, and toast, Josie told Ted about the lying Victoria Garbull (or Malliet—or whatever her name was), her parties selling shoplifted clothes, and Josie and Alyce's surprise visit to her home.

"Basically, we busted her and put her out of business," Josie said. "We promised not to tell the police."

"Think she believes you will keep your promise?" Ted asked.

"Not if Frankie found out how Victoria really makes her living. I think she killed the blackmailing nurse."

"How did Frankie know Victoria was shoplifting?" Ted asked.

"Three years ago, Victoria was badly hurt in a hit-and-run accident. She was taken to Holy Redeemer Hospital. Frankie was a nurse there at that time, and she had a talent for ferreting out people's secrets. I believe she found out Victoria was light-fingered. Frankie didn't need any special detecting skills. I figured it out, too."

"You discount how smart you are," Ted said. He stacked their empty plates and loaded them in the dishwasher.

Amazing, Josie thought. A man who doesn't expect to be waited on. "Victoria lied about her last name to me—twice," she said. "She killed Frankie. I don't have much sympathy for my late classmate. Frankie brought on her own death. That woman liked to torment people once she learned their secrets."

"It's time to blame Victoria," Ted said. "We should tell Officer Doris Ann Norris what you found."

"Then what? It's no crime to lie about her name to me. We have no proof that Victoria killed Frankie. I doubt if Officer Norris could get a search warrant just because I saw Victoria's shoplifted clothes. Even if she did, Victoria has had time to get rid of the stolen goods."

"I'll go see Victoria," Ted said. "She has this household on edge."

"And tell her what? That your girlfriend thinks she's a killer? It won't work. Victoria has enough nerve for two crooks. It's been honed by her shoplifting."

They'd cleaned the kitchen. Josie poured them more coffee while Ted folded his bedding and piled it in the armchair. She sat down next to him on the couch and rested her feet on the coffee table.

"Let's go to the police," Ted said.

"No. The police were sure the killer was Laura Ferguson. They looked at the video, saw Laura had the same scarf, and thought she had a motive to murder Frankie."

"Josie, I'm not saying the Venetia Park police are right, but you can't fault them on that. Laura had a very good reason to kill Frankie."

"No, she didn't. Her daughter is pregnant and sick," Josie said. "Laura wants to be with Kate. She wouldn't let anything jeopardize that. Victoria has no children, no husband, and she could lose everything if she's caught shoplifting. The Venetia Park police still haven't found Victoria. They didn't suspect her. They've already arrested Laura and she's going on trial. Do you think they'll risk their case when this quick arrest makes them look good?"

"How good will they look when Laura goes free?" Ted asked.

"Even Renzo, Laura's own lawyer, is giving her the 'juries are unpredictable' speech. Laura thinks he's not sure, either." Josie leaned her head on Ted's shoulder. It felt good. She enjoyed talking with Ted. He was so reasonable, so concerned. He didn't try to bully her.

"Suppose you're right, Josie, and Victoria's the killer," Ted said. "If she murdered Frankie, she can kill you, too."

"She surprised Frankie. I'll be on guard. Victoria won't hurt me, not with her nosy neighbor Chuck looking in the windows. She's not stupid. I'll get the information I need, run out of her house, and call the cops. Then the police will set an innocent Laura free. And she can be with her pregnant daughter, who needs her."

Josie smiled, her happy ending neatly tied with pink ribbons.

# Chapter 35

"Wake up, Ted. We're late," Josie said. "We have to take Amelia to school."

"Huh?" Ted, bleary-eyed and bristly-bearded, sat up on the couch and nearly knocked over his coffee cup. "What time is it?"

"Time to leave. Past time. We should have left five minutes ago. I'll call Mom and see if Amelia's ready."

Ted sprinted for Amelia's bathroom while Josie called her mother. Jane answered the phone. "Amelia's finishing her toast. We'd still be asleep if Stuart Little hadn't awakened me demanding breakfast."

"We overslept, too," Josie said. "The house must be under a spell. Send Amelia straight to Ted's car. We'll be right out." She ran to her bedroom and threw on her clothes.

"I'm almost ready," Ted called from the bathroom.

"I'm putting on my coat," Josie called back.

She heard Amelia's feet pounding down the stairs, then her footsteps crunching across the snow. There was silence. Then Amelia galloped back up the front porch and slammed through the front door.

"Mom!" Josie heard her daughter's distress. "Something's wrong with your car. The locks are frozen. Somebody turned your car into a snow cone."

"A what?" Josie fell over her purse on the living room floor.

"Come see." Amelia tugged on her mother's hand.

"Let me get my hat," Josie said. "Where is it?"

"Your hat's on a kitchen chair. Harry's sleeping on it."

"Perfect," Josie said. The cat had made himself a warm nest in her knit hat. He grumbled when she moved him to the floor. Josie's hat bristled with Harry's wiry hairs. She didn't have time to pick them off. She slapped the hat on her new, chic hair and ran outside.

A cold, bright sun shone down on Josie's car. The battered vehicle glittered, locked inside at least two inches of ice.

Icicles dripped from the bumpers. The doors were frozen shut. Even if she could break the ice on them, the locks were frozen. The windshield wipers would have to be chipped out of their ice prison. The tires were frozen to the street.

"That rotten old woman," Josie whispered.

"Who?" Amelia said.

"Mrs. Mueller. She did this to get even with me."

"Hate to say this, but I don't think so," Amelia said. "Follow the shoe prints." She pointed to their snowy lawn. A second V overlaid the first one from yesterday. This time, the prints didn't stop at the pile of snow that had fallen off the roof. They continued over the fallen snow heap to the edge of the house.

Josie walked alongside the footprints. Someone had walked—no, tiptoed, from the shape of the prints—up to Amelia's window. The trespasser hadn't been after Amelia, but the hose and water tap beneath her window. Josie saw a full set of shoe prints by the tap.

"Looks like the person turned on the hose and sprayed the car," Amelia said. "You can see the squiggly hose marks on the lawn, like a long, skinny snake. Look at the tracks on the other side of the V. Those prints don't go near Mrs. Mueller's house. They run off in the other direction. Mrs. Mueller's prints are at the edge of the yard, where she yelled at us. They're bigger than these and her boot sole is different. Go look."

Josie did. Amelia was right. Mrs. Mueller's boot print was at least a size larger and her boot sole had a waffle pattern. Josie couldn't blame the vandalism on Mrs. Mueller, no matter how much she disliked the woman.

"Mom, we're late," Amelia said. "It's cold. We can't wait for your car to melt. Ted can drive me. His car didn't get iced. He's parked around the corner."

Josie could see the Mustang's tangerine tail. "You wait by his car," Josie said. "I'll go get Ted's keys and warm up the car. Don't mention my car, or you'll be even later for school."

"But, Mom," Amelia said.

"I'll tell Ted about it later," Josie said. "We have to get you to school right now. If you're late, you'll have to deal with Mrs. Apple by yourself. Do you want that?"

"No," Amelia said.

Josie guessed that her daughter would rather avoid the formidable Barrington School principal. Josie suspected Ted would insist on going to Victoria's house for a direct confrontation. She would learn more if she saw Victoria by herself—with Chuck hovering in the background as the unknowing chaperone.

Josie's front door slammed shut. Ted ran toward them, keys in hand. Josie gave her daughter a last warning. "Remember, Amelia. My car is my business. Not a word to Ted about what you saw on the way to school."

Ted swiftly navigated the back roads to Barrington, avoiding the major traffic jams, and pulled into the school's circular drive as the bell rang. Amelia jumped out and waved good-bye.

The return trip to Josie's house was equally fast, but not as frantic. They had pulled in front of the house when Ted's cell phone barked. He parked, listened, then said, "I'll be right there. Think he'll make it?"

"What's wrong?" Josie asked.

"A pug named Max tried to catch a UPS truck. The truck ran over the little guy. I have to help Chris with the surgery on his hip. Do you want to come with me to the clinic? You'll be home alone."

"I'll be fine," Josie said. "You've made sure Amelia is safe at school and that's my big worry. Go save Max."

Ted kissed her absently and drove off. He was too pre-occupied to notice Josie's car sparkling at the curb like a four-wheeled zircon. Josie saw a single blind slat lift at Mrs. Mueller's, then drop quickly. The old woman must be dying of curiosity about Josie's carsicle.

Josie examined her car closely, looking for a crack in the ice. She took off her glove and tried to pry a frozen chunk off the door handle. She broke a nail.

She was stuck, just like her ride. Her car wasn't moving until the next thaw. In St. Louis's capricious weather, that could be tomorrow or two months. Either way, Josie was without a ride.

This day just gets better, Josie thought, shivering beside her ice-encrusted car. Her mother's door opened and Jane marched down the sidewalk in short, angry strides. Her outfit would have scandalized Mrs. Mueller, if the two women had been on speaking terms. Josie bit her lip to keep from laughing at the spectacle of her mother in an old red winter coat, a pink-flowered flannel gown with a ruffle on the hem, and brown fleece-lined boots.

"Not sure the boots go with the gown," Josie said. As soon as the words slipped out, she regretted them.

Jane was in no mood for jokes. "Josie Marcus, how many times have I told you to put that hose away in the garage?"

"Mom, I'm sorry. This is my fault. You're right."

Jane seemed somewhat soothed by Josie's admission of guilt. "Is your car damaged?"

"Not that I can see. But unless there's a sudden warming trend, I can't drive it."

"Then call that police officer, Doris What's-Her-Name. I fell back asleep after Amelia ran downstairs."

"Good. You need your sleep," Josie said. "There's too much going on. You tire easily."

"No I don't," Jane said. "I'm fine, thank you. Are you

sure You Know Who didn't do this?" Jane wouldn't even say Mrs. Mueller's name.

"No," Josie said. "The culprit has smaller feet."

"Figures," Jane said, and snorted. "I'd better get dressed."

Josie trudged inside and made herself a cup of coffee, then called Officer Doris Ann Norris's cell.

"My car's been vandalized," Josie told her. "Someone froze it."

"That's a new one. I'll be right there."

In the time it took Officer Norris to arrive, Josie wondered who'd turned her car into a block of ice. Was it Rosa or Trish from the lingerie store? Did they even know where she lived? Josie didn't think so. Mrs. Mueller literally hadn't set foot on their lawn.

That left—ah! The double liar who lived in the house with purple shutters. When Victoria wasn't icing her enemies, she iced Josie's car.

Officer Doris Ann Norris didn't bother to hide her smirk when she examined Josie's car. "I can charge whoever did this with vandalism, if we can ever catch them," she said. "But I don't think we will. Looks like a kids' prank to me."

"Why don't kids put burning bags of dog doo on porches, like they used to?" Josie asked.

"Is that what started the trouble with your next-door neighbor?" Officer Norris eyed Josie shrewdly.

Josie blushed. "Well, it didn't help," she said. "But she snitched on me first. She told Mom that I—" She stopped. She was a grown woman with a child, seething over an ancient grudge with a silly woman.

"I sound ten years old, don't I?" Josie asked, and managed a grin.

"Maybe a mature nine," Officer Norris said. "If you locate the vandal and you have proof that person iced your car, call me."

Josie left her frozen car to check the snow tracks on her lawn. She studied the double V of shoe prints. They were smaller than Mrs. Mueller's. And they had a pattern of intersecting curves. Victoria could have made those last night. If so, she'd leave boot prints on her own lawn. Josie could go over there now and check. Then she'd have her.

Revenge was a dish that tasted best cold.

Victoria would feel like she was buried under ice when Josie finished with her.

# Chapter 36

Josie's breath came out in steam puffs as she powered along the shoveled sidewalk. For all she knew, steam was coming out of her head—or even flames. Never mind that the temperature was five degrees. Josie didn't feel the cold. She was hot with rage.

Officer Doris Ann Norris had finally left, still smirking over Josie's frozen car.

It was 10:20 in the morning and Josie was ready for the first phase of her attack. She was certain Victoria had killed Frankie. Then, when Josie got close, she'd thrown blood on her car and iced it. Her vicious murder had put an innocent woman in jail. Her petty acts of revenge had uprooted Josie's peaceful life. Ted had to sleep on her couch as a bodyguard. Amelia was banished upstairs to her grandmother's home for her safety.

Josie felt like a fool. She'd believed Victoria. She really thought the woman had a sick mother and tried to help. She'd been conned. Josie wouldn't fall for another of Victoria's sob stories.

She prayed her quarry had left home already—for Victoria's own safety. If she got her hands on that woman, Josie would beat her the same color as those stupid purple shutters. She wasn't afraid of her, either. Josie was armed with pepper spray. She'd take her down like the lying dog she was.

Josie walked to the skinny house faster than she'd expected. She slowed as she turned the corner and took time to scout Palmer Avenue. Victoria's yellow Miata was not parked in front of the house with the purple shutters. The driveway was empty. Good. She was gone.

She stomped up the front steps, hoping One Buck Chuck, the chatty neighbor in the charcoal house, would come out for a talk. His red front door opened seconds after Josie rang Victoria's doorbell.

Josie breathed a sigh of relief as Chuck popped out. Bright-eyed and bald, he looked like a chipmunk in a barn jacket. Today, he wore boots instead of house slippers, so Chuck must have been planning to go outside. His lips were flapping before he got to Victoria's house.

"You just caught me on my way to the supermarket," he said.

Josie hadn't caught him at all. Chuck had detoured for a talk on the way to his car. She gave him an encouraging smile. "Hi, Chuck. Is Victoria home?"

"Your friend?" Chuck said. Was he fishing for how well Josie knew Victoria?

"That's the one," Josie said. Your neighbor, she thought. The one the police wanted but couldn't find. The shoplifter who posed as a disabled woman in a wheelchair. The misbegotten liar who threatened my home. You can't see past that pretty exterior, can you, Chuck? Victoria's hidden her true self behind a curtain of silky white-blond hair.

"She's gone to work," Chuck said. His face was innocent of suspicion. He was eager to give Josie the news. "Second time she left today. Victoria was up in the middle of the night. Woke me about three. Not on purpose, mind you. She's a considerate neighbor. But it gets so quiet on this street at night. I heard her shut the front door."

"Slammed it, huh?" Josie said.

"No, she closed it quietly. I only heard Victoria because my ears are sharp. Teeth, not so good. But I'm not going deaf like a lot of men my age." Chuck puffed out his chest, proud of his auditory powers.

Josie didn't want to discuss Chuck's hearing. She steered

him back to Victoria. "Wow, that's impressive if you could hear her door shut when you were upstairs in your bedroom," she said. "You must have ears like a cat's."

"Well, to be honest, I wasn't in my bedroom. My prostate has me up and down all night," Chuck said. "But you don't want to hear about that."

Definitely not, Josie thought. She kept smiling and hoped Chuck would keep talking.

"I was going down the hall on one of my nightly commutes to the commode," he said, "when I heard Victoria close her front door. I looked out the hall window and saw her running across her lawn. She didn't take time to walk down the front steps. Victoria took a shortcut across the snow-covered grass. That's dangerous, you know. That snow gets slippery when it melts during the day and then refreezes at night. Guess she's younger and more surefooted than I am. She doesn't have to worry about breaking a hip at her age. But she will."

Chuck paused to savor Victoria's future downfall.

"So you saw her cross the lawn," Josie prompted.

"Right," Chuck said. "Then Victoria hurried down the street. I leaned over to see which direction she was going. I wasn't being nosy. I was being careful. Maybe someone was threatening her and that's why she was moving so fast. Neighborhoods have to be alert to stop thieves and rapists."

"The police say Neighborhood Watch programs are important for crime prevention," Josie said.

"Exactly," Chuck said. "I was worried she might get mugged or attacked or something. She's an attractive young woman to be walking alone late at night. I was relieved when she turned east."

He pointed toward Josie's street.

"Those are quiet, residential streets that way. If Victoria had been heading toward Manchester Road, I would have been more worried. Lots of traffic on that street and"—he lowered his voice—"some of those cars are from the *city*."

Like many locals who didn't live in St. Louis, Chuck believed the city was a criminal haven.

"Can't imagine what she was doing taking a walk at that hour of the night," Chuck said, "but it's not my place to ask. Still, I felt uneasy. I waited up for her like a worried mother, pacing the hall and checking the window. I didn't fall asleep until I saw her come back. She was gone nearly an hour. 'Course I didn't say anything to Victoria about watching out for her, and I hope you won't, either. Young women today have an independent streak. She'd think I was interfering."

Good old Chuck, Josie thought. He was a better observer than a video camera.

"You're right about her being independent," Josie said. "I have an idea where Victoria was going at that time of night."

That last sentence was the only honest one she'd said to Chuck. She felt mildly ashamed, but not enough to stop using him. Not until she had all the information she needed. Josie had a daughter to protect. "Was Victoria wearing my favorite scarf? The black-and-white one?"

"Sure was," Chuck said. "Has those flowers on it. Looks pretty with her long, pale hair. For some reason, she only wears that scarf when she goes out at night."

"That's why she bought it," Josie said. "I bet she was wearing her dark coat, wasn't she?"

"How'd you guess?" Chuck said.

Victoria was dressed exactly like the woman Mrs. Mueller saw smearing Josie's car with bird blood—and like Frankie's killer.

"Well, thanks, Chuck. I'll catch up with Victoria when she comes back. You expect her home about two o'clock?"

"You can set your watch by that young lady," Chuck said. "Leaves home at nine thirty sharp. Comes back at two o'clock. Modeling must be a job with bankers' hours. Pays well, too. She brings home lots of bags from fancy shops. Well, she's got the figure to wear pretty clothes. Might as well have fun while she's young. Parties, shopping, things like that.

"Speaking of shopping, I'd better head for the grocery store. I'm out of coffee and peanut butter and Wesson Oil is on sale two for one." He held up a fistful of coupons. "Nice talking to you."

Josie waited until Chuck drove away. Then she crunched down Victoria's shoveled and salted porch steps and found the boot prints that he'd said Victoria had made on the lawn last night. Josie thought the prints seemed smaller than the trail left by Mrs. Mueller's massive Russian-winter boots at the edge of her lawn.

These soles had a pattern of intersecting curves instead of Mrs. M's waffle-pattern boots. Josie wondered if the boot prints leading to Amelia's window had the same distinctive curves.

She was glad to hear that Victoria was still leaving home at nine thirty and returning at two o'clock loaded with shopping bags. She must have been hunting five-finger discounts—and holding shopping parties to sell her loot. Victoria had broken her promise. She hadn't stopped shoplifting. She'd double-crossed Josie and taken away her ride. Worse, Josie had stupidly given a murderer a break. Well, Victoria wouldn't get a second chance.

Josie barely noticed the cold on her walk home. Now she was warmed by red-hot thoughts of revenge. She had enough to put Victoria behind bars. All she had to do was make a phone call.

# Chapter 37

"I've found the evidence!" Josie shouted into the phone. "I found Frankie's killer. I know who vandalized my car! I can take you there. I can—"

Officer Doris Ann Norris stopped the landslide of words. "Whoa! You can tell me who you are for starters."

"Josie Marcus. You were at my house this morning. Remember, I had—"

"The cool ride," Officer Norris said.

Josie didn't say anything. She didn't think her situation was funny.

"Is that what you call a frozen silence?" Officer Norris said.

Josie didn't trust herself to answer.

"I shouldn't be making jokes when your car is out of commission," Officer Norris said.

Finally, the woman got the message. Josie hadn't had to say anything offensive, either.

"Now, take a deep breath and start talking," Officer Norris said. "Slowly. So I can understand you."

The words poured out of Josie in a second rush. "Those shoe prints in the snow in my yard. The ice on my car. The bird blood on my windshield. I know who did it. Victoria. The police looked for her, but never found her. She's a shoplifter, too. And a killer. You can arrest her after two o'clock today. You can have the credit."

"I'm still not tracking this," Officer Norris said. "Let's

try once more from the top. Tell me who this Victoria is, what she did to you, why police were looking for her, and why I should arrest her."

The third time, Josie was able to slow down and explain herself better.

"Her real name is Victoria Malliet," Josie said. "She was in the restroom at Plaza Venetia when I found Frankie Angela Martin's body in the handicapped stall. Victoria was in a wheelchair. She said her name was Kelsey, gave a false name and address, and ran away. Rolled away, actually, in the wheelchair. The police were looking for her in connection with Frankie's murder."

"Which has been solved," Officer Norris said. "The suspect is in custody and awaiting trial. So we don't really care if this woman gave you a false name."

"She gave us false names twice," Josie said. "She wanted to get away from the police and from me. She's a shoplifter. She wears a big dark coat to look fatter than she really is. She puts on two or three layers of stolen clothes and hides them under her coat. No one suspects a disabled woman."

"So she wheeled herself over to your house last night?" Officer Norris asked.

"No!" Josie said. "She's not really disabled. She used the shopping mall's wheelchair to make it look like she couldn't walk. The wheelchair was a disguise.

"I tracked down Victoria to her home. She lives in the house with the purple shutters on Palmer Avenue. I talked my way into her home. She has a living room full of stolen clothes. She sells them at parties at her house. Victoria is the vandal who damaged my car by hosing it down so it was covered in ice. I have her boot prints for proof."

"Proof of what?" Officer Norris asked.

"Proof she was at my house, using my garden hose to turn my car into an icicle," Josie said. "The boot prints on my lawn match the boot prints in the snow on her yard. We could arrest her for vandalism."

"We? Since when did you get a badge?" Officer Norris sounded annoyed with Josie's presumption. "Why would a woman in your neighborhood walk over and vandalize your car?"

"Because she's a murderer. She killed Frankie Angel."

"Did you see her do that?"

"No, but she was in the handicapped stall at the time it happened."

"You think," Officer Norris said.

"I know she's a shoplifter. She'll be home at two o'clock and you can arrest her then."

"Did you see her shoplifting any of those items at the stores?" Officer Norris asked.

"No, but—"

"Then how do you know she wasn't cleaning out her closet and piling the clothes in her living room?"

"Because the clothes still have the tags on them," Josie said.

"And you've never had an item in your closet with the tag on it?"

"One," Josie said. "Maybe two. But we're talking mountains of sweaters, skirts, and dresses."

"So what if she leaves the tags on?" Officer Norris said. "You've made a good guess. But that's not proof of shoplifting. Lots of people buy stuff, leave the tags on, and pile them high in closets and on furniture. Isn't there a hoarder TV program that shows houses with stacks of expensive items people bought and never used?"

"Victoria doesn't have receipts for those clothes!" Josie said.

"If I walked into your house now, could you produce receipts for everything?"

"No," Josie said.

"I can check her name," Officer Norris said. "I can see if this Victoria Malliet has any priors, wants, or warrants. But if we don't have any arrest warrants on this woman, I can't bust in and haul her off to jail. No judge will give me a search warrant on your information."

"Isn't there any way around this?" Josie asked.

"Maybe if I had permission to enter her house, I could

make notes on what I saw," Officer Norris said. "Then I could tell the property-crimes detectives about her. Maybe she'll confess."

Not likely. Josie knew that. Shoplifters like Victoria were cool customers—or in her case an icy one.

Josie made one last try. "Victoria stole Frankie's red dress and the tennis bracelet off her arm after she was murdered. Victoria sold them both."

"What dress and bracelet?" Officer Norris asked.

"Frankie carried a red dress with her into Desiree Lingerie. That's why she was at the lingerie shop. She was looking for a special bra to wear with a dress with a low-cut back. She bought the bra, then left with her purchase and the dress.

"She took them both with her into the handicapped stall. Victoria found the body before I did, but never said anything. Instead, she stole the dress and took Frankie's diamond tennis bracelet. Victoria sold the dress at her house party and the tennis bracelet at a pawnshop."

"And you know this how?" Officer Norris asked.

"Victoria told me."

"And you didn't tell the law?"

"I made a deal with Victoria. I said I'd leave her alone if she quit shoplifting. She has a sick mother in a nursing home."

"Oh, does she? That's original."

"We called the home and checked," Josie said. "We promised not to turn her in if she quit shoplifting. She broke her end of the deal when she vandalized my car. Now I think she may be lying about her mother, too."

Officer Norris's voice was dangerously low. "I hate amateurs meddling in police business. Hate it. *You* made a deal with a shoplifter. *You* concealed evidence in a homicide. I ought to run *you* in for interfering with a homicide investigation."

"But can't you trace the tennis bracelet?" Josie asked.

"Oh, now that *you* finally decide to share the results of your so-called investigation, you want me to do your grunt work? It doesn't work that way, amateur," Officer Norris said. It was painful to be on the receiving end of her scorn. Josie was glad the angry officer wasn't there in person. Her emotions were frightening enough distanced over the phone.

"You forgot a few things when you were meddling in an investigation," Officer Norris said. "Do you know the name of the pawnshop that this Victoria used?"

"Uh," Josie stalled.

"Let me guess—no. Since we're having a guessing festival, let me guess that Victoria took the jewelry to a pawnshop that didn't ask a lot of questions. If the police show up looking for that bracelet, the shop owner will suffer amnesia—or give us a false description of the seller. I'll bet my next paycheck the victim's husband couldn't identify the tennis bracelet even if we did find it."

Josie waited for Norris to calm down, then said in a small voice, "Victoria usually comes home at two o'clock. If I get into Victoria's house and see her, could I call you? Would you at least come over and look at her living room and the boot prints on her lawn?"

"I'm only entering that house if she invites me," Officer Norris said. "And that invitation had better be engraved."

# Chapter 38

Eleven o'clock. Three hours before Josie could catch Frankie's killer. If she kept pacing her living room like this, she'd wear a hole in the rug.

She called her friend Alyce. "Officer Norris is angry at me," Josie said. "But I know Victoria iced my car and I can prove it. I talked the police officer into meeting me at Victoria's house. I'll show her the evidence and she'll arrest Victoria."

"I hope so," Alyce said. "But in the meantime, you're carless."

"That's why I called. Do you want to make a quick trip to Plaza Venetia this morning?"

"Sure, but didn't you say Victoria was the killer?"

"I still think she is, but I want to be sure. Victoria is slippery. She might talk her way out of trouble. And if I'm wrong, I can still investigate Frankie's murder while I wait to confront her after two. I want to talk to Trish and Rosa. Are you free?"

"Justin's with his nanny. I have to be home by two. I'll pick you up in twenty minutes," Alyce said.

By eleven thirty, Alyce and Josie were at Desiree Lingerie. Amelia's skull-and-roses lingerie was now on the window models. Josie wondered if Rosa had changed the display models now that she was in charge.

She could see Rosa joking with a woman so lean Josie didn't think she even needed a bra. Rosa looked up when

Alyce and Josie entered the shop, gave them friendly smiles, and said, "Trish should be back in a minute and I'll be right out as soon as I help this woman."

"Take your time," Josie said.

She wandered toward the front of the shop and saw Trish in the alcove behind the escalator. Today, the blond saleswoman's hair did not look stylishly shaved. It shot up in white-blond spikes like a strange fungus. Trish was arguing with a skeleton in tight leather pants. His pale face was a pincushion of piercings. He had a dirty glamour, like a busted rock star.

Josie could hear them easily. Trish shook the skeleton's hand off her arm and said, "I told you no, Owen. It's over."

"So you hate me." He had his hands on his hips. His words were a confrontation.

Trish backed away, her tone pleading. "I don't hate you. But I can't associate with you anymore. I need to stay away from temptation if I'm going to go straight."

"Straight where?" he said. "Straight into a boring ticky-tacky life where you'll be like everyone else?"

"I want to be like everyone," Trish said. "I don't want to go back to your world. I almost died last time. Please, Owen, if you love me, try to understand."

"I understand," Owen said. Josie flinched at his bitter voice. "At least I'm a temptation. Good-bye, Trish. I won't bother you anymore."

He stormed off. Trish buried her face in her hands and wept.

Josie stepped back from the window and pawed through a rack of bustiers to give Trish privacy. She was examining a hot pink number when Alyce said, "Wow! Are you going to get that one?"

"No, I have everything I need," Josie said. "It's time to leave."

Alyce looked puzzled. "Are you sure?"

"Positive," Josie said. "We need to go now." Trish would be coming back any moment. Josie didn't want her to know she'd overheard that argument.

"Bye, Rosa!" Josie called through the changing room door. "We have a family emergency. Back later." She dragged Alyce out the door. Trish was still weeping in the escalator alcove.

"Don't say anything until we're in the car," she said softly to Alyce.

Inside the soft leather luxury of her friend's Escalade with the heat running and the engine purring, Josie told Alyce about Trish's tearful scene. "I thought Frankie was blackmailing her. That conversation proves it."

"Why?" Alyce asked. "Trish didn't mention Frankie or drugs. She said she didn't want to see that guy again."

"He looked like a drug user," Josie said.

"Doesn't mean he is one," Alyce said. "Maybe Trish likes low-life men. It's not noon yet. Anything else you want to do?"

"Do we have time to stop by Carlson Place?" Josie asked. "I want to find out if Victoria has a mother named Justine Garbull."

The Carlson Place lobby looked like a luxury hotel with plants, paintings, and a curved reception desk. The receptionist was as polished as the desk.

"Yes, we have a Mrs. Garbull in residence," the receptionist said. "But she's not receiving guests today."

"Is her daughter, Victoria, here?" Josie asked.

"She doesn't have a daughter," the receptionist said.

"Victoria Garbull isn't her daughter?" Alyce asked.

The receptionist looked puzzled. "No."

"Maybe you know her as Victoria Malliet," Josie said.

"Victoria Malliet told you that she was Mrs. Garbull's daughter?" the receptionist asked. "Let me get Mrs. Cassidy, our director of guest services."

She showed Josie and Alyce into a small blue room. They declined offers of tea. A cool blonde glided into the room and asked delicately probing questions. After ten minutes, Mrs. Cassidy said, "Victoria Malliet is not related to Mrs. Garbull. Ms. Malliet was in our employ, but left at our request."

"She duped us into calling Carlson Place," Josie said, "and we believed Mrs. Garbull was her mother."

"I'm not surprised," Mrs. Cassidy said. "Now, if you ladies will excuse me, I must go."

Alyce drove away from Carlson Place at 1:10. "I can drop you off at Victoria's house and then I have to go home," she said. "Are you going to be okay alone?"

"I won't be alone," Josie said. "One Buck Chuck will be watching us like pay-per-view TV, and I have Officer Norris on speed dial. I can't wait till she claps the cuffs on Victoria."

Alyce stopped at the end of Palmer Avenue. Josie saw Victoria's yellow Miata parked in front of her house. One Buck Chuck popped out of his red door like a figure out of a cuckoo clock. Josie waved at him as she rang Victoria's doorbell. Chuck stayed on his porch, watching. He didn't pretend to be doing any yard chores.

Victoria opened the door. Model slender with a silken waterfall of pale hair, the killer was stunning. No wonder Chuck couldn't keep his eyes off her, day or night.

"What are you doing here?" Victoria's harsh voice didn't match her shimmering exterior.

"I want to talk to you about the ice on my car," Josie said. "You froze my car so I can't drive it."

"I put ice on your car? Mother Nature did that, honey."

"She didn't use my garden hose. And those are your boot prints in my yard."

Victoria gave a hard barroom laugh. "Get out of here, before I call the police."

Josie stayed planted on Victoria's doormat. She could see the couch piled high with sweaters, scarves, and skirts. The rack bulged with dresses.

The sight of Victoria's loot gave Josie the courage needed. "Go ahead." She waved at the charcoal house. "Hi, Chuck." Chuck waved back and started to come toward them.

"Invite me in," Josie said under her breath. "Hurry! Unless you want Chuck over here talking your ear off." She smiled and waved again at Chuck. He was hurrying toward them.

Victoria glanced over at her neighbor and opened the door. Once Josie was inside, Victoria slammed the front door. Josie speed-dialed Officer Norris and said, "I'm in," then hung up.

"A police officer is on her way," Josie said. "You can complain to her."

Victoria did not invite Josie to sit down. The living room seats were filled with clothes. The two women stood in the vast hallway. Josie ignored the woodwork and art glass windows. She saw a brown wig and a black one on foam stands on the television. Her fingers itched to pull Victoria's blond hair and see if it was real.

Josie distracted herself by counting the sweaters on the couch. She was at twenty-seven when Officer Doris Ann Norris arrived in her police car. Chuck must have been positively levitating at this exciting spectacle.

Officer Norris knocked firmly on the door. "The officer wants to talk to you," Josie said, stuck on the inside doormat like a pair of old boots.

"I'll let her in," Victoria said. A mean smile distorted her pretty face. "I have no reason to fear the police." She threw open the door. "Welcome."

"Are you inviting me in?" Officer Norris said.

"I have nothing to hide," Victoria said. "Josie seems to think I've stolen the clothes that I collected for a charity. The truth is that my friends and I donate them to an organization for poor young women who want to look professional for job interviews." She modestly aimed her eyes at the floor, refusing to take credit for her good deed.

She said "the truth is," Josie thought. Liars love those three words.

Victoria was still spinning her tale. "Thanks to our donations, women can go for job interviews in good-quality professional attire."

Josie picked up a blue sequined dress. "What profession is this one for? The oldest?"

"Any businessperson knows that parties are networking opportunities in pretty dresses," Victoria said.

Officer Norris was writing in a small notebook. "There's nothing wrong with collecting clothes for charity." she said. "It's not a police matter."

"You told me your name was Victoria Garbull and your mother was in a nursing home," Josie said. "You said you were the daughter of Mrs. Justine Garbull."

"I'm sure there's been a miscommunication," Victoria said. "I told you that I worked at a nursing home and Mrs. Garbull was like a mother to me.".

"She can tell you she's Wonder Woman if she wants," Officer Norris said. "It's not against the law."

"The shoe prints on Victoria's lawn match the prints on mine," Josie said. "They have the same intersecting curves on the soles."

"You mean these boots?" Victoria produced a pair of black boots from a rack near her front door. Josie recognized the pattern on the soles.

"It's true, Officer," Victoria said. "I wear these boots and the soles do have a distinctive design. But let me show you something. Come on. It's just a short walk." She picked a white coat off a hall tree and started across her front lawn. Josie and Officer Norris followed her.

"These are my boot prints," Victoria said. She pointed to the prints Josie had seen earlier with the intersecting curve pattern.

They continued down Palmer Avenue, walking past three turn-of-the-century homes with wide porches and stained-glass windows. At the fourth house, Victoria pointed to the shoe prints leading to a mailbox by the street. They had the same curved pattern.

"Mrs. Morgan, who lives here, has those same boots. So does my friend Taffy, who lives one street over. These aren't rare or expensive boots, Officer. They were on sale at the Designer Shoe Warehouse and we all bought them. Black boots are a winter wardrobe basic."

She smiled at Officer Norris. Josie knew she was losing. Josie tried one more time to trap the wily Victoria. "Your neighbor Chuck said you left at three o'clock in the morning."

"I did," Victoria said. "I couldn't sleep and I went for a walk. I feel so safe here. Maplewood has good police protection. I wouldn't hurt his feelings for the world. Chuck is a nice man, but a bit of a busybody. I bet he told you I went for a walk and I hold those shopping parties. He's never been to one. They're really parties for our charity. My friends bring clothes to donate. Sometimes we try them on, like little girls playing dress-up. We drink margaritas, giggle too much, and outdo each other with how many nice outfits we can give a few less fortunate women."

They were back at Victoria's home with the purple shutters. Victoria waved to Chuck and smiled sweetly as she climbed her stairs.

At the porch she said, "Officer, I don't want to take out a restraining order against Ms. Marcus. I understand she has a young daughter and she's concerned about her child's safety. But I haven't harmed her. Could you ask Ms. Marcus to please stay away from my property? Thank you."

The voice of sweet reason quietly shut her door, leaving Josie and Officer Norris together on the wide porch.

"Sorry, Josie," Officer Norris said, and shrugged. "There's nothing I can do. Stay away from this woman and her house or you'll be in real trouble. Do you want a ride to your house?"

"I'd rather walk," Josie said.

She burned with shame. On the walk home, Josie swore she would get that slippery Victoria. And she wouldn't go after her alone. She'd call in her friend Alyce.

This time, she would fight her enemy on the battlefield Josie knew best—the mall.

# Chapter 39

"How much longer should we wait?" Alyce asked. "I don't want the neighbors calling the cops because they see a suspicious car."

Josie had spent hours seething over the humiliation Victoria handed her. Then she'd called Alyce. Together, they'd plotted revenge. Alyce had promised to go to war with Josie the next morning. Now they were waiting in Alyce's Escalade at the end of Victoria's street.

"It's nine twenty-six," Josie said. "There's nothing suspicious about two housewives in a shiny Cadillac Escalade."

"You don't look like a housewife," Alyce said. "Not with your new haircut."

"Sh!" Josie said. "There she is."

A dark, blurry figure got into a bright yellow Miata. "Follow that car!" Josie cried, and they were off. Victoria drove swiftly toward the highway.

"She's taking the west ramp," Josie said.

Alyce followed the yellow car, easily keeping pace in the light traffic. The bright Miata was quick and easy to see. The Cadillac was faster and blended in better. This highway was the gateway to St. Louis's suburban wealth, and it teemed with sober luxury cars.

"She's changing her hunting ground," Alyce said. "She's shopping—"

"Shoplifting, I hope," Josie said.

"At one of the rich new malls," Alyce finished.

Victoria's yellow Miata turned off the highway and Alyce followed the car. "She's going to the new Buckingham Mall," she said.

Buckingham Mall was a sprawl of square grayish brown stores with a fantastic fake-castle entrance. Young men in red uniforms and tall black busbies like those of the British queen's guards stood at attention at the mall entrance.

The parking lot had plenty of empty places this early in the shopping day, and Victoria parked her car four spots from the mall entrance. Alyce slowed her Escalade to let a blue Mazda back out of a parking spot as Josie watched Victoria get out of her Miata. If they hadn't been following the Miata, Josie would never have guessed the woman climbing out of it was Victoria. She looked fifty pounds heavier than yesterday.

This morning, Victoria wore her long, shapeless black coat, the same one she'd had on when she was in the wheelchair. The coat nearly covered the calves of her dark boots.

"She looks like she's gained weight," Alyce said.

The woman in the Mazda was having difficulty backing out her car. She smiled apologetically at Alyce. Alyce pantomimed to the struggling Mazda driver to take her time.

"Victoria didn't get fat overnight," Josie said. "Yesterday she was tall and slender—a size eight or ten. She's bulked up under the coat with clothes. But that's all wrong."

"Why?"

"If she's shoplifting, she would put the stolen clothes on under her coat and walk out wearing them. I doubt if she could pile on an extra camisole."

"Maybe she can stuff the stolen goods into her purse," Alyce said.

"Her purse is so small. There's barely room for a wallet and keys. But the rest of her outfit is perfect for shoplifting. Her distinctive blond hair is hidden under a wide-brimmed black hat."

"How did she do that?" Alyce asked.

"My guess? She put it in a braid and pinned it around her head. She's hidden her bangs, too. And look at her eyebrows. She's darkened them so she looks like a brunette. A heavy knit scarf covers the rest of her face and neck."

"Clever," Alyce said. "A Muslim burka would show more skin."

The blue Mazda was finally free of the space. The woman gave Alyce a friendly wave and drove off.

"Victoria's boots are flat and practical," Josie said. "She can run in those, if she has to. She's definitely up to something. Let's go see what it is."

Alyce pulled smoothly into the spot the Mazda had left empty. Josie and Alyce followed Victoria into the mall. Their quarry was strolling past the stores, studying signs and sale offerings. At a sunglasses cart, she tried on several pairs.

"Watch her," Josie said. "If she slips a pair of glasses into her pocket, we'll raise a ruckus. There are security guards everywhere."

Josie and Alyce sat on the edge of a planter. Screened by peace lilies, they watched Victoria talk to the sunglasses saleswoman.

"That saleswoman is too alert for Victoria to palm anything," Josie said. "She knows her cart is at risk for shoplifter rip-offs. I hope Victoria doesn't recognize me. That scene at her home with Officer Norris was pretty intense yesterday."

"No way," Alyce said. "I can barely recognize you in your Fashion Victim disguise. You're well hidden by your blond trophy-wife wig, stiletto heels, and Escada jacket. Is that the one you bought at a West County garage sale?"

"You have a good memory," Josie said.

"That jacket is hard to forget," Alyce said.

"I know," Josie said. "It must have cost a thousand bucks new, but I never wear it unless I need a disguise. It's bright red and covered with gold braid and buttons. I look like a general in a banana republic."

"You look like a rich woman," Alyce said. "There's no way Victoria will recognize you. She sure won't remember me. I'm the anonymous suburban mom."

Josie was saved from answering when Victoria put the

last pair of sunglasses back in its place and smiled at the saleswoman.

"Subject on the move," Alyce said.

But not very fast. Victoria continued window-shopping. Ten minutes later, she stopped for a latte at a coffee cart. Josie used that as an excuse to rest her tortured toes.

"Those heels look painful," Alyce said.

"They are. If we don't catch Victoria soon, I'll be crippled," Josie said. "The pointy toes are killing my feet." She discreetly slipped off her shoes under a table and wiggled her suffering toes. She and Alyce watched while Victoria sipped her espresso. After fifteen minutes, Victoria stood up and dropped the cup in the trash.

"She's heading toward Bluestone's department store," Alyce said.

Now Victoria was moving fast, loping through the mall. Alyce and Josie had a hard time keeping up with her, especially Josie. Her heels clip-clopped like a horse's hooves. She was afraid Victoria would notice the noise.

But their target remained oblivious. At Bluestone's, Victoria stopped at a table of sale scarves.

"Watch her," Josie whispered. "Those scarves are easy to conceal."

Victoria pawed through the scarves, picked out a blue one, and took it to the counter. Josie and Alyce pretended to examine the new shoe styles across the aisle while they watched Victoria in a store mirror.

"Rats," Alyce said as Victoria paid for the scarf. "Why is she doing this?"

"Maybe she can put some stolen merchandise in her Bluestone's bag," Josie said. "She chose a counter right by that guard there, so store security can see she's Miss Trustworthy Shopper."

Victoria took the escalator upstairs to the better-dresses department.

"I hate getting on an escalator in heels," Josie said, wobbling onto the moving stairway. "But we have to follow her."

Spotlighted at the top of the stairs were three black sequined sheath dresses, displayed like fine art. "Look at those dresses," Alyce said. "A size zero, a two, and a four. Who wears them? There's not enough material to make a decent bandage."

A bored security guard, who was almost as skinny as the display rack, leaned against a nearby pillar. He was staring off into space.

"Did you see the price tags?" Josie asked. "Three thousand dollars each."

"Move quick," Alyce muttered. "Target at two o'clock."

Josie and Alyce shifted to a rack of black pencil skirts. "I'd get more use out of this skirt," Josie said, holding one up as a shield to hide herself from Victoria. "I have a lot of blouses I could wear with it."

She peered over the skirt top at Victoria, who was carrying three black dresses. She had stopped to examine the expensive sequined sheath, then moved on. When Victoria left the rack, only two dresses remained. The security guard was still lost in his own world.

Josie slipped back to count the sequined sheaths. "She took the size zero. No way she could wear that size."

"But she could sell it to her skinny friends," Alyce said.

Victoria approached a saleswoman, who was talking on her cell phone. "Can I try on these three dresses?" she asked.

The saleswoman nodded absently and pointed toward the dressing room. She didn't stop her conversation or count the dresses.

"If I was mystery-shopping this store, that saleswoman would get black marks," Josie said. "She's a shoplifter's delight. Victoria has four dresses. The saleswoman should take the dresses from the customer, count them, unlock the dressing room door, and show her inside. These dressing room doors aren't even locked."

"We'll have to try on some clothes to watch Victoria," Alyce said. She handed Josie the black skirt.

Josie waved to the saleswoman, who was still on the

phone. She held up the skirt. The saleswoman nodded at her, and Josie and Alyce went into the dressing room area and opened the beige louvered door to a double room.

Victoria was in the dressing room next door. They could see her feet under the partition.

Josie and Alyce pretended to discuss the skirt.

"I think it's a little tight at the hips," Josie said. "It's not fair. I've been dieting for weeks. Do my hips look fat?"

"Definitely not," Alyce said.

"I need a bigger size," Josie said.

Josie and Alyce continued their pretend conversation until they heard Victoria's dressing room door open. Josie opened her own door and saw Victoria slowly walk out of the dressing area. Josie nipped inside Victoria's dressing room, then reported back to Alyce. "She left three dresses hanging on the hook," she said. "The black sequined number is missing."

Alyce surveyed the department. The saleswoman was still on the phone.

"Victoria didn't buy that dress," Alyce said. "She can't be wearing it. The sequined dress is too bulky to fit inside a scarf bag. How is she stealing it?"

"I don't know, but she is," Josie said. She watched Victoria move slowly through the better-dresses department. Her long, loping gait had become an awkward lumber.

Then Josie knew where the dress was hidden. She couldn't let the store personnel—or Victoria—see her sound the alarm. She crouched under a clothes rack and screamed, "Stop! Security! Stop the woman in the black coat. The one with the hat! She has a stolen dress."

Josie stood up. The guard at the top of the escalator was now fully awake. He saw Victoria and tried to block her from getting on the escalator. Victoria was moving faster now, walking with a graceless waddle, like a heavily pregnant woman.

The skinny security guard tried to stop Victoria, but she shoved him into a frail silver-haired woman with a mass of shopping bags. Mrs. Silver fell into a rack of sheer evening blouses. The guard landed on top of her. The woman, the guard, and the clothes rack tumbled down together.

"My arm!" Mrs. Silver screamed.

The guard, tangled in a mass of chiffon and hangers, reached for his walkie-talkie. Victoria had safely made it to the escalator. She stepped carefully around two chattering shoppers, then rode serenely down the long moving stairs.

"Oh, no," Josie said. "She's not getting away this time."

She shoved past the talkative shoppers and reached for Victoria, who was nearly at the end of the escalator. Josie's high heel caught in the moving stairs and she landed on top of Victoria in a flying tackle.

Victoria fell headfirst onto the hard floor. "Oof!" she said as the breath was knocked out of her. She started to sit up. Josie walloped her with her purse and sat on top of her.

The security guard had freed himself from the rack of blouses. He radioed for help for the silver-haired shopper, then ran down the escalator.

"Ma'am, ma'am, are you okay?" he asked Josie.

"I'm fine," Josie said. "Congratulations. You've caught yourself a shoplifter."

"I don't know what you mean." The guard looked confused.

Josie sat up and pointed to the dazed Victoria, sprawled on the hard floor. Her hat had flown off and her long blond braid had uncoiled like a braided snake. Her coat had slid up. The expensive black sequined dress glittered between her legs like a demonic afterbirth.

"This woman here," Josie said. "On the floor. She was trying to walk out with a three-thousand-dollar dress between her knees. You caught her."

# Chapter 40

"You caught Victoria fair and square," Officer Doris Ann Norris said. Mrs. Mueller peered out her bedroom window at the spectacle of a police officer on Josie's doorstep again.

"I didn't catch her," Josie said. "Bluestone's security guard did. She was trying to sneak out with an expensive dress. The guard saw her acting suspiciously and called the Venetia Park police."

"Yeah, right," Officer Norris said. "While we're discussing suspicious behavior, you just happened to be shopping in the store."

"I'm a mystery shopper," Josie said.

Josie didn't feel like dancing to celebrate Victoria's dramatic capture. She was glad the shape-shifting shoplifter had been caught, but she was bruised by the fall down the escalator.

"Well, this is no mystery," Officer Norris said. "The store caught her with a dress that cost three thousand bucks. Victoria can't claim she wanted to buy it. Not when she was waddling around with it shoved between her legs. She's sure no size zero. I can't believe zero is a dress size."

"It is, if you're a Chihuahua," Josie said. "Do you want to come in for coffee? You'll freeze on the porch."

"I'll take a cup for the sake of your neighbor," Officer Norris said. "She's going to fall out of her bedroom window watching me on your porch."

"Good," Josie said.

Officer Norris followed Josie into the warm kitchen. Josie poured coffee and popped two of Amelia's cookies on a plate.

"You don't have to do that," Norris said. But she ate the cookies.

"It's a thank-you," Josie said. "You believed me when I said Victoria had stolen those clothes."

"I never said I didn't believe you," Norris said. "I said there wasn't any proof she'd been shoplifting. The prosecuting attorney couldn't make a case just because someone has a roomful of clothes with tags on them. I tried to convince her. She wouldn't go for an arrest."

"Victoria wouldn't be in jail now if you hadn't made notes on all those clothes in her living room," Josie said.

"The property-crimes detectives are adding up the loot. So far, the total is thirty-five sweaters costing up to five hundred dollars a pop, forty dresses—not one less than five hundred dollars—and assorted pricey skirts and slacks. All the clothes still had the tags on, which makes it easier for us. The stores have identified the merchandise as stolen—and they're still finding more."

Josie raised an eyebrow. "She had expensive taste."

"It's definitely going to cost her," Officer Norris said. "Looks like Victoria stole more than twenty-five thousand dollars. That makes her shoplifting sprees a Class B felony. Plus, when she got caught with that three-thousand-dollar dress at the store and tried to run, Victoria pushed a woman into a rack of clothes and broke her arm. She caused a bodily injury during the commission of a crime, and that will increase Victoria's penalties. Oh, and the bigger stores have her on video, too. Juries like videotape. She'll need a good lawyer to avoid fifteen to twenty years in jail."

Josie didn't bother hiding her satisfaction. Her car was still a frozen lump. Her knees ached from the fall. Her pride was hurt. But she'd made sure Victoria was caught and jailed, nice and legal.

"Is your car still in cold storage?" Officer Norris asked.

"Yes," Josie said. "And it will stay there. More snow is expected this weekend."

"We can charge Victoria with vandalism for the ice on your car," Officer Norris said.

"What about murder?" Josie asked.

"Sorry, homicide didn't find any connection between Victoria and the victim's death. There is no evidence. We couldn't even find that black-and-white scarf you said she had. Victoria is a shoplifter, not a killer. She'll be locked up a long time."

"Maybe my car will be thawed out by the time she's free," Josie said. "I want her charged with murder, not vandalism."

"Not gonna happen. Look, Josie, I chewed you out for meddling in a police investigation." Officer Norris gave Josie a stern stare. "You deserved it. You don't want to hear this, but your friend Laura Ferguson is flat-out guilty. She killed that woman. She's in jail and she should be. The Venetia Park detectives arrested the right person. Laura Ferguson had motive, means, and opportunity."

"But so did Victoria," Josie said.

"How do you know that?" Officer Norris gave Josie that laser stare.

"I—she—she was in the hospital when Frankie worked there. Victoria was hurt in a hit-and-run accident. It was in the paper, if you don't believe me. Frankie liked to torment people with their secrets. She could have figured out that Victoria was a shoplifter."

"Did it say that in the paper, too?" Officer Norris said.

Josie shook her head.

"I don't approve of your stupid amateur sleuthing," Officer Norris said. "If I catch you doing it again, I'll run you in. Leave the investigating to the pros. You have a daughter to worry about. Laura Ferguson is guilty. Let it go."

But Josie couldn't. She knew Laura was innocent. She knew her friend needed to be with her ailing daughter. Josie had narrowed her investigation down to the two lingerie saleswomen, Rosa and Trish. Both had had deadly reasons to hate Frankie.

Josie needed to know which woman was guilty.

She still had to talk to one more person connected to the killing—the heroic Cody John Wayne. He had been in Desiree Lingerie the day Frankie was murdered. He was the director of security at Sale Away. It was his job to notice people and their actions. Cody was a trained observer. Josie had to see Cody today. He might know something that would free Laura.

She started out the door for Sale Away and remembered her car was frozen. She couldn't drive there. She pictured the nearly deserted Sale Away parking lot, feral dogs roaming the bleak, potholed asphalt. She couldn't ask her mother to drive. It would be stupid to go alone. Ted could take her. His bodyguard duty ended with Victoria's arrest.

Josie missed him. She liked their cozy domestic mornings. Mentally congratulating herself on her wise decision, Josie called Ted's cell phone. She was relieved there were no background barks, meows, or growls.

"No patient emergencies this morning?" Josie asked him.

"I'm at home," Ted said. "Chris told me to take the day off. Are you free? Want to go somewhere fun?"

"I still don't have a car," Josie said. "I'd like to go somewhere, but a trip to Sale Away won't be fun. I don't want to walk through that parking lot alone with those dog packs. If you go with me, I'll take you to lunch afterward. My treat."

"You don't have to bribe me to be with you." Ted switched to a bad cowboy imitation: "I'll saddle up my Mustang, ma'am, and be right over."

Ted's vintage car was a cozy haven on a cold winter day. His hello kiss was equally warm. "How are you?" he asked. "How's Amelia?"

"She's back in her own bed with Harry snoring beside her. I think Mom was glad to see her go back home, too. She and Stuart Little have their set routines. They like to watch television together."

"I'm worried about you," Ted said. "You took a nasty fall yesterday."

"Just bruises," Josie said, and shrugged. "They'll heal."

"Does it bother you that the security guard got the credit for catching Victoria?" Ted asked. "You did the actual work. I saw him being interviewed on television, acting like he was a great detective."

"I'm glad," Josie said. "I can't be seen on camera. That takes the mystery out of mystery-shopping. The guard validated my story when he took credit for capturing Victoria. He was my insurance, in case Victoria escaped shoplifting charges. If store security caught her, Victoria couldn't accuse me of stalking her."

"Clever," Ted said.

"Oh, it gets better," Josie said. "Since Alyce and I had an unpleasant shopping experience at Bluestone's, the store gave us both one-hundred-dollar gift certificates plus a day of beauty at the store salon. A massage, facial, and manicure will pamper my bruises."

"You don't need a day of beauty," Ted said. "You're beautiful the way you are. The killer is still out there. Do you want a bodyguard tonight?"

Josie warmed to his words. He believed Laura was innocent, too.

"Thanks, but I've imposed on you enough."

"Josie, it wasn't an imposition," Ted said. "I like being with you and Amelia. I'll sleep on the couch tonight if you want."

"Amelia needs her routine, Ted. These last few days have been hard on all of us. Last night I fixed her favorite comfort food for dinner, macaroni and cheese. We played with the cat. We turned in early. Tonight, my big plans include doing the laundry. We need a few nights of dull, normal things so Amelia will feel safe."

"What do you need?" Ted asked, his voice husky.

Whoa, Josie thought. This is going way too fast. Time to put the brakes on.

"I need you to drop me off at the front door of Sale Away," Josie said. "I have to find out if Cody has the key that unlocks Laura's cell door."

# Chapter 41

Sale Away was an outlet store in purgatory, where shopping was a punishment. Customers grimly filled carts with items prized for low price rather than high style. Josie wondered if they had been condemned to search for bargains.

Ted drove twice around the potholed parking lot. He saw no sign of the head of Sale Away security in his golf cart, or the pack of mangy dogs.

"I'm coming inside with you," he said.

"Please, wait in the parking lot," Josie said. "Cody doesn't know you. He'll talk better to a lone woman."

"What if he attacks you?" Ted said.

"In a store with staff and customers around?"

"If you're not out in twenty minutes, I'll come looking for you."

"Thirty," Josie said.

"Twenty-five," Ted countered.

"Okay," she said. "But there's no need to worry. I'll be inside a store, protected by a hero."

Ted's face fell. "And outside, too," she added. She dashed out of the Mustang's steamy interior and ducked inside the building. A young woman with a flour-sack figure pushed by Josie and smiled. She had no front teeth.

Josie watched herself walk through the sliding doors on a closed-circuit television. The security guard at the entrance nodded at her.

"I'm looking for Cody John Wayne," she said.

"He's in his office in the back of the store," the guard said. "Straight down Aisle Eight, ma'am. Plumbing supplies."

Josie felt dwarfed by the aisle's shower stalls, their glass doors already coated with soap scum. Showerheads stuck out of wall displays like monster appendages. Josie wondered if the dusty sinks would ever come clean.

The plumbing-supplies aisle dead-ended under a sign that said RESTROOMS. Josie smiled for the first time in Sale Away.

Cody was in his office with the door open. He looked less than heroic at his desk, munching a massive bear claw. Pastry flakes decorated his chest.

"May I help you?" He brushed off his uniform shirt.

"I was at Desiree Lingerie in Plaza Venetia the day you picked up your wife's order." Josie sat down uninvited in his flimsy guest chair. Cody glared at her. Josie's smile faltered. "That was the day Frankie Angela Martin was murdered. My friend Laura Ferguson is in jail awaiting trial for killing her."

"I believe we had this conversation the other day, ma'am," Cody said. "I couldn't help you then, and I can't help you now."

"You might," Josie said. "Laura didn't kill Frankie. She has to get out of jail. Her pregnant daughter is sick and she needs her mother."

"Like I said, I'm sorry for her trouble, but I can't help."

Josie reached into her purse for the news story with Victoria's photo. "At least take a look. Have you seen this woman before? Victoria was at the mall the day Frankie was murdered. I think she is Frankie's killer."

Cody put down the pastry and studied Victoria's photo. "I can't say she's familiar. Why show me?"

"I thought you might have seen her at Plaza Venetia when you were there. She's a shoplifter. Maybe you've come across her at Sale Away. In the line of duty."

"You think someone who looks like her would shop at this store?" Cody's scorn singed Josie's eyebrows. "Did you get a look at our customers? Most live in trailer parks. Hell, half look like they live under bridges. This classy blonde wouldn't be caught dead shopping—or shoplifting—at this store. Let me tell you for the last time: I don't know anything about that lady's murder. I don't go into restroom stalls and suffocate women with plastic."

Josie froze. "How did you know she was suffocated in a restroom stall?"

"Huh?"

"I said, how did you know Frankie was suffocated in a restroom stall?"

"It was on TV," Cody said.

"You said you never watch TV news because you couldn't keep the stories straight."

"Then you must have told me," Cody said.

"No, I said Frankie was murdered at the mall. I never mentioned a restroom. You just told me how she died and where."

"My wife must have said something."

"No!" Josie said.

Cody turned angry. "Why are you bothering me, lady? The police already caught the killer. They're a hell of a lot smarter about crime than a—what are you, exactly?"

"Mystery shopper," Josie said.

"Well, you better leave that mystery to the professionals. You're slandering this Victoria, calling her a killer. What did she do to you?"

"She threatened me and my daughter."

"How? Did she call you? Send letters? Or go to *your* office?"

"She put blood on my car windshield. Then she took a hose from my yard and drenched my car. It's still covered in ice."

"I still don't see how that threatened your daughter," Cody said.

"I saw her footprints in the snow leading to my daughter's bedroom window. Victoria was trying to get my garden hose, but I didn't know that. Our house was in an uproar." Josie felt small and foolish. "You have a son. You must understand."

Cody's face turned stroke red. "What do you mean by dragging my son into this?"

He stood up. Josie realized he wasn't much taller than Laura. Or Mrs. Mueller.

Mrs. Mueller, who looked like a Russian general in her bulky winter coat.

Mrs. Mueller, whom Ted had mistaken for a man.

Mrs. Mueller, who had provoked Josie's mother into a shouting match. Jane had waved a butcher knife in her kitchen, swearing she'd kill the woman.

The Jane scene was replaced in Josie's mind by Amelia, upset that Josie couldn't see the details that made Harry a classic tabby cat. *No, Mom, you're not looking,* Amelia had insisted.

Josie saw the details now. All of them. Cody John Wayne, a man gunned down by carjackers and taken to Holy Redeemer Hospital. A hero tormented by Frankie because he wore panty hose on cold nights.

Cody, a father who loved his son, Tyler Dylan Wayne. The newspaper headline said Tyler was a hero like his father: HEROES RUN IN THIS FAMILY.

Frankie had taunted Cody about his hero son. Josie's hairstylist was sure the teenage Tyler was no hero, that he'd let his friend Randy drive drunk and crash his car. Had Frankie pushed Cody to the brink, the way Mrs. Mueller had driven Jane to make threats of murder?

"I have work to do," Cody said. His face was unreadable. "I need to make the rounds of the parking lot. Now, if you'll excuse me."

Cody reached for his outdoor gear in a precarious pile on the wall hook. The cheap hook was loaded with heavy winter wear and pulling out of the Sheetrock. Cody yanked off his fleece-lined blue uniform jacket. The hook came out of the wall in a shower of dust. A long, dark coat and a black knit muffler fell to the floor. In the pile, Josie saw a silky black-and-white scarf.

*"You don't see the details, Mom,"* Amelia had said.

Now Josie saw these details: Cody didn't look as big without his bulky uniform jacket.

Cody had worn a dark coat on the day of the murder. Like that coat on the floor. A coat that could be either a man's or a woman's in a grainy mall video. If a man in a dark coat hid his face with a head scarf, he could easily be mistaken for a woman.

Cody had killed Frankie. He had the best motive possible: She was tormenting his son.

Josie swiped the scarf off the pile on the floor. "You followed Frankie into the restroom and killed her. You wore this scarf to cover your hair. The police thought you were a woman."

"You're nuts," he said. "That scarf is a present for my wife."

"Then why didn't you give it to her?" Josie said. "Why hang it on a hook in your office?"

"Because I—" Cody reached for the nightstick on his utility belt and swung at Josie. She ducked.

"You don't want to hurt me," Josie said. "There are too many people around."

"Is that so?" Cody said. "Did you have trouble getting back here through the crowds of customers?" He swung the heavy nightstick again, catching Josie's shoulder. She screamed and held up the guest chair like a shield.

"See how many people came running when you screamed?" he said. "Nobody. We've had wild-dog attacks on the lot. That's what I'll tell the police after I find your body in the parking lot. The bite marks will cover any bruises."

He took a third swipe at Josie and hit her shoulder again. The pain made her so dizzy, she clung to her chair shield. Her thoughts were thick and slow. She knew she had to get the pepper spray out of her purse. She backed toward the office door, holding the chair in front of her with one hand while she searched in her purse for the pepper spray with the other.

Kleenex. Wallet. Keys. She threw them on the floor.

Cody's nightstick caught her upper arm again. Josie went down, still holding her purse, and hid her head under the chair seat.

Cody whacked the chair seat, splitting it in two. Josie ran out the door, jamming the broken chair in the doorway.

She dashed for the plumbing aisle, but Cody was too close. He reached for her long knit scarf. She slipped from his grasp and fled into the women's restroom, barricading herself in the handicapped stall.

"Josie!" he called. "Come out. You can't get away."

Josie slammed the lock shut. I've trapped myself in the restroom, she thought. I'm going to die like Frankie.

Cody beat on the stall door with his nightstick. Slam! Slam!

Dents appeared in the thin metal. Josie frantically searched her purse.

Pack of mints. Lipstick. Hairbrush. She threw them on the tile.

Slam! Pound! One hinge tore away from the wall.

"Cody!" Josie cried. "Stop! What if someone comes in?"

"I'm pursuing a shoplifter," Cody said.

Keep him talking, she thought while she searched her purse. Grocery list. Coupons. Compact.

"Cody, it's not your fault," Josie said. "Frankie threatened your son. Any parent would understand."

"She said my son was no hero," he said.

Slam! Cody had dropped the nightstick. Now he used the metal trash can as a battering ram.

"My boy, Tyler, came into the emergency room, drunk and out of his head with pain. I was there when he babbled about his friend Randy. I had to hold him down. 'I shouldn't have let him drive,' he kept saying. Sometimes Tyler thought he was talking to Randy. He shouted, 'No, Randy! Don't go so fast! You don't have a license. Please, say something!'

"Then my son started crying. He knew Randy was dead. Tyler had tried to save Randy from the burning car, but it was too late."

Slam! The trash can smashed the stall door again. The second hinge held. Josie put her weight against the door to brace it.

"Frankie heard him crying and screaming, the miserable bitch. My poor boy still has nightmares. He quit drinking. He was trying to get his life together again when the phone calls started. I picked up the extension and heard a woman ask Tyler, 'How are you, hero? Better? How's your friend? He'll never get better, will he?'

"I knew it was Frankie. I said I'd go to the police if she didn't stop. She laughed. I offered to sell the house and give her the money. She said, 'I'm not asking for money. Go to the police. Do you really want them to know what happened? What about your insurance company? Randy's parents will sue your socks off. Or should I say your panty hose?'"

Slam! The trash can hit the door again. Josie felt the jolt through her whole body. The hinge still held.

"She kept calling Tyler. She wouldn't stop. He was falling apart. He was drinking again. I begged her to stop and she laughed. When she made those remarks about my boy in the bra shop, I couldn't take any more. I had to save Tyler. If it meant the end of my life, so be it.

"I followed Frankie to Deep Designer Discounts. She saw me. I was afraid she'd complain to store security, so I bought that scarf for my wife. Frankie didn't notice me until she was out in the mall again. She said she'd tell the truth about my son. I said I'd kill her.

"She said, 'Try it. I'm going into the one place you can't follow me.' She flounced into the women's restroom. I put on that scarf and looked like a lumpy old lady. I followed her inside."

The silence was deafening. Josie was so caught up in Cody's story, she'd stopped searching through her purse. Now her fingers felt a plastic rectangle. Her cell phone.

Slam! Cody smashed the stall door again. The final hinge was coming loose. Josie started to speed-dial 911, then realized by the time help arrived, she'd be dead. She braced herself against the dented door and kept searching for the pepper spray.

"Frankie didn't have time to bolt the stall door. I pushed my way in and killed her."

Slam! Josie felt that one through her teeth. The last hinge popped. Josie's fingers found the pepper spray in her purse as Cody ripped away the stall door.

His hair was wild. His eyes were infinitely sad. "You understand, don't you? You'd do the same thing."

"Yes," Josie said. She sprayed him right in his eyes.

Cody howled like a wounded dog and clawed his face.

# Chapter 42

Josie was stashed in the Sale Away manager's office, wrapped in a blanket. Five hours after Cody had attacked her, she still couldn't leave the store, and neither could Ted. When the police arrived after the 911 call, they'd immediately separated Ted and Josie. She was allowed to sit in a lopsided chair in a nearby office. Ted had been banished to the stockroom.

Ted had been the real first responder. He'd waited in his car for an uneasy twenty-three minutes. Then he couldn't take it any longer. When he didn't see Josie coming out the front door, he ran into the building and questioned the entrance guard.

"You looking for the cute little lady?" the guard asked. "She went to the security office, best I know. Haven't seen her on my TV monitor here, shopping in the store."

Ted raced down the plumbing-supplies aisle and glanced in Cody's office. He saw the destruction: the hook torn out of the wall, the coats on the floor, the wrecked chair in the doorway. He didn't need to follow the trail of tossed purse contents to find Josie. He could hear screams and metallic clangs coming from the women's restroom.

Ted slammed into the restroom just as Cody ripped off the stall door and Josie sprayed her attacker in the face.

She'd speed-dialed Officer Doris Ann Norris, while Ted called 911.

When the first carload of police officers arrived at Sale

Away, the entrance guard sent them straight down the plumbing-supplies aisle. Cody was rolling around on the restroom floor, rubbing his eyes and screaming, "I'm blind! I'm blind!" The bent, battered stall door was propped against the wall. Ted was holding Josie as if he'd saved a Ming vase from tumbling off a shelf. Josie shivered and shook so badly that her teeth chattered.

That's when Officer Doris Ann Norris had arrived. Cody had recovered enough to say that Josie was a shoplifter who'd stashed "something valuable in her coat. I was trying to arrest her."

"What was she stealing?" Officer Norris asked.

"I don't know. But it was valuable."

"Where is it?"

"She hid it," Cody said. "I don't know where. I can't help find it. I can't see."

Officer Norris didn't find any shoplifted item and neither did anyone else. The guard who had been at the entrance said he never saw Josie come out of the back area. "She just went straight inside the security office," he said.

Josie wondered if his open country-boy face counted for him or against him.

Officer Norris could see one thing clearly: The destruction in Cody's office and the women's restroom far outweighed the cost of anything Josie might have stolen.

The police called the paramedics. Cody's injuries were serious and the paramedics said he'd made them worse by rubbing his eyes. They strapped his hands to the stretcher to keep him from doing more damage and rushed Cody to the emergency room at Holy Redeemer. A uniformed officer went with him.

A second ambulance arrived for Josie. A paramedic with a shaved head said her uncontrollable shaking was probably shock. He thought Josie's shoulder was bruised, not broken. He recommended that she see a doctor at the hospital.

Josie, who had bare-bones health insurance with a sickening co-pay, settled for an ice pack and a musty blanket from the Sale Away shelves. A cup of bitter sugared coffee helped control her shivering. Josie's shoulder worked well enough that she could sign the papers refusing medical attention.

She told Officer Norris a different story than Cody: She said the head of Sale Away security had attacked her when she accused him of killing Frankie Angela Martin. Josie said Cody had used a head scarf as a disguise at the mall. He was the "woman" on the grainy video who followed Frankie into the Plaza Venetia restroom. He had a good reason to kill the former nurse: Frankie Angel was tormenting his son.

After the paramedics released her, Josie was escorted into the manager's office down the hall. The manager, Mr. Higgins, had brought Josie the blanket and sugary coffee "on the house." Josie wondered how Sale Away had the nerve to charge for that brew, which tasted both burned and boiled. The coffee was so strong it nearly dissolved the foam cup.

The frightened Mr. Higgins kept wringing his hands and repeating, "I don't understand. Mr. Wayne had such good references. I checked them myself. Our store policy is not to pursue shoplifters. If they leave the building while security is in pursuit, they could get hit by a car."

Or eaten by dogs, Josie thought. The manager's monologue was getting on her nerves. "I told Cody that," Mr. Higgins said. "I told him the pursuit wasn't worth the risk of a lawsuit."

She was relieved when Officer Norris called him away. Josie listened to a flaccid string version of "(I Can't Get No) Satisfaction" and thought it was the perfect sound track for Sale Away shoppers.

Josie hoped Officer Norris believed her this time. When the two Venetia Park detectives who'd investigated Frankie's murder arrived, Josie took that as a good sign. The rumpled Detective George Waxley was doing his Columbo impersonation, pretending that he didn't have a clue. His impeccably dressed partner, Detective Michael

Yawney, didn't bother hiding his disgust with the store, its stock, and its staff. Josie wondered if the handsome Yawney would need medical attention to uncurl his lip.

Detective Yawney made Josie repeat her story until she lost track of how many times she told it. Around noon, someone brought her a limp sandwich. Josie thought it would take more than two detectives to solve the mystery of the gray meat between the stale bread slices. She ate the sandwich anyway.

Officer Norris stopped by periodically to check on Josie. At two o'clock, she gave Josie permission to call her mother. Jane would have to pick up Amelia at school. Josie's cell phone was still part of the restroom crime scene. Norris let Josie use the office phone.

Jane, after a flurry of worried questions, promised to pick up Amelia. "I'll speak to you, young woman, when you get home." Josie felt like she was bringing home a report card with a D on it.

"I won't be long, Mom," Josie said. It wasn't the first or the last untruth she told that day.

By three o'clock Josie had signed a statement for Detective Yawney. She'd recovered enough to feel restless.

Mr. Higgins was still wringing his hands. "I don't mean to be rude, miss, but my first shift has to cash out their registers. I need my office. When are you all going to leave?"

"Good question," Josie said.

When Officer Norris dashed back in, Josie asked, "May I pick up my wallet, please?"

"No, that trail you left is still being photographed by the crime-scene techs," Officer Norris said. "Including your keys and lipstick."

"If I knew my lipstick was going to be immortalized, I would have bought a better brand." Josie's giggle was too high.

Officer Norris turned eyes like flamethrowers on Josie. "Is that a joke? Because I'm not laughing. In case you've forgotten, a woman was suffocated—and that's a horrible death. Today, you accused a hero of murdering her."

"Has Cody been arrested for murder?" Josie asked.

"He's being booked for agg assault with a deadly weapon."

"But Frankie's dead," Josie said.

"The aggravated assault case is you."

"What was the deadly weapon?" Josie asked.

"The bathroom door. He hasn't been arrested for Frankie's murder. He asked for a lawyer and won't talk."

"Can I go home, please?" Josie asked.

Officer Norris left, her body bristling with annoyance. At three thirty, she returned with Josie's purse. "I think everything is in there. If I were you, I'd wash it before I used it. That bathroom floor looked disgusting. You can go now and so can your friend Ted. He's in the hall."

Ted was waiting with open arms. Josie ran straight into them. He hugged her until she said, "Ouch! My shoulder."

"You must have some nasty bruises," he said. "Let me drive you to the hospital."

"Can't afford it," Josie said.

Josie and Ted walked out of the store at 3:35, some five hours after they'd entered. "What if your shoulder is broken?" he asked.

"Then you can X-ray and set it."

"I'm an animal doctor," he said.

"Exactly. Your patients can't talk, so you have to be better than people doctors."

"My practice doesn't include people," he said. "And I'm not practicing on anyone, especially you. But I won't argue with you now." He had his arm around her—carefully. Josie enjoyed being cherished.

"Where do you want to go?" Ted asked.

"Home," Josie said. "I'm bracing myself for the lecture already."

"How mad will your mother be?" Ted asked.

"Once, when I was in first grade, I wandered away from Mom at the old Famous-Barr department store. A saleswoman found me and paged Jane. Mom collected me at the information counter. She nearly fainted with relief. When we were out of the store, she said, 'Young lady, if you ever scare me like that again, I'll kill you.' I'm expecting a similar lecture."

Out of the corner of her eye, Josie saw movement on the edge of the parking lot. Three shadowy figures loped across the lonely expanse of asphalt. The dog pack. She felt in her purse for the canister of pepper spray and realized the police had it now.

"I see them," Ted said. "I have my spray."

"Ted, I still want to thank you for your help. You've spent your day off stuck in a storeroom because of me. I'd like to take you out to dinner tomorrow night."

"I'll go to dinner with you anytime," Ted said. "But I want to take you and Amelia ice-skating at Steinberg Rink. It's a local tradition."

"I'm a terrible skater," Josie said.

"Me, too," Ted said. "I think that's also a St. Louis tradition. I may spend more time falling on the ice than skating on it. Please, Josie. Say yes."

Josie remembered when Amelia had pleaded with Josie to let her father, Nate, take her ice-skating. Josie had refused because Nate had been drinking. But Amelia could go with Ted and Josie. "We'll all go tomorrow night," she said.

"Deal," he said. They sealed it with a kiss on the bleak parking lot. The troublesome shadows at the edges disappeared.

# Chapter 43

Josie folded Amelia's cotton shirt and added it to the stack of clean laundry on top of the dryer. She'd carry the clothes upstairs tomorrow morning. Tonight she needed to soak her bruised body in a hot bubble bath. Josie's shoulder, back, and knees ached from her encounters with the escalator and Cody John Wayne.

Josie dragged herself up the basement stairs until she heard the kitchen phone ring. Then she broke into a run. A call at this hour was rarely good news.

She answered with a timid, "Hello?"

"Hello, yourself!" The stern Officer Doris Ann Norris sounded almost giddy. "Guess you heard the good news on TV tonight. He confessed."

"Who?"

"Who do you think? Cody John Wayne. Don't tell me you've forgotten him already."

Josie was confused. The last time she'd seen Cody, he'd been on his way to the hospital, clawing at his eyes and screaming that he was blind.

"He confessed to you?"

"No, to those Venetia Park detectives. The hospital washed out his eyes first. The docs say Mr. Wayne will see again. He made the pain worse by rubbing pepper spray into his eyes, so he's in a world of hurt."

"Me, too," Josie said. "He bruised my shoulder."

Officer Norris skimmed past Josie's complaint and kept

talking. "The going-blind scare must have put the fear of the Lord in Mr. Wayne. Venetia Park got him a public defender. When Mr. Wayne calmed down, Detective Yawney told him about the evidence they had from the Plaza Venetia murder. The crime-scene techs found a shoe print on the floor."

"How?" Josie said. "The Plaza Venetia bathroom didn't seem dusty."

"There was wet tile near the sink and the floor wasn't that clean. They got a shoe print."

"Cody's size?"

"His size and his shoe. The right shoe was marked by a deep cut in the sole."

A deep cut in the soul. That sounded poetic to Josie's fogged brain, until she realized Officer Norris meant there was a distinctive cut on Cody's shoe sole.

"He was wearing the same pair when they took him to the hospital. Crime scene also found two hairs on the victim's body. Short, brown ones. Her husband's hair is darker. They're doing DNA testing now, but they're sure they'll get a match.

"Once Mr. Wayne found out the police had evidence, he confessed. His public defender nearly had a cat in the interview room. The lawyer did everything but throw himself on top of his client to shut him up, but Mr. Wayne wouldn't stop talking. It was like when a plumber opens a blocked drain. The words gushed out. I'm hoping his lawyer cuts Mr. Wayne a decent deal."

"Me, too. I knew Frankie," Josie said. "She was an evil woman."

"So I heard," Officer Norris said. "It's too bad Mr. Wayne is looking at jail time. If you ask me—and no one will because I'm low on the totem pole—that woman drove him to it. But I'm not supposed to blame the victim. Murder is wrong and he killed her."

After delivering her argument for clemency and then refuting it, Officer Norris seemed surprised by her outburst. "I'm sorry. That was unprofessional."

"But true," Josie said. "Now that Cody has confessed, are they going to let Laura Ferguson go?"

"They will. Probably first thing in the morning. These things take time, Ms. Marcus."

It didn't take Josie any time to fall asleep after a long hot soak in her bath. She was alone tonight. Jane had offered to let Amelia sleep upstairs, then drive her to school in the morning.

As Josie expected, Jane had had sharp words for her daughter. Then she took the sting out of her lecture by adding, "Amelia wants to cook with me this evening. She can stay overnight and I'll take her to school. You need your sleep."

"Can I bring Harry?" Amelia asked.

"If he behaves himself," Jane said. "No running and chasing Stuart Little. No banging against my furniture. And you"—she pointed to her daughter—"go downstairs and get some rest. Your eyes look like two holes burned in a blanket."

Josie went, but she was too hyped on adrenaline to fall asleep. She puttered around, dusting and tidying, then did laundry until Officer Norris called. That put Josie's mind at ease and she was finally able to sleep. Josie awoke after ten the next morning, when she heard a thud on her porch. Then the doorbell rang.

Josie was too sleepy to answer it. Terrible things disguised as gifts had been left on her doormat. One of the worst was a dead rat buried in the pretty paper of a shoe box. Harry the cat came out of Amelia's room and stared at her. He seemed too uneasy to sit down next to Josie.

"Morning, cat," she said. "Did Amelia drop you back here while I was asleep? She must have fed you, too, or you would have been in here earlier, demanding breakfast."

The doorbell rang again. Then twice. Three times. That sent Harry into full alert, ears up, eyes wide. He trotted to the living room. Josie followed him. Harry circled in front of the door and growled. Josie heard the sound of a car driving away. Good. Whoever had been on her porch was gone.

She lifted the living room blind using the Mrs. Mueller

method and peered out. A cardboard box the size of a television squatted on Josie's porch. She opened her front door and approached the box carefully.

GIFT BASKETS BY GILDA — OPEN IMMEDIATELY, a red label on the box commanded. There was no other message.

The box was too heavy for Josie to give it an exploratory shake. She dragged it across the threshold into her home, left the sealed box on the boot mat, and went for a butcher knife. Now she was prepared for anything inside it, good or bad.

Harry sniffed the box carefully. He didn't growl this time. He sat next to the box.

"Okay, Harry," Josie said. "You've checked it for me. Let's let 'er rip."

She slit the packing tape along the top with the knife. The box was stuffed with enough foam peanuts to feed every plastic squirrel in Missouri. Josie pushed them aside and heard the crinkle of cellophane. Inside was the mother of all gift baskets, wrapped in blue cellophane, decked in ribbons, and packed with goodies.

Josie carefully lifted out the basket while Harry chased a foam peanut. The basket bulged with bounty: chocolate truffles, smoked salmon, roast turkey breast, cashews, maple-crunch popcorn, cheddar, water crackers, pepper relish, honey mustard, summer sausage, a bottle of Cristal— the champagne of rock stars and celebrities.

This would make a lavish feast after tonight's skating session.

Josie opened a blue envelope and a check for five hundred dollars fell into her lap, along with a note from Laura Ferguson. "Dearest Josie," it read. "You cleared my name and restored me to my family. I cannot thank you enough. Lang and I hope your next shopping experience will be more pleasant than your recent visit to Desiree Lingerie. Fondly, Laura."

Josie dialed Laura's home number. A man answered. "Mr. Ferguson? It's Josie. I got your wonderful present. That was a feast in a box."

His voice warmed instantly. "Please, call me Lang. We're glad you like it, Josie. I know you want to talk to Laura, but she's with our daughter, Kate."

"How is Kate?"

"She's better now that her mother is with her. Laura will stay with her until after the baby is born. Kate needed her mother and you made that possible."

"I was glad to help, Lang, but you didn't have to pay me."

"We didn't pay you, Josie. We just want you to get your-self a little treat. You saved our family. I'll tell Laura you called. And thanks again."

Josie cut herself a sausage sandwich and ate a few ca-shews. She called Alyce and gave her an update.

"Congratulations," her friend said. "I saw the news on television: Frankie's killer has been arrested. Laura Ferguson is free. Your daughter is safe. You must be so relieved it's over. Now you can rest on your laurels."

"Hope that's good for bruises," Josie said, and helped herself to a chocolate truffle.

# Chapter 44

Stars shone like diamonds on jewelers' black velvet. Bare tree branches reached for their soft glitter like greedy fingers. St. Louisans believed Steinberg Skating Rink was one of the city's most romantic sites. Tonight proved they were right.

Josie felt out of place among the confident skaters gliding around the ice. She couldn't control her feet. She felt clumsy in her clunky skates. She was cold. Woman up, she told herself. Get out on the ice and enjoy yourself.

She moved gingerly onto the slick surface, her ankles like rubber in her rented skates. She stayed close to the safety rail—but not close enough. Two steps out on the ice, Josie slipped and nearly fell on her bottom. Ted deftly caught her, then lost his balance. The two of them landed together on the ice, laughing.

Amelia skated up to them, her stride smooth and controlled. "You two make a great pair." Josie's daughter laughed so hard, she almost fell down, too. Josie and Ted used the railing to pull themselves up. Josie kept one gloved hand on it, hoping she would feel more at home on the ice. You got the first fall out of the way, she told herself. No major damage. It was rather fun.

"Can I go skating on my own?" Amelia asked. She circled around them, then slid to a smooth stop. How did her daughter learn to skate like that? She seemed so natural on the ice.

"Yes," Josie said. "Stay in sight where I can see you."

Amelia skimmed across the ice as if she'd been born with skates.

"Thank goodness my daughter didn't inherit her mother's grace on the ice," Josie said, brushing off her cold jeans. "She must get her skating talent from her Canadian father."

"Grace had nothing to do with your fall," Ted said. "You've had a rough couple of days. Don't forget you were bruised from that tumble down the escalator and hurt in the attack by Cody John Wayne."

Two teenage girls in bright pink coats skated by, moving effortlessly around them.

"The escalator bruised my knees," Josie said. "Cody whacked my shoulder with a nightstick. This time, I landed on my rump. I have bruises front and back."

"You look good in purple," Ted said, and Josie gave him a small shove. He caught the side railing, slipped, and hung on.

"Is that what you did to poor Victoria?" Ted asked. "Did you shove her down the escalator?"

"No, my heel caught and I fell on top of her," Josie said. "Knocked the breath right out of her. I hope she has a few bruises of her own. But she's in enough trouble. She's looking at fifteen to twenty years in jail."

Josie didn't bother hiding her satisfaction. Her car was still a frozen lump. Her knees ached from the fall at the store. Her pride was hurt. But she'd made sure Victoria was caught and jailed, nice and legal.

"Hi, Mom! Hi, Ted!" Amelia yelled as she made another circuit of the rink. They waved to her.

Ted skated to a deserted part of the rink. "Josie," he said. "I love you."

"I—"

She couldn't bring herself to say the other two words. They were so dangerous. Do I love Ted? she wondered. I love his brown eyes and the set of his broad shoulders. I like the feel of his well-worn flannel shirts and his gentle way with animals. I like that he's the right age for me, not too young or too old.

It's too soon, a voice whispered. Unless that was the sound of skates on the ice.

I don't like how I make hasty decisions about men, Josie thought. It took me a while to get over Mike and now I've fallen for Ted.

It's too soon, she heard again. But that couldn't be the sound of skates. No one was near them. She was hearing her own doubts. Should she listen to them?

"Josie, say you love me," Ted said.

His plea made Josie dizzy. Did she love him? Was that what she felt? Maybe. But there was something else. Was it joy? Fear? No. It felt like confusion.

"I don't know anything about you," Josie said.

"Yes, you do. You know I'm a veterinarian. You've met my partner, Christine. I'm thirty-five. I'm still paying off our clinic expansion, but I meet the payments every month.

"I like animals and so do you. I have a Lab and an orange cat named Marmalade. I rent a two-bedroom house decorated with pet hair. I like snakes a little too much for your taste, but I promise I'll never bring you a reptile— well, one with scales. Can't vouch for the two-legged reptiles I encounter."

Josie was laughing now. "I mean, I don't know anything personal about you. You're not married. Were you ever?"

"Once, way back in veterinary school I gave a woman named Leann an engagement ring. We were supposed to get married after graduation. But it didn't work out. I wanted a small-animal practice in the city. Leann grew up on a farm and liked working with large animals. We each went our way, literally. She moved to Kirksville and I went to St. Louis. No hard feelings."

"What about your family?" Josie asked.

"One brother. With any luck, you won't meet him."

"What's wrong with him? Is he a thief? A drunk? A drug dealer?"

"He's an idiot," Ted said. "He loves stupid practical jokes. He almost got fired for a stunt he pulled on some co-workers with Super Glue. I nearly killed him after he tried one of his stupid pranks on poor Festus. I don't want him around."

"And your parents?" Josie asked.

"Mother lives in Florida. She has a second marriage made in heaven—for her, anyway. Mom married a plastic surgeon. My stepfather whittles on her constantly when he isn't injecting her with Botox and collagen. I'll see Mom in a few weeks. I usually ask for a photo before I pick her up at the airport. Every time we meet, she's a new woman. I barely recognized Mom when she came here for her last visit."

"Will she stay at your house?"

"Never," Ted said. "She says I'm so grown-up now that I make her look old. She can't abide my house. Mom doesn't like dogs or cats. She doesn't like pets, period."

"How did she produce a son like you?"

"I take after my dad." Ted became serious. "I'm sorry you won't be able to meet my father. He died ten years ago. Heart attack. Dad would have loved you. There, is that enough about me?"

Ted had his arms around her, sheltering Josie from the cold winter wind. Josie took a deep breath, gathered her remaining courage, and said, "Ted, I love you. But I never told you about—"

Ted stopped her with a kiss. "I don't want to know about the other men in your life. I only care about Josie Marcus, the woman with me now. She's magnificent."

"But I have a history of bad decisions when it comes to men," Josie said.

"You make bad decisions? Don't you remember that I have an ex-girlfriend in prison for murder?" Ted asked.

"I didn't forget," Josie said. "I figured you wouldn't want to be reminded."

"At least none of your ex-boyfriends murdered any-one," Ted said.

Three boys whizzed by. One jostled Josie and she fell on the ice again. The boys didn't look back or stop. Ted reached for her. "Are you hurt?" he asked.

Ted tried to lift Josie and he fell, too. They sat on the ice, laughing and holding each other.

Amelia skated over to them and said, "I see you're back where you started. Can I help you up?"

"I'll do it," Ted said. He pulled himself up by the railing, then lifted Josie. She moved gingerly. Her bruised bottom was cold. Her shoulder ached. Her knees were too cold to feel any pain.

Ted took her hand. They started skating, moving together on the ice.

"See," Ted said. "We both slipped, but we got up again. Look how good we are together."

They skated hand in hand. Slowly, gracefully, they circled the rink, enjoying the glow of the city lights against the night sky.

# Epilogue

The spring thaw brought an unexpected warming trend in the icy relations between Jane Marcus and her neighbor. Mrs. Mueller apologized to Jane and reappointed Josie's mother to her usual committees. Mrs. Mueller and Jane were civil to each other, but their friendship lacked its old intensity.

The ice on Josie's car melted sooner, after a freakishly warm day in February.

Laura Josie Chadwick arrived February fifth. The healthy baby girl weighed seven pounds six ounces. Kate named her daughter in honor of the two women who'd helped her during her difficult final trimester.

Three months later, Grandma Laura Ferguson was reinstated as manager of Desiree Lingerie. The chain's headquarters gave her an apology and a raise and expunged all criticism from their records.

Rosa happily gave up her manager's title in return for weekends off at the store. She remains assistant manager at Desiree Lingerie, working at the pay level she enjoyed as manager. Saturdays and Sundays, she helps at her family's restaurant. Rosa used her pay increase to consult an immigration lawyer.

Josie had jumped to the wrong conclusion about Rosa's father: He wasn't the only man named Hector Maria in St. Louis, and he'd never applied for that restaurant job. Rosa's parents were in this country legally. Rosa was a United

States citizen, and under the immigration laws, Rosa's parents were "immediate relatives." The lawyer filed the proper petitions and applications to get them green cards. Rosa's parents are now legal residents.

Trish quit as a sales associate at Desiree Lingerie to become a uniformed officer in the Rock Road Village force. She is working toward a degree in law enforcement at night. Josie sees Trish occasionally going into St. Philomena's Church for Narcotics Anonymous meetings, but never says anything. Trish pretends not to see Josie. Josie never found out why Trish attends the meetings. She reminds herself that she was wrong about Rosa's father. All she knows for sure is Trish's past is not her concern.

Dr. Tino married his receptionist, Shannon, the Saturday before Mother's Day. Their son, Tino Junior, was born seven months later.

Cody John Wayne pleaded guilty to manslaughter. The judge felt that the hero was remorseful and had been subjected to "extreme provocation" by the victim. "That does not justify your crime, Mr. Wayne," the judge said in a severe tone. "There were other solutions. You could have gone to the police for aid." Cody was sentenced to ten years in prison. With good behavior, he may be released in five. Dr. Tino, Frankie's only surviving family member, did not protest the sentence.

Cody's son, Tyler Dylan Wayne, was relieved when the true story of the fatal car accident came out and he was no longer a hero. Tyler goes to meetings at Alcoholics Anonymous. He has been sober for 362 days so far.

Victoria Eva Malliet (who falsely claimed she was Victoria Garbull) was sentenced to twenty years in prison for a Class B felony. The police found nearly forty thousand dollars in stolen goods in her home. She was forced to sell her house to pay for her attorney's fees and to make restitution to the stores.

Chuck never forgave Josie for the loss of his fetching blond neighbor. A middle-aged couple bought Victoria's house on Palmer Avenue. Chuck came over several times to talk to them, but they claimed to be hard of hearing. Chuck still tips the pizza deliveryman Big Al one dollar.

Officer Doris Ann Norris was promoted to property-crimes detective for her work on the felony shoplifting bust.

The Bluestone's department store security guard received a letter of commendation for the capture and conviction of Victoria Malliet, along with a five-cent-an-hour raise. If he works every day for the next twenty years, he might make the money he saved the company when Victoria was prevented from shoplifting the three-thousand-dollar dress.

# Shopping Tips

**Measuring pain:** Some women rank shopping for a new bra with mammograms and other painful female experiences. One of my friends needs at least one martini before she marches off to a department store lingerie department. Shopping for lingerie isn't my favorite pastime, either. I've shopped on my own, facing mind-numbing choices: underwire? Padded? Front closure? Back clasp? Seamless? Strapless? Soft cup? Sports? Low-cut demi bra or safe matronly over-the-shoulder boulder holders? A short tour of the racks and it's enough to make strong women sag—and I'm not talking about the sad gray lingerie I'm wearing.

But I don't have to be alone in this search. I can consult a bra fitter. I've been to department stores where the fitter used a tape measure and to Intimacy, where the fitters used their eyes to figure my size. Personally, I'd go back to Intimacy again. I spent about the same at both types of stores, but the fit was better at Intimacy.

**No hot times for your bra:** Dryer heat kills bras. Ask the experts. They'll recommend that you wash your bras by hand. But if you don't have that kind of time, invest in a lingerie bag, fasten your bra clasps so the hooks don't catch in the bag mesh, and drop your bras in the washer. Then air-dry them. You'll get longer wear.

**Squash may not be good for you:** Curvy women like Josie's friend Alyce often resort to minimizer bras to make their breasts look smaller. Some fitting experts say minimizers only maximize the pain. Instead of squashing, buy a bra that lifts your breasts higher. This will make your torso look longer and slimmer.

**Help yourself—and help fight breast cancer:** You can buy martini glasses, bracelets, baby clothes, bikinis, and a host of other items to support breast cancer awareness and research, especially around Mother's Day and Breast Cancer Awareness Month in October. One such site is www .advantagebridal.com.

**If only we knew this in high school:** The average American woman's breasts change size and shape some six times in her life: when she gains or loses weight, when she quits exercising or starts working out more, when she uses birth control pills or hormone replacement therapy, during pregnancy and nursing, and if she gets breast implants.

The average bra size? A C-cup, and many women wear Ds. That information comes from Susan Nethero, founder of Intimacy bra shops, in her *Bra Talk* book.

**Headlights and dimmers:** Some women are embarrassed when the outlines of their nipples are visible through their bras. Some resort to Band-Aids to hide their "happy nipples" or "headlights." Those work, but pulling them off can be painful. Gel cover-ups with names like Dimmers and Bra Discs will give you a smooth line in your bra.

**Let it show:** Women who think their nipples are nothing to hide try products such as BareLifts, adhesive stick-ons that are said to lift breasts and realign nipples to a high position. Lingerie departments may carry these adhesive stick-ons, or you can check them out at www.bare lifts.com.

**Afterglow:** I can't decide if this is tacky or tantalizing. Maybe it's both. LuminoGlow makes glow-in-the-dark lingerie. www.glowinthedarklingerie.com.au.

**Hot mamas:** Pregnant friends complain that once they start to show, they are consigned to the cutesy ghetto, expected to wear maternity clothes in nursery styles and colors. These women tried to tell the stores that they were carrying a baby—they hadn't turned into one. Lingerie for new mothers was dreary.

HOTmilk Lingerie seems to understand the difference between babes and babies. They sell bras with no wires to inhibit milk production, no stitching or seams to irritate sensitive nipples, and "quick release clips" for easier breast-feeding. HOTmilk has lingerie, camisoles, nightwear, as well as a charity called Knickers for Africa to help elevate the status of young women. www.hotmilklingerie.co.uk.

**The end of Swamp Thing:** Many woman enter menopause as early as their midthirties. They know the horror of waking up in the middle of the night in wet bedclothes, clinging to a damp pillow. NiteSweatz's line of "moisture wicking" products are designed to help with this problem. NiteSweatz makes sleepwear, day wear, gowns, cover-ups, even pillowcases. For more information, go to www.nitesweatz.com.

**Don't want to pay NiteSweatz prices?** Try a "moisture wicking" T-shirt. They're supposed to soak up sweat, and they work night or day. Nike's Dri-FIT is one of many similar brands.

**My grandma wore a girdle:** God rest her soul. That rubber girdle must have been an instrument of torture in the St. Louis summers, no matter how much baby powder she used. Many modern women prefer to tame their curves with shape wear such as Spanx. There are styles ranging from "below the knee shapers" to "high-waisted panties" that reach to your bra band. You don't have to suck in your gut at the beach, either, with "slimming" swimsuits. Check out the styles at www.barenecessities.com.

**Women are not the only ones who suffer to look slimmer:** Spanx makes a line of men's "moderate control cotton compression" T-shirts and tank tops. Available at www.barenecessities.com.

Read on for a sneak peek at the
next novel in Elaine Viets's national bestselling
Dead-End Job Mystery series,

## *PUMPED FOR MURDER*

Coming in hardcover from Obsidian
in May 2011.

Helen Hawthorne wished Eric Clapton would shut up. She didn't want to listen to him croon about cocaine.

"She don't lie. She don't lie . . ." Eric sang.

Enough, Helen thought. She sat up in bed and pulled up the black satin sheet over her breasts. She didn't want to be totally naked for the first fight of her marriage.

Phil, her husband of thirty-three days, looked lean and white against the dark sheets. She admired his young face, a startling contrast to his silver-white hair. His eyes were closed as he listened to the music.

Here goes, Helen thought. As soon as I open my mouth, our honeymoon is over.

"I hate that song," she said. "Clapton sounds bored."

Helen waited for Phil to defend his guitar hero. He gave a lazy stretch, sat up and said, "You're right."

"I am?" Helen raised one eyebrow in surprise. Her husband worshipped Clapton. He even had a "Clapton Is God" T-shirt. Helen expected Phil to be struck by lightning every time he wore it.

They'd spent the sizzling September afternoon in his bedroom, listening to Clapton sing about hopeful love, hopeless love, and shameful, sinful love while they indulged in legal, married love. The cool music and green palm fronds shading the window turned Phil's bedroom into an oasis at the Coronado Tropic Apartments.

Phil reached for the CD clicker and switched to an old

favorite, "White Room," with the howling guitar sound. "There. Is that better?"

"Much," Helen said.

"You have to admit the guitar riffs in 'Cocaine' are elegant," he said. "In his defense, Clapton thought he was singing an antidrug song."

"Not to me," Helen said. "Sounds like he's in love with the White Lady."

"You and a lot of other people," Phil said. "You heard the audience cheering in that live recording. That's why he quit singing it for a while. Coke was the evil lady of the eighties, and 'Cocaine' was her anthem. When Clapton brought the song back for his North American tour, he added 'that dirty cocaine' line for his backup singers. It's my least favorite Clapton song. He sounds depressed."

"Did you ever use coke?" Helen asked.

"Did I *what*? I. Hate. Coke." Each word was a separate sentence. Phil threw back the sheet, slipped into his white robe and paced up and down. With his silver hair, he looked like an agitated ghost.

"I hate the whole cocaine culture: the destruction, the corruption, the killings. I worked a case here in South Florida in the mideighties, in the days of the cocaine cowboys."

"Sounds very *Miami Vice*," Helen said. "I loved that TV show."

"*Miami Vice* was a Disney movie compared to Miami then," Phil said. "Coke isn't romantic pink sunsets, throbbing sound tracks and drug dealers' yachts."

"I wouldn't know," Helen said. "I was in high school back then. Our wild St. Louis drug scene was kids smoking pot under the bleachers."

"I'm only five years older," Phil said. "I was a PI trainee on my first major case. I was only twenty-one, and my hair was blond. They thought I'd be good at finding a sixteen-year-old runaway because I looked young. Her name was Marcie. I was supposed to bring her back to Little Rock."

"Did you?"

Phil was still pacing the terrazzo floor in his bedroom, avoiding their scattered clothes.

"I tracked Marcie to some clone of Studio 54, then bribed the doorman with a hundred bucks. Put the bribe on my expense account. Thought I was quite the stud."

"You are," Helen said. She tried to put her arms around him, but Phil shook her away. He seemed anxious to make this confession.

"I followed Marcie into a club packed with half-naked people. It looked like every club then: tropical neon and a shiny black bar with mirrors. Behind the bar, Tom Cruise wannabes mixed flashy cocktails."

"Sounds interesting," Helen said.

"It wasn't," Phil said. "The crowd was mostly fat, balding men, Don Johnson look-alikes with designer stubble, and very young women. Couples were having sex everywhere: behind the curtains, in bathroom stalls, even right on the tables."

"Ew," Helen said. "I want to wash my mind out after that image."

"Well, I can't. I also can't forget the black bowls of coke. They sat around like party favors."

"What happened to Marcie?" Helen said.

"I don't want to talk about it."

"Did you find her?"

"Yeah," Phil said. "I found her. I sent her home—in a box. I'd like to forget her. I'd like to forget the whole ugly decade."

Phil seemed to shut down. He stopped pacing and sat down on the bed next to Helen.

"It must have been horrible for you," she said.

"It was no fun for Marcie, either. She didn't deserve what happened to her."

Helen traced the outline of his thin, slightly crooked nose with her finger and kissed the bump where it had been broken years ago. "Let's talk about something pleasant: our new detective agency. Do you still like the name Coronado Investigations?"

"It's perfect," Phil said. "Classy with a retro feel, like the Coronado Tropic Apartments. Our office could be a set for an old private eye movie: the rattling window air conditioner, the monster gunmetal gray desks, the battered file cabinets. I can see Bogart sitting behind my desk in a wifebeater undershirt, drinking cheap whiskey."

"I'd rather see clients," Helen said. "Our savings will run out soon. We have to find some. How do we start looking for work?"

"That's what I asked Ray, my PI friend. I had breakfast with him this morning. I was working while you slept in. He's a retired cop who's with a big agency now."

"You were supposed to tell me what he said when you came back," Helen said.

"It's not my fault. I was distracted by this tall brunette with great legs."

Helen tucked her legs under her. "There. The distraction is gone. Why should he help us? Aren't we competition?"

"Not really. He works for a huge agency that specializes in private security. It started as a small shop run by two friends and grew. Ray says we need a PI license and a computer. I already have both. We need insurance, and we have the money for that."

"What about me?" Helen said.

"The state laws on private eyes are changing. We can get you in under the wire as my trainee, but you'll have to take classes. So will I, if we want the business to succeed.

"Ray says we have another important asset—our reputation. I'm glad we went back to St. Louis and cleared up your troubles with the court. That's out of the way."

*Troubles with the court.* Helen felt like a boulder had been lobbed at her gut. She'd divorced her lying, cheating ex more than two years ago. That was how she wound up in south Florida. She was on the run, avoiding an outrageous divorce settlement. A St. Louis judge had given her greedy ex-husband, Rob, half of Helen's future income.

Helen had hidden in Fort Lauderdale, working jobs for cash under the table. Rob had tracked her down, demanding fifteen thousand dollars. With the help of a St. Louis lawyer, Helen had cleared her name with the court.

"Has Rob shown up in court to contest the new divorce settlement?" Phil asked.

Helen felt her mouth go dry as Death Valley. Alkaline dust seemed to coat her tongue. "Uh, no. The process server can't find him. My lawyer published all the legal notices. Rob never appeared."

"He disappeared at the wrong time," Phil said. "Your legal troubles are over."

"Almost over," Helen said. "I didn't file any taxes while I was on the run. My St. Louis tax attorney is working on that problem."

"We'll be free soon," Phil said.

Helen felt a second boulder land on her back. Rob was never going to show up in court. If she was lucky, no one would ever see her ex-husband again. Rob was dead, and she'd helped bury him. His death had been an accident, but Helen couldn't tell anyone except her sister, who'd helped hide the body. She couldn't even tell Phil, the man she loved. She'd have to carry that crushing burden the rest of her life. She hated keeping a secret from her husband, but if she told Phil, she'd ruin an innocent young life.

"What's the matter, sweetheart?" Phil asked. "You look pale."

"Nothing," Helen said, adding yet another lie to the layers of deceit. "What else did your PI friend tell you?"

"Lots. Maybe too much. I'll tell you more as I remember it. Ray suggested I hang around the courthouse and watch for new case filings. He says I should find a small, hungry law firm and do its investigative work. Our business will grow with the firm's."

"What do we do in the meantime? Live on love?"

"Find our local niche," Phil said. "Florida has more private eyes than any other state except California."

"Because this is such a rootless society?" Helen asked.

"Partly. Also, a lot of old cops retire down here. They live on their pensions while they start up their own agencies."

"Makes it tough for us," Helen said. "We don't have their investigative skills."

"We have our own advantages," Phil said. "Old cops can be set in their ways. They're used to getting what they want through the power of the badge and don't learn how to coax information out of people. You're a genius at getting dead-end jobs."

"Thanks, I think," Helen said.

"Low-paying jobs are good ways to observe subjects. The people who do the work see things the bigwigs never do. They're more likely to talk. You've worked as everything from a hotel maid to a bookseller. You're a good listener."

"You're good at disguises," Helen said. "I've seen you look like an outlaw biker, a homeless man and a businessman. A cop looks like a cop no matter what he puts on."

"Ray says we could try to specialize in background checks or insurance-agency work."

"So we follow some guy suing someone because he hurt his back, and catch him mowing the lawn."

"Something like that," Phil said.

"Sounds boring," Helen said.

"Could be," Phil said. "Is it any duller than standing at a shop counter?"

"I guess not," Helen said. "Maybe Margery has some ideas to make a more lively living. Our landlady has a stake in our future, too. Our office is in her apartment complex. Is it time for the nightly poolside gathering?"

"It's seven-ten," Phil said, checking the bedside clock. He pulled on his jeans. "Should be just starting."

"Wait. We haven't fed the cat yet," Helen said, buttoning her blouse. "Thumbs is at my place."

"Are you sure it's a good idea to keep two apartments?" Phil asked.

"My tax attorney said no major lifestyle changes until we get the IRS settlement," Helen said. "Besides, keeping my own apartment and sneaking into yours makes marriage seem illicit."

A furious cat greeted Helen at her apartment door with loud yowls of protest. Thumbs was mostly white with gray-brown patches. His giant six-toed front paws gave him his name. Thumbs followed Helen into the kitchen. He flipped over his food bowl with one huge paw.

"Hey! That's not nice," Helen said.

Thumbs stared at her with angry green eyes.

"I should know better than to lecture a cat," she said, pouring his dinner. Thumbs edged her hand out of the way and buried his face in his food.

Helen found a box of white wine in her fridge, rummaged for a can of cashews and headed outside.

The Coronado Tropic Apartments, built in 1949, looked like a white ocean liner. A hot breeze stirred the palm trees in the courtyard and small waves rippled the pool's tepid water. Margery Flax and their neighbor, Peggy, were stretched out on the poolside chaise longues like Victorian maidens.

The real maidens would have fainted for sure if they'd seen Margery. Helen's seventy-six-year-old landlady was wearing purple rompers. Her long tanned legs ended in eggplant espadrilles. Marlboro smoke veiled her face. Her sunset orange fingernails glowed through the cigarette smoke.

Margery's face was wrinkled, but she wore her age like an exotic accessory. Her steel gray hair ended at a necklace of charms. Helen saw martini glasses, wine bottles, olives, lemons, wineglasses, drink stirrers and a small corkscrew, all about the size of a beer cap.

"Cool necklace," Phil said.

"It's called a statement necklace," Margery said.

"Looks like yours says it's time for a drink," Phil said.

"Drink!" came a raucous voice. "Drink!"

"Pete's learned a new word," Peggy said. Her Quaker parrot was perched on her shoulder like a corsage. Pete was the same bright green as Peggy's long gauzy dress. Both lived at the Coronado and gave the old apartment complex its exotic color.

"And a useful word it is," Margery said. She raised her wineglass in a salute to the gray-headed parrot. "Let's drink."

"Good boy," Peggy said. "Here's your reward." She gave the bird a bit of broccoli. The parrot dropped it on the pool deck.

"Poor Pete," Helen said. "That's some celebration when all you get is broccoli. Can he have a cashew?"

"Sorry. That's on his no-fly list," Peggy said. "He's still two ounces overweight."

Helen closed the lid on the can of nuts and stuck them under her chair.

"Bye," Pete said, sadly.

"We came here for help," Phil said dragging a chair over to the group. "Coronado Investigations needs to specialize to succeed. Any suggestions?"

Peggy said, "Based on my past experience with men, you should investigate potential spouses and lovers. Right now, I'm dating a good guy, but my friend Shelby from work is looking for a detective. She's having problems with her husband, Bryan. About a year ago, she bought him a gym membership. Bryan has lost twenty-five pounds. He works out seven days a week. He's got a killer body."

"What's wrong with that?" Helen asked.

"Shelby hasn't had sex with him since he started looking good. She's convinced he has buffed himself up for another woman."

"Or man," Phil said. "Fort Lauderdale may have more gays than San Francisco."

"Whoever it is, Shelby needs an answer," Peggy said.

"Sounds promising," Phil said.

"I think you should help families," Margery said. "The average person can afford you better than they can a big agency. You can investigate when the family can't—or won't—go to the police."

"Like finding runaways and deadbeat dads?" Phil said.

"Partly," Margery said. "My mechanic has a problem. Gus thinks his brother's suicide was a murder. He wants to hire an investigator to prove his brother was killed. He died in the eighties."

"Opening a cold case can cost a lot of money," Phil said.

"He's got it," Margery said. "Gus charges me eighty bucks an hour to work on my car. He specializes in vintage restorations."

"I thought your Lincoln Town Car was fairly new."

"Then I'm the vintage restoration," Margery said. "You want the job or not?"

"What's his number?" Phil asked.

"I have him on speed dial." Margery opened her cell phone and hit a number.

"Gus?" she asked. "You still want that detective? I've found a good agency—Coronado Investigations." She listened a moment, then asked, "Can you meet him at his repair shop?"

She looked at Phil. He nodded. So did Helen.

"It's *they*, Gus," Margery said. "You're hiring the best team of shamuses in South Florida. They don't come cheap, but you can afford it after my car bills. What did you do last time on my Lincoln—a heart transplant? Coronado Investigations will see you at seven tomorrow night."

Peggy had her own cell phone out. She snapped it shut and said, "Shelby also really wants you to start looking into her husband, Bryan's, activities. She'll stop by at seven tomorrow morning before she goes into work."

"Amazing," Helen said. "We got two jobs sitting by the pool."

"Enjoy the honeymoon," Margery said. "It won't ever be this easy again."

# LOOK FOR THE BOOKS BY
# ELAINE VIETS
*in the Josie Marcus,
Mystery Shopper series*

### Dying in Style
Josie Marcus's report about Danessa Celedine's exclusive
store is less than stellar, and it may cost the fashion diva
fifty million dollars. But her financial future becomes moot
when she's found strangled with one of her own snake-
skin belts—and Josie is accused of the crime.

### High Heels Are Murder
Soon after being hired to mystery-shop a shoe store, Josie
finds herself immersed in St. Louis's seedy underbelly.
Caught up in a web of crime, Josie hopes that she won't
end up murdered in Manolos...

### Accessory to Murder
Someone has killed a hot young designer of Italian silk
scarves, and the police suspect the husband of Josie's best
friend. Josie tries to find some clues—because now there's
a lot more than a scarf at stake, even if it's to die for...

### Murder with All the Trimmings
Josie Marcus is assigned to anonymously rate year-round
Christmas shops—easy enough, she thinks, until she learns
that shoppers at one store are finding a deadly ingredient
in their holiday cake. Josie must get to the bottom of it all
before someone else becomes a Christmas spirit.

### The Fashion Hound Murders
Josie Marcus has been hired to check out a pet store's
involvement with puppy mills. When the employee who
clued her into the mills' existence shows up dead, Josie
realizes that sinking her teeth into this case could mean
getting bitten back...

**Available wherever books are sold or at penguin.com**

OM0010